SINS OF THE FATHER

a Logan Falcone thriller

Michael Reid, Jr.

SINS OF THE FATHER

a Logan Falcone thriller

Michael Reid, Jr.

Edited by: a.r. merlo

Sins of the Father

H Q T

PUBLICATIONS

Cover design: John Apostolopoulos Digital Ink Group.

Interior design and layout: a.r. merlo.

ISBN 978-0-9973500-0-5

CONTENTS

To Molly, for hooking me up with limitless contacts.

To Ashley for always being present to answer my annoying questions.

To Kyle for explaining how planes don't go Mach 14,

and to Kristin for basically writing my scenes involving the helos.

Chapter 1
THE CANDYMAN

Aden, Yemen

A child runs unseen down a narrow street, weaving through hundreds of people hiding from the scorching sun. The weather had been sweltering for weeks, but at least outside there was a breeze. The boy slowed, as the subtle smell of lemon and roasted nuts leapt into his nose. It was his favorite treat, a love cake, the only thing that could keep him from his mission. He inhaled deeply and scanned the area with his eyes. He searched past several vendors as they yelled while simultaneously wiping the sweat from their foreheads. Finally, he spotted the distraction to his left. His mouth watered as he imagined the sweet, sour treat crunching in his mouth.

Whap! A metal spatula slapped the table next to him and the vendor hollered for the young boy to move along. Instinctually, he ducked behind an adjacent food stand and crashed through a group of men drinking tea; giggling as he snuck away unseen. He turned down a steep and narrow alleyway. He was almost there, to an apartment a recluse called home; a ghost the children called the Candyman.

David Westbrook sat with light cascading in from the cracks at the front door. His eyes were glued to a jumble of numbers and letters as they flashed across the screen to his left. A larger, brighter monitor sat in front of him, and a third one displayed a three-dimensional map of the Middle East, extending as far east as China. On the map were hundreds of dots, some small and blue indicating limited activity, others large and red showing tremendous activity. He was pinging computers by the thousands, his algorithm working flawlessly as it began to create a picture of which computers were playing nice and which had ulterior motives.

"*El-khair!*" the young boy yelled as he burst through David's apartment door. The intense sunlight pierced the room, causing dust in the air to glow in the multicolored rays of light.

"Get out," David hollered, shielding his eyes, and shooing the boy to leave.

"*Biddi, Biddi!*" the boy exclaimed.

"You always want something but you never give me anything good," David responded, frustrated that the boy was once again bothering him during peak hours.

"*Beddak?*"

"Of course I want news, but you never deliver. I work alone Amal. Each time you tell me something, I have to follow up. It's how this works."

The young boy laughed and pointed at a box in the corner of the room. He held up two fingers, "*Ethnain.*"

"In English, Amal."

"Two for this."

"You tell me what you found and I'll decide."

The young boy, barely ten, always tried to negotiate his rates with the Candyman but it never successfully worked out. Nonetheless, he paused and rubbed his chin as if deep in thought.

"Okay Amal, leave now. I don't have all day," the impatient agent said as he spun his chair toward the desk and watched the numbers continue to scroll across the screen.

"It's good, it's good!" the boy said, shuffling toward the man.

Quickly, David sprung to his feet and stood well above the small boy from Yemen, his t-shirt sticking to his chest and abdomen. "Tell me now." The look David gave Amal was one meant for the men he often interrogated after hearing these "good" reports.

"I hear about a man in the mountains. Very powerful. Nobody knows his name but he's training hundreds to attack U.S."

"That's not even worth one," he said, holding up a finger.

"I know! That's not what I have to tell you. There's a man in the city. Today only. He will know. I hear a man on the street say he will be here."

"Where?"

"The port. A ship coming."

"Name?"

"Lady Phoenix."

"Okay. You can have one now, and two more—if this is all true," David said, softening his demeanor and rubbing the boy's head firmly. "Come back next week and I'll let you know."

Amal ran to the corner or the dark, lifeless room. He tore open a small box and grabbed a bag of blowpops.

"Amal. Grab me one," David said with his back to the

boy. Once again, his full attention was on the data flashing across the screens.

"*Shukran*," David said, smiling to Amal as they both unwrapped their candy. "You have a green! That's my favorite."

Amal lifted it toward the man, offering a trade.

"No, no. You've earned that. I'll see you next week my friend," David said and reached his large hand out, the boy took it and squeezed as hard as he could. David smiled at the effort.

Amal placed the candy in his mouth. The tart, sugary combination immediately made his mouth water and his eyes light up. He skipped out of the room, but only after giving David a high five. Once again, the room was completely dark, but this time the Candyman was focused on darker thoughts.

It was 1300 hours when David arrived at the port in Aden. He wore a small brown satchel over his right shoulder and held a digital monocular in his left. It only took him minutes to find the Lady Phoenix, which he quickly learned was heading for America in three days. He stood behind the tall legs of a loading crane as it lifted cargo containers onto the large ship, creaking under the stress of a particularly heavy load. Every ten minutes he would remove his Ray-Bans and lift the monocular to his eye, scanning the ship. Finally, after over two hours, he saw a group of five men.

They were as conspicuous as could be, all wearing yellow hardhats, all wearing overalls and thin white shirts, and all sporting beards of various lengths; except for one. His hardhat was white, pristine, and his clothes were meant for a lunch meeting at a five-star restaurant rather than the deck of a cargo ship. His gray pants and custom tailored white button-up seemed staunchly out of place.

As David walked toward the parking lot, he soon spotted his mark's car. It was the only luxury car in the lot, a black AMG Mercedes, parked perpendicular to the many other cars. David walked past a few port employees, nodded at them, and made a direct path to the Mercedes. As he approached, he reached into his bag and grabbed a small black device. He visually scanned the immediate area, as well as the horizon for any individuals who could be watching. By the time he reached the Mercedes, he was confident there was nobody providing security for the meeting on the boat.

David pressed the small device gently onto the door of the car. Within seconds, the doors unlocked and disengaged the security system. Quickly, he climbed into the spacious backseat and laid on the floor, the intense heat and thick, stagnant air immediately caused his heart to beat more rapidly.

He closed his eyes and focused on his dark, one room apartment, his data, and the map full of dots displayed on his screens. David ached to make sense of it all. He had thousands of data points. He knew all came together, but couldn't build the algorithm in his mind. His dual degrees in mathematics/electrical engineering and computer science from MIT should have helped, but without a fresh set of eyes looking over the information, it was tough to get perspective. It had been nearly four years since he heard an American voice. The data was too large to send, and too sensitive. He was forced to send small, encoded pieces back to the U.S., which were often overlooked due to the agency back home not having the full scope of the numbers. This is what led him to his unique form of interrogation. That's the only intel the suits back home listened to.

David lay uncomfortably still on the black carpet, his heart beating forcefully and rapidly. Sweat had saturated his thin clothing and began to moisten the floor of the car. He fought the urge to move, knowing the man he waited for was more likely to be coming with each second. Finally, he heard the actuators from the doors unlocking.

Bright sunlight entered the car as the driver's door opened. David could smell the man's cologne before he even entered. The man sighed heavily and dropped hard into the leather seat. He pushed the start button on the car, leaving the door open for a moment. David felt the fresh air wash over him and he silently took a deep breath. Cool air from the air conditioner reached his left arm, leg, and torso; a chill encompassed his body.

Thump, he heard the tight seal of the Mercedes' door close and slowly they pulled away, the sound of rubber over gravel gave David a rush.

David waited several minutes enjoying the comfortable air as his heart rate slowed to normal. He knew the drill. David reached quietly into his messenger bag and pulled out a black blade. He also removed a syringe full of his homemade "candy."

The car stopped for a traffic signal, and David shot up from the floor. Using his right hand, he grabbed the driver's chest and slammed him hard against the seatback. His left hand held the blade tight against the driver's throat.

"Don't move," he told the man calmly in Arabic.

"What am I supposed to do?" the man squealed as the light changed to green.

"Turn right and drive until it ends."

"I'll tell you nothing."

"I doubt that," David said as he bit down gently on the syringe between his teeth.

Quickly, the driver lurched forward, but David was faster, removing the knife from his neck and slamming him back into the seat. It was terrifying how both spindly and strong David's long arms were, as if they were hydraulic and carbon rather than human.

"Drive," David growled, as he noticed a streak of bright red running down the knife toward his hand, as he held it firmly against the driver's neck.

It took several minutes to reach the end of the road, but in that short time, blood had run down the blade handle onto David's hand; a metronome of viscous fluid dripped down to the floor of the car, becoming lost in the dark carpet. David was worried. His drug typically took thirty minutes for a full effect.

"Pull over," David said as he looked to the right and left, seeing nobody in the dark, lonely alleyway. This was one of several locations around the city that David had commandeered over the years. He found it much easier to have a variety of "facilities" enabling him to get to a location he knew was safe. He also knew his questions would never get answered without a certain amount of aggression. He tried leading with the nice guy approach on many occasions, but that only wasted time.

"Get out," he demanded and pulled the blade away when the driver's door opened. David got out and looked at the man for the first time up close. He was middle-aged, about five-foot-ten, and wore a thick, manicured beard. He also saw the crimson stains on the man's shirt had completely saturated his collar and advanced in a tapering streak to the level of his heart.

"Walk," David said, directing him with the knife toward a dark doorway of the building to their right. It was shadowed by its own height, the sun already descending behind the structure. The prisoner listened without hesitation.

Inside the room smelled of rust, despite the lack of steel. There were two wooden chairs and a small amber light hanging from the center of the room over plywood floors. As they walked deeper into the void, the wooden floor became peppered with dark spots, increasingly becoming larger and more dense as they approached the chairs.

"There," David said, pointing at the dark chair. The prisoner approached and the smell of iron filled his nose. His eyes became wide and he hesitated, thinking to run as he realized what the dark stains were.

"Please, no. I have children. I know nothing, I know nobody. I was at the port today for a friend. You must believe me!"

"I know you called someone in the car. Who was it?"

"A friend."

"Sit down," David said, glaring at the man and pointing the knife directly into his face.

"You'll kill me," the mark said with a trembling voice.

"Not if you talk. So, talk."

"I have no informa—"

David hit the man hard in the face with the handle of his knife, splitting the skin just under his right eye. Quickly, David took the syringe and jammed it into the man's arm, pressing the plunger down hard.

"You'll sing now," David said, wiping the spattering of blood off his dirty white shirt.

"Ha ha ha," the man began laughing as he plopped down into his chair. "I've done drugs before, sir. They gave me a lot of things for a moment like this."

"See, you're talking already. You can't help it, can you?"

"This is nothing. You won't make me talk. I've taken everything. Truth serum is useless, infidel."

"I'm not sure if you're just a bigger pussy than most, or if it's the loss of blood, but you're talking early. You'll die soon, either way."

"I talk for nobody! I told you in the car," he said and spat at David. David took off his shirt, revealing his lean body. He wound his moist shirt tightly and *whap!* He snapped the prisoner in the chest, splitting his skin. *Whap!* He did it again. *Whap, whap, whap!* He did it several more times leaving small wounds in the man's chest through his bloodied shirt.

"Stop!" the man yelled and covered his chest with both hands.

"What's your biggest secret?" David asked as he sat backward in the chair, leaning on the back of the seat playfully, his head resting on both hands.

"I slept with my wife's sister. Her son is mine. Nobody knows I give her money."

"Interesting," David said, laughing and sitting up, as the man sat staring at the floor, reviewing what had just come out of his mouth.

"It was a joke," the man finally said, looking up and stretching out his arms as he struggled with a smile.

"No, it wasn't. You see, the drug I gave you is my own cocktail so to speak. You haven't had any experience with this. I promise you."

"What?"

"Have you heard of the Candyman?" David asked, and waited for the reaction. He had a reputation, having been in the Middle East for over a decade, moving from one large city to the next. The terrorists had begun to hear rumors about a CIA operative who used atypical techniques.

The mark began to cry silently, several tears ran down his face as his mind drifted through horrific stories he heard over the years: the dismemberment, the burning, the waterboarding, hunting down family members and murdering loved ones. However, none of this was true. Most of the time, David let them loose after they talked. From there, the terrorist organization would likely do the torturing and killing as a retaliation for them speaking with the

Candyman.

"So, talk."

"I was there to look at a ship."

"I know that much already."

"It was for a man from Saudi Arabia."

"Name?"

"I don't know."

"Tell me more than that," David said as he showed the black blade to the prisoner again who still stared at the floor. David lowered his head in a search to find the captive's eyes.

"That's all I know about it," he said, wiping his hands together.

"What do you know then?"

"An attack in the U.S."

"Where?"

"Los Angeles."

"When?"

"This month."

"Who's involved?"

"A dozen men."

"Do you have any names?"

"Only three."

David took out his bag and grabbed a notebook and a pen. "Write their names, and anything you know. Where they stay, what they plan to do, as much detail as you can."

Several minutes went by but the prisoner had written down two pages of information and given it to David. It consisted of three names, six addresses, and a tentative plan for suicide bombing several college campuses around Los Angeles. David looked the intel over with care before locking eyes with the prisoner who sat calmly in his chair. The prisoner was pale, his shoulders rounded forward, and he was taking slow, quick breaths. The left side of his shirt was covered in blood, and slowly dripped down to the floor, adding to the stains.

"Do you even have kids?" David asked gently.

"Only the one from my wife's sister."

"He's taken care of?"

"Yes."

"That's good." David stood up, took his shirt, wrapped it around the man's neck, and began to pull it tight. The prisoner didn't even fight.

David walked out into the night air and stretched his arms high above his head. Shirtless, he began his walk across town where he would make an encrypted phone call stateside. He knew this was something they'd want to hear immediately.

Chapter 2
TRAPPED

Washington, D.C.

Logan sat on a couch at home. Samantha left an hour earlier for work, which meant he had nothing to do but wait for a phone call that may or may not come. It had been a year since Amir Patel had slipped away, but the bitterness was still palpable. Every mission he did with his team felt as if it might be the one that would grant him revenge. He ground his teeth at the thought of their next encounter, as he watched President Pierce give a speech about how "we've defeated terrorism." Logan understood more than anyone, this was a lie.

Logan's phoned began dancing on the wooden coffee table distracting him from the thoughts that reverberated daily in his mind.

"Logan," Secretary Smith said as he heard the phone connect.

"Thank God. I can't stand listening to this speech anymore."

"I need you guys to come in. We've got a hot call."

"Be there in twenty."

Logan and his men, Lonnie, Dubs, and Migs, all met at the designated house ten miles outside D.C. It was a small home, owned by a someone who owed Secretary Smith a favor. After General Jenkins was found to be a high-ranking security threat, as well as the handler for Amir's terrorist cell, Smith wanted Logan's team to be completely under the radar. Five people knew about the team, and they all kept it locked down. Not even Samantha knew about their safehouse, or their missions.

"What up, Logan?" Lonnie asked as he entered the small living room and plopped down onto the couch. "You see that shit on the news?"

"Yeah, I saw it."

"Terrorism is dead. You haven't heard?" Dubs asked from the kitchen with a mouthful of chips.

"You gonna get soft my dude, eatin' that shit. You know why the ladies love me so much?" Lonnie asked, lifting his shirt, showing his abdominals to the men for the hundredth time.

"That impresses me less than that speech from President Pierce," Dubs said, pointing at the TV with the bag of chips.

"You keep eatin' big boy," Lonnie said, pointing haphazardly at the snack.

"Gentlemen," Secretary Smith said as he entered the home. "Sorry for the delay, but when the president speaks, everyone wants to talk about it. Took forever to get those politicians off me. I can't believe he's made this his platform," the secretary mumbled the last sentence to himself.

"No problem boss," Migs said, standing up to shake his hand.

"Okay Logan we've got a bad one brewin'. La-La Land. Apparently as many as twelve terrorists planning on suicide bombing a bunch of college campuses. I need you out there ASAP."

"How credible is the source?"

"He's one crazy son-of-a-bitch. Been dug in so deep in the Middle East I don't have a clue where he is. All I know is he calls from time to time with intel that's never wrong. He's the real deal."

"How long?"

"He said two weeks, but we can't risk the wait. You're on a flight tonight out of Dulles; got two rooms and a black Suburban waiting at the airport."

Secretary Smith set his briefcase down and opened it, grabbing a file from inside and handing it to Logan. Smith knew the entire country had capable FBI, and local anti-terrorism task forces, but the intel that came with a possibility of grabbing Amir Qasmi, went directly to Logan's team.

"There's only three names," Logan said, sighing and handing the file to Migs.

"That's the hard part. You'll need to find the remaining nine. Likely they'll be in and out of those addresses."

"If not?" Dubs asked, his baritone voice rumbling in his chest.

"Take what you can get. Something's better than nothing. Get some info out of these guys before you send them to *Allah*."

Los Angeles, California

It was just past 0100 and the moon was full and high overhead. Logan and Dubs sat in their SUV watching the outside of a small single family home in the back corner of a subdivision outside of Los Angeles. It took three days of surveillance, an additional car, and several hundred dollars in bribes, but they finally counted thirteen individuals who were entering three addresses on a regular basis. The only problem was they rarely met in groups larger than four, and never larger than seven. However, this night Dubs and Logan counted nine in this house, and Migs and Lonnie sat outside a second home just south of Pasadena, which had the remaining four.

"How we lookin'?" Logan asked into his radio.

"Same shit," Lonnie joked as he watched the only house on the block with the lights on. "Oh, wait a minute," Lonnie said intensely. "Sprinklers just came on," he said, smirking. The neighborhood Lonnie and Migs were in was affluent, with large homes, well-manicured lawns, and regular patrols from a uniformed cop.

"Still counting four?"

"Yup," Migs said from within a hedgerow just behind the large home. He had a perfect view of the kitchen where four men sat at a table, conversing and referencing several pieces of paper.

"We're counting nine here," Logan said. "Ten minutes to execute."

"Roger," Migs said.

"Yut," Lonnie affirmed, grabbing his Glock 23. He pulled the slide back engaging the weapon, the metallic sound acting as a switch. His body was becoming tense, his breathing rate accelerated, and he closed his eyes for a moment, imagining the scenario that would be taking place in the next few moments.

"Rent-a-cop," Lonnie said when he opened his eyes. He slid down in his seat and hid from view as the neighborhood police officer slowly cruised by.

"Okay, that's the 0130 check," Migs whispered.

The policeman turned the corner and Lonnie exited the car. He took a drink of vodka, then splashed a few drops on his purple shirt. He unbuttoned several buttons revealing a gold chain and a tank top beneath. He approached the front door to the home and rang the doorbell.

"You got their attention," Lonnie heard Migs through his small earpiece. "They aren't moving though. Hit it again."

Lonnie rang the doorbell two more times.

"Oh yeah. Now you pissed 'em off. You've got two comin' at ya' hot," Migs said as he rose from his prone position and slowly moved toward the house; unseen in his black gear.

"Hey man, what up?" Lonnie asked as the door whipped open; a short, bearded man standing in the doorway. "Does Reggie stay here? Heard he was throwin' an after party."

"No Reggie here. Do you know what time it is?" the man asked, as the smell of vodka wafted toward him from the black man standing on his front step.

"Naw man, I'm just chillin', but you sure he doesn't stay here? This is the address he told me," Lonnie said, pointing up toward the numbers above the arched doorway.

The Middle Eastern man made the mistake of taking his eyes off Lonnie to look at the numbers.

Wham! Lonnie struck the man hard in the face. He reached down and drew his Glock, placing two rounds silently into the terrorist's head as he walked into the home, dragging the man out of the way and closing the door behind him. While that was happening, Migs had moved in through the back window and double tapped the two terrorists that remained at the table.

Lonnie rushed into the house and quickly cleared the family room and kitchen, while Migs went upstairs in search of number four.

"Clear," he whispered as he checked a bedroom. "Clear," he whispered after clearing a second bedroom and the Jack and Jill bathroom between. Migs peered into the master suite and saw a glow from the opposite side of the bed.

"Get your hands up!" Migs hollered and Lonnie heard, rocketing up the staircase and through the hallway.

Pop, pop! Migs' Glock flashed, sending two shots through the bedding and into the last terrorist. Lonnie ran into the room and around the bed. He ripped a bloodied phone from the terrorist's hand.

"Not fast enough. You lose," the terrorist said as he smiled through red tinted teeth, the glow from the phone illuminating his face.

The text had already gone out: "RUN! RUN! RUN!"

"You gotta move now!" Migs said loudly into the comms. "Can't wait for us. They got a text out."

Dubs left the car and sprinted up the street in silence, going around to the back of the small, dated home as planned.

"Holy shit!" Dubs said as he watched shadowed figures scrambling behind the curtains.

"Damn it," Logan said as he leapt out of the SUV and knelt in the grass forty yards from the house, his suppressed M4 assault rifle up and ready.

Pop, pop! Logan shot, dropping a terrorist immediately as he tried leaving the front door. Someone from inside the home quickly slammed the door shut. Logan heard a yell followed by the lights in the house going out.

Pop, pop! Logan heard the odd sound of a silenced Glock, as Dubs shot a terrorist climbing out a window in the back of the house.

"Two down," Logan said.

After that it was still for several minutes. The moonlit homes and surrounding area became eerily still following the initial rush.

"ETA?" Logan asked softly.

"Five minutes out!" Lonnie yelled over the wind noise from the rented sedan as he raced down Highway 5 toward Sun Valley.

"Copy."

"Dubs hold it down. When they get here we're gonna breach in the front."

"Roger."

The five minutes passed slowly and the humidity was causing sweat to run down their arms and onto their palms.

"We're here," Lonnie said as he turned off the headlights, rounded the corner, and parked the car quietly. He and Migs came running toward Logan who never took his eyes off the one-story home.

"Okay, here's how it is. Migs you've got point. I'll throw bang, you enter first, Lonnie is two, I'm three. Dubs has back side. We can't risk frag, might set off any explosives, yut?"

"Yut," the men responded.

The three men tactically moved to the front of the house. Logan knelt near a large bay window in the front. He shot at it with his silenced sidearm, then threw a bang grenade into the room. The blast sent glass confetti outward from every window in the house, while the noise disoriented the terrorists inside. Migs breached the door with Lonnie and Logan close behind.

One by one they secured the terrorists, not shooting them, but rather tying them together in an awkward circle.

"Clear!" Migs said, entering the living room.

"Clear," Logan said, scanning the bathroom and first bedroom.

"Clear," Lonnie said, checking the master bedroom.

"Seven's the count Dubs, plus two down. Come in."

"Copy," Dubs said and approached the rear door.

Logan watched as one of the terrorists braced himself behind another.

"Hold, Dubs," Logan said as he walked toward the mass of bodies tied together in the living room. "What's your secret?" he asked the cowering terrorist.

"No English."

Whack! Logan hit the man hard with the rifle, sending a spray of red across the already stained carpet. Logan walked toward the back door and immediately saw the problem. Connected to the door handle was a complex electronic rig, wired to a stack of charges.

"Dub's come around front."

Logan walked back into the room and drew his pistol, popping two rounds past the terrorist's head, the heat from the lead singing his beard, but not drawing blood.

"Anyone else wanna play games?" he asked forcefully to the men on the ground. We're not in the business of taking prisoners. Tonight was a generous night."

"Damn straight," Lonnie said, looking down at the men tied together.

"Lonnie, I need you to take a look at the back door. See if there's something you can do with that."

"Got it."

Logan walked around the prisoners, looking each one of them over, trying to determine the hierarchy, who was weak, who was the strongest. Finally, he settled on the one he felt was the leader.

"Him first," Logan said, pointing to a middle-aged man, a beard more black than gray, and well built. Fear didn't know this man well.

Dubs reached down and cut the man loose, then dragged him to the back of the house.

"Who's the group you're fighting for?" Logan asked the man as Dubs held a gun to the back of his head. "Do you know Amir Qasmi? Where are you from? Who gave you this mission?"

The man just sat and stared at Logan from his knees. Not a single question got a rise out of the man.

"We got our intel from a man in Yemen. Does that sound familiar to you? He turned on you. You know who that might have been?"

The man only smiled.

"Take 'em all," Logan said toward Dubs.

The assault team dragged the terrorists out two by two into the back of the Suburban and piled them up.

"You two head back in and make sure we didn't miss anything. Meet us at the warehouse," Logan said to Lonnie and Migs.

"You got it boss," Migs said and the two men jogged back to the house.

Lonnie and Migs checked the closets, under the furniture, the cabinets. They cut open the mattress and the couches, finding nothing. The two men made quick work in the attic, but it was immaculate, not even an old cardboard box to be found. The last place they checked was the basement.

"Got a torch?" Migs asked as he held out his hand toward Lonnie. Lonnie reached into his belt and pulled out a flashlight.

Migs began walking down the wooden stairs into the mouth of the darkness. Dust danced in front of the flashlight, appearing as small bioluminescent bugs flying toward the LEDs, gaining in number with each step down into the old basement.

"You smell that?" Migs said, pausing and turning around to face Lonnie who was still standing at the top of the stairs.

"No."

"Come on," Migs said and turned back down the stairs. With each step, he gradually saw more of the small dark basement as he scanned the area with his light. He reached the final stair and felt it give. He lost his balance and grasped the railing. Stepping back, he released the pressure from his unstable footing.

Boom! Migs was thrown into the air, slamming into the wooden ceiling as the stairs were catapulted from the concrete below. Lonnie was thrown back into the hallway, his body making a large hole in the drywall as his ears bled and failed to perform. He was concussed, and felt as if he were outside of his body as he tried to stand on his feet. He peered down into the fire filled tomb below, slowly beginning to process the situation.

As Lonnie stood, the heat from the blaze began to burn his exposed skin, and the nitrogen burned his nose. He was immediately taken to a warzone in his mind. It was such a dichotomy, to be in a small home outside of L.A., but feeling as though he was in war torn Iraq.

"Migs!" Lonnie yelled. "Migs!" he tried again. The noxious smell coupled with the concussion made him sick and he turned to vomit into the hole in the wall.

He grabbed his comms and yelled, "Dubs you gotta get back here now!"

"What's going on—"

"Migs is dead! The whole fuckin' basement blew. I can't hear you, my ears are all fucked up! Just get here now!"

Lonnie sprinted through the house, upturning tables, running into the garage looking for a ladder, anything to help him get Migs out. He ran outside, and by the grace of God, there was a garden hose. He turned on the water and nothing happened. The neighbor had a hose also, so he ran next door and grabbed it, attached it to the hose he had, making it long enough to get into the house. He stood at the top of the stairs and sprayed water down into the inferno where the stairwell used to be. He imagined Migs in a corner waiting for him to help. He hoped Migs was yelling and he just couldn't hear the cries for help, or, even better, laughing at how panicked the typically smart-assed Lonnie was.

Several minutes passed and the fire had died down, revealing the truth. Migs was lying on the floor at the base of the stairs. Lonnie jumped down and went to his friend. It was useless to try. He had a massive head wound which likely killed him instantly. He never felt a thing.

"Lonnie you down there?" Dubs yelled from the doorway, his large frame eclipsing all light that was coming from upstairs.

"Dubs?" Lonnie asked, reacting to the sudden change in light. He picked Migs' body up and threw it over his shoulder. He walked over the smoldering remains of what used to be the stairs.

Dubs knelt in the doorway and reached down toward his friends. He was able to grab Migs' body, and pulled it up though the doorway.

He held Migs, the nearest thing he had to an older brother, close to him and sobbed into his singed clothes. He began to hear sirens over the cracking of wood and the hissing of water from fractured pipes in the basement. He gently laid Migs down and reached into the basement for Lonnie, who quickly sprung up. The two men carried Migs out, placing him into the back of the Suburban where the terrorists had been moments earlier.

"Get out of here fast. Go to the safehouse," Dubs said to Lonnie whose eyes still appeared glazed over. Lonnie nodded, understanding what Dubs was saying, but still not hearing the words.

Dubs waited until they drove a few blocks away and felt

confident the cops weren't following them. He was struggling to keep his emotions in check, but his best friend was laying in the back of the car, dead from a booby trap in the basement of the terrorist's home. He picked up his phone and called Logan, after he stopped screaming, and finally found a way to stop his hands from strangling the steering wheel.

"What's the situation?" Logan asked while sitting in a room next to where the seven terrorists sat tied up facing the wall.

"He's dead Logan."

Silence. Logan was stunned, enraged; guilt overwhelmed him. *I should have been there.* He hung up the phone and kicked a steel door open. Walking into the large warehouse, he could see the Middle Eastern men as they each sat with their hands behind their back and legs tied together.

The same terrorist from earlier began to chuckle, then laugh, and stomped his boot down firmly onto the concrete floor several times.

"God is good! Is he not my brothers?" he exclaimed, his words echoed in the brightly lit warehouse. "I know what happened American. Your friend went downstairs. You think you know everything but you don't. You think we know anything? We don't. Ask us. We won't tell you a thing. We serve *Allah!*"

Logan walked quickly toward the man who spoke and reached down with his gun. He paused, briefly, making sure the man knew fear as they locked eyes. Logan shot twice. The blood spatter on the concrete was a close match to the rust stains that already painted long streaks down the tall walls.

Logan walked to the next man. *Pop, pop!* He skipped the next and went on to number four in line. *Pop, pop!* And went the fifth, sixth, seventh in the line, all receiving their two shots in the head without a chance to talk.

"I've got three rounds left," Logan said to the last terrorist who sat in horror with blood from his friends spattered all over his face and clothes. He spat a few times, as the salty iron taste of blood leached into his mouth from his moist lips.

Pop! Logan shot the man in the left knee. The terrorist screamed out in pain.

"Tell me information. Who sent you? Where did you get your orders? How were you contacted? What was the go signal?"

"I know nothing!" the man said, breathing heavily and rocking back and forth.

Pop! Logan shot the man in the shoulder. "Tell me something and the last bullet will send you to *Báb al-Jihád* or whatever heaven you so desire."

"Him! He knows all."

"The funny guy?"

"Yes, yes. He knows all. He gets all on his phone."

"Where's his phone?"

"Always with him."

Logan walked to the man who sat lifelessly leaning against the wall, the smirk now absent from his face. He searched him, finding nothing.

"Search, it's there!" the man insisted nodding his head toward his former leader's backside. Logan reached down the man's pants and found a phone in between his buttock. Logan then raised his gun and shot the last terrorist in the head. He decided not to do anything with the phone until Lonnie arrived. He was the best with bombs and booby traps.

Logan sat, allowing tears to roll down his face as he thought about Migs, and even shed a tear for Sherman, his sniper teammate he had lost years ago. Logan bore the burden of both, and started to wonder why he was the one always surviving.

Lonnie arrived at the warehouse, quickly running inside. His boot squealed as he stopped and froze thirty feet behind Logan who was sitting in a folding chair directly in front of the seven dead terrorists. Logan sat with his Glock in hand, pulling the trigger over and over again, *click . . . click . . . click* like a metronome, its faint sounds reverberating off the concrete walls. It had been ten minutes since a 40mm round left the chamber, but his finger was on autopilot.

"Logan?" Lonnie asked quietly as he slowly approached the leader of their unique assault team. "Hey man, you alright?" Lonnie asked as he finally reached Logan, standing at his side and looking down at the visibly distraught soldier.

A moment later Dubs came charging into the room like a bull seeing red. "I'll kill those mother fuckers!" he said, searching the room with blind rage, failing to see the terrorists had already been assassinated. His eyes were bloodshot as he spat, his face glistening in the wake of tears and sweat. "What's going on!" Dubs yelled, confused when he finally spotted Lonnie.

"Hey man take a walk," Lonnie said with his hands held gently up toward Dubs.

"Take a walk? What the hell am I supposed to do with that?" he asked as his eyes began to well up, his face already red. "I can't get the smell outta my nose, man!"

"Where is he?" Logan finally spoke. He looked down at his gun and realized he was still pulling the trigger.

"The Suburban," Lonnie said, reaching down to place a hand on Logan's shoulder. But, before he made contact, Logan slipped away and strode toward the SUV.

"You stay in here," Logan said to Dubs aggressively pointing a finger into the large man's face.

Logan made his way to the car in the night. The full moon was perched high above, giving him all the light he required. He opened the rear doors and was greeted by the awful smell of burnt flesh, hair, and clothes; then the horrifying sight of Migs. It wasn't even his friend any more, instead, a blackened and tangled mass which could have been anything; but he knew who it was. He reached into his pocket, grabbed his phone, and took several pictures. He sent them to Doyle Smith with a text that said, "Tell President Pierce terrorism is alive and well. We lost a good man tonight."

He walked back into the warehouse and went to his chair, sitting in front of the bodies once again, and stared at the web of flesh and spattered blood.

"This is all we got," Logan said, holding up a phone. "It was on that one," he said, pointing to the first man he shot. "Whatever's on here better be worth the life of that man out there."

"Nothing's worth that man out there," Dubs said defiantly.

"Damn straight," Lonnie said in agreement.

"Let's get the hell outta here," Logan said as he stood and walked out of the room. They left the warehouse together, wrapped Migs in a large tarp, and laid him gently into the back of the Suburban. None of them said it, but they all felt it should be them who brought Migs to Arlington.

Chapter 3
DEUX

Paris, France

President Pierce stood in front of a podium draped in red, white, and blue. The president was in Paris for the groundbreaking for *Deux*, the larger, more intricate Eiffel Tower. Over his right shoulder, an American flag; to his left, the French flag, both equal in height, and lazily flapping in the warm breeze. He smiled politely and raised a hand into the air. After several moments of applause, he gestured for the French president, Renee Bari, to join him at the podium. When she did, the crowd reached a fever pitch and the two of them wrapped an arm around one another and waved.

"Thank you," he projected over the crowd. "Thank you for the warm welcome," President Pierce finally spoke after two minutes of applause.

"I'm here, as you all know, to celebrate the triumph over evil." Again, he had to pause as the crowd of thousands hollered over the loudspeakers placed all around the venue.

"Evil. It's taken many forms over the centuries. In our lifetime, terrorism is a word that has become synonymous with evil. It strikes without warning, it destroys our families, our way of life, our physical realities. Last year, on Bastille Day, the people of France were shown the true depth of this evil. Behind me used to stand a symbol of France, but now, the earth behind me is a scar on this beautiful country, and a constant reminder of a battle waged by evil." A steady but present stream of boos emerged briefly from the crowd. President Pierce paused, dramatically, and then looked over the crowd and smiled. "But today I'm here with President Renee Bari to tell you the tides of war are changing!"

The crowd erupted and the two presidents once again stood embraced. President Bari motioned for something off camera.

"Behind this piece of paper is our plan for constructing the new vision of France!" President Bari said with enthusiasm in her voice. She reached toward the large easel and grabbed one side of the cardboard paper that covered the detailed rendition of the new structure. She paused, and motioned for President Pierce to grasp the other side so they could hoist the paper away together.

"*Trois, deux, un!*" she said as the crowd joined in.

The cardboard was pulled away and a massive OLED screen displayed a turning 3D model of the new structure to be built. It was similar to the Eiffel Tower, having four strong legs that arched upward exponentially, but in this model there was a rotation to the steel construction that made it appear a corkscrew. The top also opened wider, giving it a top-heavy appearance. But it was elegant and spiritual, as if bending toward the heavens. The screen went dark, and a light show erupted on *Deux*, which would accompany the structure at night.

"You see we *are* winning the war. We *are* driving the terrorists back to where they came, and they aren't regrouping, they are defeated. I can confidently say that it's been six months since we've seen a terrorist attack on U.S. soil, and one year to the day since we've witnessed one in France. Unfortunately, in America we've been dealing with domestic affairs. Gun violence is at an all-time high, police violence is becoming a daily reality so we're possibly entering a new era of evil. One that I plan on leading the fight against, even after I've finished my second term as President of the United States," he said, declaring himself the victor of the upcoming election in a couple short months. "Thank you President Bari, thank you France for allowing me to be a part of this historic day. To a future without terrorism; without evil," he said, raising a hand into the air with a bottled water.

"*À un monde sans terrorisme,*" President Bari said also raising her water.

President Pierce walked off the stage and toward his motorcade, which was parked just beyond the crowd. The secret service, as well as the local French police, did an excellent job ensuring the pathway was clear for him to take long fast strides to his waiting SUV. He climbed into the back and slammed the door.

"Let's see that asshole spin this!" he said to Grant Sanchez, his campaign manager.

"You looked good, sir," he responded, distracted, as he re-watched the feed on his laptop. I think you could have gone without a tie, made it look more informal, relaxed, but I think you'll look good in America either way."

"Thanks Grant. I still think we need something to put Senator Waxman in the rear view."

"You do have Nassir Ajab," Grant said, holding his breath.

"I know, I know. Just not keen on bringing in a Muslim. That might affect me in the election. Last thing I need is some ignorant citizen trying to make it seem as though I'm siding with a terrorist to eliminate terrorism."

"That sounds ridiculous."

"I agree, but I think we can both agree the press wins elections, despite our best efforts. We need as much positivity in the media as we can find. That means more things like today. The more we can bury the terrorism incidents from last year, the better."

"I think so too."

"Mr. President," Secretary Smith said after listening quietly for several moments via the speakerphone.

"Yes Doyle," the president said, arms folded, face pensive.

"We've heard of another cell in the U.S. They're going to be attacking out west, L.A. area. I've got someone on it. They went dark three days ago, so hopefully we will hear back soon."

"How many is that since Amir Qasmi escaped?"

"Seventeen cells."

"We're not slowing them down at all are we?" President Pierce asked, combing his fingers through his hair.

"My honest opinion?" Secretary Smith asked.

"Please."

"I think you need to stop these speeches. When an attack happens, things will look much worse. You're making it seem as though we have everything under control, but in reality, we are flying by the seat of our pants. Matter of fact, we're incredibly lucky to have been getting the intel we've been getting. One of these days we're gonna miss something and you'll be in sad shape."

"Okay, okay. How are they communicating?"

"We're watching the deep web. A lot of chatter on

there, but our best intel is coming from our guys in the Middle East."

"You think I should see what that I.T. guy has to say?"

"Nassir Ajab I'm assuming?"

"Yes."

"Couldn't hurt to listen, but I don't trust anyone after Jenkins blew up in my face."

"Thanks Doyle. Anything else?"

"No, sir."

"Have a good afternoon then."

The presidential limousine pulled up to the Hotel InterContinental Paris Le Grand. President Pierce sat motionless, staring at the back of the leather seat in front of him. His look was blank, deep in thought, quickly running variables through his mind. He was always analyzing situations, thinking several moves ahead. In his mind, the only move he had left was to sacrifice his queen; to allow his opponent close enough to strike, then attack.

"Grant. Get Nassir on the phone. I need to finally hear his proposal."

"Uh, of course, sir," Grant said, closing his computer and grabbing his phone. "Now?"

"Yes."

Grant dialed the number and spoke to an assistant of Nassir Ajab. After several moments, he handed the secure phone over to President Pierce, who immediately sat upright and cleared his throat.

"Good evening Mr. Ajab," the president said with a smile.

"Hello Mr. President. I just watched your speech online. Very moving. I would like to congratulate you on your successes thus far. But as I've discussed with your staff, I think your concerns are far from over."

"I'm not ignorant. I'm aware the threats are still out

there," he said, glancing toward Grant. "So, what do you propose for us?"

"I want to help you monitor internet traffic. Try to determine the sources of terrorist activity, origins of messages, et cetera."

"I'm not certain that can be possible. To allow a private company access to our internet security, develop codes, inserting them into our servers. I'll have to pass on that for now."

"Mr. President we have a new type of computer. It's quantum technology, the first of its kind."

"Go on," President Pierce said, sitting back into his seat.

"Do you like baseball Mr. President?"

"It's America's pastime."

"Could you hit a ninety-nine mile-per-hour fastball?"

"Not at my age, but when I was nineteen I'd have given it a go."

"With our tech, you could. Let me explain. Imagine having the ability to slow the ball down to the point where it was almost standing still. You could read the rotation, the words, you could even count the seams. Mr. President, you could put your bat down, walk out to the ball, and study it as it came toward the catcher."

"What's the point Mr. Ajab?"

"Our technology allows you to go through data thousands of times faster than current binary coding systems. We can easily decipher codes, track data, monitoring incoming and outgoing traffic, and even scan the not-so-nice bits of information in the dark web."

"I'd really have to think about this Mr. Ajab."

"You have an election coming up am I right? The last thing you want is another incident on your hands."

"Is that a threat Mr. Ajab?" President Pierce said loudly in the back of the SUV as he sat up and leaned forward.

"I'm sorry Mr. President. I don't want you to take it that way. I'm truly a fan of yours, despite my lineage."

"And that is?"

"My family is from Saudi. I'd love to rectify the recent findings released by congress, regarding the involvement of Saudi Arabia in the events on September eleventh."

"I appreciate your time Mr. Ajab. I know you're a busy man," he said, dismissing the reference to the recently released records that caused a substantial amount of social unrest.

"Anything for you Mr. President. You have my number and please, call any time. I'd love to be of assistance."

President Pierce exited the vehicle without saying a word, walked into the hotel, rode up the elevator, and into his suite. He collapsed deep into a pillowy couch, and traced the carved trim work in the room with his eyes, trying to clear his mind. The beauty in the design was lost on him. He only looked for the patterns, the mistakes, the general use of space and how it could have been done differently, if not better. President Pierce didn't want to look back on his time in office and think about what could have been done better, what should have been done differently. He needed every advantage he could find.

President Pierce finally allowed himself to close his eyes.

Knock, knock, knock. Slowly, he pulled himself out of the soft couch and walked toward the white double doors.

"What is it?"

"Secretary Smith, sir. A video call," said the secret service member holding a computer.

"I'll take it in the room please," he said, stepping aside and allowing them to bring in the screen. The secretary, as well as the president, waited patiently for the secret service to clear the room. Secretary Smith had requested a private audience prior to them notifying the president.

"What's the news Doyle?"

"I heard from one of my men, sir." Secretary Smith held his phone up to the screen revealing the haunting image he received from Logan.

"What am I looking at here Doyle?"

"The body of Miguel Martinez. A marine, a pilot, an American hero; killed by a terrorist cell in Los Angeles."

President Pierce's heart sank. "That damn Waxman is gonna eat this up! I'm done for."

"Henry!" the booming voice of Doyle Smith came through loud and clear, as if he was still shouting coverage on the football field from his days back at Georgia. "The incident has been cleaned up. The official story is that a meth lab exploded in a home just outside of L.A. Unofficially, I'm one man down with this strike team. Beyond that, there was another riot today in Chicago over police brutality. You've got a few looming issues when you return. In my opinion, the larger of the two is the situation with this incident in L.A."

"Thanks for the information Doyle. I apologize for my reaction. I was out of line. No excuse for that. See you stateside tomorrow and we can discuss it more."

Chapter 4
ALIVE

Unknown location, Yemen

The room was hardly big enough for Amir to lay down. Even in the fetal position his feet touched one wall, and the top of his head touched another, however, this cell was pleasant compared to what he endured during his first several weeks in captivity. He'd lost forty pounds, his hair had fallen out, and he was forced to eat scraps from discarded food and drinks the soldiers had given him. The beatings weren't bad, he often allowed his mind to drift away, back to the America that existed before his days in the Army, to a place that made him mentally strong. But, after a while, they broke his mind as well. He cried the tears he wished he cried when he was a boy being called a terrorist. He cried the tears he was too proud to cry when his mother died of cancer. He cried the tears he thought he cried for his father's brutal murder and for the choices he made afterward. But now, he lay in a room and felt no emotion. He was a shell waiting to be filled, inhuman.

Bang! Creak. His door slowly opened revealing a dimly lit hallway. Amir stood, knowing if he didn't, he'd feel the sting of cold steel on his face or the ache in his stomach from a boot. He followed the silent guard down a hallway, turning toward a brightly lit room with white walls and a white tiled floor—easy to clean. But this time things were different. His mouth became dry, his heart raced, and nausea took over his body. He began to dry heave only to be struck by a guard waiting inside. *I did everything right!* he thought but dared not say. Amir tried to lay down, but they grabbed him from the floor and stood him up, only to pound him in the stomach when he took his own weight.

"Stand!" the man barked at him.

Amir's eyes darted all over the room looking for a sign, a hint at what he was supposed to do in this new situation. Usually there was only one chair in the room, which meant he was going to be beaten, followed by questions. Other times, no chair, which meant he would be asked to do physically demanding tasks until he failed, which would lead to physical punishment. This time there were two chairs, and a stainless steel table between them.

A door opened on the far side of the room, a door Amir had never witnessed open in the months he had spent in the underground facilities. He'd seen at least half a dozen concrete basements, and never the sun. When he was transported, he was blindfolded, gagged, beaten until he lost consciousness. He began to take a step backward and was met by a boot in his back, driving him forward. He crashed into the heavy metal table causing one of the chairs to fall, making the sound of metal on tile ring their ears.

"Get up!" a man yelled at him as Amir struggled to his feet.

Amir stood just in time to see a well-dressed man with a sharp nose and deep set eyes walk through the door. The way he moved was calculated, each step a reproduction of the last, and his Italian leather shoes scraped gracefully across the tile that had seen so much horror. Even the man's hair was perfect, not a strand of his salt and pepper out of place. He walked to the table and stared into Amir's eyes smiling, subtly. The man looked back toward the doorway and a second, younger man entered the room. He was just as handsome as the first, but his eyes were filled with rage. This young man took the rifles from the two guards and then left the room.

"Do you know who I am?"

An entire minute went by before anyone spoke. Smiling, the well-dressed man spoke again. "Do you know who I am, Amir?"

"No.

"Ah, but you do. Think harder."

"I don't know, sir," Amir said softly.

"Do you remember General Jenkins? I have to imagine you do, it wasn't *that* long ago you took his life."

A wave of memories flooded back in. DuPont Circle, a purple heart, Saint Louis, and Logan. It made Amir feel nauseous again.

"I can see you remember. Don't bother answering. I want you to feel comfortable. The man walked toward the chair that was still on the floor. "Allow me to grab this for you." He bent down and held his tie to his chest as he raised the chair back upright, placing it next to the table with just enough space for Amir to slide in and sit.

"Sit with me," the man said as he walked to the other chair and sat. Amir slowly lowered himself into the chair, watching the two guards in the room while doing so.

"Amir, we both want the same thing: respect. I know

that's why you joined the Army. I know that's why you excelled. I also know that's why you did such excellent work leading your team under Jenkins."

Amir became uneasy in his chair.

"Sorry to bring his name up again, but you see that's how we met. You texted me from his phone. It's what brought us together. Do you know who I am?"

"No."

"My name is Karim, but the name is not important. Would you like to know what today is?"

"Yes."

"Bastille Day!" Karim said with his hands out to the side raised high into the air and smiling. "What happened one year ago today?"

"I don't know," Amir said softly, his mind was empty, exhausted, and malnourished.

"I understand. You've been through a lot with these men here. I hate what they do; do you know that?"

"I don't know."

"Look at me Amir," Karim said, leaning onto the table with his light gray suit. "I care about you." They locked eyes for a moment, and Amir looked down at the floor.

"Amir, I have respect, money, power. I am smart and motivated. You are too. I can see it in you. I want nothing more than for us to work together. Do you hate these men? What they did to you?" he asked, pointing at the two guards in the room, but his eyes stayed locked onto Amir. "Can I earn your trust today?"

"How?" Amir asked, hopeful, but guarded.

Karim removed a nickel-plated 1911 from his waist. "I know you've seen one of these before. Maybe not as nice," Karim said, twisting the weapon on the table, the bright LED lights in the room reflected in the rubies that decorated the grip, "but it works the same." He slid it across the table toward Amir. The metal scraping metal acted as flint for Amir's soul.

The two guards in the room dove toward the table but Amir grabbed it quickly and stood. Life had returned within. He felt a wave of strength overwhelm him, as if the gun gave him the forty pounds of muscle he lost, his confidence, and allowed him to feel emotions once again. Rage is what he felt, revenge was what he wanted. He raised the gun and double tapped both guards in the head in quick succession. He then turned toward Karim and pointed the gun at him.

"Amir, put the gun down," Karim said calmly.

"Why? You did this to me. All of it. Didn't you?" Amir said, spitting the words out between his teeth as his rageful eyes burned a hole through the calm man. Amir was trembling, the gun barely able to stay on target as his adrenaline began to dissipate.

"No. I need you to trust me. Drop the gun and we can talk more. I want you to be the man you want to be. Respected, feared, admired."

Amir began to lower the gun slowly.

"Taj! Enter!" Karim demanded, and in walked the young man from earlier, holding a rifle and pointing it toward Amir. "This is my son Taj. You will be his helper. He will train you. You will run a camp soon. If you'd like. You will perform the duties Taj has done for years. I trust you with my son's job. Is that enough?"

Amir threw the gun and sat back into the chair. Karim walked around the table and grasped Amir's shoulders gently.

"You are my son as well now Amir." He bent low and kissed him on the head, the smell was putrid, thick, but the gesture was important. "Whatever you need I will provide. Do not hesitate to ask. But, I will ask a lot from you as well."

Amir couldn't help but cry and nod his head.

"You are hungry, yes?" Karim asked, motioning once again to the doorway as he walked back to the opposite side of the table. Two men brought trays of fruit and bread. "Eat slowly, Amir. You don't have to finish this all today. We'll get you healthy again. People will fear and respect you soon my son."

Chapter 5
A VOICE OF THE PEOPLE

Washington, D.C.

Logan stared at the floor in his basement, elbows on knees, and a half-drunk beer sweating onto the floor, forming a thick, dark ring in the concrete. To his left, a small refrigerator, and to his right, twelve empty bottles standing at attention. This had been his routine for three straight days since the funeral at Arlington, where they buried Migs' ashes. Nobody really knew how Migs wanted to be buried, the topic hadn't been brought up, but they all agreed he was already halfway there after the incident. The ceremony still had a casket, still had the stars and stripes draped on it, then folded and handed to his mother and father as she cried softly for their only son.

Logan sat recalling the events of the funeral, the conversation with Migs' mother, how he had to explain to her Migs had been involved in a "training accident" which left him unrecognizable. He hated the lie, but it was the only way to keep their task force a secret.

Samantha came down the stairs, breaking the white noise from the house fan as her feet gently slapped the concrete floor. She was apprehensive, nervous to come downstairs for the past three days, allowing him the space he clearly needed; but she was scared for him. Slowly she walked up behind Logan and gently stroked his upper back with her nails. He flinched, initially, then reached back and firmly grasped her hand, pulling it away gently.

"Please don't Sam," he said softly, but firmly.

"What can I do honey?" she said, fighting to hide the sadness that was cascading down her face.

"You'll never understand what it's like to be that close to the one who dies. I've had it happen so many times now. I don't think I'm supposed to die."

"Please don't talk about it like that. It scares me."

"You don't think it scares me? Am I supposed to just watch everyone around me die?"

"I—I don't know what to say!" she said, covering her mouth and sobbing. "I'm happy you're with me. I don't want you to die!"

"I don't know what to say either. Maybe just let me be for now. I'll come up soon," he said, taking a long drink from his beer, stopping because he had finished it. He set it neatly into a row that promised to grow as the evening turned to night.

Samantha turned and walked toward the stairs, pausing for a moment to pull out the pregnancy test she had taken while he was in Los Angeles. She opened her mouth, for a moment thinking the news might turn him around. The thought of a mini Logan could have made him happy. She paused and allowed herself to fully grasp the stress he was under. She convinced herself she had plenty of time, and walked upstairs.

Chicago, Illinois

Senator Herman Waxman was an Illinois native and still loved the land of Lincoln. Early in his political career, he decided it was important to show people he wasn't about the glamorous lifestyle and big government homes the public office often came with. Instead, he lived with his mother and his two daughters in the house in which he grew up. A year before he ran for his first election, his wife died in what ended up being a rare viral infection caught too late. The fact that he was a single parent resonated with voters, and ultimately within the Democratic Party. After serving in the Senate for four terms, he was quickly thrust into the limelight after the terrorist attack in Chicago.

Senator Waxman had consistently talked emotionally about the attacks in Chicago, aggressively pointing the finger at those who he felt were responsible: President Pierce, Secretary of State Doyle Smith, and various members of the FBI and DHS for not acting on intelligence they knew existed. The senator could really charge people up emotionally. Unfortunately for the local PD in many cities around the country, he had ignited a fire within the citizens that bred hate, rioting, and crimes across racial and ethnic lines, and, even had certain groups committing acts of violence against the police. It wasn't Senator Waxman who provoked this behavior. He was only trying to get people to care, to open their eyes and ask questions, to act instead of complaining as bystanders.

Senator Waxman stood in front of an immense crowd in Grant Park. The sun was resting high in the sky, as if trying to catch a glimpse of the wonderful speaker as he walked toward the wooden podium. The roar was deafening and the senator smiled warmly, his bright, white teeth were a stark contrast to the dark skin he received from his Brazilian mother.

"Good afternoon Chicago!" he said excitedly, his thick, baritone voice penetrating the crowd's chanting of "Waxman, Waxman, Waxman!"

"Oh, this will always be my city!" he said, raising his hands and clapping, pausing briefly to wipe a tear from the corner of his eye. He was every bit an emotional man, but it was passion that made him that way, not weakness.

"I have a heavy heart today my people," he said and the crowd responded by quieting down, some even sitting into their folding chairs or on blankets. "I see so many of us hurting each other. So much anger, frustration, bitterness; and for what? This country is about coming together in times of need, and in times of prosperity. You heard President Pierce say we are winning the war on terrorism—"

"Boo!" the crowd groaned and interrupted Waxman at the mention of the republican candidate.

"Now you see? That's exactly it. The president is doing his job. He's making an effort to get rid of these murderers, but unfortunately it was too late for some of us. I don't need to remind people here of the devastating effects of terrorism. All I have to do is walk down beautiful Michigan Avenue a few miles to a place where the city is still scrambling to clean up the mess from just this year. In my opinion, things could have been done to prevent it. I haven't been quiet about that, and when I'm president, you had better believe I will continue to speak openly and candidly about the need for continued anti-terrorism work."

The crowd cheered loudly again, some banged bells, drums, and blew horns. Others waved flags and held up signs supporting Senator Waxman.

"One thing President Pierce hasn't directly addressed in great detail, is our current problem in this country. It frustrates me to see our local police departments so abused and falsely accused of crimes against civilians. Don't get me wrong though. A corrupt cop is worse than any civilian criminal, but let's face it. They've gotten a bad rap in recent months, and I'd appreciate it if we could all go home tonight and teach our children how important it is to respect the law, rather than making them the bad guy. We've all seen the movies, and if there were as many bad cops in real departments as there are in Hollywood, we'd be in serious trouble.

"What I think it all comes to is this. Very simple. If we treat each other with the respect and dignity we want to receive, everyone would be happy. Let's all try to be a bit better at it. I will lead by example. I vow that from this point forward, my campaign will not negatively attack President Pierce in any way. I will only speak on my platform and leave it at that. Occasionally, politics can get ugly and I want to be as respectful of my competitor as I can," he said, smiling over the crowd who caught his joke.

"Thank you Chicago! I'll do my best to move the White House here when I take office, but I'll admit there are a few things I can't do," he said with a smile and a wave, exiting the podium and walking toward the rear of the stage, ultimately entering a waiting car. As he pulled away, the crowd continued to cheer as a local band took the stage and began to play for the crowd.

Chapter 6
A BROKEN MAN

Washington, D.C.

Doyle Smith paced the floor of his office, playing with his class ring. The years since football weren't kind to his body, and when he was under stress, he ate fast food and the salt inflated his hands, making the large ring impossible to remove. He had the University of Georgia football game streaming online, trying to distract him from watching the clock, but he couldn't hear the announcer over his own thoughts.

After Migs' funeral, Logan had given Secretary Smith the terrorist's cellphone in hopes they could gather some intel. Doyle was apprehensive about those around him since Jenkins, so it took him several days to find a technician good enough and proven enough to do the job of analyzing the data from the phone. Doyle was promised he'd receive any intel from the phone in three days. It was Saturday, and it was the third day.

"Mr. Secretary," Margaret his administrative assistant said through the phone.

"Yes?"

"You've got someone here to see you. Won't give me his name."

"Thank you, send him in please."

A moment later a slender man with glasses and dressed in loose fitting clothes entered the secretary's office. Everything about him was black, his shoes, pants, shirt, and jacket, even the rims of his glasses were matte black.

"Everything you need from the phone is on here," he said, holding up a small flash drive.

"So you were able to find something?"

"Yeah, a few things. Emails, contact names, a few IP addresses from where messages were coming from."

"Can we track the IPs? Get a location?"

"Check the data on the flash drive. You'll know how to get in touch with me if it doesn't make sense. But it will."

"Thank you." Secretary Smith shook his hand and allowed the man to leave without another word.

Doyle ran around his desk, turned the Georgia game off, and placed the flash drive into the computer. Thirty seconds later he saw two files: aerial photos and contacts. He immediately called Logan.

"Hello," a weak voice said on the other end. Secretary Smith checked the time, 1430.

"Logan, this is Doyle. How you doin'?"

"Never better," Logan said, grunting and sitting up from the couch.

"We got a big lead on that phone. I'd like you to round up the boys and meet me." Doyle paused, realizing Logan wasn't himself. "How much time you need Logan? Realistically."

"Three hours."

"I'll call the others. You get some rest. See you in three hours."

Logan ran upstairs and quickly jumped into the shower. He'd been in the same clothes for four days, and could smell himself when he moved. He took a deep breath to slow his heart as he stood in front of the foggy mirror, seeing himself for the first time in two weeks. He had dropped several pounds and was soft where he should have been firm. He lifted his right arm and flexed it, noting a decreased responsiveness of his biceps. He sighed, frustrated with himself for not staying strong and focused on his commitment to the cause.

Logan grabbed his razor, shaved twice, making sure he appeared in control. He then threw on some clothes, searching for the tightest shirt he could find in order to fill it out. Once he was moderately satisfied, he went downstairs and into the kitchen.

"Wow honey. You look great," Samantha said, smiling at him from the living room. She walked toward him and squeezed her body right next to his, feeling the warmth of his skin, but the ice in his soul.

"Thanks," Logan said, working the coffee maker.

"You heading out?" she asked as a pit grew in her stomach.

"Doyle called. He needs us to come in."

Samantha's smile faded. She assumed it had to do with work, but actually hearing the words made her nervous.

"Are you sure?"

"What the hell's that supposed to mean?" he asked and squeezed the handle on the coffee pot as he slammed it firmly back onto the warming plate. He leaned onto the counter with outstretched arms, supporting his torso.

"You've been hurting Logan. Are you sure you should go back?"

"When's a good time Samantha? Should I take my time? Go talk to someone?"

Samantha turned and sat on the couch stunned. She had tiptoed around him for days, not speaking to him, and what little conversing they had, Logan gave very short, distracted answers.

Logan was trying to control his anger, but being vulnerable wasn't easy for him. She cared for him and was scared, but he needed to be strong. More important, he needed to seem solid. Not only for her, but for his assault team, for Secretary Smith, for the moments where he'd face another terrorist.

Logan poured a large cup of black coffee and sat on the couch with Samantha.

"I'm sorry," he said as he put his hand on her leg.

She looked up at him and immediately saw he was still very drunk. She could always tell if something was off about him. "You're gonna need a ride."

"I'll be fine sweetheart," he said, smiling widely and taking a drink, the steam rolling up over his face. "Wow, that's hot!" he said, burning his tongue and pulling back from the molten coffee.

She responded with a slight smile and a tilt of her head, allowing her brown hair to cascade down toward the arm of the couch. He chuckled.

"Fine. I'll call Migs," he said, slipping into habits formed over the last few months. Migs had lived the closest and they often rode together. The smile quickly evaporated from both their faces. Samantha was scared, not knowing what to expect as Logan sat staring into his coffee, the only thing in the room as dark as Logan's thoughts.

"I'll call Dubs."

"Logan," Samantha said, bending forward trying to catch Logan's eyes. "You can talk to me," she said after he allowed her to see his once bright, green eyes, which were now bloodshot, hollow, alone. The memory of who he was just a few weeks earlier trickled into her mind, and she was left with a pain in her stomach for who he now was.

"I love you, Logan."

"I love you, too."

It took thirty minutes after the phone call, but Dubs arrived, beeping his horn in the big truck.

"Dubs!" Logan said as the big man pulled up in the driveway. "See ya' later sweetie," he said, kissing Samantha on the cheek.

"How you doin' big guy," he said, hugging Dubs. As the men embraced, Dubs looked to Samantha. She slightly shook her head back and forth, a look of concern on her face.

"Good man. Hanging in there. How you been? I texted you here and there but didn't hear from ya'."

"Yeah my damn phone broke. Pretty sure I got pissed and threw it right after things went down."

Once again Dubs looked up toward Samantha who sat on the porch steps, glistening tracks running down her cheeks as she struggled not to break down in front of Logan.

"Alright Sam, I'll bring him back in one piece."

"Thank you, I know you will. Say hi to Jackie for me."

"Will do. She says hi already. Give her a call. I'm sick of being the middle man," Dubs said, winking and waving as the two men climbed into his big truck.

"When you guys gonna move in together?"

"Never!" Dubs yelled playfully from the truck as he sped away.

The drive was quick, but awkward. Dubs knew Logan wasn't in a good place but he wouldn't say anything. Dubs felt strange calling out the man who saved his life, the glue that held the team together. In the brief moment while driving to the meeting house, with the strong aroma of coffee in the air from Logan's aluminum cup, Dubs realized just how short their time together had been; and how well they all knew each other. It had only been a year since they met. Logan had been the instructor for a course on counter-intelligence when all hell broke loose, and they were forced to hunt down a terrorist cell.

"We've done a lot in the last year," Dubs said, breaking the silence.

"Seventeen terror cells since Amir."

"That's a whole lot of frequent flyer miles."

"Mhm," Logan said as he stared out the window.

Twenty minutes later they arrived at the safehouse where Lonnie waited inside with Doyle.

"How we feelin'?" Doyle asked as the two men walked in and sat down at a small kitchen table. "You sobered up?" he said, looking directly at Logan, frustration in his tone.

"I'm good," Logan said playfully, inside he was boiling. It was an unnecessary jab from Doyle.

"Logan, we've got some good stuff from that cellphone. Take a look," Secretary Smith said, opening his computer. "Five solid leads on men, all known to be in Yemen or the surrounding areas. Based on some of the pings on computers, we flew a satellite and got two infrared shots of what looks to be training centers in the mountains of Yemen."

Doyle opened the files and showed them the infrared images of two terrorist training centers, as well as a list of five contacts with their pictures.

"I've been told these are new locations that haven't been seen or heard of before. By the size and heat signature, they're likely the largest to date."

"What's the plan then Mr. Secretary?" Lonnie asked. "You want us to fly out there and bust this place up?"

"Not at all. Your intel is gonna save lives gentleman.

We're blowing this compound off the earth. I've already reached out to Captain Myers, the executive officer of the supercarrier Gerald Ford. He's going to be executing an airstrike sometime in the next two days. As soon as I get the reports I'll let you know. Fair enough?"

"Yes, sir," the men all seemed to say in unison.

"Okay. Well you all get home and rest. We've likely got a busy time ahead of us. Expect a retaliation if this camp is as big as we think it is."

Chapter 7
AMERICAN

Sana'a, Yemen

The late afternoon heat felt foreign as Amir hid in an alleyway. Hot was a relative term for Yemen's largest city, Sana'a. Amir would have loved to walk its streets, admire the incredible architecture, and imagine the sculptors working. But that only happened in a life before Saint Louis, before Jenkins' death in the darkness, and the text message that sent him to the other side of the world.

The sounds of the bustling streets were deafening—too many frequencies, randomness, unpredictably coming from all directions. He couldn't process the auditory stimuli, let alone the intense light from a sun he hadn't seen in months. He knew very little of the language, and even less about the culture, but he was in the large city with Taj Al Muhammad. Amir was to learn all he could from Karim's son in order to assist in running the training camps and interrogating prisoners, even though Amir felt he learned that part well enough already.

"Amir, come!" he heard Taj call from a street fifty meters to his right. Amir waved and forced a smile, then looked down at the ground and clenched his teeth, trying to ignore the sounds, forget the wind on his skin. He opened his squinted eyes despite the searing sun. A moment later, he confidently strode toward the shorter, muscular Taj.

"Amir this is a friend we can count on in Sana'a," he said, gesturing to the man in front of them. The third man was very small, thin, and his eyes darted suspiciously.

Taj looked at Amir and held up his hand, wiggling his pinky back and forth. Taj then nodded his head toward the small man. Amir picked up on the hints, and immediately saw the man was missing both of his pinky fingers. Amir snapped his gaze back toward Taj who winked.

"Tell Amir what you've told me."

"I see planes fly from the south."

"All of it," Taj said playfully, like a master to his obedient dog.

"They are American planes. Fighters, with reserve fuel beneath. I see them now four days in a row."

"What's that mean huh?" Taj said, pushing the man away. "Come on American," he spat the words at Amir. "That's what makes you valuable. He never saw these planes before. Where are they going? What for? Where are they coming from?"

Amir stared at Taj, his stomach spasmed as he heard questions being thrown at him over and over again. It reminded him of being interrogated by the large men in the underground room he was beaten in time and time again. Amir was frozen in a world so bright, so loud, so quickly moving around him. He wasn't sure what Taj wanted from him.

Taj sighed, placing his hands on his hips. "I'm not going to beat you my friend," he said and raised a hand to Amir's shoulder. "I truly just need your input. What do you think my brother?"

"Training ops. They are training for a mission. If they're flying it daily, then it's happening soon. Extra fuel means distance. They came from the south, could be carrier borne aircraft."

"You think they are planning an airstrike here?"

"I wouldn't know. They could be practicing in the mountains for similar terrain, or they could be preparing for something here. What's worth striking here?"

Taj smiled and slapped Amir on the back, causing him to flinch. "We need to get you relaxed my brother. Come, let's grab a drink and talk to my father."

"It's illegal here, right?" Amir asked, scared.

"You've got a lot to learn, American."

Chapter 8
DEATH FROM BELOW

First Lieutenant Alex "Reflex" Pines was sitting in the rear of his FA-18 watching the radar as Commander "Crank" Heinz flew to each checkpoint. It was a moonless night and the sky was blanketed in thick clouds that extended from horizon to horizon. Even at 600 knots, the clouds seemed motionless as Reflex traced their undulations, searching for a break in the pattern as his heart raced the swirling engines he straddled. On occasion, the Haraz Mountains of Yemen poked their dark, jagged peaks through the cottony surface, hinting at the dangerous world that lay below. But, at 30,000 feet everything felt emotionless, and the comfort given by Eagle Two, the wingman to their right, was immeasurable.

As he looked toward the other FA-18 Super Hornet, he saw the heavy ordnance it carried: two JDAMs, four AIM-9X air-to-air missiles, and an external fuel tank. He also saw the concentric rings from the twin General Electric F414s churning the orange glow.

"So, how'd you get your callsign, wizzo?" the Commander asked the young weapons systems operator, wizzo, for short.

"Long story, sir," Alex responded as he blinked hard and sighed, frustrated with himself for feeling so anxious.

"No sense in us not talking. We hardly know each other son," Crank said with a fatherly tone into the comms.

"I'm sorry, sir. We were out one night and a waitress walked by with a tray full of drinks. She got bumped, spun around, and a beer fell off the tray. I caught it in the air and chugged it. She turned and was mad as hell. Said I owed her $2.50. I told her it was gonna break on the floor anyways so what's the difference?"

"And?"

"Yeah, I went home with her that night, no big deal," Reflex said, laughing a little with pilot.

"I know damn well that's not the full story Lieutenant."

Alex paused for a moment not wanting to reveal the real reason the guys back at flight school gave him the name. "Okay, they also call me Reflex cause of my gag reflex, sir. Everything triggers it; except flying."

"Well there ya' have it. The real story," he said with a chuckle and a short pause. "Stick with the first one. Much more satisfying."

Alex and Commander Heinz had logged about seventy flight hours together since Reflex replaced the Crank's former WSO. During that time, they learned each others tendencies, but many conversations below decks helped stamp out their respective roles. Alex learned quite a bit from the veteran, but he still felt green. This was their first mission together, dropping JDAMs onto a confirmed terrorist compound in the mountains of Yemen.

"Sir, we're three seconds out from waypoint Charlie," Reflex announced.

"Roger that," he said as he gripped the flightstick more firmly preparing for the next maneuver.

"Eagle Two, Eagle One. Tac right to Delta at 125," Crank said into the comms.

"Eagle Two, tac right," Reflex heard them respond in his headset.

The two fighters rolled right ninety degrees with a snap and immediately changed their heading, allowing Reflex an expansive look at the cloud cover below. It was calm, beautiful, hard to imagine the horrors being planned in the valleys underneath.

"Eagle Two, this is Big Brother. You've got an approaching bandit on radar, bearing twenty-five degrees, approaching at a high rate of speed. Recommend a course alteration and you've been cleared to go weapons hot," said an anonymous voice from the Boeing E-3 Sentry, which was cruising at forty-thousand feet, two-hundred miles behind them. It had been scanning the skies for the aerial mission.

"Copy that Big Brother. How long to intercept?"

"Three minutes," the man said in a flat tone, as if he were reading from a boring script.

"Eagle Two we're gonna come off our flight plan for a moment. We might need to say hello to a new friend." The flight team accelerated to 850 knots, a boom reverberated off the mountain peaks below.

"Break left," Crank said, and both planes banked toward the left in an airborne tango, their steel bodies seemingly glued together as long, orange halos screamed from their power plants.

"Hick . . . hick . . . hick," the men in Eagle One both said as they clenched their bodies firmly against the five-g turn.

"Sir, we have two bandits," Reflex said as they snapped back, leveling out of their turn.

"Eagle Two, we're cleared for weapons hot. Feel free to engage," Crank said firmly into the comms. "Eagle Two, break right to separate."

"Reflex!"

"Sir," Alex responded nervously, his gloves feeling moist and his breathing more labored.

"You know why I got my callsign?"

"No, sir."

"'Cause I don't fuck around, son. I'm about to abuse this plane, pull every g outta this fi-i-i-i-i-i-ne piece of engineering. You ready?" he asked with the confidence of a man who'd been there before.

Alex's hair stood up on his arms. He felt a fire ignite inside him and wanted to flex his body harder than he ever had. His mind became focused, the fear melted away, and he knew his roles: to watch the radar and to manage the weapons; Crank was gonna shred the sky.

"Yes, sir. Crank it."

Crank went into a steep descent, while Reflex watched the radar closely.

"One coming toward us bearing 090. Range forty miles and closing quickly," Reflex said calmly. He was separate from the reality of the moment. He had gone back to training, to flight school, to the simulator. He was focused only on the immediate: the fear of failure no longer existed.

"Hard right," Crank said a split second before he turned hard toward the bogie to intercept.

"Copy," Reflex said and toggled off the safeties, dropping his visor down to assist with target acquisition and guidance. "Twenty miles and closing."

"We're gonna dive down to twenty-thousand feet, then once we intercept, we'll come hard left and climb to try and engage from behind," Crank said calmly.

"Copy."

"After that, just shoot that son-of-a-bitch out of the sky so we can get on with our primary."

They were accelerating downward, and Reflex watched as they flirted with Mach 2 before Crank pulled back on the stick, bleeding off speed, sending both the men hard into their seats as they maneuvered to engage the bandit.

"Hick . . . hick . . . hick," the men said as Crank climbed aggressively, and banked.

"There's two," Crank said as he saw a pair of twin afterburners glowing in the darkness above him.

"Eagle Two, we've got a pair," Crank said as he finally pulled in behind the enemies.

"Copy Eagle One. We're preparing to engage our target . . . Eagle One we've got one over."

"Engage Eagle Two, then come to me, over."

"Copy."

"Big Brother this is Eagle One. We've got three aircraft in our current airspace."

"Roger that Eagle One, we're seeing that too. Can you ID?"

"Negative."

A split second later, the two planes Eagle One had engaged both rolled out and began a deep descent, one turning right, and the other, left. Without hesitation, Crank followed the aircraft to the left.

It was slow motion for Reflex, even his eyes seemed to blink slowly as he tried to lock onto the diving plane in the darkness. It was a deadly game of tag; the FA-18 Super Hornet's payload of AIM-9X Sidewinder missiles being their explosive hand.

"Big Brother, Eagle One. I've engaged a Terminator, over."

"Copy Eagle One. You're still clear for weapons hot."

"Reflex, how we doin'?" Crank groaned as he rolled right forcing them hard into their seats.

"He's in and out of lock," Reflex said as he watched the

SU-35, a Terminator, maneuvered aggressively.

"Eagle Two," Crank yelled into the comms, "We've got a bogie coming around our back."

"Copy, Eagle One."

"We've got a lock!" Reflex shouted.

"Fire!" Crank said forcefully and without hesitation.

"Fox Two!" Reflex said, sending the first missile whistling into the dark night.

The SU-35 barrel-rolled left spitting bright orange flares into the air before banking aggressively left, causing the missile to fly beyond its intended target. The missile then turned hard left to pursue.

"Locked. Fox Two!" Reflex said as they stayed engaged behind the hostile. As the second missile flew into the night, the intense glow from the rocket blinded them temporarily. A moment later, an explosion of metal and fire spread across the night sky.

Crank whipped the FA-18 hard right to avoid the debris, "Wooohooo!" he let out a primal scream as he leveled the plane, then began a steep climb.

"Eagle One we're engaged with hostile two. Break right."

"Roger Eagle Two." Crank turned hard right and the second SU-35 drifted into Eagle One's sight. Another AIM-9X whistled, several flares launched from the second SU-35, but despite the counter-measures, the missile detonated on target; a second fireball illuminated the sky.

"Eagle One we're missile locked!" The voice sounded panicked in the radio as they struggled to make evasive changes in directions. The Russian-made SU-35 was incredible, moving rapidly to stay behind them, its radical wing design made it superior in maneuverability, but only slightly.

"They're firing!" Eagle Two screamed as they launched flares, peppering the night sky in bright light and sulfur.

"Eagle Two come around bearing 210 degrees," Crank said as he prepared to engage the bogie. Crank watched intensely as his wingman helped him engage. "Okay Eagle Two. Hard left and we're in."

"Reflex get a lock," Crank said, eerily calm under the stress of the situation.

"Got it."

"Fox Two—"

Suddenly the SU-35's nose went vertical but the plane didn't climb. Instead, it seemed to stall in mid-air. Crank tried to decelerate but it was impossible to match the aeronautics of the Russian fighter and they blew past the Terminator, losing their radar lock.

Crank dove hard, accelerating toward the mountains. He turned sharply right, attempting to circle around behind the SU-35 once more; this time trying to keep a larger distance.

"They're firing," Eagle Two hollered. Flares spat out angrily into the darkness but they had no effect on the incoming missile, and Eagle Two burst into a ball of fire.

Crank and Reflex sat silently, both wishing to see a parachute in the glow of the wreckage.

"He's circling around us from above," Reflex said as he caught sight of the glow from the Terminator.

"Fuck this guy," Crank mumbled as he dove hard into the clouds below.

"Sir," Reflex said, remembering the mountains that lived within the pillowy cloud layer.

"Just keep an eye on him."

Crank began flying through the clouds, between the peaks, and even popping back above the clouds to establish where he'd fly next in order to avoid the dense grouping of mountain peaks. He was slowly making his way back toward their original objective, to drop their payload.

"We're getting close to bingo," Reflex said, checking the fuel gauge.

"I hear ya'," Commander Heinz said as he glanced at the gauges for himself, noting how low on fuel they were, and dove down into the clouds once again. "Where is he?"

"Our five o'clock high," Alex said, continuing to track the SU-35.

"Fuck bingo," Crank said as he throttled up the afterburners to level five and climbed, turning the FA-18 vertical and accelerating toward the heavens. After climbing for three-thousand feet he quickly rolled the plane 270 degrees and began an aggressive banking turn as he decelerated and spotted the SU-35.

"Can you lock?"

"Yes, sir."

Crank accelerated once again trying to catch the fleeting SU-35.

"He's accelerating away," Crank mumbled through gritted teeth. He fought the urge to chase him, to kill him, but remembered the mission. He turned right, slightly, and entered the bombing run.

Beep, beep, beep! The warnings began to scream in the cockpit.

"We've got multiple missile warnings!" Reflex said, looking at the radar.

From the valley below, one, then two, four, six, surface-to-air missiles punctured through the clouds, their bright orange rockets seemed to start the cottony clouds on fire. Upward they screamed through the night air chasing the Super Hornet. Crank throttled down the engines, reducing their heat signature. He then released flares and banked hard right, pulling upward on the stick, smashing them hard into their seats at six-gs.

"Two detonations!" Reflex said as he spun his head

around attempting to see how many missiles still followed them.

"Copy," Crank said as he executed a steep descent back toward the mountains, using gravity to help them accelerate into the clouds.

"I'm gonna get us close to that peak. Drop the ordnance," Crank said as he looked through the cockpit glass toward the looming mountain just ahead of them.

"Three, two, one, away!" Reflex said as he released the JDAMs.

The aircraft screamed over the top of the mountain, barely one-hundred feet above the peak, then Crank dropped the nose slightly and decelerated into the valley below.

"Three detonations!" Alex said through shallow breaths.

"Easy Reflex. I need you to stay cool."

The two men were on edge, gauging their position and where their next waypoint would have been. The mission was dead, but at least they weren't. They needed to get back to the carrier quickly.

"We've got four more incoming!" Alex said, scanning the radar, then looked out of the cockpit window toward the abyss below. From the darkness, a glimmer of light multiplied into four and they began to grow larger as they raced upward from the valley.

"Eject, eject, eject!" Commander Heinz yelled into the comms as he pulled the ejection handle. Barely a second later the FA-18 was incinerated by three separate missile strikes.

Both men launched upward into the violent wind.

"Agh!" Alex's head snapped back hard against his headrest as he was blasted by 500 knot winds. Thankfully, he had his face shield down from acquiring targets. His arms were pulled back behind him and he felt a pop and searing pain in his left elbow and shoulder. He was disoriented, lightheaded, struggling to breathe as his parachute opened in the thin air twenty-thousand feet above sea level. Finally, he saw the flames of their FA-18 as they descended slowly toward the valley below.

He scanned the sky, the mountains appeared as waves fixated across an endless horizon. He found east by the dark purple hues of an early morning far away. The subtle colors of the sky and the dark silence below was almost comforting as his parachute rustled high above, greeting the ever-thickening air as he descended into the valley.

The comfort was short lived. He began to hear voices yelling from far below, indistinguishable at first, but then several individual voices emerged.

Pop, pop, pop . . . pop, pop, pop, he heard from below as bright tracers flew upward from the valley, like long sparks from a demonic fire. Alex tracked where the shots were going, and saw Commander Heinz approximately one-hundred yards away, lazily floating downward, seemingly unconscious.

Alex began to feel nauseous and quickly removed his facemask. He vomited down the front of his flight suit and struggled to find adequate air between heaves.

Pop, pop, pop. More tracers streamed into the black sky as he watched his squadron leader helplessly descend under fire. Fortunately for Alex, nobody below seemed to notice him.

Several minutes passed, and Alex finally began seeing details of the ground below. The rocky surface seemed to be approaching more quickly than he'd imagined as he braced for impact.

Wham! The seatpan struck the ground with bone rattling force, and Alex fought to roll toward his uninjured side as the parachute stretched itself along the ground, still catching a small amount of wind.

Pain reached out like devilish tentacles all over his body, stinging his neck, his low back, his ankles, but mostly his left arm.

"Grrrr," he growled in pain as his shoulder reduced itself in the impact with the ground. His elbow, however, was a flaccid mess. He could see a large step-off in his forearm, indicating he likely broke both the radius and ulna.

Quickly, Alex sprang into action. He grabbed the medical kit from the seatpan, drank the entire liter of water, trying his best to avoid the shock that was surely setting in. Next, he holstered his sidearm, and dug into the rest of the kit. He took quick inventory: flashlights, signal mirrors, flares, radio, multi-purpose knife, emergency blankets, and water purification tablets. Finally, he saw a couple small packs of Sour Patch Kids, his favorite candy. It was odd how comforting the candy was. It almost made him smile as he knelt on the red-brown earth of the Haraz Mountains.

He took the knife and ran to the parachute, cutting out a long piece of the Paracord. He then found two long straight sticks, and placed them on either side of his forearm. Next, he wrapped several lengths of the parachute cord around his arm and the splints to stabilize the fracture. Last, he cut a large triangle from the parachute and made himself a sling and placed his left arm into it.

Alex looked toward the mountain peak above. It was bare, devoid of any cover; no trees, no large boulders. Beyond the peak to the east, the sky lacked stars, and the indigo hue brightened even more. Looking down toward the valley below, he saw few trees or shrubs, but plenty of rocky outcroppings that grew larger at the lower altitudes.

Alex stumbled, slipped, and crawled down the steep rocky mountain. His lungs burned, his muscles ached, and his head was thumping from the lack of oxygen. In his twenty-six short years, he'd never been to the top of a mountain. His throat burned as he tried to swallow but all moisture had been taken from him. For a brief moment, he thought it would have been better had his left arm been amputated during the ejection. The dead, painful weight was forcing him to feel sick, and his gag reflex had gotten the best of him on more than one occasion, making his dehydration even worse.

Pop! Alex heard a gunshot echo all around him. He froze behind a cluster of small boulders. He heard his heartbeat as blood flowed through his head, which made it even more difficult to decipher the voices in the distance. His head hurt more as his heart rate increased.

Pop! Pop, pop, pop! Pop! Pop! He heard a series of shots. It was clear there were several types of weapons being used. He looked at his own sidearm, the Glock 19, and he knew it had been Commander Heinz who fired the first shot; but there were now several guns. Alex began to scan the horizon in every direction, looking for movement. The sun was finally cresting over the peak and he was relatively exposed.

He leapt from his hide and bound his way down the steep slope, each step jarring his arm and causing a searing pain in his head. He felt it, but ignored it, knowing that his only salvation was getting as low as he could as fast as he could. He reached a ledge that descended twenty feet to the next solid piece of ground. He quickly glanced right and left, seeing the drop-off extending at least two-hundred yards in each direction. He sat on the ledge, and counted to himself.

"One . . . two . . . three."

He jumped, landing onto a rock and twisting his ankle inward, a loud pop accompanied the inability to move his joint.

"Come on!" he growled as he reflexively tried to reach his ankle with both hands and feeling the pain in his elbow come to life again. For a moment, he rested, trying to decide if he should move any more. He sat next to an outcropping with a small crawlspace below. In front were several bushes. The combination would provide cover from any angle.

The sun was still rising to his back as he sat against the mountain in darkness, surrounded by a dense grouping of vegetation. He closed his eyes, tried to control his breathing, and thought of home.

He fell asleep, the stress and pain finally getting the best of him. Alex dreamed of the day he saw his father's motorcycle, a twisted, scarred mass of metal and fluid, as it sat in his father's garage. He saw his father, a man Alex tried to emulate with his own career. He was always excited to hear his dad talk about what it felt like to fly, to bank hard and let physics throw him down into the seat of his F-16. His father was an Air Force pilot, but died when Alex was only eight. It wasn't his career that took his life, but a drunk driver.

Alex heard his father's voice, *the only thing close to flying is riding that bike.* Years later, he was glad his mother had kept it. Alex took the Yamaha Seca 550 and rebuilt it after he joined the Navy. He promised himself he'd ride it after his first tour. But now he lay silent, asleep on the mountains in enemy territory, dreaming of the bike he'd likely never ride. At least he got to share the feel of flying with his dad.

Alex woke to the sound of gravel under boots and the metallic sound of a weapon bouncing in a man's hand. It was amazing how much more effective fear was than coffee. He was more awake than he had been in hours. He tried to move, but the pain in his ankle proved unforgiving.

He groaned, almost imperceptively, but he may as

well have told them exactly where he was. The footsteps stopped. He heard a radio, some chatter in Arabic. Suddenly a half dozen ropes came over the edge of the cliff where Alex sat. He knew they couldn't see him, but the harsh sunlight from above made Alex nervous. He watched as several men began rappelling the twenty feet down to where he was.

When the men hit the ground, Alex stood from his hide with his gun in hand. *Pop, pop, pop.* Alex shot six men in quick succession before they were able to get their guns into the air. Several more Arabic men were descending the cliff behind him. *Click, click* the Glock was empty, but Alex was still trying desperately to shoot the men as they rappelled.

Whack! The butt of a rifle struck Alex hard across the face and he crumbled to the ground. As he lay flat, staring at the white sky, several shadows came in from all directions. They began to pull at him, kick him, grasp at his clothes and gear. They were stripping him of everything from his gun to his clothes. He was lying naked, twelve-thousand feet above sea level. His face was a red mess, the ground around him quickly turning a darker shade as his blood mixed with the earth. His left arm rested lifelessly on the crumbled rock, and his ankle pointed at a grotesque angle, which made him begin to gag. He heard the man talking over him, but couldn't make out a word. He was shivering from shock, fear, and the temperature was nearly freezing.

Finally, Alex was picked up by a half dozen of the men, who carried him to an open area where several vehicles eventually pulled up. Dozens of armed men piled out of the surrounding landscape and began climbing into the off-road vehicles. Alex was thrown into the back of a truck where a blanket laid haphazardly in the back. He crawled to it, seeking the promise of warmth but as he lifted it, he began to scream. The mutilated body of Commander Heinz lay beneath, hardly recognizable.

Alex remembered staring at the bloodied face of his father as he lay on the side of the road. The accident that took his father happened just down the street from their home, and Alex witnessed the entire thing. He heard his father's bike and raced to the sidewalk. His dad always popped a wheelie to make Alex smile, and it always did. When the truck came barreling through the stop sign Alex hadn't seen the wheelie, but the bike did go into the air. He ran as fast as he could, screaming. The smell of iron and the sight of blood was much different than in the movies. The police caught the guy who ran a red light, but the thirty-year sentence hadn't lasted. He was out in twelve.

"You motherfuckers!" Alex screamed out in anger as he crawled toward the back of the truck. He was projecting his feelings as an eight-year-old boy. Alex heard his father's voice, he heard Commander Heinz briefing him before the mission. Hundreds of conversations, training flights, meetings all flooded his mind as he continued to stare at his squadron leader; and think of his father.

The door swung open and the bright light of day blinded Alex to the assault that was incoming. A soldier quickly struck Alex in the head, using the grip of his gun like the head of a hammer. Alex was unconscious; his mind free of the horror; for the moment.

Chapter 9
THE AWAKENING

Amir sat in the front of a Land Rover as Taj drove quickly through the mountains of Yemen in the dark. The road, if it could be called that, was full of boulders, holes, and quick switchbacks, but Taj refused to use his headlights. It was the middle of the night and he didn't want anyone flying overhead to see them.

"You realize they have infrared capabilities, too," Amir said as he held onto the roof with one hand and the center console with the other. He wore his seatbelt, but it didn't seem to help steady him in the car seat.

"I understand," Taj said with a bright, white smile easily seen through his dark beard.

"You're having fun?"

"Amir, we are quickly becoming friends!" Taj exclaimed. "You know the things that make me happy!"

Amir smiled as he watched Taj enjoy himself.

"You know we couldn't come out here because it was dangerous before. Now it's safe."

"What's different?"

"You remember the planes?"

"Yes."

"We knew the planes were likely coming for our new compound. But don't worry. We took care of it."

"What does that mean?"

"We shot them out of the sky," Taj said, dangerously taking one hand off the wheel, pointing into the sky with his hand in the shape of a gun. He bounced around hard in the seat with one hand on the wheel, like a rider on a bull. "America thinks they own the world, that they know everything, but my father is a smart man, Amir. You know that?"

"I do."

"He placed defenses up. We saw the planes coming from a long way off. We even scrambled our own fighters. My father purchased SU-35s. Best fighters in the world. Plus, we had a dozen mobile surface-to-air sites all over the valley. The Americans didn't stand a chance."

Amir sat stunned, impressed by Karim's resourcefulness, as well as his preparedness.

"Are you upset American?"

"No, impressed."

"Good. Because I have one more surprise for you when we get there."

"I'm not sure I like surprises," Amir said, recalling his time as a prisoner, guessing how he should respond to each new situation.

"Amir, I will tell you one more thing," Taj said, stopping the car to look at him. "You have much more to learn about what we're planning. Your man, Jenkins, he wasn't very progressive. He lacked the vision my father has. You on the other hand, I think you'll better understand."

"What does that mean?"

"We are beyond the whole bombing thing. It's overdone.

Granted, it does stir the pot and elicit fear, but it's too small scale," he said, smiling once more, but this time, full of pride. "My father will let you know, when he feels you are ready."

Taj put the car back in gear and continued the long drive.

The bouncing ride went on for hours. The men stopped more than once to fill the gas tank with fuel from several five-gallon canisters they had strapped to the roof. Amir had waited days to see what Taj was so excited to share with him, and now, there was a second surprise.

"Here we are American!" Taj said, stopping in front of a massive three-story building. The sun was meandering its way through the dozens of mountain peaks giving the illusion of a multi-sunrise. The morning light allowed for a dramatic first impression.

The building was well constructed and situated deep within the valley, sporting expansive 360-degree views from towers at each corner of the structure. It was at least one-hundred yards long. At the center, there was a large satellite dish array, pointing their concave surface toward the heavens in a variety of directions. Amir also noted several sentries at each of the four corners, as well as a dozen guards on the grounds between the building and a fence.

"Are you ready for surprise number two?" Taj asked, rubbing his hands together and winking.

"Sounds good," Amir said slowly, concerned at the look in Taj's eye.

"We caught an American pilot!"

"How?"

"Survived an ejection. He's broken, but we don't need him to walk or write. We just need him to talk; and you're gonna help me do it. Ready?"

Amir slowly nodded and felt a cold shiver race up his spine.

"Amir, this way," Taj said, signaling him to follow. Amir had frozen in front of the main gates, locked in a staring match with a dead-eyed security guard. Amir looked away, and the guard smiled as he watched Taj's protégé walk away.

"Great location in the valley. Very wide, can see for kilometers in any direction. Nobody can drive up to us, fly under darkness, nothing. We have total supremacy here. But let me show you something just in case," Taj said, leaning in and smiling, his breath heavy with tobacco.

They walked to the furthest corner of the compound, then away from it in a northerly direction for approximately ten minutes. Amir's feet stung from burst blisters. He hadn't worn shoes for months, and initially they were a pleasant change, but after walking in Sana'a they had rubbed him raw and bloody.

"We've arrived!" Taj said with his eyes squinting as the sun finally peeked over the eastern range.

"Where are we?"

"Below your feet is an escape tunnel. It gives us a head start toward the closest range," he said, pointing to the mountains behind him toward the north, at least a mile away.

"How deep is the tunnel?" Amir asked.

"You'll see. It's where we're going in!" Taj said, kneeling and wiping away sediment from the top of the painted steel door. He lifted firmly and it began to swing open rather easily. Amir quickly saw the massive steel door was hydraulically assisted.

"After you," Taj said as he smiled and stepped back.

Amir stood at the edge of the opening, staring at a vertical concrete cavern. Small arched sections of rebar had been placed into the concrete, making a pseudo-ladder that Amir began to climb. The concrete tube descended into the earth, barely wide enough to accommodate him, even in his malnourished form. Slowly he descended. His hands began to ache from squeezing the metal rods, his skin a fragile covering, and his muscles were atrophied, causing his forearms to burn, then go numb. Finally, they hit the ground. Amir looked up to watch as Taj jumped from three rungs above. All light ceased to exist in the concrete tube.

"How'd you get all this built?" Amir asked, bewildered at the engineering feat.

"Oh, Amir. Now's not the time to talk boring engineering. Follow me," Taj said. He was strange, serious, in a way Amir had never seen. Taj strode down the hall with a purpose, his hands were clenching and releasing, over and over as he took deep breaths in, and forcefully blew them out. They reached the end of the brightly lit tunnel and found three guards standing post, each of them recognizing Taj and unlocking the doors, staring at Amir as he followed. Amir recognized them from before and a familiar ache ripped through his abdomen.

"Where is he?" Taj asked as soon as the door closed behind him. The area was very clean, completely concrete and steel. The lights above were minimal, but somehow cast a bright white light, allowing everything to be seen clearly.

"Cell three," a guard said and pointed them in the right direction.

"Have you not been here before?" Amir asked, limping, his ancient calf wound beginning to reveal itself. He had been compensating in the way he walked to avoid the pain in his feet, but sacrificed his calf.

"No. But I helped design it." Taj stopped and looked at Amir. "You need to understand we are much larger and wealthier than any organization they've talked about on Fox News, American. We have three more like this in the mountains of Yemen alone. Unfortunately, you've been to one, and several of our older, smaller places throughout the Middle East."

Amir tasted bile at the thought of being dragged into an SUV, his hands and feet tied together, and a wet sack placed over his head during those trips to different facilities. It was like breathing through a straw for hours, and when the dust landed on the sack it stuck, covering most of the small openings in the fabric. Never had his lungs burned so bad.

"I can see I've upset you, please forgive me. Those days are far behind you my brother. You're on the other side now," Taj said, grasping the taller Amir on both shoulders firmly. "Now I need you to be ready for this. You don't speak. You just listen and watch. Understand?"

"Yes," Amir said as his anxiety was replaced with excitement. He was once again being groomed for leadership.

Inside the six-by-six concrete box lay a man in darkness. They had put Alex in a kurta shirt and linen pants, both made of thin cotton, which provided little warmth. Alex laid on the concrete floor humming, his song highlighted with staccato by the shivering of his body.

"Infidel," Taj said sweetly, bending down to address the pilot. The ceiling was only five feet tall forcing them to lower themselves. "Time to ta-a-alk," he sang to the pilot and reached toward him, only to pull his hand away when Alex reached out for help.

"Get up," Taj said and backed away, allowing the pilot space to get out.

It was painful for Amir to watch the man stand. Alex's left hand was swollen, bruised, his fingers barely recognizable. His face was also swollen, but the bruising had begun to turn yellow and green in dramatic contrast to the dried blood in his hair and near his right eye. Alex took weight only on his left leg, clearly indicating something was wrong with his right. Finally, Alex was erect, his shoulders rounded forward on his left side, an automatic response to his damaged arm, which made him appear a few inches short than his normal six-foot-one.

"Walk," Taj told Alex as he and Amir followed behind. Alex hopped down the hallway, his right hand balancing against the concrete wall.

As if answering Amir's unspoken question, Taj said, "Broke his own right leg and left elbow, but we broke his face." Taj fought the urge to slam the American pilot into a wall, bounce his head off the floor, and torture him right there in the hallway. However, he knew the orders from his father: to gain any intelligence they could in the fight against the infidels.

They entered the interrogation room and Amir began to sweat. There were only two chairs, both steel, and the floors were tiled white—the only tiled floor he saw in the entire complex. Tile wouldn't stain like concrete when the blood started to hit the floor.

"Time to talk Lieutenant Alex Pines," Taj spit out the name trying to sound as American as his tongue would allow.

"Lieutenant Alex Pines, U.S. Navy. Number 432564532. DOB December 11, 1988."

"You're very good at reciting the basics. But I want more. Did they tell you I was coming?" Taj said as he paced the room, not looking at Alex who sat in one of the chairs.

Amir was standing in the far corner of the room, recalling the times he spent being assaulted by the guards. He'd already seen three of his former guards within the facility's walls.

Taj walked up to Alex and kicked the legs out from under the chair forcing Alex to fall, landing on his left shoulder and elbow.

"Ughh!" Alex growled in pain and grasped the elbow. "Lieutenant. I'm sure your commanding officer wouldn't like that you fell from your chair." Taj paused and looked down at Alex. "Ah. You don't need to worry. I had forgotten your C.O. died after we shot him. An easy target really. You know it's incredible we didn't see you. We looked. I think it was a sign from *Allah*. You were meant to talk. You need to talk Lieutenant," Taj said, squatting down right in Alex's face.

"Get in your chair!" he yelled, accompanying his words with spit that landed on the prisoner's face. "Pretend I'm your commanding officer now. Would you hide things from me?" Taj said and pushed Alex back to the ground as he struggled to get to his feet.

"I could hold you down forever," he whispered into Alex's ear, loud enough for Amir to still hear it. "You wouldn't be the first American soldier to aid in our cause. You see that man over there?" Taj said, pointing toward Amir. "He was in the U.S. Army. An impressive service record, but now he's with us. Many others have been with us too. Some in high positions, some in low. We love them all." Taj spoke as he helped Alex back to the chair.

"You see lieutenant, we can help you. It doesn't have to be this way—"

"Lieutenant Alex Pines, U.S. Navy. Number 432564532. DOB December 11, 1988."

Taj hammered the lieutenant across the face and blood trickled from the wound above his eye. "Just so we are on the same page. I don't strike you out of frustration. No, no. I'm just beating the devil out of you. That stubborn force that won't let you be who you should be."

Crack! The sound was knuckle on bone as Taj struck him a second time, spraying blood onto the tiled floor.

"Amir!" Taj said, gesturing toward the corner. "Tell him what we'll do if he doesn't talk."

Amir approached slowly, fear building within him as he watched Alex roll on the floor in pain. He tried to speak more than once, but couldn't find his voice. Finally, after Taj motioned for him to speak, the words finally came.

"They won't let you sleep. They'll beat you with regularity, make you feel violated as you sit naked on a cold chair. They may burn your skin, or suffocate you with a wet bag and allow dust to block the few holes large enough to allow air to penetrate. You'll learn what they want to hear, and they'll punish you for it. Just when you think you've understood the pattern, they'll change the game. Your cell will be your bathroom and your bed. Your injuries will stay forever. You will talk one way or the other."

Amir stood silent now, anger coursing through his body as he stood with clenched fists. He hated his past, he wished he was strong like Alex Pines.

Whack! Amir punched Alex in the stomach. The sensation of his soft tissue giving way was satisfying to Amir, as if it was Alex's will giving way to force. "Talk now!" Amir yelled as he secretly begged the pilot to give in early, rather than endure the crude punishments Taj surely had in mind. Before he realized it, he had struck Alex three more times, each in the head, and the soldier was unconscious.

"Enough!" Taj said, grabbing Amir who spun around and raised his hand to greet him. "Relax, Amir. It's over for now," he said, smiling and grasping Amir's bloodied hand in his own, wrapping his thick, callused palm around Amir's bloodied knuckles. "I had no idea, Amir. You have passion for the cause! Welcome my brother."

Amir rested on a soft bed inside a large room they had waiting for him. His mind was cluttered with confusion. He was sure he felt empathy for Alex, but he wasn't sure why he wanted the pilot to talk. Was it because he was for the cause as Taj said? Or because he knew what Alex would have to endure. *Do I want to help him?* Amir thought, confused at the idea. He hadn't helped anyone in years; not since his father died.

He felt sick and sprung up from the bed. He scrambled around the room looking for the best corner to vomit, but then he saw the door. He ran to it; it was unlocked. He found his way to the bathroom but by the time he got inside he felt better. The idea of being free, trusted, placed in a room that didn't lock, was incredible. He decided it was time to help someone, but he didn't know who.

Chapter 10

WAR GAMES

Washington, D.C.

Secretary Smith sat at his desk in Washington, the darkness wrapping him like a cocoon, as he grasped for the illusion that the real world wasn't there. But it was, and it was bad. He just received a call from Captain Myers the X.O. of the supercarrier Gerald Ford. They had two pilots who were killed in action, and two who ejected, but hadn't been heard from. The speed at ejection exceeded the safe limits, according to their overwatch group in the Northrop Grumman E-10. This meant probably four KIA, without executing the main objective. Sure, they had shot down two bandits, Terminators, Russian built SU-35s, which U.S. intelligence had no idea would be in the area. But worse yet, there were surface-to-air sites seemingly everywhere in the valleys of the Haraz Mountains.

Doyle didn't know which person to call first: President

Pierce or Logan. Protocol took over, allowing him the easier decision.

"Mr. Secretary," President Pierce said as he sat up in bed. He rarely slept much between the call of duty and his campaign.

"I'm sorry Mr. President but something's happened."

After a brief pause, Pierce was out of his bedroom and into the study where he talked at normal volume. "What's going on Doyle?"

"We conducted a mission based on intel from Falcone's team. Two FA-18s were shot down over Yemen, no news of survivors. Lieutenant Alex Pines' beacon was activated but aerial reconnaissance shows no signs of life. All assumed to be KIA."

"Damn," Pierce said as he rubbed his eyes.

"Any noise from Yemen?"

"Nothing, sir. I don't think we'll hear anything either. Mission was over the Haraz Mountains, far from any city."

"How'd it happen?"

"We're trying to gather more images with a satellite over the area, so far we've seen very little, some of the wreckage, a few vehicles, several mobile SAMS."

"SAMS? How the hell did they get SAMS?"

"We shot down two SU-35s as well, sir. A third got away."

President Pierce was silent. His mental game of chess was hurled to the ground. He was unable to see any of this coming, and now there were even more variables.

"I'm coming in. Call Raymond. We need to discuss this."

There were few people in the Oval Office at five in the morning. President Pierce, Secretary Smith, and Vice President Raymond White, a narrow-shouldered, smooth talker from New York City. The three men sat comfortably in the relative darkness, the sun beginning to light the room with the orange glow of a warm summer morning.

"What do we know, Doyle?" Pierce asked, breaking the short silence as the men sat on couches, black coffee in their hands.

"Not much. As I told you, we've scrambled a satellite for imagery, gotten a few photos of mobile SAMS, identified the compound's location, and found the wreckage of four planes, two ours, and two theirs."

"We know the location of the compound?" Vice President White asked.

"Yes. Confirmed with IR images. There are warm bodies all over the place. That was the main objective."

"Why don't we launch another attack? We have infinitely more intel now. Why we didn't have this before is beyond me!"

"Raymond, we don't have confirmation of four KIA. They might be holding one of ours in that compound," Doyle said, interrupting the vice president.

"That's the last thing we need right now, Ray. The terrorists would release that to the press so fast. We need to confirm what happened."

"We should bring General Anderson in on this," Doyle said. The president appointed General Mitchell Anderson head of Joint Special Operations Command after he aided Logan in the capture of Amir and his terrorist cell.

"I think that's a good idea," Pierce said and stood up, putting on his suit coat. "Get back to me when we get a plan together."

"Will do, sir."

"And Doyle, don't tell Falcone. Not yet. We can't have him flying off the handle."

"You read my mind, sir," Doyle said, lying. He planned on calling Logan immediately.

"Doyle, one more thing," Pierce said, rubbing his hands

together. He had spent the last hour trying to re-establish his chess game, the pieces seemingly incomplete. "We now know of at least one massive compound. Logan's executed raids on over a dozen terrorist cells here in the states, and the terrorists we interrogated, at least the ones who talked, said they got their information in the dark web. You think we should bring Nassir on?"

"I think it would be worth a look."

"Okay Doyle. Let's vet him out. See what comes up. If he's clean, we'll bring him in."

"Sounds good, sir."

"Now if you gentlemen don't mind," he said, gesturing toward the door. "I've got a speech to prep for. Waxman really got me after that speech in Chicago. I lost six points."

Doyle walked outside taking a deep breath of the humid air, and immediately he began to sweat. He always sweat, but the heavy humidity and the stress of calling Logan were all acting against him. He wasn't scared of Logan, just his response to the situation. Since Migs died, he had been in a terrible place. He looked at the trees that stood unmoved in the stagnant air as he pulled out his phone. He dialed Logan, knowing their cellphones were secure.

"Hey Doyle, what's the news?" Logan answered. Doyle could tell Logan's mind was sharp, and heard him breathing heavily.

"You busy?"

"Just wrapping up a run. Getting my shit together Mr. Secretary," he said with a smile as he wiped his brow.

"I've got some news," Doyle said, sighing. "Our airstrike failed. We might have four KIA."

"What?" Logan said, sitting down on the curb and spitting.

"They were ready. SAMS and Russian SU-35s attacked

them. They got two of the three fighters, but then a SAMS shot Eagle One from the sky. Eagle Two got it from a bandit. We know for certain Eagle Two didn't eject, but Eagle One did. We haven't heard from them, unsure of their status but are presumed KIA."

Silence lasted for a while as Doyle allowed Logan to process the intel.

"This isn't on you, Logan. It's on me. I rushed the op. I wanted to hit these bastards on their turf quickly and aggressively."

"No Doyle. It's on me. I killed the prisoners. We could have gotten something from them. I know we could have. But after Migs—"

"Logan," Doyle said forcefully, stopping Logan's thoughts. "You can't allow yourself to think that way. You're the reason dozens more attacks on civilians haven't happened. I—we need you on your A-game." Doyle sighed and closed his eyes. "I told you we don't know if we have four KIA. I'm calling General Anderson."

"A black-op?"

"Yeah. Boots on the ground. See what we can find."

"I want in," Logan said, standing. His heart was pounding and life surged through him as if the words were fuel, and the mission was a new battery.

"Exactly why I called," he said, sighing heavily. "I don't think you're ready. I realize you feel responsible but we need you stateside in case we have any fallout from our attempted attack. Please Logan. Don't fight me on this. I'll keep you in the loop, but you know as well as I do, General Anderson has very capable people."

Logan clenched his teeth. He hated being sidelined, but he also knew Doyle had a good point. "Fine. But I swear to God if they find out one of the pilots is alive, God help anyone who stands in my way."

"We'll cross that bridge when we get there, Logan. Talk soon."

Doyle called General Anderson.

"Mr. Secretary," General Anderson said from his new office in Washington, D.C. He hated everything about it, except his framed American Flag. They hadn't allowed him to bring his collection of rare military rifles that decorated his former office walls, stating it was a danger. He fought the rules, but only superficially, instead he used them to decorate his home.

"Hello, General. How are things?"

"Terrible. We lost two birds," the general grumbled as he leaned forward in his chair.

"That's why I'm calling. You haven't heard anything from Eagle One?"

"Nothing."

"Neither have we. I talked to the president this morning. He green lit a spec-op for you to get boots on the ground. Investigate the area, determine if we have four KIA, or maybe we've got some POWs."

"That's some pretty hostile territory."

"I agree, sir. Send your best."

"Will do Mr. Secretary."

"One more thing, Mitchell," Secretary Smith said, using the general's first name. "Logan wants in but I'm not letting him."

"Why?"

"He's the one who found the intel leading to the strike. General, they lost Migs a few weeks back."

"Shit. Breaks my heart to hear that. I liked that kid." General Anderson paused, briefly reflecting on the Saint Louis mission and remembering how well Migs handled himself. He was, after all, the man who convinced Logan not to shoot Amir behind the hotel.

"Logan's a damn good soldier. I'll take him and his boys any time you see fit."

"Good to know. He already threatened me. Said if we find evidence one of the pilots is alive, he's going."

"Well I say we let him."

Secretary Smith paused, sighed, and responded shaking his head. "Me too."

Chapter 11
SHARPSHOOTER

Pittsburgh, Pennsylvania

Dinah sat at her computer in the early morning light, the sun entered the window acutely, casting a glare on the screen. She sipped her coffee as she opened the web browser. She hated checking social media, but was bored and killing time before her husband woke up. He worked with SWAT, and the previous night he was called in to raid a drug house where forty kilos of heroin was seized. He had woken her up at four in the morning to tell her the news. At the moment, he was too excited to sleep so they made love until the sun came up. Once she saw the sun, she couldn't go back to sleep.

She scrolled down her Facebook feed, most of it being from the previous night; nobody posted at six in the morning on a Sunday. She clicked on several shared posts about a variety of things, useless stuff really, but anything to keep her mind occupied. Then Dinah saw her husband's post.

He was standing in their bathroom, pointing the camera at the mirror. The caption: "Going hunting tonight. If you're a bad man and you see me coming you better run. I can shoot from a long way out." It made her sick. He was wearing all black, his SWAT lettering standing out as he held a handgun in one hand, the phone in the other, with an AR-15 hanging from a tactical strap at his chest. He had on a black, knit hat, and his beard was trimmed neatly, but even that was black. His eyes were sinister and his upper teeth were biting down onto his lower lip, distorting his handsome face.

"Rami!" she yelled toward the bedroom. "Rami!" she yelled again.

The tall muscular man came barreling out of the room, still naked from just hours earlier. He had the pistol from the picture in his hand as he scanned the room.

"Dinah, what's the problem?" he asked, his heart still pounding as he placed his gun down on the wooden end table, staring at her with wide eyes.

"This!" she responded, pointing aggressively at the screen. "I told you Rami, I don't like these pictures. They make you look so evil."

Rami smiled and walked to the computer, looking at the image he took of himself only hours ago. "I want people to know I'm not playing games, Dinah."

"What if someone we don't know sees this? You're a Muslim. People see this, and then they see *this*," she said, clicking on an image of both of them after mosque, both of them in traditional clothing. "People will place these images together and call you a killer."

"I am. I've killed a few bad men Dinah. I'm not proud of it, but I'm not ashamed. I do my job, my love," he said, squatting down and looking into her dark brown eyes.

"Can you at least make your posts private?"

"I'll consider it," he said, leaning toward her and kissing her lips gently. "But think of it this way too. I'm changing the conversation. A Muslim man on a SWAT team taking out the bad guys. We aren't all terrorists Dinah."

She hugged him and he lifted her easily off the floor as she squealed and kicked her feet playfully, allowing him to take her back into the bedroom. They spent the next few hours there together, skipping breakfast and sleeping through lunch, both finally finding some restful sleep.

"I've got to go," Rami said as his powerful, callused hands stroked Dinah's body lines.

"Be safe my love. For both of us," she smiled and placed his hand on her stomach.

"Do you think it will be a boy?" he asked, smiling wide.

"I just want a healthy baby, and a husband who can raise it well."

"I love you," he said sweetly, their eyes stayed fixated on one another, as if a secret force had bonded them together. "And you too!" he said, quickly moving toward her belly and kissing it repeatedly as she giggled, his kisses becoming ticklish even with his trimmed beard.

"Can't wait for you to be home," she said, whining as he leapt from the bed and frantically dressed. He only had five minutes before he had to leave.

"Me neither."

Rami got into his Challenger and revved the engine. He had wanted the Hellcat but the budget Dinah had placed him on since getting pregnant left him with the V8, which he supercharged anyway. She wouldn't know the difference, but he loved the whistle of the supercharger once it hit at two-thousand RPMs; and screamed at four. Dinah also didn't know how much it would cost to replace the tires every five-thousand miles, due to his constant wheel spinning.

It didn't take long for him to get to the station. They

lived close, which allowed him to spend as much time as he could with Dinah. He exited the car and felt the thick air enter his lungs and he began to sweat. He walked into the station and was greeted by full applause. Word had spread from the previous night's drug raid, and someone had printed a large image of him in full SWAT gear, the same image Dinah had scolded him for that morning.

"Hey superhero!" Eric Nelson, his sergeant, said and slapped him on the shoulder.

"Come on guys," Rami said and smiled, throwing his thick arms in the air.

"Come on what, *sharpshooter*?" Eric said, looking around the room for confirmation. "You got three of those bastards last night, didn't you?"

"It got real, really fast," Rami said, recalling the night's events.

It was hard to decipher the events during the raid. They had entered the house, and were greeted with a barrage of gunfire. Rami dove into the home, rolling to the far corner, out of the shooter's line of sight. Quickly, he vaulted toward the hallway where the gunfire was originating. He peeked around the corner, seeing one shooter. Instantly, Rami shot him in both shoulders. He watched as the man tried to raise one arm, and then the other, panicking as he finally felt the searing pain and saw Rami. A second assailant exited the room and tried to run down the hallway. *Pop, pop!* Rami shot him in the back of the knee and the right shoulder. Rami stayed low and ran to the room the two men had left.

"Clear!" he yelled back to the rest of the SWAT team and they entered the home. Rami saw a third perpetrator in the bedroom at the end of the hall. This individual was armed with an automatic weapon, looked to be an Uzi, but Rami couldn't make it out completely. His view was obstructed by a table that had been placed on its side. He took his time, controlled his breathing, and shot three rounds into the table. A metallic sound followed a yell, as the man behind the table dropped the weapon. The remaining elements from the SWAT team charged into the far room, clearing it, taking the last four men unscathed. Seven men arrested in all, along with the 40 kilos of heroin.

"We heard, Rami," the sergeant said, breaking Rami's thoughts of the previous night.

"Rambo! Rambo! Rambo!" they started chanting, as his face turned red.

Chapter 12

CSAR

Haraz Mountains, Yemen

It was dark, a sliver of an old moon barely lit the surface of the mountains as two MH-60 helicopters flew quietly through the valley. The pilots, however, didn't need light to see, their FLIR tech used infrared imaging to paint the HD picture they used to fly. The route was planned by JSOC, two FA-18s, and FA-18Gs had escorted the helo in, providing cover and jamming tech for the spec op, ensuring their safe arrival. There were no surprises this time, as the satellite imagery used was from just hours earlier.

Lieutenant Solomon White sat with his squad. The Seahawk banked hard, almost scraping the earth, as it flew low in the valley of the Haraz Mountains. Solomon could barely see the second Seahawk, a gunship carrying two 7.62mm machine guns and a pair of door-mounted .50 calibers.

The Haraz Mountains ascended higher and higher the deeper they went, and the Seahawks would become sitting ducks for man-portable air-defense systems, MANPADs, due to poor maneuverability at high altitude. The SEAL team was going to have a long hike ahead.

"Ten mikes out Lieutenant," the pilot said to Solomon, breaking the silence they'd been under since refueling on a lily pad called Iwo Jima, a WASP class ship that sat in the Gulf of Aden. "We're on our own from here," the pilot said, reminding the SEAL team the FA-18s were going to remain in a holding pattern and wait to escort the empty helos back to the fleet.

"Check down," Solomon said to the seven men he operated with. Silently, they all readied their night vision and slung their M4s, two picked up their M249s, a light machine gun, and Blue placed his Barrett 50 across his back, preparing for the rope descent into darkness.

Sergeant Mike "Blue" Williams was the best marksman Solomon had seen. They'd worked in the same squad for four years, and on more than one occasion, Solomon witnessed him shoot a target at over 2,000 yards. Blue was a quiet man, grew up out west, and used to hunt with his grandfather in the mountains. His dad had been dead to him for years. He left Mike and his mother when Mike was a small boy. They called him Blue because when he was young, his grandfather used a fifty-cent piece as a target for him to shoot. They often went to the mountains, placing the coin a thousand yards out, and Mike would shoot targets in hundred-yard increments working out toward the thousand-yard goal. Mike wanted to join the military desperately when he was young, to be just like his grandfather, a sniper in the Army. "I won't allow it unless you can hit that silver, son," his grandfather would say over and over again through tobacco stained teeth. Mike hit that coin when he was seventeen. His nickname became Five-O, then, and ultimately the name morphed to Blue four years later after he completed BUD/S, earning marksmanship, and becoming part of Solomon's team.

The helo began to descend while the gunship remained approximately two-hundred feet above the rocky earth below, scanning the horizon for any indication of danger. No FA-18 could save them there, no other helo was inbound, and MANPADs came without warning. Everyone was on high alert.

A small, red light turned on, and Solomon dropped his black rope into the mouth of darkness; a flailing lifeline he would soon descend, leaving the comfort of the aircraft for the vulnerability of the cold, quiet, hostile mountains below. Seven more lines dropped and seconds later they were all boots on the ground.

"Alright, four-by-four. We got twenty klicks to Reflex's beacon. We don't go weapons hot unless we're engaged."

Methodically they made their way up the mountain and overlooked the large valley below. A sea of mixed green and black flooded their eyes, as the NVGs used the light of the moon to bring it all to life. As they walked, the horizon began to turn a brighter shade, decreasing the contrast to the point of irritation, so Solomon ordered them to stow their NVGs.

Soon it was 0700 and they were on location, hiding behind rocks in a large grouping of jagged boulders. Scanning the horizon, the valley to their south, and the peaks that extended in every direction, Solomon and his team saw no immediate threats.

"Blue you get high up on the ridgeline and watch toward the north. Whiplash, Lucky, Ghost, you three spread out to the east. Mayan take the rest west. I'll go check the seatpan."

Solomon waited for his men to set a perimeter. It was likely hostiles were waiting to ambush a search and rescue ream. The SEAL team knew from the aerial recon the compound was to the northeast, but it was eighty miles away. They would see anyone coming from a long way off, unless they were hidden in the infinite square acreage of the red, stone mountains. Solomon knew the seatpan could be booby trapped, and the beacon could be an invitation to the ambush.

"In position," Blue said, scanning the area below. "No hostiles, no Reflex."

"On, location," Solomon heard from the two groups to the west and east.

"Copy," Solomon softly, his tactical throat mic picking up his silky-smooth voice loud and clear. His voice is what made his wife fall in love with him. He thought of her, Lacy, and his little girl, Rachel, for a brief moment before pressing their memory deep down, focusing on the task at hand. If he wasn't focused, he may never smell his wife's perfume, feel her warm breath on his neck, never swing his daughter around in the air again. Even though she was eight, she still loved him to do it, and he was surely capable with his vise-like hands and thick arms.

Solomon began snaking his way toward the beacon, watching for trip wires, signs of disturbed earth, and IEDs. Blue helped some, scanning where he knew his friend would likely go, but he also watched the horizon with his 12x scope.

"Hold, Sol," Blue said as he scanned the area twenty yards ahead of his team leader. "Something shining in the bush at your eleven o'clock."

"I see it," Solomon said and immediately turned and went right of his intended path.

It took five minutes and three more course corrections, but he crossed the two-hundred yards to the beacon. He sighed when he got there. None of the survival gear was present. He'd seen it before. Likely Reflex was already dead. Solomon scanned the immediate area, noting an exposed wire.

"We've got an IED. I'm gonna set a charge," Solomon said, reaching into his back and placing a block of C4 onto the ground near the beacon and seatpan. He ran back the way he came, turned, and detonated.

Everything exploded, the C4, the IED, and the beacon. The blast echoed in the mountains for a dozen seconds and Solomon called command.

"Hercules, this is Sol."

"Copy Sol," the JSOC commander said into his comms.

"No body. We've got IEDs all over the place. I destroyed the beacon and seatpan. Those were the only items on site and they were booby trapped."

"Roger. Proceed as indicated."

"Copy Hercules."

"On me," Solomon said, and the SEAL team began returning to their lieutenant. He scanned the forward area as his men meandered through the vegetation, the IEDs, and bounded in and out of hides.

"Sol we've got movement in the north," Blue said as he looked through his scope, while the east and west teams moved back to Solomon.

"What you seeing?"

"Dust, looks like maybe two vehicles comin' fast," Blue said as he stared down his scope.

"Hercules we've got nobody in the area, correct?" Solomon said to command.

"Correct, Sol. You're the only ones."

"We've got hostiles inbound from the north," Solomon said to his men who immediately stopped and turned toward the north.

"Ten kilometers and closing," Blue said quietly as he lay prone. He knew they'd fight. Solomon always fought.

"Weapons hot," Solomon said. "Same positions, focus fire to the north. Keep a perimeter. Blue I'm coming to you," Solomon said, and they all retraced their steps making quick work of getting back in position.

For several minutes, Blue and Solomon watched the approaching vehicle. It morphed from two to four, a convoy of approaching threats, bounding and steering their all-terrain vehicles over the rough landscape. The vehicles rode single file; the ridgeline was too narrow for them to spread out.

"What's the range Blue?" Solomon asked as he watched through his own 4x scope, the enemies appearing several miles out through the haze of the atmosphere.

"Three kilometers, tops," he said without thought. He'd looked down a scope his whole life.

A whistle; distinct, familiar, and deadly, rang out from above.

"Incoming!" Ghost yelled into the comms as he heard the artillery first. The men all got low just before the mortar round hit the site several hundred yards from any of them. This happened a second and third time. Each round was getting closer to the eastern most group of men, Whiplash, Ghost, and Lucky.

"We're moving," Ghost said as he signaled to Whiplash and Lucky. Methodically they moved down the mountainside, one moving around the other, a constant weaving that they'd rehearsed, that they'd used on dozens of live ops, to stay moving and covering one another.

"Blue!" Lucky said. "Eyes on the spotter. Five o'clock high."

Blue quickly pounced up from his prone position, turned, and began to scan the mountainside. He returned to prone.

It was difficult to gauge for distance, the mountains always gave the illusion of proximity due to their enormity, but Blue loved to shoot in the mountains.

"Got 'em," Blue calmly said and began calibrating the rifle for wind and distance. Twelve-hundred yards, no wind through the valley in the early morning. He took a breath and let it out; again, he took a breath and let it out, holding it. He squeezed gently on the trigger.

Boom! A shot rang out and the concussion wave sent dust into the air around his muzzle as the Barrett recoiled into his sturdy shoulder. Blue waited only a few moments, but he knew the round landed true as he watched the spotter collapse, his binoculars falling from his face violently.

The mortars stopped, but the valley came to life.

"Hostiles approaching from the west!" Mayan said as his team began peppering rounds down toward the approaching danger.

"Put a round in the front car," Solomon said to Blue who returned to watching the convoy.

Boom! Another shot from the powerful rifled crackled through the mountain range like rolling thunder. The front car in the convoy stopped abruptly, the .50 caliber rounds piercing the radiator the aluminum block with ease, planting itself into the camshaft. The convoy halted.

"Moving to the west," Solomon said to Blue as he left. "Keep me posted."

Solomon raced down the steep mountainside and into a flanking position from the north. "Mayan, I'm to the north of the hostiles."

"We've got eight at our twelve."

"I'm moving, cover me," Solomon said and began to tear through the dust covered landscape, bound over rocky terrain, and race toward the hostiles shooting blindly toward his men. He barely felt the ground and heard nothing but his own breathing as his M4 rattled softly in his hands.

Within a minute, he saw several of the hostiles, but took his time, finally counting eight. Four of the hostiles were grouped close together, the other four, spread wide across the gently sloping landscape; and all were focused on his men. Solomon pulled the pin on a frag grenade. Throwing it toward the group, he counted to three, ensuring his shots would come at approximately the same time as the detonation.

Solomon squatted, pointed his gun toward the closest hostile, *pop! Pop, pop! Pop!* He began to shoot. *Bang!* The frag rang out, putting down four. *Pop, pop!* Solomon struck the last man with a double tap of his M4.

"You're clear down here," Solomon said as he watched over the eight hostiles, ensuring they were dead before moving back to Blue.

"We've got eyes on the mortar team," Ghost said quickly. "Three-hundred yards to our two o'clock."

"Proceed with caution," Solomon said, allowing the men to hunt.

Ghost, Lucky, and Whiplash began to weave their way toward the unsuspecting group who struggled to re-acquire the Americans.

The SEAL team got to within fifty yards, unseen.

"Whiplash, you get the far right, Lucky, grab the guy in the middle. Three, two, one," Ghost said as they strategically placed lead through the air. The three-man artillery unit was neutralized.

Ghost silently scrambled toward the artillery site and made quick work of placing a charge onto the remaining mortar rounds. He scurried back toward the other men. A moment later, the entire valley echoed, destroying the artillery site.

"Artillery's down," Ghost said into the comms.

"Blue, you got a clear shot at the rear truck?" Solomon asked, his breathing labored as he returned to his friend.

"Yes, sir."

"Hit it."

The .50 cartridge exploded as the firing pin ignited the powder. The precise ratio of the weight and rifling of the barrel placed the perfect amount of spin on the smooth bullet. The muzzle break shot flames and hot gas as the round belched out of the rifle, giving it the look of an angry dragon. Through the air, the honed projectile sang out, scorching the thin air as it arced toward the target vehicle.

"Let's roll," Solomon said and the group of SEALs began working their way through the valley, bounding over rocky outcroppings as they quickly moved toward the convoy. Blue remained behind, providing overwatch for the team.

It took an hour, but eventually the SEAL team worked their way close to the convoy.

"Look good, still nobody spotting you. Three-hundred yards out," Blue said calmly as he panned back and forth from the team, to the convoy. The SEALs were covering a lot of ground, and they were in a low position, tracing the ridgeline on which the convoy sat immobilized.

"Two-hundred yards. Hold," Blue said quickly and the team dropped low and waited. They could hear faint voices, yelling, as they scrambled to move the rearmost truck in an attempt to flee.

"Hostile approaching," Blue said as he began to control his breathing once more. The team raised their weapons and scanned their zones, each knowing their shooting responsibilities without having to discuss it.

In a moment, a man fell down the steep slope toward them, his chest displaying a massive cavity from Blue. *Boom!* A moment later the sound of his .50 caliber reached the team. The sound was like a starting gun. They raced up the incline toward the hostiles. As they reached the ridgeline they caught the entire convoy by surprise.

"Drop your weapons," Solomon yelled in Arabic. "Drop your weapons!" he yelled again shooting a round into the rearmost vehicle. Ten Arabic men dropped their weapons, but three tried to raise theirs. Blue immediately responded by placing a round into the chest of a man. The slap and thud heavy lead made on flesh was unnatural. Solomon and Ghost took the other two non-compliant individuals out.

"Hercules we've got ten hostile prisoners," Solomon said into the comms as the team began searching and securing them to one another, hands behind their backs, and bags over their heads.

"Copy that Sol. Advise exfil at location Bravo."

Solomon referenced his map, noting Bravo to be twenty kilometers south. He paused, assessing the situation. He looked over the ridgeline, and saw that it eventually extended toward the south. "Thanks Hercules, out."

Solomon searched the trucks. One by one he entered the rear of each, noting their cavernous space and moving to the next. The final truck caused him to pause. The entire floor was stained, a thick streak of the dark matter painted a detailed picture of death.

"Bring that one here," Solomon said, pointing to the eldest member of the convoy, a man barely thirty with dark, bloodshot eyes. He was fearless, angry at the SEAL team's trespassing.

"What is this?" Solomon asked, pointing to the stains. The man refused to speak, spitting into the bed of the truck and smiling. Solomon asked again, this time in Arabic, "Ma hdha?"

The man smirked, gathered phlegm from the back of his throat, and spit it into Solomon's face.

Quickly Solomon grasped the man by the hair and

placed the prisoners face directly onto the dark smear, the smell of blood quickly entered the man's nose as he tried hard to fight the pressure from the large black man's hand pressing down onto his skull. After several seconds, the man gave up the fight, sighed, and began to chuckle. Solomon didn't need this man to talk, he just hoped the prisoner would have been a bit compliant, making the search and rescue op more productive.

"Take 'em back," Solomon said to Ghost who grabbed the prisoner and roughly brought him back to the rest of them. All the prisoners sat on the ridgeline, unable to escape. The SEALs had taken their shoes and blindfolded them for good measure.

Solomon took out a bag and a knife. He scraped at the floor of the truck bed, removing some of the superficial blood stains and placed them into the bag. He was hoping they could run DNA and determine if it was Alex Pines.

"We'll take the second truck," Solomon said to the men. "Have these assholes push that one over the edge," he said, referring to the lead truck Blue had disabled.

They took the two functioning trucks, splitting the SEAL team and the hostiles evenly between the vehicles. A short while later, the SEAL team silently bounced their way down the ridgeline as the truck's suspension groaned in the difficult terrain. Solomon reached toward his pocket, which held the bag containing the blood scrapings from the bed of the truck. Hopefully, they could get it to Germany that night, and have an answer by the next week. Interrogating the hostiles would go easier with evidence. Ghost was driving the truck as they headed toward Blue who waswaiting patiently, watching them approach via the ridgeline.

Solomon's head snapped right as instinct took over when he heard the *whap, whap, whap* of the rotors of a Russian KA-50, the Black Shark. The attack helicopter rose from below the ridgeline as it strafed sideways, facing the small convoy.

"Bail out!" Solomon yelled into the comms as rockets jettisoned the aircraft a moment later.

Boom! Smoke and flames played the lead, and shattered rocks and debris the encore, as the SEAL team tumbled down the opposing slope, banging against rocks and red earth, eventually settling two-hundred yards below; all seven narrowly escaping.

"Blue?" Solomon asked for his sniper.

"I've got him," he responded. "He's circling the damage."

"Okay. Ghost, Lucky, hit 'em with the LMG and draw his attention. We'll all get at least three shots with the 40mm. Make it count. Hustle back here if we've failed, and hope he doesn't find us," Solomon said, his smooth face giving way to dimples as he smiled broadly.

Slowly the team worked their way up the two-hundred-yard incline, spacing every twenty yards between them. Their thighs ached, but they didn't concede as they continued to ascend, crouched, their weapons up and focused. They began to hear the propellers whirling overhead, a comfortable breeze sweeping down the ridgeline, as dust cascaded downward toward the men, causing them to squint to keep their eyes safe.

"He's facing north. Go," Blue said as he eyed the Black Shark, its dark brown color matching the mountainside.

"Move!" Solomon shouted into the comms and the men raced the last fifty yards to the edge of the ridgeline.

Boom! The gas tank on one of the vehicles exploded, causing the Black Shark to maneuver rearward, and over the steep descent on the south side of the ridgeline. Suddenly the SEAL team found themselves less than thirty yards from the ominous monster floating above, the wind making their movements more labored, and their escape much more unlikely. Helos were a death sentence for infantry, their ability to slowly search and destroy from above with little weakness gave the men a chill. It was the first time Solomon's team felt vulnerable, unprepared. Nobody knew these hostiles would have access to attack helicopters.

Solomon aimed his M4 toward the beast above, its dark shadow easily seen contrasting the brilliant blue sky. The smoke from the vehicles started to flow down the mountainside toward them like oily dry ice.

Thump! The sound of a 40mm grenade barely registered as Solomon took the first shot. Quickly, several more thuds sent cylinders spinning toward the metal beast. Ghost and Lucky began to throw controlled bursts of fire toward the Shark as well, banging rounds off the metal hull. Just before the pilot reeled around to investigate, Solomon's grenade struck.

Bang—an otherworldly scream from the metal, and a hole appeared followed by a shower of shrapnel and spark. Three more struck true, creating matching black holes in the dark brown shell. By now, the men had shot their second 40mm grenades toward the aircraft as it struggled to gain its bearings, not realizing the shots were coming from directly below. Again, the explosions struck home and the helo banked toward the north and out of sight, a small streak of smoke marking its path.

"It can't maneuver well up here," Solomon said, remembering the ridgeline was 12,000 feet according to the maps they studied prior to deployment.

The team ran to the crest of the ridgeline and sat low, hidden from view.

"He's still there, below the ridge on the north side, trying to gain control. They're all over the map," Blue said as he continued to watch.

"Fire at will," Solomon said as adrenaline filled his body. Like Spartan warriors at the Hot Gates, they would defend this narrow pass to the death if they had to. He ran between the vehicles, took a knee, and pointed down fifty yards at the erratic helo as the pilot struggled with the stick. The man wasn't paying attention to anything else. He was oblivious to the special forces unit above, each trained killer fixated on the vulnerable Black Shark.

Thump, thump, thump, thump, thump, quickly they all unloaded their 40mm one last time as Ghost and Lucky shot continuous fire toward the windscreen and propellers. Even Blue got involved, firing downrange toward the rear propeller, striking true and causing the steel mammal to spin wildly as it descended deep into the abyss that was the north side of the ridgeline. Three-thousand feet below it struck the earth in a hellish scream of twisting metal, bubbling paint, and death.

"Gonna take a bit longer now, Blue," Solomon said as he watched the aircraft below. "Rendezvous at checkpoint Delta. We need to get to a better position down in the valley. We'll move toward exfil Lima."

As they walked, the sun tried to battle the ancient dance of another day, as it began to sink below the Haraz Mountains, its well-painted, abstract swirls of red and orange on the endless canvas across the sky. Solomon noticed it, but it reminded him of his wife. She always sent him pictures of beautiful sunsets. He did what he could to keep focused by reaching into his pocket, grasping the plastic bag that held the only hope they had in determining Alex's end. Solomon knew it wouldn't bring any leads. Even if it was Alex's blood it meant nothing. It wouldn't tell them he was captured, or if he was even alive, only that he bled, and knowing the situation they were in, it was likely he bled a lot.

Chapter 13
MEDUSA

Seattle, Washington

Nassir was sitting in his large office where floor to ceiling windows allowed a panoramic view of Lake Washington. The early morning sun reflected off the water like thousands of camera flashes. It was quiet, relaxing, until his phone rang.

"Hello Grant," Nassir said with a smile as he answered his phone.

"Morning Nassir. Hope all is well."

"It might be, depending on the news you're bringing," he said as he walked toward the windows, taking in the beauty of a virgin morning.

"He's decided to look into you, see who you are, where you came from, business deals. You understand."

"Progress Grant. That's great. How quickly will that go? I'm confident they won't find anything. I'm born here, raised by good parents. I don't even have a speeding ticket."

"I'm just an advisor. I have no idea how long things like that take."

"Listen. You and I both know it's in his best interest to use my tech. Terrorism isn't dead. Never will be. I'd advise you to continue to remind him we need to stay ahead."

"I'm sure he's getting it from all sides already," Grant said, checking over his shoulder as he heard noise coming from down the hall.

"You guys lost another five points I saw," Nassir said, digging into Grant.

"Did we?" Grant responded sarcastically, annoyed with the young engineer's sales pitch. The campaign was slipping, people were falling in love with Waxman, and it was becoming apparent he could rouse the people.

"Hmmm," Nassir said playfully. "Maybe I should be talking to Waxman's people. They'll likely be in the White House soon."

"The election is still a few months away."

"Precisely my point. By then, several attacks could happen and you'd have missed out on the opportunity to stop them. I'll tell you what," Nassir said, sitting back into his brown leather chair. "I'll go ahead and send you what we get from scanning the dark web. If he feels it's appropriate, he can act on it. If not, that's on him."

"Seems fair."

"Good. But Grant, being able to scan all incoming and outgoing data is what this system is designed for. Our system can also plant super RATs into their systems. I need the president on board."

"A super RAT?"

"Sorry, Grant. Industry term. It means Remote Access Terminal. We could control their computers, send messages, access their accounts without their knowledge. But with our quantum tech, it could be a lot more invasive, and undetectable."

"Like I said, Nassir. I'll do what I can."

"I'll reach out to you again soon."

Nassir hung up the phone and opened his computer. Immediately the display came to life. He motioned across the screen with a swipe of his hand, and the data appeared on the far end of his office on a massive white wall, twenty feet high and forty feet wide. He looked over the data, particularly the incoming bits their own team was assessing as possible terrorist communications. It was eerie looking over their codes, lacking the ability to translate what they were saying, if anything. Nassir's group hadn't deciphered the codes the terrorists were using. It was all useless information in their hands, but in the hands of the government, it could prove limitless. Nassir needed the connection. It was an obsession, a game he needed to win, like many other games he'd won before this.

In high school Nassir quickly became the person everyone went to for homework hacks. He'd program a calculator, a phone, a tablet to work complex formulas, hide crib sheets, or connect them all to a hidden network for answer sharing; at a premium. It was how he made his first ten-thousand dollars. Each hack, each connection to the network grabbed him a few dollars, so by the time he was seventeen he had seed money to start his side business, which included coding.

He would code anything from RC cars and drones, to web applications. He would charge a fifty-dollar hourly rate to rewrite coding for applications, making them run more efficiently with less errors, and all the while, he would pack away the knowledge. If he saw a way to expand an application, build upon a piece of tech, he wouldn't share it. Instead, he placed it onto his own hard drive, storing it for himself; just in case he'd need it later.

His small business was worth well over one-hundred thousand dollars by the time he was accepted into MIT's engineering program. It was there he discovered the limitless possibilities in material science, and it was there he secretly stashed away the ideas he would later use to develop Medusa; a three-dimensional processing chip giving him his valuable quantum computer.

Medusa was like nothing else before. Its computations worked in qubits, rather than the standard bits, allowing for zeros, ones, or zero—one to be present simultaneously. However, this wasn't a novel idea, qubits had been used before. So has the unimaginably cold environment the processor was housed within, a temperature at nearly minus 273 degree Kelvin, also known as absolute zero in the universe. The entire computer was shielded from electromagnetics, and was supported on one thin aluminum pole, so it wasn't grounded to anything outside of itself.

Medusa gathered its lovable name from its structure: twelve tentacles composed of circuits numbering in the hundreds, snaking out of the three-dimensional plasma. Within the chip itself, an inorganic plasma of Nassir's design, allowing electrons to flow freely in any direction they chose, or, they could be manipulated to flow like water, creating an infinite number of communicative pathways, instantly and simultaneously, over the tens of thousands of circuits that surrounded the chip. Nassir had the enclosure for the chip built with leaded glass. He argued it would reduce the chance of radiation infiltrating the sensitive environment within. But, in reality, he wanted to watch the gentle blue glow as the electrons jockeyed for position during computations; the losers releasing their energy as a glow, only to be recycled once again and thrown back into the fray. It was mesmerizing, pulsing, alive.

He reached toward his computer screen with an open hand. The images on the screen shrank down as his hand closed. He walked back to the windows and looked out over the water once again, now seeing only the grays and blues of an overcast sky.

"How quickly things could change," he said to himself. He smiled, realizing what he had said. The flawless morning giving way to rain had brought hope to the creative engineer.

Washington, D.C.

President Pierce stood on the lawn of the White House as he looked over the media staff, each person sitting with recorders, pen, and paper. He wore a tailored gray suit, a dark blue tie, and a clean shaven face. He was rested, confident, as he readied to address the country. It had been a few weeks since Senator Waxman's statements in Chicago, where he challenged President Pierce to match his commitment to a clean and focused campaign. The statement had been well received in the public eye, most Americans had been sick of politics for years; the constant bullying, lying, and finger-pointing had gotten out of control in recent decades. In fact, a poll had been taken regarding whether Americans understood a politician's platform, and over fifty percent were clueless as to what each person planned to do in office, but they were nearly ninety percent accurate when it came to allegations against a particular politician running for office.

Pierce smiled as camera shutters slapped closed all around him, the crisp mechanical applause was something he hadn't gotten used to.

"Good morning," he said as several pens stood to

attention and readied themselves to meet paper. "I'm here to address the recent proposal brought forth by my friend, Senator Waxman. I think it is a noble idea, a grand gesture to place our respective political platforms first. Recently, we've seen a poll which reveals some sad statistics regarding what voters are remembering from our campaigns. Unfortunately, where each of us stand on the big issues isn't what's being talked about, or remembered come time to vote."

He paused, briefly, frustrated in the moment, but his eyes, his body language revealed nothing he felt inside. His hands seemed tied, Waxman had polarized the entire country. The senator had his finger on the pulse of the American people, the liberal media, the movement of acceptance. If Pierce didn't agree, he would surely take a monstrous hit in the media, followed by a dramatic impact in his approval numbers, and likely his voters as well. He would seem a soulless bully, out to smear the name of a good man.

"This is why I've agreed to his plan for a positive, surgical campaign, focusing on the issues and where I stand; not where my opponent stands, or what may be in his past." Pierce smiled and looked into the row of cameras. "Let's face it. He's a good man, but hopefully you find me a better leader. Thank you," he said, smiling again and walked quickly back toward the White House. Secretary Smith and Grant, his campaign manager, accompanying him after several strides.

"It's better to beg forgiveness later than smear your name now. Waxman is squeaky clean, nothing in his history. He's a single father and a hard-working man. We haven't found anything worth making you look like a monster by disagreeing at this point," Grant said in the Oval Office.

"I know. Still scares the hell out of me. Feel like I'm under his thumb now, like I can't step out of line."

"You won't lose any points with the statement that's for sure. For now, that's all we care about."

"No it's not," Doyle said, speaking up and walking toward the president's desk. "We've got word from Yemen. SEAL team took heavy resistance, had seven or eight prisoners, but then a Russian attack helo changed all that. Almost took out the whole team."

"What the hell are we dealing with Doyle?" President Pierce said frustrated; his chess game still under attack. "I can't even think about the campaign while this shit's going on!"

"I agree. If Americans find out about our failed mission, about our KIA, it'll be bad. The election is only weeks away," Grant said, sighing.

"More than that, sir," Doyle said, staring at Grant. "If we can't stop an attack here on U.S. soil, you might as well kiss that second term goodbye."

"What do you want from me Doyle? I've already stopped talking about the end of terrorism," President Pierce spat at his secretary, the words vibrating the round walls in the office.

"What about Nassir?" Grant asked as his body tightened, not allowing air to escape his lungs. His conversations directly with Nassir had been secret.

"We've more or less vetted him. He's Saudi by way of his parents. He's first generation American, attended MIT, Stanford, computer engineering. He has no ties to the Middle East, his father was an engineer. No other family of note. Non-religious, his social media is pretty bland, a few photos of drinking in college ten years ago was the worst we saw. His website is quite impressive as well."

"NSA clear him?"

"Not yet, but I can't imagine it'll be long," Doyle said finally sitting into his chair.

"Let's set a meeting with Nassir, NSA, FBI. Get us all in the same room so he can tell us what he's got. And Doyle, let's make it soon. I've got an election to win."

Chapter 14
GHOSTS

Arlington, Virginia

Logan sat next to a marble headstone, a bottle of Jack Daniel's resting on the ground, staring through the darkness of a moonless night. The enormity of the cemetery was lost on him at Migs' funeral service, and, even before that, when Sherman was laid below years earlier.

"Hey man, I haven't talked to Heather in a while," Logan said to the white marble sitting to his left. "I don't ever know what to say to her."

Logan took another drink from the bottle, and thought to pour a shot onto the grass, but he stopped himself, respecting the hallowed ground he rested on.

"She looks good though, we're Facebook friends, whatever the hell that's worth," he grumbled, his words slurring as he leaned into the headstone as he tried to feel supported.

"I lost another one," Logan said, a tear rolling down his face. Lieutenant Alex Pines; a wizzo on an FA-18. I'm losing my touch Sherman. Why the fuck is everyone dying because of my mistakes? Huh? Shit," Logan said, smiling and slapping the cold marble. "I thought I heard you giving me shit for a minute."

Logan's insides went hollow, an ache filled the void and reminded him he was still alive, no matter how much he drank. *When's it my turn!* he screamed inside.

Two days earlier, he heard the news from Secretary Smith. The SEAL team had prisoners, but they were disintegrated by rockets as they sat tied together in the back of a truck. The SEAL team leader found blood in the rear of a covered truck, the results: positive for Alex Pines, and his squadron leader, Commander Heinz. All were now presumed KIA because they hadn't heard a word from a terrorist group to negotiate terms. General Anderson, as well as Secretary Smith, had concluded even if Pines had survived, he would have been tortured and killed. They came to that conclusion due to the aggressive nature of the hostiles the SEAL team had come in contact with.

The grief was all encompassing for Logan. Four pilots lost on his intel, and Migs' death a month before, was a one—two punch leaving Logan reeling back into the emotional cage he found himself in after he lost Sherman. As he sat on the soft, moist grass he felt no physical pain, no shiver in his body, despite the unusually cold evening, as the wind gusted rhythmically causing him to slump forward against the force. But this time, the wind had caught him off guard, tipping him back just enough for him to lose his balance. He reacted, reached toward Sherman's headstone and grasped it to stabilize himself.

"Still there for me, brother," he said to his sniper teammate who lay six feet under, eternally sleeping with his sharpshooter metal and the tattoo of his love, Heather.

Footsteps approached. Logan heard the subtle crunch of flattening grass with each step. Logan sprung to a kneeling position as his adrenaline brought him as close as it could have to sobriety in the moment. He couldn't make out which direction it was coming from, but he heard them, which meant it was likely upwind. He drew his gun and pointed it into the narrow space between headstones, visions of a dark night in Iraq played back in his mind.

Logan and Sherman had been tasked with providing long-range recon on a small village outside of Baghdad. The intel stated this particular town was a depot for radicals who moved into the city, bombing civilians and American soldiers, whoever came first. It was a silky, black night, eerie light filtered down from gray clouds above, providing a masking to the light from the three-quarter moon overhead. A force recon team was infiltrating the town, demolishing all questionable facilities. Logan lay prone, scanning the area, scouting for his shooter, Sherman.

"I see IR beacons coming from the south," Logan said, looking through his monopod from a thousand yards away, observing the squad of force recon Marines entering the city.

"Got it," Sherman said, as he lay prone, his rifle pinned to his shoulder, his shooting finger sliding toward the trigger, gently caressing the steel frame like a lover.

"Halo, we got a heavy machine fifty yards ahead," the lieutenant said to Logan.

"Copy Reaper." Several seconds passed as Logan scanned the village below, looking for the hostile. "Eyes on."

"Execute," Reaper said coldly.

"Copy," Sherman said as he calibrated for the five-mile per hour wind coming from right to left. He also had to decide whether the close proximity of the structures would have any effect on the round.

Boom! A shot rang out as Sherman decided the effect would be negligible.

"Moving," Reaper said as his men slithered quickly through the town, like a short, pulsing cobra in the night.

Pop, pop. Logan heard gunfire in the distance as the Marines downrange engaged the enemy. More popping, but this time erratic, uncoordinated; unfamiliar explosions from guns he barely recognized rang out. It seemed like hundreds of rounds were blistering the air as he frantically searched for targets Sherman could put down.

"What we got, Logan?" Sherman asked, his voice flat and calming.

"Nothin'," Logan said. Panic washed over him and made it difficult to concentrate on the green haze through the night vision.

"Take it easy brotha'. We got this," Sherman said, sensing his teammate's distress. Logan knew Reaper and the strike team well; they were all part of the same company.

"Hostile!" Logan said eagerly. "Approaching from the west, slowly, he's trying to flank."

"Got 'em," Sherman said as he placed his crosshairs on the crouched teenage boy.

Boom! One shot; one kill.

Logan's heart began to accelerate as he scanned back toward the direction the hostile had come from. Twelve more targets were moving up the street in an attempt to flank his strike team as they cleared homes. Logan and Sherman couldn't see Reaper and his team. They hadn't for some time, which meant they were likely moving through the town successfully, however, it made the team vulnerable.

"Reaper, you've got a dozen hostiles approaching your entry point at the main road," Logan said into the comms.

"Copy, Halo," Reaper quickly responded from inside a home they had cleared only moments earlier.

Boom! Sherman sent lead downrange, striking the first hostile, causing the rest to scramble in a panic.

"Hostiles broke into the city," Logan said to Reaper as he watched the remaining targets scramble around homes, sprint toward their point of origin, or simply run down the street flailing their gun erratically to gain more speed. It must have been hilarious for those watching at their forward operating base, but in the moment, Logan was nervous for Reaper and his squad.

"It's too unpredictable," Logan said to Sherman.

"We've got our orders. Sit and watch," Sherman responded, his eyes unblinking as he stared down into the town through his narrow viewing window. He was like a scientist looking into a foreign world through his microscope, disconnected, studying, waiting for the moment something happens.

"Halo, Reaper's down," a familiar voice from one of the squad members crackled through their headpiece.

"Repeat?" Logan said as blood rushed through his ears, adrenaline supercharged his heart and he was enraged.

"Reaper's down. We've set a perimeter on the building. Our grid is A-3, the far east side of the town. Significant hostile presence closing in from the west and north."

Logan stood and stowed his ranging scope, grabbed his M4, and began sprinting toward the city. Sherman followed a moment later, hiding his M40 beneath his shirt. He ran after his teammate, topless, through the warm Iraq night.

"What the fuck?" Logan said as he glanced back spotting his shirtless teammate. He quietly laughed at the sight of Sherman running into the city, his tanned torso glistening in the omnidirectional light from the cloud cover above.

Finally, the two-man team found themselves entering the westernmost edge of the city.

"Halo, to your west," Logan said to the fire team. "Guide us in."

"You've got half a klick to us, stay off the main road, advise moving north and sweeping in. We've got good eyes that direction and will see you coming."

"Roger, we've activated our strobes," Logan said.

Sherman and Logan moved north along the westernmost aspect of the city. They knew they'd be safe there, having come from that direction themselves. After only a few minutes, they hit the northwest corner of the town. Slowly, they moved eastward, scanning the dark town for hostiles. Shooting, for the most part, had stopped, leaving the town in an eerie silence as their boots gently kissed the loose stones and fine dust in the streets.

"Agh!" Logan heard a grunt as Sherman grasped a hostile, and in one motion jammed his KA-BAR deep into the man's throat, silencing a potential alarm. The man dropped to the ground, blood appearing as an oily river oozing from the wound and into the earth.

Moments passed slowly as the two men moved silently, methodically through the city at a southeasterly vector, clearing homes, and seeing no hostiles.

"We've got your beacons," Logan heard through the comms.

"Copy."

"Head directly south, there's a large group of hostiles in that direction. We've counted fifteen locals, civilian. Be advised."

Logan and Sherman separated, each moving south down parallel streets, less than two-hundred feet between the two of them, but it may as well have been miles. They'd always been right next to one another, hearing the breath enter each other's lungs. They were used to being separate from a unit, but not from each other. Logan felt naked, Sherman was shirtless, and they were now being watched over by the strike team. It was a complete role reversal; nobody was in their element.

Logan spotted hostiles first, a group of five. He stayed crouched, found cover behind a building, and quickly eight shots rang out from his M4, striking true on every target.

"Five down," he said as he ran toward the next street to the east, two-hundred feet further from his teammate.

Pop, pop, pop, pop, pop, he heard friendly fire coming from the west; Sherman. "Three down," he said.

Then it happened. Too many hostiles to count began pouring out of homes around Logan, more came from south of the strike team's location; all came crashing down on the Americans. Later the Marines found out some of the homes in the town had underground tunnels that were capable of hiding dozens of fighters, but in the moment, their training took hold.

Logan systematically retreated toward his teammate, shooting and then moving, shooting again, and moving, always making sure he didn't stay stationary for more than twenty or thirty seconds. The strike team aided his maneuvers by focusing their fire toward the north, eliminating dozens of hostiles. Finally, Logan was reunited with Sherman. The two men reloaded, and without speaking, knew.

They spun up from their hide and shot into the darkness, their hot, lead flesh seekers finding target after target. It was incredible, the poetry in their motion, one shooting while the other moved, the other providing cover while allowing the other to reload. Hostile after hostile cried out in the night as metal pierced their clothes and flesh, creating a hellish orchestra of pain and agony, all the while, unseen hostiles were moving in from the south.

"We're being overrun!" the strike team said through the comms as Sherman and Logan began to move southward through the city once more. Immediately, they saw the situation. Dozens of hostiles surrounded the home in a semicircle, peppering it with gunfire as Marines from within did their best to shoot outward, throw grenades, and one Marine even deployed smoke toward the west.

Logan and Sherman fired on the hostiles, making quick and easy work with those unlucky groups to the west and east of the building that housed the Marines.

Click, click, click, Logan's M4 failed him. Having lost count of the shots he'd taken, he dropped to a knee in cover and searched for another magazine, but came up empty.

"Clear to the north. Move!" Logan said into the comms to the fire team who burst from the home, carrying Reaper. Logan ran toward the south, a sidearm in his hand. He crouched, one knee on the ground, and readied himself for whatever came toward him as the force recon group carried out their leader, their friend.

Pop pop, pop pop, his M45's crisp sound reverberated off the houses he sat between, as he ended two more lives. More assailants came, and Logan responded with flashes of powder, heat, and lead; the prologue to an endless sleep for several more hostiles. Again, he clicked an empty magazine.

Vulnerability took hold as Logan knelt alone in the alleyway, as three enemies quickly turned the corner seeing the young Marine. Without warning, Logan was grasped from behind, thrown flat onto his back, and stared up at a shirtless Sherman. With one hand, he held Logan down while the other pointed an M4 through the alleyway, shooting the three hostiles. He grabbed Logan by the shirt and with one powerful move, lifted him to his feet. The entire strike team evacuated the city toward the east, Logan and Sherman ran to their sniper post and grabbed their gear before heading to their exfil.

Logan was kneeling in the graveyard, just like he had in that alleyway in Iraq, no Sherman to save his life; but his clip was full.

"Logan," he heard a booming voice say. He didn't respond, scared he was imagining Sherman's voice.

"Logan," a man said again, this time a little clearer, the voice reverberating in Logan's own chest.

"Who's there?" Logan asked loudly, trying to cover the fear that found its way into his voice.

"Dubs."

"Over here," Logan responded, too shocked to ask the question of how.

Dubs finally saw Logan, the shell of a man he used to know. He was drunk, dirty, lazily holding the gun on his lap, his left hand still grasping the neck of a bottle.

"What the hell, man?" Dubs asked softly as he sat on the other side of Sherman's headstone, unable to look at the man he idolized. It was traumatizing for Dubs to see Logan so vulnerable, so defeated and weak.

"When's it my turn?" Logan said, tears rolling down his face. "When do I get to fucking die?"

"What?"

"Everyone around me dies. Not me."

"Logan you're not making sense," Dubs said, annoyed.

"Reaper, Sherman, Migs, Alex Pines, Commander Heinz, two other pilots I don't know, dozens more who served with me. When do I get to die?"

"None of this is on you. Any of us can say what you're saying, Logan. I'm telling you this as a friend, no bullshit, and you know that's hard for me to do." Both men paused silently. "You need to talk to someone about this before you do something stupid."

"What's that supposed to mean?" Logan said, frustrated at the suggestion.

"You know what the fuck I mean. Samantha loves you, she needs you! Not this lifeless person you've become; and you need her. She's strong Logan, she can help you. Shit. I can help you. What you wanna do, brother?"

Brother, the word resonated with Logan. He had so many brothers over the years, so many men he served with, good ones, friends. "I need to sober up," Logan said, trying to stand.

"Let's get the hell outta here," Dubs said as he read the headstone. "So, this was your guy, huh? The one you told me about?"

"Yeah, Sherman. Big ass boy, never saw him miss."

"Tell me about him," Dubs said as the two men walked out of the cemetery, Logan telling stories the whole time.

Washington, D.C.

Two men sat in an SUV watching the outside of a modest home, waiting for a phone to ring. It was 0300, but both men felt no fatigue by the hour or day, or the darkness of the night. They hadn't talked for hours, just sat, watched, and waited. Finally, a red LED on the dashboard lit. The driver turned on the radio, and immediately they heard two familiar voices.

"Hey Samantha, sorry it's so late but I found him."

"It's no problem, I couldn't sleep anyway. Where was he?"

"Right where you said he might be."

Samantha didn't speak for several seconds as emotions

cascaded through her body like a relentless waterfall. She struggled to find words of hope, sorrow, thankfulness that Logan was alive and he had a friend like Dubs.

"Thanks, Dubs."

"We'll be home tomorrow. He's gonna talk to somebody."

"What can I do?"

"Nothing you aren't doing already. Be supportive, listen when he talks, talk when he doesn't, and call me if it gets to be too much."

"Thank you."

The men in the car pulled away after hearing the conversation between Samantha and Dubs. There was nothing else to be gathered at that moment about Logan, or his team. They had the anti-terrorism group reeling, their leader on edge. It was good news for Karim's men; their own sinister plans had yet to begin.

Chapter 15
REFLECTIONS OF A TRAITOR

Yemen

Amir sat, waiting for Taj to enter the interrogation room. For weeks they had talked to Alex Pines, and for weeks he said nothing. However, Amir had seen the signs of a break: the rolling of his eyes, the sweat, the firmness to his features as he struggled in the chair, slumped shoulders, crossed feet, and the fear in his bloodshot eyes. Alex hadn't slept more than five minutes at a time. It was worse for Alex that way, to fall asleep, allowing him to relax the mind for a moment, and then suddenly get sprung back to life with loud music, bright lights, and physical stimulus; whether it was an electric shock, cold water, or piss.

"Amir my brother!" Taj said as he entered the room. "*Assalamualaikum.*"

"*Assalamualaikum wa rahmatullah,*" Amir responded in kind, blessing Taj more greatly than he was blessed. It helped with the solidarity of the radical men, to encourage them to bless one another, the initiator receiving more blessings than the responder.

"I think today we break Alex Pines," Taj said, inhaling deeply. "The guard said he was whispering to himself last night, crying out as well. Today you talk to him. See if he listens to your voice, American."

Taj walked toward the door on the far side of the room and knocked, signaling the guard to grab Alex from his small cell. Not more than two minutes later, Alex walked in, mostly under his own power, his wounds beginning to heal. He finally took partial weight on his leg. His arm, still lifeless and stiff, often experienced throbbing and searing pain from his elbow to his neck, like electric fire every time he tried to extend it. The guards knew that, so on occasion, they would force his arm through range of motion and Alex would respond by gnashing his teeth, vomiting, or passing out.

Taj and Amir already sat waiting for Alex, who slowly waddled into the room, sitting in the third chair that sat straight across from the two captors.

"You are well?" Taj asked, smiling.

"Alex Pines—"

"We know already Mr. Pines. I'm not going to hurt you today. I'm not even going to talk to you. He is," Taj said, gesturing toward Amir who sat staring at Alex, his rapid heart pounding forcefully against his chest.

Amir's physique was returning slowly, as he was able to eat normally once again. The last time he interacted directly with Alex it led to a physical intervention. If he were to get violent this time, he may break Alex for good. Amir had been confused, unsure of his own emotions in the moment.

"Lieutenant Pines," Amir said casually. "May I call you that?"

Alex nodded and failed to match Amir's unwavering gaze, looking down at the floor for relief.

"You should know I lost my father years ago. It wasn't pretty, so I'll spare you the details, but it changed my life completely. Lieutenant, Alex, I was in the U.S. Army, decorated, respected. I was enlisted but I had the ear of the officers all the way to my X.O. I was a leader, a damn good one, but the moment he died changed my life forever," Amir paused, watching Alex for signs of weakness. None.

"This was your first assignment? Greenhorn. We know a lot Alex, hope you don't feel uncomfortable. It was a noble attempt. You guys did an impressive job with the SU-35s we dispatched, but our SAMS were tricky; borderline unfair I realize. Just too many. My first deployment was Afghanistan, and I'll tell you something, what a mind fuck that was. I'm first generation Pakistani, and I was forced to see my father's homeland through the eyes of my rifle for the first time as I killed men my father might have known. I was gung-ho American before that, full of pride, wanting to prove myself as a citizen of that country. You know what happened when I came home?"

"No," Alex responded; Amir had won. A fluttering in his stomach told him to press on, to really lay the story on thick, try to elicit emotion from the young pilot.

"My father was murdered by an American, right in front me when I returned stateside after finishing my tour. A racist monster beat him to death while I sat staring in a mirror in the bathroom, struggling to recognize my own face. When I came out, I saw what had happened and I snapped. I killed the man and two of his friends. I stayed with my dad until the police cuffed me and drove me away. I got my revenge, but not my career. Thankfully, a man named Jenkins came to me, saved me, helped me become who I am."

"A traitor? A shameful man who prides himself on the revenge he took?" Alex asked, looking up.

"I have no pride. It died in a restaurant, and again, in a room like this," Amir said, rage billowing in his chest.

"Your father died in vain. He came to America intent on a better life for you, and now you pissed it away. How proud he must be," Alex said and spit on the floor toward Amir.

"Your father died too, am I right?" Amir said, trying to turn the tables.

"A drunk driver killed him."

"Don't you want revenge?"

"No, I want justice."

"Is there a difference?"

"My name is Lieutenant Alex Pines, U.S. Navy. Number 432564532. DOB December 11, 1988."

Amir launched from his chair striking Alex hard. Blood and spit hit the floor just moments before the pilot landed hard, unconscious, in a sickening slap of flesh. Amir walked quickly toward the door, ripped it open, and ran down the hall.

What have I done? The thought reverberated through his mind, as he ran through the corridors, down the rounded concrete tunnel, and finally found the vertical access Taj brought him down when they arrived at the compound.

It hurt to breathe, his lungs felt as though they were being singed by glowing embers, his hands and face were numb. He felt like crying, like screaming out into the darkness as if he were trapped deep down inside himself for years, but hadn't known it until now. Alex showed him the light he'd refused to see; for years he avoided looking back, burying thoughts of his father and his mother who'd died following her battle with cancer. He'd been a wreck after her death, the steady insults at school had been exponentially worse after she was gone. She always heard him, listened, made him stronger. After she was gone, he needed to find a way to prove himself; the Army.

He thought of boot camp, of his company, his C.O. Colonel Hardy and how he trusted Amir more than any enlisted man in the company. He recalled his own pride, and the emotions he lacked came surging back as he told Alex about his father. He missed his pride more than he missed his mother.

Finally, Amir opened the hatch and began breathing the fresh mountain air. The afternoon was cold, fall had begun to show its true form, and he stared at the cloud of moisture leaving his lungs. Memories of years spent in the suburbs of Chicago flooded back, so many he couldn't pick out a single memory from the hundreds. His abdomen began to cramp, his body began to sweat as he thought to run, to tell everyone what was happening in the valleys of Yemen; but there was nowhere to go, no one to trust. *What did I do?*

After a walk, Amir had gathered himself enough to head below once more and face Taj. Slowly, he worked his way around to the main entrance. The guards recognized him, letting him in without any questions asked. Amir felt empowered by the freedom, his gait became relaxed, his body stretched like a flower toward the sun and he stood tall with every inch of his six-foot-four frame.

Quickly, Amir stepped through the halls in the concrete underground searching his partner out. He knew by this time Alex had been placed back into his cell, but for good measure, he walked past. He paused at the door and nodded to the guard who smiled broadly at Amir, silent praise for the assault he delivered on the pilot. Amir felt warmth in his insides, and an itch to attack the guard, to end him. The two stood, staring awkwardly, the guard's smile had reduced to a forced smirk at his leader. Amir stared through his dark eyes, eyes that to most would have seemed lifeless and demoralizing.

"Amir!" Taj said louder than conversational volume from down the hall.

Amir held the stare until the guard looked away, Taj providing the excuse. Amir strode away toward Taj, the only man he feared.

"I'm sorry, my brother," Amir said, sighing heavily. "I thought I had him."

"Amir, you know nothing. My father said it was better that way, but what does he know? Do you see him here?" Taj said, glancing around playfully, a look of bewilderment on his face as he threw his hands in the air.

"I think you can keep a secret, Amir. Come, walk with me."

The two men walked up the concrete stairs, through the main level of the compound, and out into the bright late afternoon sun. Neither man talked, Taj leading Amir toward the truck they rode in together.

"Get inside," Taj said as they reached the vehicle.

Off the compound they went, into the mountains, driving for what seemed like three hours. Taj was unusually silent the whole time, despite Amir's attempts to get him to talk.

Finally, they stopped at the peak of a ridgeline several thousand feet above sea level. The view was incredible, highlighting rocky outcroppings pressing upward in failed attempts to reach the heavens. The ground in the valleys was smooth, rolling, pillowy dust, seemingly untouched for centuries.

"It was a place like this they filmed the American movie, *The Martian*," Taj said, breaking the silence. "Just another example of the west doing as they please. The ground had been untouched, like this. Beautiful, isn't it?"

"Yes," Amir said still taking in the foreign landscape, trying to grasp its scale. The horizon went on forever, as did the red-brown earth, like a sandy river through high walled banks; its movement ancient, patient, slowly making its way toward the sun.

"For generations, the west has come into our lands, forced their will, made us relocate, and divide our historic homelands between themselves like some kind of game. My father began a movement Amir. One that fulfills our destiny. We are ushering the end times, the final battle to be held here, in the Middle East. We have been very successful Amir. We have brought the entire world here to fight our small skirmishes, in order for the greater good. We are doing God's work, Amir."

"You've told me all this before. What is your father hiding?"

"My father doesn't believe in the party line, and neither do I," Taj said, smiling, finally showing his teeth for the first time on the trip.

"I'm confused," Amir said, looking at Taj rather than the view.

"My father and I don't believe in a war that will usher in the end times, Amir. We think it's a wonderful way to convince individuals to die for our cause, to sacrifice themselves all over the world, but we just want to see the west fall. If that happens, we will inherit quite a bit of business."

"So, what's your true plan?"

"Cyber warfare."

"Why?"

"Because if you control the internet, if you control the servers, then you control everything! Imagine, we want corn production to cease in the U.S., we attack the seed production plants, the fertilizers, the farming equipment itself through a malware update. You want to make millions?

Simply control the trending stocks, futures, anything you desire. Do you want power to go out in New York? In Chicago? Or Los Angeles, so those wonderful Hollywood movies can still be produced? How about all of them at the same time? Abracadabra."

"How do you gain access to all that?"

"Simple, they give it to us."

"There's no way the U.S. government allows access to everything."

"Amir, you are so shortsighted. Have I shown you nothing? We are capable of everything. You think this pilot means anything? He doesn't. Anything he tells us will likely be useless to our main objective, but why not try and gather as much information as we can from the enemy? Knowledge is power my brother."

A knot formed in Amir's abdomen. He felt powerless. Even if he did get away, what was the point? He looked out into the infinite landscape, again trying to imagine its end, wondering how he could find his way out of the mountains if he ran.

"Would you like to hear a joke, Amir? A funny story perhaps?"

"Sure."

"You may not find any humor in it, but Jenkins was a pawn in our chess game. We intended for him to serve a purpose, to sacrifice himself for our cause at whatever point we desired. We were going to blow the whistle on him, distract the ones we needed to at a point in time when it became necessary. So what, if anything, would that have made you?"

Amir was trembling, the gravel beneath his feet danced rhythmically as his heartbeat pounded against his chest wall, exaggerated by the altitude. He looked at the ground recalling the years he worked for Jenkins, from the Middle

East to the U.S., from gathering a team, to killing Vladimir in Italy when the teammate had been lazy, allowing himself to be discovered. *Was Vladimir sacrificed? Was I the executioner for their game?"*

"You know my father controlled Jenkins, but do you know how?"

"No," Amir said, struggling to exhibit restraint, but the only thought reverberating in his mind, *push him down the ridge.*

"Jenkins killed a lot of soldiers. One directly, shooting him in the head with his service weapon while my father interrogated him. He then gave us the location to their forward operating base, and, where it was weakest. We bombed it, killing an additional fifty-three men. My father truly is a great man, a wonderful talker, a masterful leader. Wouldn't you agree? American?"

"Why do you call me that?"

"Because that's what you are isn't it? You weren't born here, you certainly don't know our pain, our struggles. You're learning though."

"Yes, I am."

"One more funny anecdote. Your friend, Logan Falcone." The name made Amir's nerves stand on end. If he hadn't been shocked by Taj's secrets before, he certainly was now. "He's running around like a wild bird, trying to catch these worthless cells in the U.S. We're watching him, sacrificing our people so the U.S. stay focused elsewhere, while we work toward out true intentions. He'll be useless soon. Would you like to kill him?"

"What?" Amir was shocked. The last time he thought of Logan had been before arriving in Yemen. It seemed so long ago, a different lifetime. Amir had been respected once, loved, had dreams and aspirations. At least he was beginning to remember the man he used to be.

"We are watching him, and his team," Taj said, smiling. "In fact, one of them is gone, died trying to eliminate a cell we planted in L.A. They are so ignorant, Amir. Even President Pierce is saying terrorism is dead."

"Why are you offering me Logan? How could I even get close to the man?"

"In time my American friend. I just wanted to set the table."

"Why take me out here to leave me in suspense?" Amir asked in frustration. "Am I going back to the states?"

"My father is a great man, Amir. You owe a lot to him," Taj said, ignoring Amir's question.

"I understand—"

"No, Amir, you don't," Taj said, his voice dropping low as all playfulness melted from his tone. Even the wind gusted as Taj turned toward Amir, looking at him for the first time since leaving the compound nearly four hours earlier.

"You don't know, because I never told you. I intended to kill you. But only after I made you suffer. I planned to torture you until you forgot who you were, until you died inside. I saw you as an American, a traitor to your heritage, someone to make an example out of. But then my father showed me his larger plan. He explained you were capable of being an ally, rather than an enemy. Praise be to *Allah* for my father."

On their way back, Amir knew he needed to escape, but didn't know when, how, where he would go. For hours he reflected, he thought about his options but the only one that seemed likely was to convince Karim he needed to go stateside and kill Logan himself. He would have to wait, to pray, for the opportunity to present itself. He wasn't sure how much longer he could hide his new feelings; especially the one that started as a whisper and began its crescendo toward screaming, *Who am I?*

Chapter 16
AWAKEN THE FUTURE

Washington, D.C.

Nassir arrived early, as he always did, and took time to navigate the open lobby. He paused at the memorial wall that was embossed with dozens of stars carved out of the solid concrete, representing a member of the CIA who had been lost in the line of duty. He imagined the memorial would have included more stars, but knew his only reference point was how Hollywood portrayed the life of a CIA operative, and that made Nassir smirk.

He moved toward a bench that rested against the wall and sat. He was comfortable in his tailored suit. He sat up straight, his face relaxed, and his mind clear. He watched people as they came and went through the lobby, trying to establish who worked there, versus those who were simply passing through, as he was this morning.

"Mr. Ajab?" A young woman in a business suit

approached the young engineer.

He nodded and smiled. "Hello."

"Please come with me. They're ready for you."

She didn't walk as much as she glided through the halls, up an elevator, and through a corridor. Each step of the way required a pass, a retinal scan, or a fingerprint. Nassir was mesmerized by her grace as her heels rarely clicked, and never scraped, as she raced over the stone floors.

"Leave your phone with me Mr. Ajab. It's policy," she said, smiling as they reached a pair of wide, wooden doors. "Wait here," she said, placing his phone in a box, locking it, and handing him the key.

"Who says you don't have another key?" he asked playfully.

"Who says it'll be your phone when you come back?" she responded and waved behind her as she walked away, her hips swaying side to side, more than they had been while she led him to the meeting.

Nassir stood and waited, thinking of how bad he wanted to see the mysterious woman when he left. He noticed several cameras in the corridor, and knew those were the few security measures he was allowed to see. A moment later, the door opened.

"Mr. Ajab," Secretary Smith said and outstretched his meaty hand, crushing the much smaller Nassir's.

"Mr. Secretary."

"We've got a full house today, Nassir. Wow us."

Nassir entered the dimly lit room, which was prepped for the presentation. A large SmartBoard was on the wall in front of the room, turned on, and waiting for Nassir to present.

"I'd like to introduce Mr. Nassir Ajab. Engineer and inventor of a new type of quantum computer. He feels it may help us with national security, allowing us to decipher more of the communications the terrorists are using in the dark web."

"Thank you Mr. Secretary." Nassir smiled as the door closed behind him. He heard several actuators engage electronic locks in the door they entered, and the room was secure.

"Mr. President, I didn't expect to see you here," Nassir said, smiling and walking quickly toward him, shaking his hand. "So nice to see you in person."

"Thank you, Nassir. I'm interested in getting your project started immediately, so long as you can prove it's worth our time and energy to move forward." President Pierce anchored onto Nassir's hand and bore a hole in him with his eyes.

"I understand, Mr. President," Nassir responded as he pulled his hand away. His heart quickened, mouth became dry, and he couldn't remember how to begin. At a much slower pace, Nassir moved toward the front of the room.

"Good morning," he said, the pleasantries falling on distracted ears. "This is Medusa," Nassir said, pointing toward the screen as his presentation began. I won't bore you with the backstory, but it's capable of performing sixty times as many calculations as the fastest computer to date. I looked up the figures this morning. Other quantum computers are restricted by their processor design. Mine is markedly different. So much so, I don't even plan on writing the patents, since studying them would reveal how it's made. Have you heard of Moore's Law? Computing speeds won't catch up to Medusa for years. In fact, we've begun to see a drop off in the acceleration of computing speed, simply because the hardware isn't advancing in ways which would allow the speeds to continue to increase at that rate any longer. The exception to this, is Medusa.

"How this works for you? My computer cannot be

hacked. It operates on a platform which other computers can't access. Medusa, however, can access any computer on the planet. Do you remember when Blu-ray players came out? They could upconvert conventional discs to a higher digital quality. Medusa is similar to that idea, being that it can play in the lower realms of computing." Nassir smiled.

"You're still not telling us why we should use it. Sure, it's faster, sure it's not hackable; you claim. But what is the logic behind using it?" Bill Whiteside asked.

Bill was the head of the CIA, and a skeptic of everything new. He understood what worked, having been through quite a few generations of tech over the years, and sat through countless sales pitches. He hated wasting time, but even more so, he hated being talked down to, being treated like he was not intelligent enough to understand.

"I'm sorry, sir. I'll get to that right now. I hope you don't take this the wrong way, but I like to respect the persons I'm addressing. What is your name?"

"Bill," he responded with crossed arms, and a more cross tone.

"Bill, what we can do with Medusa, is monitor all incoming traffic, including the dark web, and decipher it in real time. This will eliminate lags in response time, and give us the unfair advantage for once." Nassir watched the men in the room, like efficient pieces of machinery they were all banging through scenarios, working Medusa versus what they currently used. Nassir knew they had the algorithms he lacked in terms of deciphering the codes.

"I've got some correspondence we red-flagged. If you'd like a chance to decipher it with your tech, I'd love to give it to you," Nassir said, pulling up the files on his computer.

"Where did you get this information?" Bill asked, looking at Secretary Smith.

"The dark web. As I said we scan it, but truth be told, we

haven't been able to decipher a lot of it. Seems we need a Rosetta Stone to crack it open."

"May I?" Bill asked as he walked to the front of the room, hand outstretch as Nassir placed the flash drive into his hands. "I'll be back," Bill said and strode out of the room.

"Nassir, Chuck Renfro, NSA. Why haven't you gone public with your tech? You could make billions from investors, private firms, you name it."

"As I told Mr. President during an earlier conversation, I want to help the U.S. I want to show my lineage doesn't define me. I'm Saudi by way of my parents, but American by birth and upbringing. I'm not a terrorist, as many would argue these days."

"I see," Chuck said, glancing toward the president.

"Please, tell us more about the technology," Secretary Smith said, breaking the silence.

"Love to," Nassir said, smiling as he unbuttoned his suitcoat. "Bill seems to have my presentations on that flash drive. I'll still explain, but the visuals are what really make the presentation engaging. Either way, here goes—"

Beep. An infinitely small noise proceeded Bill launching himself back into the room. In his hands, several sheets of paper held overhead.

"You, out!" he yelled, pointing toward Nassir, rage and panic in his eyes.

"Bill what the hell's going on?" Secretary Smith asked as he stood from his chair and walked quickly toward the head of the CIA. Doyle grabbed the paper and began to read. He devoured the first page while Nassir stood, unable to move, his heart pounding and sweat beginning to saturate his shirt. Inside he willed himself to move, to initiate the first step; momentum and muscle memory would take over from there. But, he also wanted to know what was on the paper. What had made the director of the CIA burst into a room?

What made the man's eyes pop from his cleanly shaven face? A face that never revealed emotion.

"Mr. President," Doyle said as he waved for the Commander-in-Chief to join the even smaller meeting within the room.

"My God," President Pierce said as he looked at the secretary. Pierce quickly walked to Nassir. "Thank you, son. We'll be in touch," he said, extending his hand. "You've given us something pretty incredible. Now, you must leave."

Nassir walked toward the door where the woman from earlier stood, his phone in her hand as she waved it side to side. She was smirking at him, but he was somewhere else altogether. He placed the key in her hand and she furrowed her brow, the flirting was clearly not going to happen on the way out. Nassir had been successful, but to what end? What had they seen that made them abruptly end the meeting?

As Nassir exited the facility, he saw a quote on the walkway beneath him:

> We celebrate the past to
> awaken the future.
> —J.F. Kennedy

The phrase caused Nassir to quake, as if cold water ran down his spine. He smiled. Whatever those men had read from his intercepted communications was clearly important. Better yet, they may allow Medusa to assist with intelligence on a grander scale. *Awaken the future,* he thought as he took a picture of the quote and strode away, confident he would hear good news soon.

Chapter 17
HERO

Pittsburgh, Pennsylvania

The mosque was full, as it typically was during the week for *asr*, the late afternoon prayer time. Behind Rami, tall windows stretched toward heaven, as light entered the room through slits in the wooden blinds, creating the illusion of a long, golden stairway. He knelt facing east as his large, muscular body used every square inch of the space he was allowed on the carpet. The floor was covered in a series of cream-colored archways, reminiscent of domes that adorned the architecture of the Middle East. The remainder of the carpeting was blood red. Rami encroached on those around him, but they didn't mind. It was welcomed; the big man was their prince, the one who represented the entire Muslim population in their community.

The community rallied around Rami because he was respected, trusted by everyone due to his position with the

Pittsburgh SWAT team. He was single handedly changing the way the public viewed Muslims. What wasn't going well, however, was the civility in the entire community. Murders were on the rise, riots, looting, and all groups of people seemed to be involved. Senator Waxman had often talked specifically about the Pittsburgh area during several of his speeches regarding the civil unrest. It was as if humans couldn't live without conflict, the vacuum in the absence of terrorism had bred a new problem.

As Rami bowed forward, his phone began to vibrate. He was the only person allowed to have a phone during prayer, and it would only ring if there was an emergency. He quietly stood, and walked from the room. It was easy to exit, a place close to the doors was typically reserved for him by the members.

"Hello," he said quietly, his voice like stones rolling in a truck bed.

"Rami, we need you to come in. Massive looting downtown. There was a protest, turned bad. Three people shot already and we don't think it's an accident."

"Who's on site already?"

"Nobody from SWAT. We're rallying the team now."

"Meet up with you at the precinct."

Rami hung up the phone, frustrated that he couldn't finish his prayer, but even more so because he had to leave his family. It wasn't the first time, and he knew it wouldn't be the last.

"Sorry sweetheart. Got a call. Have a friend bring you home," he texted Dinah and jogged out of the mosque toward his car.

By the time Rami arrived at the precinct twenty minutes later, the building was in panic. Dozens of officers were wrangling with protesters, looters, persons who'd committed assaults. The jail cells were almost at capacity. There was blood on the floor, on the chairs, on the desk where an officer stood, wide-eyed taking in the scene, his light duty status not allowing him to help wrestle the dozens of men and women who were fighting with arresting officers. Other policemen were leaving in waves, riot shields on their arms, and helmets with thick plastic faceguards, like futuristic Spartans readying for battle; only these men and woman had fear in their eyes and a hesitation in their step.

"Sarge!" Rami yelled, his voice blasting through the loud background noise of the precinct.

"Rami, get your ass over here!" Sergeant Nelson yelled sternly.

"Rami we've got to get you out there. Gear up. You and the team aren't assigned to the riot. You're looking for a rogue assassin. I hate to say it, but people are calling it a terrorist attack. Murdered twelve already."

"Where is he?"

"We're not sure. Somewhere downtown, he keeps moving. It's premeditated without question. He's been waiting for another riot to strike. News outlets are eating it up, spinning it against President Pierce, saying terrorism isn't dead. Agenda pushers. People are dying and they are talking politics!" he said, grinding his teeth and spitting on the vinyl floor.

Rami looked at the ground.

"What's the difference!" Sergeant Nelson hollered over the noise as he looked toward Rami who smirked.

"There's blood everywhere, what's a little spit too? Reminds me of some shit you'd see in a bad movie. Find this son of a bitch and pray he isn't screaming *jihad*."

Rami stood for a moment, stunned at his sergeant's matter of fact tone.

"Didn't mean anything by it Rami. No offense. I meant it in the best of ways. We haven't had a terrorist incident in a year. We need this to be a wild card." Sergeant Nelson slapped his hand on Rami's solid shoulder. "Go."

Rami paused, taking in the scene as the SWAT vehicle reached downtown. A sea of people surged forward, placing themselves directly against the riot shields, smoke billowed at varying heights from gas grenades thrown into the crowd at intervals; they failed in their intent. Again, the wave of flesh began in the rear cascading forward as the people in the front slammed, willingly and unwillingly alike, hard into the shields with a sickening slap of flesh. The police stood firm, a breaker wall protecting the rest of downtown Pittsburgh from the onslaught of looters, protesters, and themselves.

A lone scream became viral. A panic in the crowd followed and the sea of people parted as if Moses himself had fallen upon them, calling out to God. From Rami's elevated position high on a hill above the human corral, he saw it. Two people laid on top of one another, their bodies twisted together in a sinister embrace, blood staining the concrete beneath as they struggled to breathe. The crowd was literally clawing at the walls of the buildings, smashing the glass storefronts rather than the shielded police officers in a wild attempt to clear the streets.

Pop . . . pop . . . pop. Rami heard the familiar sound of gunfire echo down the street.

"Two shooters," he said to the SWAT team as they raised their weapons and began descending toward the thousands below.

"Split the street. Three with me, you guys clear the north buildings, we've got the south," he said as they quickly approached.

More panic set in as the crowd saw SWAT approaching. "They're shooting us!" a man cried out and pointed toward

Rami and his men in their charcoal gear, SWAT written across their backs, AR-15s at the ready but fingers off the triggers. Suddenly, the crowd moved toward the SWAT team.

Rami was caught off guard and wrestled to the ground. He felt hands groping his body, his waist; he realized they were grasping for his sidearm. Rami fought to breathe, the mob of people created a vacuum, the air inside putrid, hot, lacking oxygen. He aggressively turned, swiping his rifle across the sea of bodies that enveloped him. He saw the drab, featureless sky of a late September evening, as a cool funnel of air reached his face. He breathed deep, reached down, and crushed the hand that grasped for his sidearm. He pressed his massive frame hard into the crowd of people, like Samson and the pillars; one last feat of strength before death.

"Aaahhh!" A primal scream exited his lungs, and fresh air quickened his heart. "Get back!" he hollered to the crowd like thunder and lightning, everyone cringing in fear of the large, dark man. He found himself with his back to a brick wall, the remainder of his men on the ground fending for themselves.

"I said get back!" he hollered again. This time, the erratic crowd heeded his warning as he raised his rifle, eyes focused ahead, finger on the trigger. The crowd slowly melted back, allowing the remaining members of SWAT to stand on their feet.

Pop! A shot rang out striking one of the members of the SWAT team in the back of the head. His helmet had been torn off when they were assaulted. Once again, the crowd of people raced toward the buildings, alleyways, and on top of one another, trampling those too weak or slow to move out of the way.

Rami sprinted across the street. He saw the window, the only one that was open. Quickly he sprinted up four flights of stairs, skipping up three at a time, his plyometric workouts paying dividends. He exploded through the door to the third floor and sprinted west down the hallway.

Pop! The sound was much louder, he knew he was close.

Bang! He kicked the door in and saw the shooter kneeling a foot away from the window, carefully positioning himself behind objects not to be seen. He turned and saw Rami. Quickly, Rami grabbed his own sidearm, and—*bang, bang*—placed two shots into the shooter's leg and arm. The shooter dropped his gun and leaned back against the wall, blood trickling out of the small entry wounds, masking the damage beneath the surface. It was incredible how insignificant a gunshot wound appears at first.

"Come on brother, rejoice with me," the dark-skinned man smiled as he saw Rami. "We are the same. Death to the infidels."

"We're not the same," Rami said as he knelt next to the man. "You embarrass Islam, you embarrass your family, you embarrass your cause. Lazy, predictable, greedy."

"You are weak," the man said, grimacing, his welcoming eyes turning as dark as his soul.

"And you're dead unless you tell me where your friend is," Rami said.

"You're smart though, my brother. He's across the street. Fourth floor, but good luck. He's got a head start now."

"And you're worthless. Bargaining for your life? You're no jihadist or you'd die here rather than give up a brother. Lazy, predictable, greedy, and now a murderer who used radical Islam to feed your cravings." Rami stood and reached for the radio.

"Shooter down," Rami said into the radio. "South side of the street, fourth floor, that's where the second shooter is, but you need to move. This guy gave him a head start."

"I'm not de—" the shooter tried to say loud enough to

be heard through the radio, but Rami cut him off, placing two rounds in his head for good measure.

Rami knelt at the shooter's window and scanned the building across the street. He saw a window, again open, on the fourth floor. He shot at the windows immediately to the right and left, placing one round into each of the three to the immediate east, and west, the glass showering those on the street level. He didn't care whether they received a few cuts and bruises, they tried to kill him. He saw a blur of something moving across the glassless openings.

Pop, pop, pop, pop. Rami shot round after round quickly and accurately through each window heading east following the shadowed figure. Three more quick shots ahead of where the fleeing gunman would be, and he saw the shadowed figure collapse to the ground. He stood, placing his own rifle across his back, and walked back down to street level.

As he exited the building the crowd was still, silent, watching the large dark figure walk through the street; the picture of unholy rapture. Cellphones came to attention as everyone thought to chronicle the spectacle that single handedly saved his SWAT team, killed two terrorists, and protected the angry mob from further assault. He continued to walk through the crowd, the people parted but jockeyed for a better angle to capture the beast.

Rami finally reached the line of riot shields, a phalanx any ancient army would have pissed on.

"Fuckin' Rambo," one of the officers said, smiling and laughing at Rami.

Rami held it together, the only giveaway was how firmly he grasped the grip of his sidearm. He wanted to crush the officer, to grab his riot shield and swing it at him in an attempt to remove his head from his body. It had taken a long time for the community to trust Muslims again. Rami had worked hard to change the tides in his community, to disarm the public perception, to get himself in the position of SWAT and to become a sharpshooter. He knew his position was safe, but his exposure was too great. He saw the phones pointed at him, he knew social media, Dinah's words echoing in his head. He realized he could be exposed, could be studied, analyzed, questioned, interviewed. He would be a hero, which was the one thing he didn't need.

Chapter 18
TRAPPED

Aden, Yemen

Amal was crying, scared, and angry with himself all at once. He sat on the floor in front of several faceless, nameless men who had promised to kill his family had he not helped them find the Candyman. The floor was cool, despite the warmth that evening. He saw stars through the roof of the shack he was stashed in. They locked the small boy inside the structure the day before to ensure he couldn't warn the American who assassinated so many of their allies.

"Amal, you did well. Your family will be safe. *Allah* as my witness," the strange man said as he squatted down to look Amal in his eyes. Amal could smell the tobacco and betel nut on his breath.

"Amal, this man works against us. It is good for him to die," the man said playfully rubbing the soft, thick hair on Amal's head before standing.

The faceless man gestured toward an associate who quickly came forward. A glimmer in his hand told the horrific story before it was even written. Amal saw it and leapt to his feet. He ran left, but was met by another man standing with his arms and legs wide, blocking the young boy's escape. He quickly turned around and tried to run again. Nothing. A third man was standing there, his eyes disdainful. Slowly they moved in on the young Amal, his heart pounded against his ribs, and his breath was panicked. He searched frantically for another way out.

"Ahhh!" Amal screamed, racing toward the man with the saber, wildly flailing his hands as tears rolled down his face. Amal made the decision to fight, to not go quietly into whatever afterlife he was surely being ushered into. In a moment, Amal's piercing scream was silenced: A swift death for the young spy; a body for a warning.

Washington, D.C.

Secretary Doyle Smith sat in his office trying to ignore the overwhelming number of calls, emails, and text messages he was receiving about the events in Pittsburgh.

Doyle had listened to the news as he waited for more actual intelligence. The damage, however, had already been done. The men who shot fourteen people, including a member of Pittsburgh's SWAT team, were being called terrorists. The word stung. He had warned the president months ago it was a bad idea to have his reelection platform include "the end of terrorism." Nobody could make that promise, not in this age, not when the Middle East was a never-ending game of leapfrog for who's who in terrorism. The U.S. had been successful in deterring attacks, but that was largely thanks to Logan and his team with the help of men like David Westbrook providing critical intel.

The two shooters weren't on any watch lists, weren't part of any intel reports, nor was there any intel pointing to an attack in Pittsburgh. By all accounts, this was an isolated incident, spurred on by two murderous individuals, neither of which had been to a mosque in the last ten years. In vetting them out during the early hours following the incident, the FBI had found no contact with known terrorists groups, no search queries or emails on their computers related to radical terrorism, but they did find several hits for things such as: building a good hide, improving shooting accuracy, and the best ways to kill someone.

As Doyle sat as his computer, one email caught his eye; it was from the Candyman. He quickly sat at attention and read:

> I've got another one for your team. Chicago. Six men and a woman. Their mission is very odd. To rouse public distress, add to the chaos. Not sure how they're going to do that. I'll send names in a separate message. I also heard about Pittsburgh. I questioned people on my end, and they gave me nothing on Pitt. Not sure where that one came from, but I'm sorry.

Doyle immediately picked up the phone and dialed Logan.

"I figured you'd call," Logan said as he sat in his kitchen, Dubs staring at him from across the table. Arlington was several days behind them, but Dubs hadn't left his friend. He was watching him, talking with him, making sure he got clean.

"It's unrelated to Pittsburgh. You've gotta go to Chicago. There's seven people we need to talk to. We're not sure what they're doing, but Candyman reached out. I've got their names. Let's get you there tonight."

It was 2200 hours when they arrived at O'Hare, but when the domestic flight put wheels to concrete, the team of three had all the information they needed. Secretary Smith had taken the liberty of finding the address of the supposed terrorists and sent it to Logan.

"It seems too easy," Logan said as he grabbed his bag at the baggage claim.

"What does?" Lonnie asked, scanning the people around him, monitoring them for suspicious activity. It was something he constantly did since Logan taught him to read people's movements.

"All seven share the same address. No other known places. Says they've been there for two months."

"Does seem weird," Dubs said softly, thinking about his friend Migs.

"We aren't kickin' the door in. They likely know what happened in L.A. and are trying to lure us in." Logan looked at the address again. "Highland Park. It's a damn nice area too."

"Let's roll," Lonnie said and walked toward the parking lot.

An unmarked Suburban was waiting for them in the parking lot. In the back were three duffel bags, each with a matching set of gear: two Glocks, an AR-15, vest, NVGs, helmet, an LED torch, comms, a variety of non-lethal grenades, and relatively limitless ammo already loaded into magazines.

It was an easy drive to the wealthy suburb as they traveled in silence. The plan for the night was to gather intel on the residence, determine how active it was, and if any of the terrorists were actually there or if it was a ghost house—a fake residence used by terrorist cells. Logan had run across these situations before, and tracking these groups down proved to be a difficult thing. Often times, one of the marks would come to the ghost house to ensure it was still in good order, no water leaks, break ins, and so on. In fact, Logan had staged a break in at a residence several months earlier to smoke a terrorist out. Once they saw their mark, they tracked him and brought down the whole cell.

Upon arriving at the Highland Park home, the three special operatives saw it was very active even for 0030 hours. Lonnie scouted the windows and within moments noted six individuals, most of whom were in the kitchen.

"I can ID them all," Lonnie said, putting down his binoculars and looking toward Logan who sat in the rear of the SUV by himself.

"Too easy," Logan said, staring at the house, pondering why they would so carelessly sit in a well-lit home, congregating around a kitchen island. "We need to find the seventh."

Logan reached into the bags and grabbed the Glocks and the radios, handing them out like Halloween candy. Dub's turned the car off and exited first, followed by Lonnie, and then Logan on the far side of the vehicle.

The men quickly moved across the street, checked for perimeter security systems, and hopped a wrought iron fence that encircled the property. Quickly they moved through the darkness on the south end of the home, which sat twenty feet from the neighboring home's brick exterior. Both structures provided ample shadow from the bright lights that lined the picturesque street.

They moved in silence, looking through windows on the first floor, seeing nothing more than darkness in each of the other rooms. Lonnie, dressed all in black, circled back around front, to ensure all six of the terrorists were still in the kitchen.

"We've got six," he said quietly into the comms, and

made his way back to the north side of the home into the darkness beneath an oak tree.

"We need to get inside," Logan said when he and Dubs met with Lonnie under the large tree. "Take another lap, look for an open window, try the door, but don't open it," he said as sternly as he could in the silence of the back yard.

The weather had gotten colder since fall marched steadily onward, September was giving way to October, and the noisy night creatures no longer sang. The three men remembered the explosives on the back door of the home in L.A.—all of them resting, for a moment, thinking of the friend they lost so recently. None of them admitted it, but this mission felt awkward, vulnerable, without Migs.

The first floor offered one entrance, a window that rested a few inches open in the family room. Logan took point, reaching high toward the old window. It was likely an original to the house, but, because it was cool outside, the wood wouldn't be swollen and squeak as he pushed it open.

He opened it. *Ssssshhhhhh,* a subtle hiss from the wood and wax almost urged them to remain quiet and take the home back from the evil individuals. With a push upward from behind by Dubs and Lonnie, Logan was in. He got to his feet, held up his Glock in the darkness, and scanned the room. A black grand piano sat in the corner, old wooden couches with flowered upholstery decorated the softly painted room. In the darkness, it appeared to be a pale blue, but if Logan needed to shoot, the muzzle flash would show its true color. Quickly he cleared the room and turned to the window, helping his teammates enter. Now all three were inside, their odds improving by each moment.

The original wooden floors beneath their feet played well, not a creak to give away their presence as the three-man team slowly cleared endless numbers of rooms on the main floor making their way toward the kitchen. A narrow staircase promised danger as it lifted steeply toward the second floor, the crown molding guiding their eyes toward the cavern above.

"I'll clear upstairs with Dubs. Lonnie, keep an eye on the kitchen."

Slowly Logan approached the stairs, ensuring if anyone died it would be him, but he knew he couldn't be killed. Life had taught him that. He had seen countless men die in his place, leaving him in his current purgatory. He wished for a death that wouldn't come. Dubs didn't know his secret wish, and would likely place himself in harm's way to protect his leader. It was the only thing Dubs knew. He was simple, honorable, loyal.

"Clear," Dubs said as he walked softly in his boots. It was eerie how graceful his power could become. He would have been a great defensive end.

"Clear," Logan said from the next room as they continued to weave their way through the square rooms of the second floor.

Hold, Logan gestured as he approached the fourth bedroom upstairs. The door was slightly ajar, as the previous three had been, but when Logan placed his hand onto this six-panel door it felt different. The previous doors had been soft and textured from century old wood grain that had been painted time and again over many years. This one was cold and firm; steel.

Immediately Logan's hair stood on end and his heart began to race. It was instinctual, the reaction could mean only one thing: danger. He was eager, excited as he pressed against the door, its steel hinges gliding smoothly over one another in silence. Inside, a woman lay on a bed. He scanned the room before entering. He couldn't hear his footsteps on the hardwood, but he felt the soft area rug underfoot as he approached the bed.

In a flash the door slammed shut behind him, and he heard several steel locks engage. Two men launched out of the closet adjacent to Logan, tackling him to the ground before he could aim at them.

"Logan!" Dubs said as he yelled, slamming the full weight of his massive body against the steel door.

Suddenly, the six men in the kitchen sprung up, submachine guns in hand and began sprinting toward the stairs. Quickly, Lonnie singed the air with a flurry of 9mm rounds, hissing until they slapped flesh.

"Three down, three comin'," Lonnie said as he evaded the response from the terrorists and retreated to the living room.

Dubs turned, went to a knee, and aimed both handguns down the hallway.

Inside the room Logan struggled, his arms being held down by the two men. He kicked one but without any leverage it was like shooting BBs at an elephant. One man laughed and spit in his face, the second man repeated the insult as they drove their knees into Logan's biceps, the pain becoming warm, the lactic acid was coursing through his system, and his muscles began to fail. Logan wanted to fight, to honor himself, to be with Samantha, but he also allowed a small thought to creep into his mind. A morbid, desperate idea, that this may be his time. He was happy it wasn't another one of his men.

"Oh Mr. Falcone," a sweet voice said, her thick accent almost sensual, in the right context. "You're not dying yet. An old friend would like to say hello first."

She leapt from the bed and squatted by his head, straddling it.

"You boys and your stupid games," she purred and grasped his head in her hands, looking into his eyes. After a brief moment, she reached for something. Logan tried to squirm, tried to get free, but his body failed him. He hadn't spent enough time conditioning his body since Migs had died. He was exhausted.

He watched the woman reach toward him. A burning sensation began in his neck, as something pierced his skin. A cool sensation entered him, spreading like tendrils from an icy vine, ushering him toward darkness. He saw Sherman, Migs, and then he saw Samantha, before everything went black.

Chapter 19
VENGEANCE

Aden, Yemen

David Westbrook had spent the night awake, nervously watching the door to his safehouse. His computers hummed in the still, lifeless night that slowly gave way to a morning void of light. The sunrise seemed delayed, with the drab, gray sky pausing the progression of the day, making the 0640 sunrise feel like 0500.

Amal was supposed to check in the previous day. It's what the plan had always been, present the intel, then meet the next day to receive the reward. He hadn't showed. It was unlike the annoying, chatty, often-times frustrating young boy; a boy David had become particularly fond of. Amal was smart, reliable, eager, and now, missing.

David had enough waiting. He threw on a white shirt, thin pants, and his pumas. He walked out into the monochromatic day and the slowly waking city. Hundreds of people were already walking the streets on their way back from morning prayers. Some were heading home, some to work, others had begun cooking creating an intoxicating aroma flowing through the streets.

David walked quickly through the crowds, knowing the route to Amal's home well. The CIA agent was a savant at memorization, but even better at coding. He often combined the two in order to memorize directions. After Amal gave him intel for the first time, David followed him home in secret. Now, he was retracing those steps.

The sunlight began to win over the clouds, as vertical sheets of yellow warmth shot down from above, piercing the gray skyscape. On the ground, however, things began to turn anxious. David saw a woman being embraced by her husband, an unmistakable sorrow filling her eyes as he hid her face. He nodded slowly at David who watched them closely. He could hear the husband whispering words of support of some kind.

David rounded one last corner, and before him the street was narrow, barely wide enough for two cars side by side. Apartments rose toward the gray sky that contrasted the rust colored street. Rarely did sun kiss the surface of the earth between these two buildings, and today was no exception. It shouldn't have today; it would have made the spectacle worse. The drab, dark street hid the details from view.

He was immediately greeted by a sea of weeping souls, which stretched for three-hundred yards in front of David. At the end of the road, all had borne witness to a small boy who hung from a rope. Most knew him from the neighborhood, some loved him. Others were terrified, worried that their son or daughter could be next, their empathy overwhelmed them as they stood wailing and trying to understand.

David moved closer, his instinct losing to emotion. He knew it was Amal, he knew why he was dead: to set an example for the rest. Soon, David was pressing his way through mourners, through Amal's friends and family members, until he stood twenty feet from the boy. David had trapped himself, no way of escaping if he were attacked, and the attackers wouldn't think twice to kill innocent. He saw a sign, "Traitor," draped around the boy's neck; Amal's neck; a candy wrapper stapled into his frail chest as well.

David turned, working against the tide of people, pressing himself through the crowd. His mind was outpacing his heart; rage was powering his detached body. He knew he was compromised; he knew they would soon come for him. His computers would lead to Secretary Smith, to Logan and his men. He had to get word out to them, and almost more important, he had to kill the men who killed Amal.

Crack! The sound like a whip echoed down the narrow street as a supersonic round from a rifle smashed into the street below, sending rocky shrapnel into the bystanders. A scream quickly caused panic, as David tried to get out of the fishbowl they all stood in mourning just a millisecond earlier. In this place, everyone was conditioned to events like this, they didn't freeze in a panic, they ran for safety. Like cockroaches in the light, they fled for cover.

David knew the shooter would be elevated, likely on the top of the building. He also knew there was more than one, but what concerned him more was his tech back at the safehouse.

David ran. He made it to the end of the street, sprinted down a hill toward his neighborhood, long legs birthing longer strides as his athletic shoes seemed to enhance his cadence. He rarely ran during the day in Yemen, it would have given him away. At night is when he exercised through the streets. His heart and lungs were in great shape, but running all out for over two miles eventually overwhelmed him.

He stopped, leaned against a wall, and closed his eyes for a moment. He saw Amal's face. The boy who quickly learned about the English language, about American baseball, about respect and negotiations from the Candyman. David allowed himself to grieve, to feel sorrow, in order to enhance his rage once more. His soul was satisfied, his mind focused.

He pressed himself off the wall and began moving the last mile toward his safehouse. He was an easy target, a tall, spindly man, thin from his nightly runs and rarely eating a full meal; but he was freakishly strong, especially during interrogations. He stayed in the shadows as much as he could, but little was left untouched by the sun in this area, and by now, the gray morning had given way to a bright, white spotlight following David's path.

A half-mile from the apartment he encountered his first adversary: a small man in glasses, sharply dressed and standing stationary in a sea of moving bodies. He stood out like a buoy in the waves. David responded quickly, turning down an alleyway and gaining a better position behind the untrained killer. David knew the streets, he had to for a situation such as this. David came up from behind, grabbed him around the throat with his arm, and silently took him into the alleyway. David was a panther, stealthy, deadly, strong. With one quick flick of a blade, the enemy was no more; and now David had his gun.

David released the clip, counted fifteen rounds, and slammed it back into the gun. He pulled back the slide and began an assault on his own turf. A second man walked down the street ahead of him, sunglasses gave him away. David quickly raised his gun and fired twice, the shots echoed through the streets, only a few heard the sound of another man losing his life. David's energy surged, as if death, gunpowder, and rage fueled him.

A Mercedes van was parked a block from his home, one he'd never seen before. He could see everything that was out of place in the streets he called home for nearly two years. Without hesitation, he raised the gun once more. *Pop pop, pop pop!* His shots came quickly, and the slap from the hammer between his double taps were indiscernible from one another.

Ping, a different sound came from the weapon as it spewed its final blistering projectile. David placed the gun in his waistband and ran to the car, freezing at the rear-passenger side. He squatted, and walked while crouching around the white vehicle toward the passenger door. There were no windows except those on either side of the driver, as well as the windshield, which was shattered from multiple rounds piercing through the rear of the van and exiting the window. He approached the door and grabbed the handle.

Crank! Two rounds pierced the door just above David's outstretched arm. Without a hesitation, David grabbed the handle and ripped the door open, the passenger still grasping the handle himself fell outward and tumbled onto the ground. In less than a second, David inspected the driver, two rounds had exited his head and sprayed red mist on the dashboard and flesh on the window. David then turned his attention to the man on the ground who was reaching for a radio. David grasped the man's meaty calf and clamped on. The enemy screamed and recoiled, reaching down toward David instinctually, forgetting about the call for aid. David picked the man up and slammed him hard into the van.

"How many are in my house?" David asked in Arabic, stunning the man whose calf throbbed in pain.

Bang! David threw him against the van even harder, the

man's head snapping back and denting the Mercedes. His feet kicked wildly as the slender man raised him from the ground, his anger rising with each passing second.

"Three. Three men."

"Who cut the boy?" David growled as if he were a beast, no longer human. He had seen what many hadn't, the stain across Amal's chest and abdomen through his shirt. The lack of bruising around the noose. Both were indications he hadn't died there, and he hadn't died of the hanging.

"Saad. Saad cut the child. I didn't arg—" David cut him off by striking him with the handgun.

"Where's Saad?"

"I do not know."

"Lies!" David screamed and crashed his prominent knuckled hard into the man's abdomen, then backed away, allowing the assailant to empty his stomach onto the ground.

"You're going to die anyway. Help me avenge Amal's death."

The man slowly rose and tried to gather himself. His stomach and diaphragm were in spasm, making it difficult to talk.

"He is here. In your home. But you're too late."

David picked up the gun from the ground, walked quickly toward the man, and shot him.

David didn't bother to check the clip as he raced the last block to his house. He knew the van would be the last post they would be watching from. He approached the apartment, slowly. He heard men inside and closed his eyes, listening their voices; three distinguishable pitches, but all he saw was Amal hanging.

He saw the young, innocent boy, his tattered shirt blowing in the wind, the candy he had received just a day before stapled to his chest. David felt a hole in his own chest, and his knees went weak. He allowed the gun to drop slightly as he leaned harder into the wall, wishing it would help keep his emotions up as it did his physical body. Amal had brought him the intel regarding the terrorist house in Chicago just forty-eight hours earlier. The happy boy skipped from sight, saying he'd be back tomorrow for the candy he negotiated.

David opened his wrathful eyes. He turned facing the door and kicked it, sending it into the darkness of the apartment. Tears rolled down his face as he turned to see the first man standing near the void where the door used to be. *Pop, pop!* Two shots ended the nearest man, hot mist filling the air and painting David's face like warpaint. *Pop, ching*—the sound of an empty firearm. The second man reeled back from the shot to the shoulder, but then came full steam at David.

The trespasser hit David like a linebacker, driving him through the door and back into the street where they both hit the dirt. David had grasped the man around the torso with his legs like a bull rider. When they fell, David had the advantage and drove the man's head down into the ancient ground, a crack softening the skull of the attacking Middle Eastern man. They rose to their feet, David much quicker. He placed several strikes into the soft, deformed part of the man's crown and he fell, lifeless, seizing until his nerves exhausted their neurotransmitters, and he lay motionless on the ground.

David sprinted headlong into the darkness of the apartment. It took several moments for his eyes to adjust, but when they did, he spotted a man holding a weapon.

"Saad," David stated as he stared into the man's eyes.

"I'll admit you are stronger than expected."

"Do you know who I am?" David asked, smiling, knowing his reputation proceeded him.

"David Westbrook, CIA."

Saad shocked him with the revelation. "You did your homework," David said, trying to gain control of the conversation.

"We know more than you think. You have been valuable to us for some time. I'll concede that we hadn't really planned on you being an ally. You were very good at your job so we had to adapt."

"Why'd you kill the boy?"

"It worked didn't it? Drew you out, made you irrational. You don't act out of emotion. Well, at least not until now," he said, pointing toward the outside world David had forgotten about.

David reached for his blade. Its mirror like surface reflected the light from the door and the glare from the computer screens. He honed it after each kill it made; a beauty despite its dark soul.

"No need for that my friend. I've got the gun," Saad said, pointing it playfully close to David; that was his mistake.

David's arm flailed up quickly, his fast twitch muscles driving his long arm creating a whip-like strike from the beautifully sharp blade. The gun dropped to the floor before the smirk left Saad's face. Blood spilled from the wrist wound that severed his flexor tendons.

"You're wrong, Saad," David said as he grabbed the man's bleeding wrist and squeezed it hard, his hands like a vise crushing the radius and ulna, approximating the compound fractures until they ground against one another. "What's my name?"

"Dav—ah!" Saad screamed and dropped to a knee when David squeezed his arm even more firmly.

"I'm the fucking Candyman," David said as leaned in close, his nose almost touching Saad's, as he curled his face into a sinister smile, his eyes on fire in the darkness of the room.

"Want to try my candy?" he said, lifting his voice and throwing the man's hand down onto the ground. Quickly, he walked to his desk, grabbing gauze and duct tape. He slapped the gauze down onto Saad's wounds causing him to grimace. David quickly wrapped the duct tape around the man's wrist, tightly, all the way to the elbow.

"I don't care if that hand falls off. You're not dying until we have a conversation," David said. He then taped Saad's hands together, his feet together, and placed a roll of gauze into Saad's mouth taping over that as well.

Quickly, David went to his computer, taking the three redundant hard drives and throwing them in a duffel bag along with several passports, his candy, weapons, and his honing stones. He turned to leave and saw the box of blowpops in the corner of the room. For a moment he froze, hearing Amal's voice, his playful banter for more candy. David began to walk toward the corner but stopped himself. No more would he bring children to a man's game. No more would he hide in the shadows and hope for a break. He was like a caged animal released, confused at the freedom. He now hunted for sport rather than necessity. He was good at sports, great at competition.

David threw the bag across his shoulders, walked toward Saad, and picked him up off the floor, carrying him out the secret door in the rear of the apartment. He tripped a suicide switch while leaving. After throwing Saad in the trunk of a car, he drove away. Not a minute later, his apartment was incinerated, destroying all evidence of David Westbrook, the Candyman, ever having been there.

Chapter 20
PLAYING NICE

Washington, D.C.

The Oval Office was uncomfortable, Senator Waxman and President Pierce sat across from one another on couches. To Pierce's right, Grant Sanchez, to Waxman's right, Secretary of State Doyle Smith. The sun was hot as it raced through the windows into the room, but the temperature in Washington had begun to plummet as October marched onward. However, nothing was as cold as the glares that were coming from Senator Waxman.

"What's this bullshit I can't go to Chicago and talk to my people?" Waxman said in his stern, unwavering tone. "I thought you said terrorism was dead, Mr. President?" his tone changing to sarcasm.

"I think we're on the same page in this room Senator Waxman. Pittsburgh was not a terrorist attack. We've dug deep into the shooters. They're squeaky clean psychopaths.

No connections to any terrorist groups previously known, and no new discoveries following the incident."

"You aren't telling me something gentlemen, and I'm feeling a bit underpowered here," Waxman said, looking around the room, the odds not in his favor.

"That's true, Senator," Secretary Smith said, leaning away from the senator to fully turn toward the man. "We've kept you in the dark, we've kept everyone in the dark for that matter about a secret strike team. I'm sure you remember Paris, Chicago, and nearly Saint Louis were attacked not long ago. But do you remember hearing who stopped Saint Louis?"

Waxman sat for a moment, deep in thought, remembering the days in Chicago all too well. He had volunteered in Chicago for a month after the attacks, stating it was his duty as a representative of the people of Illinois to be a part of the aid. Nobody in Washington, or anywhere in the county for that matter, had a problem with the choice Waxman had made. In fact, it had directly affected the Democratic Party's backing of him for a run at the presidency.

"I don't recall," Waxman finally said. "Maybe I was distracted."

"You likely were, but the heroes were never talked about. We never made it public. I'll tell you now. Logan Falcone, a Marine, led a group of recon Marines around the country hunting those bastards down. Unfortunately, the leader of the cell, Amir Qasmi, escaped. But that's not the point of this conversation. That small team has stopped nearly two dozen attacks since then. Mr. President, unfortunately, has gotten a bit excited about our successes, and told everyone terrorism is dead.

"Recently, we've come to realize the terrorists have knowledge of our strike team. Logan lost a man less than a month ago, and just twenty-four hours ago he was ambushed. They were working off what later turned out to be false intel, trapping the three-man team. Logan was drugged, and we believe they were attempting to kidnap him but for God knows what. Thankfully, his men are some badass soldiers and they rescued him from the home. He hasn't been debriefed yet. We're waiting for the drug's effects to wear off."

"That's quite a bit of information," Waxman said, settling back into the couch. "Why aren't we telling people about this?"

"Because we had a spy in our midst," Secretary Smith growled at the thought of General Jenkins. "We aren't trusting anyone at this stage."

"I understand you're operating on trusted intel when you advise me not to travel to Chicago. However," Waxman paused and leaned forward, elbows on knees, and looked at the pristine carpet on the ground. "However, I cannot stand to let terrorism guide my decisions. I think it's important we move forward regardless. If we live in fear, we die in fear. I'm going to Chicago, and New York, and Pittsburgh for that matter. Hell, I'm supposed to throw the opening pitch for the White Sox/Pirates game if they make it to the World Series, and they've been playing some great ball."

"All I ask is you consider our discussion, and please don't talk about our strike team. They're already a target. We don't know how the terrorists know about our anti-terrorism strike team, but the less people who hear about them the better."

"I agree," Waxman said, standing and extending his hand to the president. "After all, when I take office next year they'll be my boys too." He winked and left the room.

The remaining men sat in silent reflection, Waxman's

words echoing in their heads. He was a strong man, couldn't be intimidated by anything it seemed. He'd already experience heartache when his wife died. Maybe that was enough to numb him to mortal threats when the option of immortality was presented: the chance at a presidency. Waxman had taken a healthy lead in the polls since the events in Pittsburgh. He was ten percent up, and not a single poll was showing Pierce to be winning, even factoring in a four percent error.

"Grab Nassir," President Pierce told Grant.

"Nassir," Pierce said with a genuine smile and stood to shake the young man's hand.

"Mr. President, Secretary Smith," Nassir said, nodding his head toward the broad-shouldered African-American.

"Nassir, we've reviewed your intercepted materials, and I have to say it's spot on with the actionable intel we've provided our men on the ground. Most of which led to the capture of terrorists and stopped their planned attacks here on U.S. soil. We'd like to allow Medusa limited access to the government servers. Allow you to track incoming messages, then we can translate them, hopefully responding even quicker to threats both domestically and abroad."

"I'd be honored Mr. President." Nassir smiled, but it was forced.

"What's the problem?" Doyle asked, still sitting on the couch but reading Nassir's body language.

"It's a financial matter. The cost of development was great."

"How great?" Pierce said, crossing his arms.

"We know. It was roughly twenty million," Doyle said, disappointment on his face. "We interviewed your financial backers."

"That's accurate," Nassir said, smiling at Doyle.

"What are you getting at, Nassir?"

"I'd like a government contract. Conditional, of course. If my tech proves reliable then we sign a long-term agreement. How much is an election worth Mr. President? How much is a life worth?"

"You're out of line, Nassir," President Pierce said, a fire burning within. It was primal, visceral, and undeniable even as president.

"I'm merely putting things in perspective, sir. Please understand I meant no disrespect. I've worked hard to make this happen. Spent other people's money, borrowed, sold my tech idea to hundreds. I'm just close to making it a reality and I'd do anything to achieve my goal."

"We'll get you a contract if you keep bringing in good intel."

Nassir reached into his pocket and pulled out a flash drive. "Here's a start." He placed the stainless steel tech on the desk and smiled at President Pierce. "There was quite a few intercepts this week. Feel free to have your men look it over. Let me know when we can start."

"Today. I'll have Chuck Renfro call you later to set up your access."

"Thank you, Mr. President."

"Let's just hope you weren't lucky on the first one."

Chapter 21
FATHERS AND SONS

Chicago, Illinois

Samantha sat in an uncomfortable hospital chair at
Northwestern Hospital and caressed Logan's bruised hand.
He still had blood under his nails and deep in the calluses
of his hard hands. She didn't care about that, she just
wanted him to wake up. Behind her stood Dubs, his face
still bloodied from the encounter, refusing to wash it off. He
was on high alert after the incident at the home in Highland
Park. On the opposite side of the room was Lonnie, stunned
at the events that had transpired after hearing Dubs yell
from upstairs, reliving the events in his mind; a literal reel of
death.

The assault on Logan's team was orchestrated, planned
well in advance. Dubs had taken a knee in the hallway
upstairs, peering into the darkness before him, waiting for

the two terrorists to come up the stairs. But behind him, another five silently descended from the attic. Lonnie had charged up the stairs, his instinct was to protect his friends at all costs.

Pip pip, two suppressed shots; *pip pip,* another two, and Lonnie heard both terrorists gasp in pain, collapsing to the floor above him.

"Comin' up," Lonnie said, ensuring Dubs wouldn't shoot. Then Dubs turned to see the men spewing from the attack.

"Dubs!" Lonnie yelled just as he reached the top of the stairs. Dubs lay on his back and began firing toward the opening in the ceiling, giving Lonnie a free shot down the hallway toward those already on the ground.

"Move!" Lonnie yelled as he dropped a magazine and slammed another one into his handgun.

From inside the attic, a demonic clicking began. For a moment, neither one of the Marines registered the sound. Immediately, the ceiling began to erupt in a cloud of dust and old paint, as dozens of rounds rained down feverishly, shredding the old plank ceiling and butchering the classic wood floors of the upstairs hallway. The shooter from inside attic seemed to have x-ray vision, his rounds followed Dubs as he bound through the narrow hallway and rolled down the stairs following Lonnie.

"They've got Logan," Dubs yelled over the sound of a large machine gun still spewing out round after round.

"We got one crazy bitch in the attic. I'll draw fire, you get into the attic," Lonnie said, pointing up.

"Yut," Dubs said as the machine gun fire ceased.

They heard footsteps, one set, then quickly several more, an entire parade of people running upstairs from the basement. The basement door opened to their right, across the hallway on the main floor. Without thinking, Dubs raced ten feet to the door and hit it full force with his right shoulder. The door slammed closed quickly, broke its hinges, and down into the darkness Dubs went, riding the door like a bodyboard. Lonnie heard several grunts and screams. He sprang toward the door himself.

Looking down into darkness, he saw the outline of Dubs contrasted against the white door. He remembered staring at the basement in L.A., Migs leading their descent with his light, just before the explosion that created a void in their lives. Several flashes in the darkness began to paint a stop motion picture for Lonnie. He watched as Dubs shot into all corners of the basement, the grunting telling him Dubs was striking his targets without fail. One, two, three, four screams in the darkness, as Lonnie caught glimpses of Dubs' lightning quick movements. He was in awe of his big partner as he lay siege to the surprise attackers.

The shooting stopped, and Dubs sprinted up the stairs, reloading on the way.

"You ready?" Dubs asked as they stood on either side of the doorway to the basement. Lonnie smirked, nodded, and the two-man team slowly approached the stairway in silence. Dubs led the way with Lonnie immediately behind. Step by step they climbed the old, steep stairway, sweat streaming down their faces. When they reached the last stair, Lonnie came around Dubs to grab the first look down the hallway.

He saw nothing. Lonnie quickly sprinted and dove into the first bedroom, his Glock quickly pointing down the hall, allowing Dubs his chance to move up. He did just that, springing silently through the length of the hallway, placing himself at the end of the hall, on the far side of the access hole to the attic. Dubs placed his gun in his waist and nodded to Lonnie.

Lonnie began to shoot erratically into the ceiling, the shooter from above responded predictably. Whoever was above had clearly memorized the floorplan and began spraying round after round of large-caliber automatic fire down into the room Lonnie was in. The bullets were seemingly endless, but they gave Dubs the advantage. The mountain of a man had already jumped and grasped the joists inside the attic and easily lifted himself up into the musty cavern above.

Dubs grabbed his sidearm sending two silent flashes into the darkness, the smell of black powder erasing the must. His ears rang from the automatic fire. Quickly, he gained his bearings and walked toward the steel-door-room Logan was entrapped within. He walked as far as he could into the corner of the attic and jumped.

Dubs crashed through the ceiling, into the room, and saw Logan on the floor. He threw his gun to the ground; a painless death wouldn't be enough for them. Discipline often encapsulated the Marine called Dubs, but rage unleashed a monster. He saw three targets. He grabbed the woman, throwing her hard toward the steel door, her head snapped back and slammed against the reinforced steel. A sharp crack promised a painless death. He grabbed one of the men who still stood near Logan's body, and wrenched him forward, striking him in the face with the crown of his own head. Dubs literally tasted blood after that, his own face dripping gore mixed with sweat as he turned toward the last man. He picked him up by the throat with both hands nearly placing the man's head through the ceiling. He squeezed harder, and, even though the room was dark, Dubs watched his face turned blue. He kicked Dubs several times, each one striking hard and true but Dubs couldn't feel it. In the moment, he wasn't human. After a short time, the man relaxed, his body incapable of fighting as all the oxygen was consumed by the brain. Dubs tossed the lifeless man onto the floor. He walked back and retrieved his gun, placing a round into each of the terrorists for good measure.

Dub knelt to check on Logan. Bending his head down, he heard his friend breathing. *Thank God,* he thought, and approached the steel door, unlocked it, and walked down the hall toward the room Lonnie had been in.

"What the fuck, man," Lonnie said as he sat motionless in the room. Around him, a ring of splintered hardwood and cotton, where dozens of rounds narrowly missed the Marine.

"I hear sirens. We gotta bounce," Dubs said, gesturing toward the stairs. "Take point."

"Just tell me you see this shit?" Lonnie said once again pointing at the arc that formed around his body. "How am I alive right now, man?"

"All I know is we need to get out. Take fucking point, I'm grabbing Logan."

"His eyes are opening," Samantha said, jolting Lonnie from his torturous memory. Samantha tried to remove the worry from her eyes in the chance Logan looked at her. Several times Logan had attempted to open his eyes, but they had quickly given up the fight and he fell back into whatever state of consciousness he'd been in. The doctors said it could take several more hours, even a day, depending on the amount of the drug in his system. The situation was even more unpredictable because he'd already been driving his liver hard to process the amount of alcohol he consumed in recent weeks.

"Logan!" Dubs said firmly shaking his arm. "Falcone!" he said with a tone any drill sergeant would have approved of.

Logan's eyes popped open a bit wider but were still absent of thought, instinctual, he wasn't conscious. Sleep ushered them closed once again.

"Logan!" Samantha said in frustration, her hand squeezing at his swollen ankles and tears beginning to form a wall in front of her eyes. She didn't want to cry, she wanted to scream, to murder for her man.

His eyes opened once again, this time scanning the room a bit; he heard her.

"Logan, honey, please look at me," she said, climbing into the bed next to him and holding his head in both hands, forcing his eyes to meet hers.

After several minutes of dead air, he smiled.

"You're safe honey. Dubs and Lonnie are here. They got you out."

Logan tried to look around the room but he was weak. Lonnie and Dubs approached the bed from behind Samantha. Logan saw his men, his friends, his heroes. He smiled toward them with the limited strength he had, and nodded. Logan had welcomed death in that moment in the bedroom. Now he was forced to live.

I'm still immortal, he thought, frustrated.

Samantha began to cry. She was ashamed, never wanting Logan to feel guilty for the life he lived, but she became overwhelmed.

"Rest up Logan. We'll come back later. Glad to see you man," Lonnie said, and grabbed the larger Dubs by the shoulder and forced him out of the room.

Samantha waited for the men to leave before she looked at Logan once again, her eyes red and swollen, her lip quivering, not allowing her to form the words she wanted to say.

Logan finally found the strength to reach up and brush her hair back behind her ear. She smiled and rolled her eyes. The gesture gave her strength.

"I'm sorry, Logan."

"Why?" he asked in a whisper.

"I didn't tell you sooner," she said, reaching toward the heavy hand that brushed back her hair. She placed it onto her stomach. "I'm pregnant," she said as soft as a whisper. "I think it's why I'm so emotional," she said, snorting as she sat up and wiped her face, embarrassed.

Logan turned and faced the ceiling. Images of Iraq, of Sherman, of his spec ops with Jenkins flashed in his mind. He thought of Reaper's body in full gear, Migs' corpse, of the men he watched from his spotting scope as their lives were extinguished by Sherman. He reflected on the lives of men he fired upon, their lifeblood leaving them, the absence of a soul in a man's eyes when death took him. It was nothing now. Nothing before meant a damn thing, as he realized he would be a father.

Joy, love, the idea of a pure soul learning from him drove the poison out of his system, willing him to live. His eyes cleared almost as quickly as his mind, and the smirk he forced earlier became an emotional smile. He had a purpose. *This is why I survived*, he thought.

"Is it a boy?" he asked, looking back at Samantha.

"I don't know, yet. But I might find out at twelve weeks."

"When's that?"

"Two weeks."

He slid himself upright in bed and pulled her close. She laid against his chest, one which used to be harder, more muscular, but at least it was still warm.

"Your heart is pounding," Samantha said, smiling as her ear played as a stethoscope against him.

"I've missed you. I'm sorry," Logan said and kissed her flowery hair.

Yemen

Karim Al Muhammad paced the white tiled floor in the small room below the rocky, red valley. He sighed. It was rare for him not to come through on a promise. Logan was supposed to have been captured, brought to their facility, and offered to Amir; a token for his loyalty and hard work. The idea hadn't been part of the broad plan, but Karim knew the gesture would have carried incredible weight. For starters, it would reinforce Karim's far reaching power. Second, it would have allowed Amir closure, and may have improved his spirits. Logan was not a factor. He was being allowed to find the terrorist cells he dismantled, a decoy in a more sophisticated plan. Karim checked his watch, 0915, and sat down in a chair, waiting.

A door opened and Alex Pines was ushered into the room. Alex paused, unsure of the scenario. He had been brought into this very room dozens of times, but never saw this man. Alex always noticed the floors were clean, white, no memory of his own blood spilled upon it time and time again. It was disturbing how his mind had come to process that fact. It was as if he began to assume the physical abuse hadn't been happening and he manifested it in his head.

"Lieutenant Alex Pines, U.S. Navy. Number 432564532. DOB December 11, 1988," Karim said as the young pilot limped into the room. "Reflex!" Karim smiled as he stated the man's callsign, emphasizing the last syllable loudly, the sound piercing to the ear.

Alex slowly limped into the room and approached the table.

"Sit, please," Karim said, his warm smile oddly comforting. "You have proven to be a good soldier. I like a good soldier."

"Lieutenant Alex Pines, U.S.—"

"I know," Karim said, smiling and cutting him off. "And I can see we won't be able to go any further with our conversation. It's a shame. I was going to ask you about a motorcycle."

"What?"

"You're a fan of motorcycles, correct?"

Alex didn't speak. His mind quickly went back to his father's death, how he watched him ride his Yamaha over the crest of a hill and down into the valley every day; until the day his father was struck by the truck. He watched his father fly off the road, landing bloodied and lifeless on the grass. Flashes of the twisted, scarred metal dominated Alex's mind. The motorcycle had left a streak of red along the asphalt, a permanent reminder for almost a decade until they resealed the road. The day they fixed the scars on the road from the accident was almost as traumatic as the day he lost his father.

"It's no matter. We can get to the point." A door in the back of the room opened, and Taj brought in a man.

Alex stood, grimacing, as the pain in his ankle shot into his mind. He recognized the man entering the room: a drunk who had been released early on "good behavior," the man who drove the truck that painted the road with red, as sparks erupted, metal twisted, and a heart stopped beating.

"I can't imagine hearing a motorcycle coming, knowing it was your father, running out to watch him come to the crest of the hill where you would always feel excitement. Then have this man, this drunk, take him from you. Our justice is different here. More sincere, more . . . appropriate." Karim nodded and out came Amir, a gun in hand.

"I understand Amir has been rough on you," Karim said, sensing the tension rise and Alex's trust fall in that moment. "This is a peace offering. A way to show our softer side. We care, Alex."

Amir approached Alex, placed the gun onto the table, and stepped away. It lacked a magazine. Alex quickly picked up the gun and examined its awkward weight.

"One in the chamber," Karim said, smirking. "I guess you

could choose your worst enemy, but remember, you only get one shot," he said, pointing one finger into the air.

Alex held the cold steel in his hands. He felt empowered, dangerous, scared. There were four men in the room he could kill: The drunk driver yes, but Karim, Taj, and Amir were all more substantial targets. Killing one of them would cause an effect worth dying for. He grasped the gun firmly, turning it toward the group on the opposite side of the room.

How much blood would spray on the walls? Alex thought as he haphazardly pointed the gun away from him, his hand resting on the table. "What if I shoot you?" he asked Karim who smirked.

"I've considered the possibility. I conceded it was worth the risk for your justice."

Alex nodded. Quickly as his uninjured arm could lift, he pointed the gun at Amir. He outstretched the gun one handed, ensuring he wouldn't miss. His left arm was still a contractured, painful mass of tissue held at his side for comfort.

Amir saw the pain in Alex's eyes. He knew this moment too well. Both men locked eyes, both remembering their fathers. Amir thought about the restaurant, the blood that left his father's mingling on the carpet with the blood from his attackers, as Amir avenged his father's death. In the moment, it wasn't a choice, the men's judgment and persecution happened in seconds. Amir had been the jury and executioner. Amir knew the decision Alex would ultimately make. He wasn't scared for his own life, he was scared for Alex. If Alex pulled the trigger at all, no matter who stood on the other end, he was just like them; a murderer. Then they would have broken him.

As Amir had predicted, Alex turned the gun toward the man who stood crying, while Taj stood smiling and holding the weak man steady. Urine cascaded down the drunk man's leg, staining his pants from the crotch and down his right leg, a dark yellow pool on the white floor. He could have been dehydrated, it was the likely cause of the color, but Alex wasn't in the right state of mind. He assumed the man had continued his drinking, killing his liver, dark stained urine from a liver in distress.

Alex thought of his father, his mother who now sat at home alone, likely owning a second flag folded in a shadow box, wishing her husband and son were still alive. The thought had never entered his mind before. He'd been a prisoner for several weeks, no rescue attempts had been made, no hostage videos taken, or demands given to U.S. intelligence. One squeeze meant justice, one squeeze meant he forfeited his morality, his ethics, who he was. He tried to forgive the drunk, prayed to find him after he was released.

Alex's heart pounded hard, nearly two-hundred beats per minute, and he began to breathe awkwardly. Sweat had found its way into dry, unblinking eyes and he squinted, trying to stay focused on the evil that found its way into the room. Instinct took over, he blinked, a tear trailing its way down dirty flesh and facial hair, a pure clean line in its wake.

Amir had enough. He raised his own gun toward the drunk. *Pop pop!* Two deafening shots rang out in the small hard room, echoing through aching ears.

Alex, as if snapped out of a hypnotic state, pulled the slide back on the gun and ejected the round, allowing it to bounce several times on the floor before rolling to a stop. He slammed the gun down on the table.

"Lieutenant Alex Pines, U.S. Navy. Number 432564532. DOB December 11, 1988."

Karim smiled at Alex, his blood boiling over, but his cheeks never turned red. Instead, he sat forward in his chair, and, as if it was planned, said, "You see how committed to justice we are? We would rather bloody our hands than yours."

Karim nodded to the guard at the far side of the room who approached. "I hope you reflect on this moment. We've avenged your father. Please consider talking to us."

Alex was gently escorted out of the room by the guard. It was uncomfortable for Alex to be treated well. He was prepared to be dragged from the room, his face punished at least once or twice, and, if it was a rough night, his head would have banged into the floor and his elbow wrenched through range of motion a few times as well.

"Amir, I know I've wronged you, but you had no right," Karim said without turning back.

"I'm sorry. I thought it would help my relationship with him. Maybe he could trust me again. I was American."

"It wasn't your place," Karim turned and stood approaching Amir. Each step a click of his shoes and the sound of sticky blood pulled at his soles. "I will have Logan Falcone delivered to you, as I'm sure Taj has told you. We've had a minor setback, but our main objectives are safe."

"You are a brilliant man, Karim. I'm inspired by you . . . one day I hope to earn your trust."

"I trust very few, Amir," he said, rapping his hand against Amir's face gently. "Today you showed me your loyalty. However, your judgment was poor. Come," Karim said, gesturing toward Taj and Amir. "We will talk as fathers and sons do."

As they left the room, Karim placed his hands on each son's shoulder.

Chapter 22
HEROES

Pittsburgh, Pennsylvania

Rami was dressed in a tailored gray suit. It had been given to him by a nameless, faceless businessman, as a thank you for the events in downtown Pittsburgh. He wore a bright blue tie, a freshly shaven face, and a free haircut from his barber, Louie, who insisted repeatedly "I'm not taking the money of a hero." Rami left the money on the chair anyway, and walked out.

He stood staring into a mirror wrapped with lights. He still wore the thin paper tissue around his collar. The woman who put on his makeup shoved it there about an hour earlier saying, "The last thing you want is for all of America to know you wore makeup, even if it was for TV." Admittedly, he looked handsome, his wide, muscular shoulders filled the suit nicely and his face was flawless thanks to the twenty-something cutie who had stared so long at his face, but never saw him. Not who he really was. She saw the hero, not the man, and never met his gaze. If she had, it may have scared her. He didn't want to be here, but it was good publicity, good for the community, and his *imam* said it would be good for Muslims everywhere.

He brushed down the front of his suit, removing nothing, but he'd seen other men in the makeup room do the same thing so it felt right. He quickly pulled out the tissue around his collar and headed toward the newsroom.

The anchors' desk looked just like it did on TV, however, the chaos behind the scenes was unforeseeable. Several cameras, booms, and countless wires snaked their way throughout the large room. Scaffolding above was home to an uncountable number of lights, varying in color and intensity, covering every conceivable angle of the newsroom. As one camera went active, a red light illuminated over the top, and a prompter began scrolling through text that was read by the anchor woman. A second camera turned on, and the overhead lights changed slightly in intensity and combination, placing just the right amount of light on the anchorwoman, to illuminate her appropriately, at that particular angle.

"Hi Rami," the producer said as she slid in next to him. Her headset was cumbersome, hiding her true beauty beneath, but Rami was distracted. The amount of light was blinding, hot, and Rami felt his stomach knot and his shoulder slump.

"Hi," he managed to say as the set lights dulled a bit for the commercial break.

"You've got about ten minutes before you're up. You ready?"

"No," he said, unmoving while the middle-aged woman smirked at him.

"You'll be fine big guy. Just answer the few questions

they ask. You can't give a wrong answer. People love you!" she smacked his butt and he leapt onto his toes, looking at the woman surprised.

"Nice ass hero," she said, smiling with a wink.

He couldn't help but chuckle.

"You boys are so predictable. Figured that'd work."

Ten minutes later the studio lights made Rami feel as though he was in a large tanning bed. He began to sweat, but his expensive suit revealed nothing. Just before the cameras began to roll, someone from the set ran up and dabbed his forehead dry, his glistening skin becoming dull once again in the intense light. It was preferable to look calm, cool, steady.

"As everyone knows, a recent terrorism incident occurred in our wonderful city. This morning we have our Superman, our Dark Night, Officer Rami Salim," the anchorwoman said, smiling at him as the camera turned red.

"Hello Miss Andretti."

"Call me Sarah."

"Sarah."

"So, Rami. Everyone wants to know. How did you find the terrorists?"

"First, I would like to say on the air, the U.S. government has stated they've found no proof these two men were terrorists."

"Rami, I can see who you've voting for," she said jokingly, but he didn't laugh.

"Miss Andretti, I'd prefer not to talk politics."

"Fair enough. How did you know where they were?"

Rami thought back to the moments in the street just before he ran into the building. It was the first time he thought hard about the event in detail. He'd been distracted by the fame, the publicity, the urge to run away. Sitting at the anchor desk he wanted to forget the day, to forget the sea of people rushing toward his SWAT team, trying to disarm them, to hurt them, to likely try and kill them.

"We were actually being attacked by the rioters. We fought free, but one of our own was shot." He paused, as his mind revealed that painful moment of clarity as he saw his friend's head snapped back, life exiting his wound.

"I had no idea you were being assaulted by the rioters, Officer Salim."

"Yes, it's a disturbing thought. I realized where the shooter likely was, based on who was shot. I saw an open window. The only open window in the building. It made it easy to find him."

"Do you think the police on the scene should have noticed that? Could it have saved Officer Mark William's life?"

Rami was being put in a position he did not want to be in. The reporter was smiling, her red lips shimmering from the hot lights above. The tone in her voice revealed concern, but in her eyes was something else altogether. She was looking for a scandal, a new angle on the shooting. She wanted Rami to say someone messed up and caused even more deaths. It was another sign of the times. Everyone hated cops, they wanted to blame them for everything; she was loading a keg full of powder and waiting for him to be the match.

"Miss Andretti, the police on the scene were doing what they had to in order to stop the mob from looting and causing millions of dollars in additional damage. What are you looking for? A reason to hate more cops? To continue the rioting that allowed these idiots to shoot down into a crowd? They were amateurs. No trained shooter will shoot from one open window and then not even move. The other shooter was doing the same thing. These were two weirdos looking for an excuse to fulfill a sick fantasy. We got them;

not fast enough, but we did."

"I apologize Mr. Salim. My intentions—"

"Were transparent. You wanted me to come here and allow you to say it was terrorism, to go even further and say it was a mistake on the police not to take the shooters down earlier. But I won't allow it. In fact, I am a Muslim–American, and to say this was radical Islamic terrorism is insulting. I can tell you as a Muslim, we're all tired of being blamed at every opportunity. Read a book Miss Andretti. We're not all the same."

Rami took the mic off and slammed it on the anchor desk, his long heavy strides taking him quickly to the dressing room where he tore at his suit. He felt stupid, like a puppet dressed in white and gray, a hand trying to control his mouth; but he broke that hand. He stormed out of the dressing room in his sweat-drenched t-shirt and a pair of shorts, his dress shoes clicking hard against the linoleum floors. The hallway was lined with people, producers, make-up staff, camera men and women, audio people, and other ancillary staff wanting to catch a glimpse of the angry hero as he left the studio. He had polarized the viewers, most seeing him as a monster, rather than a hero for talking so sternly to their beloved anchorwoman. He saw the producer.

"Guess there are wrong answers after all," he said without stopping and walked into the elevator.

Seattle, Washington

Nassir sat in his large office on the third floor. He turned his desk chair to look out toward Lake Washington. It was a cold, but beautiful morning for more than one reason. What Nassir found most appealing, was the dichotomy of nature and industry: the beautiful long lines of the monochromatic building, the expansive dark blue and gray waterways, and the leaves that set fire to the forests. The clouds had given way to sunlight early in the morning and fog danced in the low points in the landscape. As the fog slowly melted, a rich mix of autumn colors had revealed themselves. The sun kissed the leaves and brought them to life, moisture on the vegetation reflected the glow from above, creating more contrast in the landscape.

"Nassir, President Pierce has arrived." The speaker on his desk interrupted his meditation.

"Please send them in."

A few moments later President Pierce walked into the room, accompanied by Chuck Renfro and Secretary Smith.

"I appreciate you coming to me," Nassir said, his eyes revealed even more happiness than his smile could.

"Not a problem, Nassir. We want to see Medusa."

"And I'd love to show you. Please, follow me."

"They're coming with," Secretary Smith said, pointing to four other men in the hallway.

"I've got room," Nassir said, smiling and waving for the secret service members to come along. "Please, close the door behind you. I've got secrets of my own here, Mr. President."

President Pierce nodded to the men and they closed the tall wooden door.

"Come," Nassir said, a playful smile on his face. He walked to the far side of the room behind his desk. The eight men stood staring at a large piece of artwork on the wall. It was abstract, mostly blue, swirls of white and gold accented with quick, violent strokes of black and silver.

"You like it?" Nassir asked, excited he was finally showing someone his device. "It's an artist's rendition of Medusa. You'll see the real thing."

Nassir reached around the left side of the image. A

hole opened in the floor, twelve inches wide and twelve feet long.

"Step back, Mr. President," one of the secret service members said and stepped forward, his hand on his weapon as he stared into chasm.

The large mural on the wall began to descend into the crevice in the floor, revealing a large elevator.

"This is the only access to Medusa," Nassir said, smiling at the secret service agent who removed his hand from the weapon. "Let's go."

"After you," said Secretary Smith gesturing with an open hand toward the steel elevator.

The doors closed silently and the metallic box descended.

"I had to do some construction," Nassir said, smiling ahead toward the stainless-steel doors, their mirror-like surface allowed everyone to see his face. "We're descending below the street level by two-hundred feet. It took a lot of planning—and money—to keep this a secret form prying eyes."

The elevator decelerated quickly, everyone's knees flexing in response. The doors snapped open and in front of them was a small atrium highlighted by a massive vaulted door.

"What the hell's going on here, Nassir?" President Pierce asked, not interested in games.

"I may be overprotective of Medusa, but I think you'll appreciate the security now that we're working together."

Nassir walked to the door, placed his hand onto a blue glass square at the far left of the atrium. A simple, but melodic chime reverberated in response to his touch.

"One more thing," Nassir said, holding up a finger and walking toward the center of the door. A moment passed and a small hole opened in the center of the door. Nassir looked into the hole. Several electronic motors began to whine and a series of metallic clicks echoed with the promise of even more adventure behind the elaborate door.

"I think we should all focus on what's behind this door for a moment," Nassir said, turning toward his guests. "The technology here is the next generation's next generation tech. Nobody has done what I've done. People won't be able to figure my tech out, unless it's spelled out for them. Not even the U.S. government and all their tech people put together. No offense.

"Medusa isn't a normal computer. Nor is it even the same species per se. My processor is my own creation, bred out of my education and experimentation in material science while at MIT." Nassir paused as the door continued to slowly open, the two-foot-thick steel offering a peek into the long, bright hallway that stretched for a thousand yards below the city, and under Lake Washington.

"It was really by accident I came across the interplay between my material and electrons. I still don't truly know how it all works. It's poetic," Nassir said mostly to himself. He hadn't told anyone of his naiveté. It was his excitement; his energy was spilling over. For years, he'd worked to perfect Medusa, to understand its capabilities, to work within parameters he didn't fully comprehend.

Secretary Smith looked at the president as the door finally opened wide enough for them to see that the adventure was still far from over. The arching hallway was raining down bright white light from the LEDs overhead. It was so well lit in fact, there were no shadows.

"We're almost there now," Nassir said as he sped down the hallway, the other seven men unhappily following.

"I have to admit," President Pierce said ahead to Nassir, "It surely is driving up the suspense. I just hope it's worth it."

"It is, sir," Nassir said, pointing up toward the ceiling

as he continued. "This is the point we cross beneath Lake Washington. I buried Medusa below water, to better protect it from outside influences, energies that could decrease the efficiency. She's a fickle lady, but that's only because she works in the realms of the impossible."

"I'm not confident I know what that means," Secretary Smith said.

"Quantum mechanics. Are you familiar with that term?"

"Not familiar, but I've heard of it."

"My machine is capable of infinitely more complex coding by allowing bits to occupy both a zero and a one simultaneously."

"You've lost me."

"That's fair. Quantum mechanics and coding are both complex in their own respect. Neither come without several years of education. Combining them hasn't really been done. As I said before, this is a different species."

The long, bright hallway finally gave way to a small, nondescript door. It was anti-climactic for such an elaborate set up. The white metal door had a mechanical, coded lock. Nassir wasted no time punching in the four-digit code. The beefy bolts quickly scraped the metal as they slid away from the door, into the wall.

Inside the last room, two small LED lights shone overhead, illuminating several grounded body suits which hung from cheap coat hangers.

"I'm sorry Mr. President, but there's only enough suits for you, Mr. Secretary, and Mr. Renfro."

"That's fine," he said, grabbing the orange rubber suit and began putting it on.

The air was cool, mid-sixties, but the suits were hot, despite their cooling systems. Immediately the four men began to perspire.

"Follow me," Nassir said as he opened yet another door

and the four of them slipped quickly inside. "Here it is," Nassir said, gesturing toward the darkness in front of them.

"Another trick?" Chuck said, annoyed as the comms went silent. Nassir turned them off in order to keep the environment as pure as possible. He reached for the wall and touched a glass panel. Thousands of tiny green and red lights came to life all over the room, like miniature monsters waking at the sound of intruders. A massive rush of wind blew through the room, gently pressing against their suits. A humming noise followed, raw energy tickled their skin, and filled their noses with an odd smell as they stood in place watching the room come to life.

Nassir switched the comms back on for a moment. "Sorry I turned off the radios. We need a clean environment. I just had to tell you something. This is my favorite part."

Right on cue Medusa came to life. In the center of the glittering greens and reds, a warming, comforting blue glow began to emerge. As if alive, it pulsed, gradually getting brighter and brighter until the whole room was bathed in electric blue light. The reds and greens conceded in defeat, drown out by the intensity of the brilliant blue. The men stood taking in the serenity, the beauty was overwhelming as the churning material inside painted pictures in shadows on the ceiling above, and the walls around it; the bundles of circuits acted as brushes.

"Medusa," President Pierce said as he stood frozen like a stone.

"Can't look directly at her," Secretary Smith said as the shadows above writhed around like slithering snakes, but his eyes were unmoved from the beauty of the material that rolled and inverted itself repeatedly in unpredictable ways.

"Now you understand," Nassir said, smiling widely as his eyes glimmered blue and white.

"Could we bring this to Washington?" President Pierce

asked.

"Not a chance. It would likely be destroyed," Nassir said, looking at the president. "Here's the beauty Mr. President. Medusa's speed is unrivaled. She can calculate innumerable things simultaneously and do it at nearly the speed of light. Thousands of computers around the world operate in clean rooms with their temperatures cooled to below freezing, but that box there," he said, pointing to Medusa, "is a fraction of a degree from absolute zero. There isn't a colder place in the universe. Moving her to Washington would serve no purpose. It's just as effective here. In fact, we could move it to the moon and it would still be the quickest computer in the world."

"I'm sold, son. You'll be an unsung hero if this keeps working."

"As long as I get paid, sir. And that my family name is kept clean."

"That last bit of information you gave us matches all the latest intel we'd been working with. I want daily updates to Secretary Smith's office, directly."

"I agree. It needs to be directly to me. I'll send it to the necessary people."

"We have a deal?" President Pierce asked, extending a hand toward the brilliant engineer and salesman.

"Absolutely."

Chapter 23
HOPE

Undisclosed location, Yemen

David Westbrook drove for almost a day with a passenger in the trunk. The sun worked against the CIA agent, as it baked his prisoner inside the enclosed space. David didn't want the man to die—he still had questions—so every hour he stopped, opened the trunk, and threw a bottle of water into the hot box, while the prisoner shielded his eyes from the blistering light.

David hated to move, to establish new connections, new safe havens, and develop a new firewall for his tech. His next destination would have only taken eight hours, however, he wanted to meander through several cities in the chance he was being followed. He was heading toward Sana'a, Yemen, a city that became a hotspot on his map of dark web activity over the last several months.

In fact, his last three moves in country were chosen using this exact method. He needed to be close to the action, and for the last several years, he'd been very successful. However, he vowed this time would be different. He'd be on his own, no more children. Amal's death wounded him deeply.

Finally, he reached the outskirts of the city as the horizon became an orange fresco, the red mountains in the distance spread before him. It was a harsh, hell-like appearance, which made him feel alone. With Saad in the back he couldn't drive into the city. The risk of being seen carrying a prisoner into an unsecured building was great. Instead, he slowly wandered through the streets in the outskirts of the city, focusing on the filth, the lifeless, the forgotten areas.

At nightfall, he decided to move into an abandoned mud brick structure he'd seen about an hour earlier. He'd waited in his car just down the street from the dilapidated residence and observed. It was quiet, not a soul had been seen, or any animal for that matter. It seemed a ghost town, except for one home several structures away, a flickering light hinted at a single soul.

David quietly exited the car, threw his duffel bag over his shoulder, and ran into the home. He cleared it in moments, having only two rooms to inspect. He jogged back to the car, his long silent strides making quick work of the fifty-yard distance. David threw the car in reverse, speeding toward the structure he just cleared. He opened the trunk and found Saad crying inside. Quickly, he grasped the man, threw him over a shoulder, and raced into the home, throwing himself and Saad inside, quietly shutting the door behind him.

David's eyes were dark, hands clenched, he rolled his head around trying to relax. He attempted to close his eyes, but a dangling boy's body was still there to greet him, forcing David to snap them back open, only to see the responsible man kneeling on the floor. One step narrowed the distance between the two of them. David quickly hoisted Saad to his feet, and plunged his bruised knuckles deep into Saad's abdomen. Air fled the murderer's lungs as his diaphragm went into spasm. David lifted him back up and repeated the attack, this time not allowing Saad to fall to the ground. He immediately sent a third left into his defenseless face.

"A child," David growled, as he threw the man to the ground and turned toward the door. He bounced his shoulders as he hopped on his toes, trying to breathe and relax. He'd never truly been emotional in times like these. It was always business, needing to get the truth, to find the next break, to gather whatever intel a guy may have. Saad was different. The terrorist hurt someone he connected with, someone he cared about. David failed Amal.

"What will you do to me?"

David walked to him, squatted low to meet the eyes of Saad who lay on his elbow bleeding from his mouth. He was dazed, distracted. He should have kept quiet.

"I'm gonna take off your fingers and toes, one by one. Peel your skin back like an animal while I force you to watch. I'll find your family, start from the youngest and move to the oldest. I promise I'll find them," he said, reiterating the point after seeing Saad's reaction to it.

"I know nothing."

"Mhm," David said as he reached behind him and pulled out his shiny blade. He held it firmly against Saad's hand near the base of the ring finger. A quick flick of his wrist and Saad's finger fell to the floor.

"I don't know anything!" he said loudly. David struck him in the face for the volume; not for the lie. He pulled back at the end of his punch, wanting to mete out the punishment, not knock him out cold.

David reached toward his bag and grabbed his secret weapon. Saad's yelling would reverberate in the calm, quiet evening. It made David nervous, forcing him back to business rather than revenge. He made quick work of injecting Saad who feigned a fight, trying to maintain some dignity but knowing he would lose.

"You're going to talk. Whether you like it or not," David said as he sat on the dirty mosaic floor, and waited for the drug to take effect.

"So that's your secret. A magic potion. How anti-climactic."

"How did you know about me?"

"Amal. Stupid question."

"How did you know to look for me?"

"We watched for candy. We know your style Candyman," he said, smiling.

David was broken, guilty, but had to press on.

"You tracked Amal to me?"

"Yes."

"What did you find out about me?"

"Nothing we didn't know already. You've been working hard for our cause. Sending information to the Americans, but we don't need you anymore."

David was stung, confused.

"What do you mean?" he asked. There was no reason to be angry or aggressive, he knew the truth would come out.

"We've allowed you to get information from us, to send it to America. We're okay with some of our people dying, for them being arrested, for you to torture men. We know you didn't go after their families. We did. It made the pawns scared of you. Made it more realistic for them, and for you. That was important."

"What's the point? What's the bigger plan?"

"I don't know."

"How can you not know!" David said in frustration, reaching with his long arm and striking the man once more.

"How's Logan?" Saad asked, laughing.

"Logan?"

"It almost doesn't seem fair how many steps ahead we are, *infidel*. He's the man in the U.S. who's acting on your intel. He's taken out quite a few of our expendable cells. Sure, if they were successful it would have been good, but bombings and shootings have gotten boring. We're moving on they say."

"Who?"

"I don't know his name."

"What do you know?"

"He's in the mountains."

"Where in the mountains?"

"Everywhere," he said, his hands sweeping wide, outstretching in front of him and around. A sinister smile arced across his face; an involuntary chill ran up David's back.

"What's he doing there?"

"Training people, sending them to America."

"How many?"

"Thousands."

"To do what?"

"I do not know."

Something triggered a memory. Maybe it was the talk of mountains, but the memory of a missing pilot quickly jumped to his mind. He had heard the rumors, discussed it with a few of his captured persons, but nobody had an answer.

"What happened to the pilots?"

"Nothing."

"Were they killed?"

"Not all of them."

"What happened to each one?"

"Two planes shot down, praise be to *Allah*. One crew ejected. We killed one on the ground. The other was taken."

"Taken where?"

"To the mountains."

"Is he still alive?"

"Yes."

David reached forward and grasped the man's throat. The strength in his long fingers clamped down hard and Saad welcomed death. He never would have spoken had it not been for the candy. He wasn't scared of David, as most of the others had been. Saad knew the secret. David wasn't someone who tortured and killed family, because Saad was the man who was responsible for those atrocities.

As Saad slowly faded, David asked him one last question. "Did Amal fight?"

Saad barely moved, but the nod affirmed David's hope that Amal raged in death.

Quickly, David grabbed his duffel bag and raced through the door and into his car. He sped away, out toward the country. His driving was erratic, foot never leaving the gas pedal as he pushed the old Mercedes sedan hard in the warm evening. The air was full of dust, but that was behind him. Ahead was clean air and his headlights lit the atmosphere. He needed seclusion, he needed a signal.

After forty minutes of hard driving, his exited the car, his sweat leaving a mess in his seat and saturating his clothes. He ran toward the foothills and quickly scaled his way toward the summit. The government had provided him a satellite phone, but he hadn't used it in several years; he hadn't heard an American voice since then either. Secretary Smith had given him a direct line, and David memorized it the first time he saw it. He dialed, and waited.

"Hello," a gravely voice answered.

"Mr. Secretary?" David asked quietly.

"Who is this?" Secretary Smith asked nervously.

"Candyman."

Smith launched himself out of his chair and sprung toward the door. The adrenaline that stood his hair on end also gave him a spring in his step.

"What's the situation, son?"

"I needed to talk. We've got a situation."

"Out with it damn it!"

"You found a missing pilot I haven't heard about?" David asked.

"No son, all KIA."

"Your intel is wrong."

Chapter 24

BROTHERS LOST, BROTHER FOUND

Haraz Mountains, Yemen

It was hot, even at eight-thousand feet above sea level. The cloud cover was non-existent and water leached from skin in the relatively thin air. Amir had gotten used to the altitude during the last few months, so he felt at home, drinking water, watching the endless undulations in the horizon. The mountains deceived his eyes, never changing, their incredible size played tricks on his psychology. The trucks drove for hours, but Amir continued to see the same jagged peaks out of his window, as if the massive landscape tracked their every move.

Amir was with Taj in the second truck. The two of them

sat alone, the lead truck was for their safety, and the fifth truck held Alex Pines. In total, there were eight trucks, full of Karim's recently trained men. Their mission: to reach another stronghold deep within the Haraz Mountains. The same mountinas that Amir had been a resident of, a prisoner within. The thought made his stomach cramp and his mind race.

As the convoy bounced along the mountain roads, Amir recalled weeks he spent in prison. The days blurred together with beatings, the "education," the sleepless nights. He remembered the day he broke, crying out, telling them about his mother's death and how he never dealt with it. Tears moistened his face as he blubbered on about how her death motivated him to join the Army. He remembered the interrogators; how they had already known everything about his service record: his time in Afghanistan, the Paktika Province, how he led a squad against three times their number, none of his men even getting a scratch. He hadn't met Taj until he was broken. He hadn't met Karim until Taj had vetted Amir out, ensuring he was capable of being another chess piece in the game. Amir had been made a knight, not a pawn, but still felt dirty, sinful, embarrassed.

Amir, just days earlier, began to feel like himself again, which scared him. He was once impulsive, bull-headed, did what he pleased, even if his superiors didn't like it that way. Amir acted on his own even though Jenkins was calling the shots for years. He planned the attacks, adding his own twists, and craved the role Jenkins sat in. Now he had stepped on the toes of Karim, killing the man Alex was meant to kill. It wasn't premeditated, it couldn't have been. Even Taj had no idea what his father had in store for the injured pilot. It was shocking, impressive, and powerful all at once, but Amir saw an opportunity to become an ally to Alex, to show Alex he wasn't the monster he appeared, at least not any longer.

The events that followed could have never been predicted. Amir was still trying to wrap his head around the fact Karim had told both Taj and himself the entire plot. Karim was trying to advance the war, to add dimension to the terror they were instilling in the west. "The hatred I have is in our blood," he said to the two men he called sons. "But we cannot continue to act on emotion. Our history was written for us, by them. Not so many years ago we were forced from our homes, by men who thought they knew better, by men who had power and money. They shuffled our homes, our villages, our countries like a deck of cards to be passed out amongst them. It wasn't their right. We are Syrian, but we are Saudi. We will crush the west, and divide them up like playing cards just as they did to us. We have the money, we have the power, we have the upper hand," Karim had said passionately as he clenched his fist.

Amir saw anger, but also guilt in Karim's eyes, because of his success while so many others were suffering, poor, still struggling to find a place in the Middle East since the Treaty of Versailles.

"Amir," Taj said, breaking the silence.

"Not *American*?" Amir said, looking toward Taj, surprised.

"I see strength in you now. My father trusts you as well. This is no small thing, brother."

"What does your father see in me?"

"A son."

"Why? There are so many other men who've been with him longer, shown more loyalty. Why did he tell me everything?"

Taj sat silent. He stared through the windshield as light flooded through his driver-side window. Amir struggled to look toward the typically heavy-handed bully. Taj seemed vulnerable, sad, distant for the first time. He was biting down, clenching his teeth repeatedly. The gossiper was holding back, and it was a struggle.

"Taj. Please. You said yourself your father trusts me. You can trust me too, brother," Amir said almost choking on the words. It felt awkward, sounded strange. A word he had never called anyone before, a burning lie tickling the end of his tongue as it left his mouth. In the few hours since Amir pulled the trigger he learned to hate Taj.

"It was a long time ago, in a place I barely remember," Taj began to speak as he lit a cigarette. He inhaled deeply through the unfiltered stick and released a long, billowing cloud toward the windshield. The smoke bounced off the glass and swirled around the car as a gentle breeze from the open windows dissipated the white cloud.

"My home then was in Saudi Arabia. We had little, but my father worked very hard. One day my mother told me to pack a bag while he was away. So, I did. She raced us to a waiting car and we sped away. I was scared, but not as scared as my little brother. We were both whipped around in the back as a man drove wildly through the streets of our home town. To tell you the truth Amir, I don't even know what the town was called." Taj paused and reflected on the moment, the fear creeping back into his mind as he took another long drag on the cigarette to calm himself.

"We made it out of the city and he drove quickly through the open desert, a plume of sand and dust thrown behind us. It was so thick and wide I could see nothing out of the rear window. I remember my mother screaming at me to sit down and put my seatbelt on. I've never gone so fast. The engine noise was horrific, it screamed for rest, but the man continued to drive hard as my mother grabbed him by the arm and shook him while screaming 'go as fast as you can!' My brother sat on the floor of the sedan, rocking back and forth, his hands covering his ears. He was humming, but I couldn't make out the song." Taj continued to smoke as he composed his thoughts.

"And then my father came. Like a hero in a Hollywood movie, Amir. He was in a truck, massive wheels, and an engine that sounded like it came straight from hell. He screamed at the man driving but the stranger didn't respond. He stayed focused on the road ahead; I think out of fear. My mother yelled for him. 'These are my babies!' she yelled to him and pumped her fist. Tears zigzagged down her face as the two vehicles slid right and left, back and forth, toward each other. I'd never seen my mother upset before."

"'Sfiyah!' I heard him yell." Taj stopped speaking and smirked. "That was my mother's name. I haven't thought of her in quite a while Amir. I miss her smile, her food. Amir, she made these wonderful sweet cakes with almonds and lemon. I can smell them cooking, brother . . . "

"Taj?" Amir said after several moments of silence.

"Brother . . . "

"Yes, Taj?"

"My brother is dead Amir." Taj flicked the cigarette out the window and sniffed hard. "My father drove ahead of us, quickly, and turned his truck to block the way. Our car slammed into the side his truck. The driver died immediately, but not my mother. She was hurt quite bad, bleeding from her face. I remember the smells, gasoline, iron, the brakes. The dust cloud finally caught up to us and filled my lungs, but I was okay. I had a seatbelt on because I was big enough to put it on myself. Aleem was not. I should have helped him."

"What ha—"

"He was crushed by the front seat during the impact. The driver's seat slid back and hit my brother."

"I'm sorry, Taj—"

"My father ran to me, picked me up, and brought me to the truck. He went back to the car for my brother. He grasped the dead man in the front and threw him to the sandy earth. He wrestled the front seat, and with the strength of ten men, ripped it from its bolts and threw it from the car, on top of the driver. Tenderly, he grabbed Aleem. I watched him stroke his hair, wipe the blood from his face, and kiss him on the forehead. He held his ear to Aleem's chest and ran to the car leaving my mother behind. 'Hold your brother!' he yelled to me as he jumped into the driver's seat and raced away back toward the city. I've never seen my father panic, not before, nor since that day. We left my mother in the desert. My father heard a heartbeat in Aleem's two-year-old chest.

"It felt like hours I sat in the truck as my father raced across the sand putting my mother further and further behind us; but I didn't care. I loved my father. He was my everything, but Aleem was his favorite. It never bothered me. Still doesn't."

"What happened to him?"

"He died in the hospital. I never got to see him once my father brought him into the clinic. We never talked about it again."

"I was an only child, Taj. I can't imagine the pain you feel."

"Amir, you asked why my father trusts you more than the others."

"Yes."

"This is why. I saw it the first time we met. You remind me of Aleem. My father sees it too. We haven't spoken about it, but I know he feels this way. I see it in his eyes. The same eyes he had when he looked at my brother in the car, the same eyes he had when my brother talked, when he performed mathematics at an early age, when he began to build with toys incredible structures. You're right to think my father an intelligent man. He is, and that trait also went to my brother."

"I don't know what to say," Amir said. He was stung by Taj's candor. A wild twist of fate had led him down an emotional road—from fear, to respect, to honor, to love, to brotherhood. Amir had been through this before. He had been bullied his whole life before the Army welcomed him with open arms. He'd led men into battle and earned overwhelming trust and respect from his commanding officers. He climbed the ranks quickly in the Army, but it seemed as though his stock rose even quicker in the mountains of Yemen.

"Say you'll never leave us like Aleem."

"I promise," Amir lied.

Washington, D.C.

It was all hands on deck in the special operations room at the Pentagon. General Mitchell Anderson executive officer of JSOC, Secretary Smith, President Pierce, and Bill Whiteside from the CIA were the heavy hitters. Everyone sat around a large, walnut table as live video streamed in from a satellite over the Haraz Mountains.

"Who gave you the intel?" Bill asked.

"One of your boys," Secretary Smith said, smiling.

"I see. Whereabouts?"

"Yemen."

Bill wrote a note to himself to look into their staff in that country.

"This the same guy we get our stuff from?" Logan asked from the back of the room. He, along with Lonnie and Dubs, stood watching the feed.

"Same guy," Secretary Smith responded, his eyes still locked on the screen. "I'll tell you what else he said that scared the shit outta me." Doyle Smith turned his wide frame around in his swivel chair, the light from the screen wrapping around his dark silhouette. "He said his last guy was big time. Spilled a lot of goods. Outside of this intel, he told me the work we've been doing against these cells has been a diversion for a much bigger plot."

"What's that mean exactly?" President Pierce asked. His terrorism-is-dead platform in serious jeopardy, and he was already significantly down in the polls.

"We have no idea. What I do know, is that our man in Yemen was told hundreds of trained terrorists have already been planted in the U.S."

"Seems as though they're waiting for a signal if you ask me," Bill said with a sigh.

"What's the signal? Any ideas?"

"Nothing. That's what scares the shit outta me. Too many variables. I'm hoping we can find a needle in a haystack that'll pop this thing right open."

"What about Medusa?" President Pierce asked, sitting up and placing his hands on the table, staring at Doyle.

"It certainly isn't going to hurt. I haven't had anything come across my desk yet," Doyle responded throwing his hands up. "Only been a couple days."

"We still need to filter out the good and the bad from the intel we get there. We can't assume every bit of intel is actionable, just like we couldn't assume that with what we were already getting. It'll help fill in gaps, coordinate with our other intel," Bill said, explaining it plainly for the president.

"What the hell is Medusa?" Dubs asked, his big voice reverberating off the walls in the dark, solid room.

"It's new tech we got from a contractor. A computer capable of intercepting and scanning all kinds of data and communications. At least that's the application we're using it for."

"Huh," Lonnie said, crossing his arms.

"We've got action," General Anderson said, pointing toward the screen as the image began to change. The wide shot jutted right toward the north, then zoomed in quickly.

"That look normal to you fellas?" General Anderson asked and smirked. He picked up the phone. "Track those vehicles to their destination. Do not lose them. We're gonna need maps, coordinates. When they stop I wanna know the size of the structure, IR scans of the buildings on location, the number of people entering and leaving, any weaponry. We're gonna need a few birds in the air to sweep for SAMS and jam radar. I want continuous satellite imagery over the area to track any changes. We need to know if there's an airstrip nearby that can send a counter strike onto what we're sending as well. Read it back to me," General Anderson listened, nodding as each point was read back to him.

"Very good. Talk soon." General Anderson hung up the phone and looked at Logan.

"You boys wanna go for a ride?"

Chapter 25
HALO

Logan sat in the driveway staring at the steering wheel. He knew the news would be hard for Samantha to hear, but he needed redemption. It was his intel that indirectly led to Alex Pines being shot down. Reaper, Sherman, Migs, but not Dubs, and hopefully, not Alex either. He was grateful for that moment with Dubs in the cemetery, the reminder that he hadn't lost everyone. Now, the possibility of Alex being alive and knowing the location gave Logan energy again. He had confidence, he had a drive, he wanted his invincibility. But he was now vulnerable. A baby was on the way and it was a distraction. He sighed, hot air left his lungs and painted the windshield a frosted white. He saw the door open and his beautiful Samantha stepped out.

Logan exited the car slowly and walked toward his wife. "I'm sorry it's so late," he said, his words leaving a white streak in the air. He stared into her dark brown eyes as the lights from the house painted her hair in browns and reds.

"It's okay, honey," she said, grabbing him and cuddling close. "It's getting so cold already," she said, squeezing.

"I know. Not even November yet."

"Ugh. I wish it were. I'm so sick of this election already."

"It's been pretty civil."

"I guess. Get inside I'm sick of being cold." She paused. "Oh, my God!" she exclaimed and grabbed his hand, placing it on her stomach.

"What the hell!" Logan said, recoiling at the awkward sensation.

"The baby moved! I've never felt it move before!"

"That's so beautiful," he said softly and dropped to his knees to get closer to the baby, forgetting his duty in the wonderful moment they were sharing.

"Huh!" She said quickly breathing in. "There it was again!" she giggled and held her hand toward her mouth as tears filled her eyes.

"Go inside," Logan said and followed her, his arms reaching around her waist in hopes of another movement.

The door closed quietly and they were warm in the brightly lit living room. The moving had stopped, but the promise of more caused them both to daydream for a moment as they sat on the couch.

"Samantha, I have to tell you something," he said, sitting up but not looking at her. Instead, he stared at his hands as he rubbed them together.

"What is it?"

"I've got to go away again."

"Where?"

"Out of country."

"What?"

"It's a rescue op. Please Samantha. Understand . . . I need this."

Samantha's eyes once again became a wall of water as she fought to keep her eyelids open against the tide of sorrow. She knew he needed something to help him get past the anger, the guilt, but she thought the pregnancy would have been enough. She knew no matter what she said he would leave.

"I understand," she heard herself say but wasn't listening.

"I've got to go."

"When?"

"Now."

He stood and Samantha stood with him, grasping him hard around the neck. It was as if she was physically trying to show him what her voice couldn't say. She wanted him to stay; she needed him to stay.

"Come home to me Logan."

"I promise," he said, knowing he was invincible.

Gulf of Aden

It had taken thirty-six hours, three flights, and a helo ride to get there, but finally Logan, Dubs, and Lonnie were feet wet on the supercarrier Gerald Ford. Logan took a deep breath as his feet hit the deck, the smell of jet fuel filled his lungs and memories long forgotten came charging back into his mind: sleeping in bunks, strange conversations, card games, mess hall, physical therapy, training on deck, training below deck, walking through the hangars, and coveting the time allowed on the internet or phone. It was a shit place, but they had always made the best of it until they got back on dry land.

"This way!" the deck boss said to the Marines as they walked across the steel deck, an FA-18's engines spooling up, anticipating the go signal. The three men were handed off to a private first class who took them below deck, and toward the briefing room.

The Marines walked into the small, nondescript room. Before them sat two squads of men, sixteen in all. At the front, a smooth shaven African-American man stood and walked toward them.

"Sol," he said, extending his hand toward Logan.

"Logan. This is Dubs, and Lonnie."

"You guys still know how to work?" Sol said, smiling, but his men behind just stared at the three strangers.

"Yut," Dubs said, his chest sticking out, an attempt to outsize the large SEAL team leader.

"Grab a seat, Marines," he said, pointing to the chairs behind him.

"Ya'll might know some of this, but we're gonna bring it all together in this room. First, some intros. We got Blue, our eyes outside. Logan, you're with him spotting. He's gonna take the high point on the south side of the compound here," Solomon said, pointing toward the paper map on the wall.

"Whiplash and Lucky are gonna lead the teams going inside. Ghost and I will lead the perimeter teams. We're gonna have ten men inside, nine men outside. Lonnie you're with Whiplash entering the western end of the compound, and Dubs, your big ass is outside with an LMG laying fire down toward the west side; when necessary. Everyone understand who they're dancin' with?"

Everyone nodded.

"Alright. Now the fun part. East team's gonna breach first. The landscape allows cover, but, Blue and Logan you'll have eyes on the mountainside. IR scopes and range Logan. Used that before?"

"Yes, sir."

"Good shit. Thirty seconds after boom, west side will blow your charge and ya'll meet in the middle. We don't know the layout. Clear every room, comms are good, green light for fire. The target is Alex Pines, U.S. Navy pilot. We're assuming they think we're coming. His challenge questions: What's the make of your bike; answer, Yamaha. What's your mascot; answer, honeybee; and what's your favorite color, red. If he's wrong, restraint and drag his ass out. We'll deal with it later.

"Once we have the target, we will move east from the entry point into the terrain. Logan, you'll paint the target while Blue provides overwatch for our exfil. We'll work up five-hundred feet of elevation, then over the ridgeline and toward one of three exfil. We wanna be in and out in ten minutes; over the ridgeline by twenty." Solomon paused. "You paint that target Sergeant." He said, pointing toward Logan.

"Yut," Logan responded with resolve, as a chill went up his back, a wave of adrenaline almost lifting him from his seat. It was time for redemption; time to bring back a lost soul.

The prop noise from the twin Rolls Royce turboprops was soothing for the men as they sat with their backs rattling gently against the steel skin of the Grumman C-2 Greyhound. They were in full gear, oxygen strapped to their faces, as they prepared to jettison the plane at 34,000 feet above sea level.

Logan sat with his eyes closed, thinking about Samantha and the baby, about how bad he wanted to get home. He felt vulnerable, apprehensive about the mission. It was brief, but he wondered what would happen if he just stayed in the plane. Then he remembered Alex, and imagined him being beaten, questioned, tortured, all because Logan gathered intel from a cellphone.

"O2 on," Sol said into the radio. "Comms check."

Each man took turns checking, then rechecking their gear. It was automatic, comfortable, and Logan was falling into habits too engrained to be called old.

The rear of the C-2 began to open, and a wave of air pressed the men toward the back door, as the pressure equalized with the thin atmosphere outside the plane.

"One mike," an anonymous voice said into the comms.

The men stood and approached the rear of the aircraft, staring at the darkness. The air was clear, not a cloud to be made out in the dark void below. The only discernable feature from the earth and space were the pinpricks of light that highlighted the sky.

Sol led the men to the back of the aircraft; to his left, Blue. They jumped together, and two by two the men jumped in one-second increments. Logan watched as each small team leapt and his heart began to pound, his breath coming quicker as the view of the mountains below became less obstructed by men standing and waiting to jump. Suddenly, it was just himself, Dubs, and Lonnie. Without a look or hesitation, the three of them jumped together.

The three-man team began their descent in silence as the air seemed to slow to a halt. Within seconds, however, they pitched themselves downward, and began accelerating toward a demonic mouth of darkness; the jagged, red earth acting as teeth surrounding a dark abyss of the valley within. The wind noise began as a whisper, but turned into a scream as they accelerated down through the thin air, their helmets slicing through the molecules as they reached terminal velocity. Each man was aware of their drop zone, a GPS navigation system accompanied their altimeter, and they were dropped within two miles of the coordinates.

Whap! The canopy snapped open throwing Logan's head forward, as the immediate change in velocity sent his insides deep within his abdomen. He squeezed his muscles tightly to counteract the stress. He was only three-thousand feet above the valley, and well below the altitude in which he could have been detected. Finally, he hit the dry, red dirt of the mountains, and quickly made his way to the rendezvous.

The twinkling sky was beautiful in the thin air. The rising and falling peaks looked like frozen waves in an endless red sea, and filtered out the light pollution from the cities rooted hundreds of miles away. Nineteen men had feet on the ground; nineteen men understood their roles. They hiked for miles through rocky terrain silently in the ink-like, moonless night.

"There it is," Sol said quietly into the comms. "Squad One, form the perimeter. Squad Two follow us in."

Solomon took point and the two squads spread out as they slithered their way down the exposed rocky slope into the valley. They were approaching the compound from the south, which provided the easiest access and showed the least activity based on satellite imagery.

"On location," Blue said into the comms as he and Logan lay prone, their cover was a complex grouping of rocky debris, likely planted there thousands of years earlier, as the mountains were slowly beaten down by the elements.

"Copy," Sol said as Squad One continued on, Logan watching their beacons blinking in the darkness through his IR scope. It took less than thirty minutes and Squad One was in position encircling the compound, prepared to fire upon the guards on the exterior.

"We've got eight armed outside," Sol said. "Mark up." Each man silently chose their prey as they'd practiced thousands of times, and executed dozens more. It was natural for them, unwavering, they knew which one belonged to them.

"Squad Two, move to breach."

Whiplash moved toward the west side of the compound with his five-man team, and Lucky moved to the east leading his four-man team.

Lonnie was nervous. He'd breached hundreds of

buildings, but his track record had been poor as of late. His last two missions nearly took his life. His heart was racing and his breathing was rapid, shallow.

"You alright, Marine?" Whiplash asked without turning.

"I'm good. Just hyped as fuck," Lonnie said, trying to seem collected.

"Don't get all Rambo on me," Whiplash responded and placed the charge on the compound wall. "Charge placed," Whiplash stated.

There was a brief moment of quiet for the team. Everyone respected the few seconds before the execution order was given. It was a moment for a silent prayer, a mental check, a fleeting thought of a loved one back home. It was business time and everyone wanted a clear head. The call was Sol's to make. He had gone through the checklist, ensuring the mission was ready for go. Blue was overwatch, Dubs had heavy fire in the west, Sol to the east. Ghost was to the north, ready to lay down anything that moved in that quadrant, and the rest had dug in strategically to monitor any guard outside, as well as cover all doors that led out of the compound. Ten men inside was enough, the compound was estimated at fifty-thousand square feet, but they weren't confident in the number of levels below ground. Whiplash and Lucky could lead a band of greenhorn recruits from Great Lakes Naval Training Facility to clear the building, but they had ten battle-tested Marines and SEALs with them.

The moment came when Sol's family leapt into his mind. His wife's bright smile, her warm skin.

"Execute," he said before deeper thoughts developed.

Boom! The charge on the east side of the building threw concrete outward and the wall collapsed.

Pop, pop, poppoppoppop, boom! Shots rang out in every direction echoing like thunder through the peaks around the compound. Eight targets down in a flash.

Lucky entered the facility first, clearing the room with his fellow SEALs, and they quickly began descending to the lowest level. "Three floors," Lucky said into the comms.

"Copy," Whiplash responded.

Boom! Detonation on the west side, and the second team entered the facility. The western team worked their way down to the second floor, clearing it, each one weaving to the next room with speed. Lonnie was smooth, collected, working with muscle memory and confidence, his fear taking a backseat to the adrenaline. He was electric, popping off round after round into rooms occupied by terrorists in training, guards, persons who'd been sleeping soundly just moments earlier, now never waking from a death that promised them eternal pleasures of the flesh.

"Second level clear," Whiplash said into the comms. One of the SEALs had stayed back to watch the stairs. When the rest of the team reached him, a pile of five bodies littered the western stairwell.

"We're coming down."

"Copy, Whiplash," Lucky said as they worked through the maze below.

The third level was dark and silent as the western team found their way to the basement. They placed their NVGs on and slowly began to navigate the lowest level. Their footsteps, gentle as they were, created the only noise to be heard. The smell of gunpowder filled the air but none of the SEALs had yet to fire a shot on the deepest, subterranean floor of the facility.

The silence left Lonnie feeling vulnerable, as flashes of the dark, nitrogen-rich basement of Los Angeles filled his thoughts. It took all his resolve not to turn and run up the stairs to the fresh air. He took a deep, cleansing breath and entered a room to his right, clearing it with Whiplash before moving on down the hallway.

"Five minutes," Sol said into the comms, the stillness of the third floor seemed to allow the noise from their headsets to echo against the cold concrete that surrounded them on all sides.

"Help." A faint voice made Lonnie's eyes open wide and his hair stand on end.

"Help." A second time the voice called out, this time slightly stronger than the first, but still barely human. It was hard to decipher which direction it came from as it reverberated through the endless maze of concrete.

The two teams methodically worked the hallways and endless rooms. They continued to hear the calls for help, coming more frequently.

Click, click, click, a tapping sound of metal on concrete. *Click, click, click* it continued, rhythmically, calling the teams toward it.

Slowly, each team made its way toward the sound, each step cautious of a trap.

"Careful," Lonnie said to Whiplash who was leading the team toward the noise. He needed to say the words to the man, even if it made him feel stupid later.

The noise became louder and louder as they worked their way to the northernmost hallway.

"Drop the weapon!" Whiplash yelled as he saw the barrel of a handgun bouncing off the floor. In front of the gun, a man lay dead.

"American," the voice cried from the small hole in the wall.

"What's your school mascot?"

"Honeybee," the voice said with a whine.

"What's the brand of your bike?"

"Yamaha," the voice said, sobbing.

"What's your favorite color?"

A long pause ensued. Alex was falling apart. Finally,

someone had come to rescue him. The mascot brought back so many memories of good times and football games, running, and his old girlfriend. The Yamaha brought back the smell of a garage, the calluses of his dad's hands as he rubbed them roughly through Alex's hair as a boy.

"What's your favorite color?" Whiplash asked forcefully, now only five feet from the low opening in the concrete, his M4 pointed at the hole.

"Red," Alex whispered as he remembered the color of blood: the blood from his father on the ground, from Commander Heinz on the bed of the truck when they were transported to a compound, and the dark crimson puddle that was left when Amir killed his father's murderer. Lastly, before the lights went out in the basement, he remembered the blood that sprayed onto Amir's face from Taj's head.

Outside the compound, Logan scanned from left to right, searching for anything bright, white, indicating warmth. Squad Two had been inside for ten minutes, and they hadn't found Alex. Then Logan saw something, someone; far west, past the perimeter, a demon from hell birthed in darkness. Logan's hands began to sweat and a flame ignited in his stomach. So many times he'd thought of the man who got away, the man who shot Dubs, a man who betrayed his country. The limp that he first saw in Iraq, then in Saint Louis, was now presenting itself there in the Haraz Mountains of Yemen. It was Amir, and he was running.

Logan sprang from his prone position and hightailed down the mountainside, his feet trying to catch up with gravity as he almost tumbled headlong down the hill. His lungs burned in the high altitude and his lack of conditioning once again beat him down. It was difficult to feel the M4 as his hands began to go numb. He strapped it around his chest and continued to bound down the mountainside.

"Logan's AWOL," Blue said calmly into the comms, breaking the silence.

"Say again," Sol said sternly.

"He's on the run, heading west. Something's got his attention."

"Dubs, get your boy under control," Sol said.

"Copy," Dubs responded and turned south just as Logan came barreling down the last hundred feet to the landing Dubs was scanning.

"Coming out, heavy one," Whiplash said into everyone's ear.

Dubs left his heavy weapon and gave chase. It wasn't hard work, but he finally caught Logan and brought him to the ground. "What the fuck, Logan? Get your shit together!"

"It's Amir, he's running!" he said with his back pinned to the ground. Dubs looked and saw the terrorist that got away. Dubs now filled with rage, but understood that the mission did not include capturing the one who got away; for the second time.

"I don't give a shit. You gotta paint that building ASAP!" Dubs said, refocused on the objectives.

Dubs was right and Logan knew it. He reached down toward his hip where the marking laser should have been, but wasn't. He reached all around his belt, but couldn't find it.

"Blue, check for laser," Logan said regretfully into the comms. He felt a wave of guilt as he squeezed his eyes shut and began to climb up the mountain, while Dubs ran to grab his heavy firepower.

Thump, thump, thump, then silence. *Thump, thump, thump* again, but this time the sound seemed to be closer. Nineteen men heard the sound, all recognized the cadence of metal swirling, churning the thin air of the mountains.

"Get up that ridgeline!" Sol yelled as his perimeter team pulled back toward the eastern side of the compound. Blue stayed in position and painted the facility with the laser guidance.

"Angel One target secure," Blue said into the comms as he held the laser steady against the long southern wall of the complex.

"Copy," the anonymous voice said from the cockpit of an FA-18 Super Hornet.

When Sol gave the go for the spec ops team to breach, an initial run had been made by four FA-18s. This first wave had long-range air-to-surface missiles that took out several SAMS' sites throughout the mountainous terrain. For three days before the mission, overhead satellites had monitored the mobile enemies surface-to-air technology, as it positioned itself throughout the valleys in an attempt to create a defensive ring around the high value compound. General Anderson insisted they were more prepared this time.

As Logan and Dubs raced up toward Blue, the sound of a helo continued to grow, echoing through the valley but becoming more distinct. Logan turned to look toward the north and the sinister sound was brought to life by not one, but three helos entering the valley. Two of the aircraft banked immediately left toward the SEAL team ascending the mountain. The third hovered above the compound and faced west. It was low, no more than one-hundred feet above the large facility.

"Give me your gun!" Logan shouted to Dubs over the wind noise and the engine whine.

"Hell no you psycho!" Dubs yelled back at his commanding officer, grabbing him by the body armor and dragging him up toward Blue.

"Five minutes out," a cracking, nondescript voice said into their headpiece. The voice was that of a god, a savior cutting through the wind to save them all.

"We've got three hostile aircraft on location," Sol said, breathing heavily as he led his men in an all-out sprint through the rocky terrain, focusing solely on the small section carved out of the ridgeline where the elevation was a few hundred yards below the rest.

"Copy," the pilot said calmly.

A moment later, strobing lights and sulfuric booms erupted in the valley; the sensory rich tag-team birthed a hellish storm, promising death and pain delivered by the attack helos. The leaded rain shattered rocks, creating finite plumes of dust and debris that the SEALs ignored as they continued their slithering, coordinated ascent; but Alex needed to be carried.

Solomon grabbed the broken man and hoisted him over his shoulder. Alex grunted and howled, but Solomon didn't listen. He scaled over boulders, crawled over the loose gravel, and scratched his way up the mountainside. Soon Sol couldn't feel his own legs, but he ignored it. Flying debris and dust blinded him and filled his lungs, making the ascent even more debilitating, but he was focused on his objective: get Alex Pines to safety.

Finally, Dubs and Logan reached Blue. "Paint it," Blue said calmly, and handed the laser to a panting Logan who spat onto the ground, because it was too difficult to swallow.

Blue steadied himself prone, ranging quickly and aiming at the lonely chopper as it hovered ominously over the facility. Blue knew the range from Logan's spotting earlier. He focused his rifle into the cockpit of the helo, finding the pilot. He took two long, slow breaths, trusting his teammates, his friends, would be invincible for a few more seconds.

Boom! His shot rang out and struck the helo, crashing through glass, missing the pilot. The front of the helo tipped skyward aggressively, and it began to reel backward. The pilot, stunned at the proximity to death, tried to steady the aircraft in the thin air. He was moving quickly toward the eastern ridgeline.

In an instant, the storm of lead and light ceased as a second helo reacted to its erratic partner. The group of two other helos split to avoid a crash, one going north and the other south. Finally, Blue watched as his target gained control and began rotating the aircraft toward the south, while he strafed sideways back to the compound.

"Sit still Blue," Sol said, the momentary reprieve was all they needed to scale the last hundred yards in the open toward the ridgeline.

"Copy," Blue said and sunk down behind the large rocky debris they used as a hide. Dubs hid with him, while Logan was forced to remain the most exposed, his sweaty hands holding the laser.

Logan heard a rumbling echo enter the valley like a large tidal wave. His heart leapt from his chest and his eyes grew wide. Again, he heard the crackle of twin jet engines blistering the sky. He wanted to scream, he wanted to jump out of his hide and celebrate, but he held himself in check; this time.

Overhead, a scream emitted, but it wasn't human, it was the atmosphere, as metal ripped through it, a tail of fire and a hand of death screamed forward into the valley.

Boom! The strafing helo disintegrated in a ball of fire, which slowly rained down onto the roof of the compound. The remaining two helos had been circling back toward the eastern ridgeline, but seeing their comrade explode caused them to panic. They both turned away, one continuing westward in an attempt to get around the mountain peaks to the north, and the other dove, nearly kissing the rocky surface in the valley as it worked its way south toward where the missile came.

Whoosh, whoosh! Two more air-to-air missiles pierced

the darkness, striking true, and sending the trio of helicopters to their rocky ends.

Two FA-18s screamed over the valley, banking hard east, their glow like angels' halos lighting up the night sky.

"Coming around from the south," the pilot said as the men on the ground listened to the rumbling thunder from the engines while the loose rocks quaked in fear.

"Copy," Solomon said, his men safe and laying low on the far side of the ridgeline, waiting for the fireworks. His eyes squinted even in the dark as he searched for the last three men who were grouped in the mountains of the southern ridge. His chest was rising and falling, straining for more air to exchange. His hands were numb and tingling and his head was pounding.

"Inbound, bearing 010. Target acquired," the pilot said as the rumbling became quiet for the moment.

The two FA-18s shot quickly over Logan, Dubs and Blue; a moment later the rumble of their energy shot down into the valley, but only after they disappeared once again into the night. In their wake, four GBU-28 Bunker Busters silently dove toward the earth, like white beasts descending into a deep, dark sea. All twenty men watched them fall, mesmerized by their parabolic curve; mute, expressionless, accurate.

The ordnance pierced the compound but a dramatic hesitation preceded the detonation. Each round penetrated deep into the structure reaching its bottom level before creating its thunderous blast. The SEAL team had seen it before, but Logan was learning on the job. He remained frozen, still pointing the laser guidance at the structure as he witnessed the compound first expand upward into the air as if the structure gasped in horror, then the first and second bombs detonated. The ground beneath him quaked, the large rock formation shuddered, and the three men backed away. Logan removed the optics from his face and saw with his own eyes the explosions from the third and fourth bomb. The structure collapsed instantly, burying itself deep inside the blast, a cloud of dust and debris shrouded the once proud structure.

Alex cried; it was really happening.

"Exfil at Bravo," Solomon said as he gathered the two squads on him.

"Copy," Blue said, gathering his gear as he slung his long-range deathmaker over his shoulder, opting for his M4 during the trek toward Bravo.

Bravo was twenty kilometers away and at a much lower altitude. Logan and Dubs did all they could to keep up with the silent Blue as he led them up over the ridgeline, down into the valley, and through the mountain pass moving from cover to cover. The light of the morning was promising a low probability of staying hidden, so they moved quickly. Logan suffered the most, but seven-thousand feet of elevation was a welcomed relief from ten. Within an hour, the three-man team caught up with the two other squads.

Alex Pines was incapable of walking. Every ten to twenty minutes the squads would exchange him from shoulder to shoulder, sharing the load. Each time the exchange was made, Alex woke, grunted, and prayed to God he'd make it out. Flashes of his father, his bike, his squad leader, his mother came to him.

"I got 'em," Blue said as the last three finally folded themselves back into the group. Blue placed Alex gently onto his shoulder and began weaving through cover as the squads worked their way deep into a canyon between two large mountains.

The sun began to rise, but the sheer cliffs to the east and west promised little direct light onto the men below, a critical reason for Solomon's choice of exfil locations. It was a much further trek, double the distance, but it promised a safer exit.

It was nearly 0900 when Solomon made the call. "Gatekeeper this is Halo, over."

"We got ya' Halo,"

"Two klicks out. Bravo."

"Copy. ETA ninety minutes. See ya' soon, Halo."

They arrived at Bravo in seventy minutes and set up a perimeter. It was quiet, which allowed Solomon to reflect. He thought about his wife and the idea of not coming home to her. "Don't you die on me," was always the last thing she wrote to him while he was gone, along with "XOXO."

"Logan on me," Solomon said softly into the comms.

It took a few minutes, but Logan presented himself in front of the officer as they hid between rocks.

"You left Blue and you made us all vulnerable." He grabbed Logan by his BDUs forcefully at the collar with both hands, shaking him once to reveal his true strength, and possible intentions.

"There's things you don't know," Logan responded unfazed.

"What I do know is, if you'd done your damn job, we wouldn't have been scattered up that mountainside with lead comin' up our asses."

Crack! Out of nowhere a fist landed on flesh. The sound of bone meeting bone ripped through the group of men. They all heard it and turned to see its cause.

Solomon stood from his hide, grabbing another large man. Dubs had heard Solomon's request for Logan, and he watched from afar. When he saw Solomon grab Logan he reacted. Soon, the two massive men were wrangling with each other. Dubs had struck first, splitting Solomon's cheek. Soon Solomon had the upper hand as he drove Dubs backward gaining momentum and throwing him down onto the ground. He landed on top of the Marine, and dropped several massive blows down on to Dubs. On the fourth swing,

Dubs grasped Solomon's arm and used its momentum to spin him to the ground, and the two men switched places. Two punches landed hard onto Solomon's face before Blue and Whiplash wrangled Dubs from on top and restrained him. Several of the other SEALs aided by keeping Solomon from re-engaging.

Logan stood shocked. He'd never imagined anyone being able to take a blow from Dubs, let alone three. Even Dubs refused to fight his restraints. He knew he'd met a monster and was lucky he struck first.

"Halo this is Seahawk One," a voice shattered the tension.

"Copy, Seahawk One," Solomon said, looking at his men and nodding.

"Five minutes out."

"Poppin' smoke," Solomon said, gesturing to Lucky who immediately threw a white smoke grenade fifty yards to the east.

"You alright?" Whiplash asked Dubs.

"I'm good," he said, feeling guilty. "Can you let me go now?"

The SEALs lifted their restraints and Dubs walked toward Solomon. A wall of flesh immediately formed between the two tall men.

"I'm sorry," Dubs said over the SEALs toward the commanding officer on the other side of the fence.

"You two need to get your shit together," Solomon responded.

"He saw someone we've been looking for. Amir Qasmi. A terrorist we caught in Saint Louis. He escaped when we brought down General Jenkins."

"No shit?" Solomon said, remembering the news and the aftermath from Jenkins being found dead in DuPont Circle. "You still compromised my men," Solomon said to Logan as the sound of propellers began to sporadically echo into the valley.

"Yes, sir," he said, embarrassed about the situation.

"You've gotta get your emotions in check. Debrief me on Amir. I wanna know what made you chase that son-of-a-bitch. I know it's been a while, so let me clue you in on something. We had eyes in the sky. We can track him, boy," Solomon said, smiling.

"For starters he shot me right here," Dubs said, interrupting and held up his shirt showing the entrance wound from the high-caliber rifle. He turned to reveal the slightly larger exit scar.

"So, you want him too?" Solomon said, smirking.

"He's a traitorous bastard. An Army sergeant turned terrorist."

"Logan?" Alex Pines almost whispered the name. It felt as though razors were crawling through his throat toward his lips. Everyone went silent as the pilot spoke. The props from the helo were gaining strength and it was hard to hear the lieutenant struggling to speak.

"Yeah?" Logan responded, looking toward Dubs.

Alex gestured with his right hand for Logan to come close. His strength was quickly fading and he allowed his head to fall back to the ground as Logan quickly responded to the request.

"I don't understand," Alex said, squeezing his eyes shut as he tried to swallow through the pain.

"What?" Logan asked, leaning in toward Alex.

"Amir. He told me he had a message for you."

Logan couldn't think, almost couldn't hear as one of the helos finally came down to the ground, a second staying airborne, providing support.

"Amir asked me to tell you everything. He saved my life." Alex said before passing out.

Chapter 26
WE LET YOU WIN

Gulf of Aden

The hours rolled by slowly as Logan anxiously sat next to Alex in the bowels of the massive supercarrier. The pilot had passed out for a second time shortly after being airborne in the helo. The weeks of torture had melted away in the familiar feeling of flight, allowing Alex to finally relax. But Logan was far from a release. In fact, he hadn't been this anxious since Saint Louis. He had seen Amir, his limp, hobbling into darkness while the enemy choppers and friendly air strike came in and blanketed the area in a bright orange glow, leaving dust, debris, and smoke. The conclusion of the assault left it impossible for Logan to see Amir, allowing his personal vendetta to slip away. But, Alex allowed him a sliver of hope; Amir had a message.

Alex stirred and Logan jumped on the opportunity.

"Lieutenant Pines," Logan said, projecting his voice

firmly. "Reflex," Logan tried calling for the pilot again.

"Yeah," he responded, not opening his eyes. His voice was as rough as unfinished concrete.

"You want some water?"

"Yeah," Alex whispered and worked hard to sit up, but his left arm was still useless. Logan helped him, as Alex winced in pain.

"You said something about a message for me from Amir."

"Yeah," Alex responded with a scowl. "He told me . . . shit." His head was pounding as he paused in thought. It was difficult for him to recall the specifics of the message.

"Just take a minute, Alex."

Alex gripped the water and took a few short sips. He found the strength to open his eyes and scanned the small, steel room, his gaze resting on Logan.

"How'd he know I was coming?" Logan asked, realizing for the first time that was likely more important than the message itself.

"He said he was supposed to kill you. You were his prize for loyalty."

"What the hell's that supposed to mean?"

"I don't know."

"What else did he say?"

Alex stared at his cup and recalled the events in the darkness. He remembered the flashes from a firearm and the ringing that followed, as his ears screamed for mercy. The concrete walls echoed the successive shots as his savior sent hot projectiles into warm bodies.

"I still don't understand everything," Alex said.

"Spit it out Lieutenant."

"Amir beat the shit out of me. He lost it a couple weeks ago when I didn't break under questioning. Then this older man came in a few days ago. Well dressed. It was obvious he was in charge." Alex paused, thinking of his own dead father, and his murderer.

"What next?"

"He brought in the man that killed my father."

"What?"

"Exactly. How the hell did he know about me? About the drunk who hit my dad? How did he get him here?"

Logan sat waiting. He knew why the man was brought. It was another technique to get Alex to open up. One crack in the armor and everything spills out.

"Did you kill him?" Logan finally asked after several minutes.

"No. Amir did it for me."

As Alex sat reflecting, Logan put the pieces together. Amir wanted to right the wrong, to build trust with Alex. Amir was smart. It seemed he understood Alex would have broken if he himself pulled the trigger. His morality would crumble, his strength soon after, and when that happened, his service to his country, and all the reasons to stay silent would evaporate.

"What happened last night?" Logan said, getting the man back on track. "What did he say about me?"

"He's a ghost. A freakish killing machine, Logan. I swear to God I've never heard of anything like what I saw." Logan's hair stood on end but he presented no noticeable response.

"Alex, you're on the carrier now. Very safe. You'll be transported to Landstuhl Regional Medical Center in Germany for rehab."

"There was another man with Amir all the time. I don't know his name. They never told me names. I only know Amir's because he told me after he said he had the message for you.

"Amir's partner came to my cell. He pulled out a gun

and told me it was time. They heard the blast upstairs from your breach. Amir came from nowhere and tackled his partner knocking the gun from his hand. My heart felt like it stopped beating as I cheered for Amir. I feel sick thinking like that," Alex said, rubbing his left arm.

"Keep going Alex."

"Guards came running toward the cell too. At least six at first. Amir raised his sidearm and shot at them. The first four went down quickly. They didn't expect him to shoot. Amir leapt over his partner, grasped him by the shirt, and picked him up. He held the shorter man close in front, like a human shield. He charged down the hallway, half lifting, half dragging the man forward as he shot repeatedly into the busy hallway. Shortly after that, everything went black."

"Went black?"

"Lights out. Amir must have tripped the breaker. But I still heard shots, saw the flash of a gun. It lit up the entire hallway at times. He seemed to be everywhere at the same time. After about two minutes, he was back at my cell with his partner. He hit the man with his handgun, knocking him to the ground. He knelt over the man, and looked into my cell. 'I'm an American too,' he said to me. 'I'm Amir Qasmi. Find Logan Falcone and tell him I helped you,' he said and shot his partner in the face right in front of me." Alex paused and reached toward his head.

"I can still hear the ringing in my ears. Then he said, 'tell Logan he's the only one I'll trust. Tell him they know everything. About the Candyman, about the spec ops anti-terrorist unit, about Migs.' He said he knew you'd be there." Alex paused again, stared at the wall. "What the hell's going on?"

"Get some rest, Alex. You did great," Logan responded. He wasn't sure how to answer the question. Logan had no idea what to do next.

He left the room as Alex reclined in his bed. Logan felt empty. The pieces were there, the message delivered, but he was confused. As he walked, the pit in his stomach grew into a chasm. He ached as his mind searched for an answer, but frustration quickly set in. He had no answers, no one to interrogate, no stone to turn. It was a dead end. Logan thought of his newfound reason to live and he desperately wanted to be home, but the muffled sounds of his rubber boots on the steel steps reminded him he was thousands of miles away.

Charleston, South Carolina

President Pierce sat alone after the final debate before the election. Both men had been respectful, allowing the other to speak, neither one advancing their cause to any significant degree. The debate was a stalemate, neither side gaining traction in the polls, the election effectively decided weeks earlier after the incident in Pittsburgh. Pierce stared at the numbers Grant gave him just ten minutes earlier. Pierce looked at his phone, 0120, and knew Waxman was likely up and looking at the latest polls as well. He called his competitor.

"Mr. President," Waxman said playfully into the phone. "Great debate tonight. Unfortunately for you, the numbers are still trending in my favor."

Pierce could hear the man smiling through the phone, but he didn't mind.

"Precisely why I'm calling. I'd like to discuss a few things with you if that's okay."

"Sure," Waxman said confused. "Now?"

"It'd be best."

"Where and when?"

"My hotel suite. ASAP."

It took thirty minutes, but the two most powerful men in Charleston were sitting in a hotel suite at the Francis Marion Hotel in t-shirts and jeans. The room was cleared, allowing the men to be alone for their discussion. Secret service men stood in the hall, a few in an adjoining room, and outside the hotel were dozens more from both politicians.

"You want something to drink?" Pierce said, smirking.

"I'm good for now thanks," Waxman said, holding up a half empty bottle of water.

"This shouldn't take long, but I needed you to be in the know."

"Shoot," Waxman said, leaning back into the soft, low back chair. It was uncomfortable, his wide heavy shoulders weren't supported and he fought to find a comfortable position.

"We had a successful attack on a terrorist compound in Yemen. Got our pilot back alive." He paused for a moment, collecting the thoughts he had wrestled with for the two days preceding the debate.

"That's excellent! You worried about a retaliation?"

"Yes," Pierce said softly and sighed heavily, adjusting his sitting position, even though his discomfort came from nervousness. His chess game with the terrorists had placed him precipitously close to checkmate.

"We've recently struck an agreement with an engineering firm, one that's developed a new form of computing. They can decipher and intercept data exponentially faster than anything we've got. It's called Medusa."

"Why are you telling me this?"

"Because everything it's predicted has happened. The firm didn't know it at the time, and we hadn't learned of its existence until recently, but they were scanning the dark web for questionable activities. They had every recent terrorism plot in their raw data. We, fortunately, had actionable intel which allowed us to stop it anyways, but now, our sources are drying up and Logan told us we hit a dead end with the compound."

"I don't understand how destroying a compound becomes a dead end."

"Nobody to interrogate. They were all killed."

"Well maybe our boys were a little overzealous. Can't blame them though, can you?"

"No." Pierce paused and reached into his pocket pulling out his handwritten notes from his debrief with Secretary Smith and General Anderson. "When the strike team moved into the lowest level they met no hostile forces. Instead, several recently deceased bodies were present. There were no lights, the power had been shut down."

"What the hell?"

"I'll tell you what the hell. Remember Amir Qasmi?"

"That's the second time you brought him up in recent weeks." Waxman recalled the meeting in the Oval Office where Pierce attempted to convince him to reduce the number of public appearances due to information coming in.

"Lieutenant Alex Pines had a message for Logan. Apparently, it was Amir Qasmi who killed a dozen trained terrorists, including what Alex referred to as Amir's partner. He also told Alex he needed to talk to Logan. The message said intel has been leaking out from the terrorist group in order to keep us distracted."

"So, they're allowing us to find their own?" Senator Waxman asked confused, his hands frozen, fingers locked together on his lap.

"Seemingly so."

"But why?"

"To hide a larger plot. Keep us busy while they sneak in

the back."

"Son-of-a-bitch," Waxman said through a long sigh and looked around the room.

"I think they're gonna attack when we're in a position of weakness. An election. The whole country is focused on what we're doing and let's face it, we're not exactly putting in the work right now. We're focused on the future."

"What do you want me to do? Why tell me all this?"

"So we're both prepared to fight back when the time comes. It may be now, it may be next week, it might be election day, or it could be after you take your place as Commander-in-Chief."

"This is heavy Mr. President."

"I agree. But we need to be ready either way."

"Mr. President," a secret service member said, entering the room. "Secretary Smith is here to see you."

President Pierce looked toward Waxman who stared blankly back, meeting his gaze with inquisition.

"Send him in."

"Mr. President," Smith said as both President Pierce and Senator Waxman stood to greet him. "Senator Waxman."

"He can stay Doyle," Pierce said, gesturing toward a third chair in the room. "I've filled him in on the debrief already."

Secretary Smith walked toward the chair and dragged it toward the two presidential candidates. "We've got some activity from Medusa, and it's not good."

Chapter 27
CHESS

Washington, D.C.

It was a quick trip home for Logan. Samantha hadn't answered the phone when he called from the airport, but it was only 0430 and hopefully she was sound asleep. He saw her car in the driveway as he pulled up to the house. He smiled as he walked toward the front door, thoughts of feeling the baby move inside her made his heart begin to quicken. Logan hadn't thought of names, but if it was a boy, he'd like to name him Sherman, if it was okay with her. For a girl, he didn't care. He just wanted a healthy baby.

The air was cool as he walked quickly up the sidewalk, his moist breath led the way, billowing upward toward morning sky and disappearing. He buried his hands deep into his coat pockets and hopped up the two steps, stopping at the front door. He sighed in the darkness, trying to control his anxiety. It was the first time he could remember feeling a nervousness associated with happiness, with joy, with responsibilities. He pulled the keys from his pocket and reached for the lock.

His insides burned. *Oh please God no*, he thought as all happiness crumbled and crashed like a pane of glass. He hadn't seen the broken door until he reached with his keys. The excitement blinded him, the man who always saw the subtleties, the nuances, the changes. A heavy footprint was left on the door; the lock useless as the wood splintered around it. Logan reached for his gun and raised it toward his chest as he breached his own home.

Logan left the lights off as he silently cleared the house. He could hear his own rapid breathing, his own pulse racing in his ears, as a drum beat in his chest. His blood felt like ice water when he entered the kitchen and saw streaks of red on the floor, the countertops, and a knife shimmering in what little light there was in the room, hinting at a battle.

He walked toward the bedroom and saw a clip from a gun on the floor. He grasped it, ejected four 9mm rounds, noting it was a clip that should have carried fifteen. A few feet away, lay the gun. He quickly turned left and entered their bedroom. The sheets were clean, but the wall was painted in blood. On the floor, a large, red stain just in front of their dresser; but no body.

Logan sat on the bed and closed his eyes, trying to piece the events together. He steadied his breathing, focusing on the evidence, trying his best not to think about Samantha and the baby. He couldn't. He kept seeing Samantha smiling as he felt the baby moving inside her the same day he left. *Where were they? Were they safe? Who can find them? I can find them. I can do this. Help me do this!*

He imagined Samantha had been in bed when the intruders entered the home. The blanket and sheets were a tangled mess; *she always made the bed*. He knew Samantha slept with her sidearm when he went out of town, and whoever entered the house wouldn't expect her to come up firing. She was a light sleeper, and always woke up fully alert. Samantha must have known whoever was standing there wasn't him.

He opened his eyes and looked toward the left side of the door, opposite the bloodstains. There he saw a scorch mark on the wood. *She used the doorway for cover.* He saw six shells on the floor just inside the room. Quickly he hopped off the bed and squatted where she had. Logan took a deep breath, her scent still lingered.

How did they stop her? He peered down the hallway, noting several fractures in the drywall and the splintered wood in the crown molding. He counted five, which meant she landed at least one shot. He went back to the right side of the bed where she slept, counting three shells. *Two more to find.* He walked back toward the doorway and looked left. Two shots were fired erratically, shredding the drywall above, the shells ejected down the hallway to the right. *Eleven,* he thought, accounting for all the rounds she fired.

He walked left out of the bedroom toward the rear of the home. The sliding glass door had been left open from the invaders. He hadn't felt the cool air entering the house until then, adrenaline made him numb to the sensations. A small pile of fallen leaves had begun to build up just inside the glass door, several leaves even venturing further into the home. *At least two more men,* he thought.

He walked his way back to the kitchen. *She's a fighter* he thought, as he saw even more blood. The knife was her weapon of choice after she broke free of their grasp. In the corner of the kitchen, between the sink and the stove, was where she made her final stand. Arterial blood spattered the cabinets, the stainless stove, and the floor below. An arc of red surrounded the corner where she crouched, swiping the blade in any direction she could, striking true more than once. Streaks of blood showed the direction they dragged her once she was subdued. *The front door.*

He ran back to the front door. On the door was another knife, but not one he had in his kitchen. It was curved with a wooden handle, its metal tarnished and pitted from years of use. A working man's blade. It pinned a handwritten letter to the rustic wood door: "You took my sons, I'll take yours. You will exchange your life for theirs. Nobody knows about this, Logan Falcone. You come alone, or Samantha, and the life she holds inside, will die. Walk outside and get in the car."

Logan had no fight left in him, no other way out. He was cornered. He walked out of the home and watched a dark Mercedes G-wagon slowly pull into the driveway, the rear driver's side door opened in anticipation. Logan quickly reached into his pocket, slid his cellphone out, and dropped it into the plants in the front of his house. He knelt, pretending to tie his shoe, and buried the device as well as he could. It was still dark outside in the early morning hours, but Logan knew whoever was in the SUV was well trained, and they were watching him closely.

As he walked, he realized it would be the last time he'd see his house, his street. He'd never smell the air in the spring when the cherry trees blossomed, or feel the humid summer air as his clothes stuck to his skin. He looked toward a tree they planted in the front yard the weekend after they moved in. "We'll watch it grow as we gracefully age, but we'll be together," Samantha joked that sunny afternoon before he kissed her. Logan reflected on the moment he felt his baby move. The only interaction he would ever have.

"Give us your phone and your weapons," a man from inside the Mercedes told Logan as he reached the vehicle.

"I don't have anything on me," Logan said, stretching his arms out toward the side. A second man sprung out of the passenger side and searched Logan. The man nodded reassuring the driver Logan wasn't lying.

"We'll find the phone," the man said, rolling up the window and drove away.

Chapter 28

A NEW SEARCH

Washington, D.C.

It had been several days since they'd returned from Yemen, and Dubs hadn't heard from Logan, so he went to their house. As soon as he saw the front door, he called Secretary Smith. Dubs hadn't moved since hanging up the phone hours earlier, he stood, fixed, a soldier on watch. The FBI agents inside felt the pressure to do things right. After all, one of their own, Samantha, was also missing.

Dubs desperately needed to know what happened, but he wasn't the problem solver in their group. That was Logan, the man who could read people, a soldier who could recreate events as they happened just by observing the evidence. Dubs was a man of action, and without something to do, he was quickly becoming overwhelmed with anxiety. He stood in the rain, praying for someone to lash out at, for an enemy to hunt. Dubs' phone began to vibrate in his pocket sending a surge of electricity through his soul; an answered prayer perhaps?

"Mr. Secretary," Dubs said as the rain fell hard onto his cold hand.

"Any news?"

"None yet. They're still inside."

"Are you just standing in the rain?" Secretary Smith asked, hearing the white noise of the rain hitting leaves.

"Yes, sir."

"It's forty degrees out Dubs. At least get your ass in the truck."

"I'll be fine. Any news on Amir?"

"Satellite images tracked him into Sana'a, Yemen. Lost him in the city. You're positive it was Amir?"

"Has Logan ever been wrong?"

"No. Never."

"Have we heard anything from your tech guy? Any intel on Logan?" Dubs asked, holding his breath. A chill ripped through his bones, but he wasn't sure if it was the rain or the emotion.

"Nothing."

"Mr. Secretary, Lonnie just got here. I'll call you when I hear something."

Dubs hung up the phone and clenched his hands together firmly, his body quaking in the effort to thaw his frozen joints. He walked toward Lonnie's sedan, which was parked at the end of a long line of government vehicles on the street.

"You good?" Lonnie asked when Dubs climbed into the passenger seat.

"I'll live."

"What they know?"

"Nothin'. Someone called in gunshots a few nights ago, but the cops that responded reported no suspicious activity."

"Dubs," Lonnie said, staring at his friend. "You know he's not dead. He's not going out like this."

"I just need to know who to kill for this."

"I'm with ya' brotha'," Lonnie said, holding out a hand for Dubs to shake.

Secretary Smith sat in his office, his mind focused on finding Logan, the man who single handedly saved thousands of lives over the past year. None of the secret team thought themselves vulnerable, but looking back, they questioned that. Logan had already been attacked in what seemed to be a set up while they were in Highland Park, just a few short weeks earlier. Doyle felt responsible for the oversight, and now, vowed he wouldn't sleep until they heard news regarding Logan—good or bad.

Logan was still on the carrier the last time Doyle had spoken to him, but the conversation was unnerving. The news had been heavy, knowing their team had been fed intel to keep them distracted from the true plot. At first, Doyle hadn't put a tremendous weight into the words, knowing they were coming from a pilot that had been a captive and tortured for weeks. He also didn't trust the source, Amir Qasmi. Even the thought of the terrorist that escaped made the secretary grind his teeth. However, now that Logan was missing, it seemed anything was possible all at once.

Doyle had many sleepless night since they began tracking who they thought was Amir through the mountains, ultimately losing him in Sana'a. He was angry, frustrated, knowing they'd been close to capturing their biggest mark. Logan would've been happy too, he needed the closure.

David! Secretary Smith thought as he simultaneously reached for his secure line. Quickly, he dialed the numbers he wrote on his desk the day David called from a satellite phone.

"Mr. Secretary," David said into the phone from a bustling, noisy street.

"David. Where are you in country?" Doyle responded, skipping the pleasantries.

"Sana'a."

Doyle nearly screamed for joy. It was serendipitous, a blessing from God that his best asset was in the city they had tracked Amir into.

"Perfect. We've tracked someone we believe is Amir Qasmi, the American-born terrorist responsible for Paris and Chicago, and he's somewhere in the city."

"Want him stateside?"

"Absolutely. And question him. Logan went missing a few days ago. Nobody has any info, but when we grabbed Alex Pines, he had a message from Amir to Logan."

"He wants to talk?"

"He did talk. Said we're chasing our tails so to speak. He said they're feeding us the wrong intel so we look one way as they plot something more grand."

"Same shit I've been hearing," David said.

"Exactly."

"Finally, someone with potential answers. I'll get it out of him."

"I know you will."

Chapter 29
THE EXCHANGE

The mountains would have been beautiful, but Logan had been unconscious for hours as the atmosphere bent the setting sun's rays into a kaleidoscope of colors. The valleys below were getting dark, but the peaks above were on fire. The small aircraft was beginning its final descent toward a nondescript airfield in a large, flat valley within the Haraz Mountains.

"Wake up," a man said as he kicked Logan firmly in the side as he massaged his hands. The enemy's hands were swollen and sore from beating Logan sporadically throughout the flight.

Logan stirred to life, awoken from his dream state where he was home, comfortable, with his wife. As reality began to seep in, his head began to throb. He tried to lift himself off the carpeted fuselage, when he became lightheaded, almost collapsing back to the blood-soaked floor. His anger grew as the events from earlier in the flight began to play themselves over in his head.

Three men had taken turns hitting Logan, while his hands

were tied behind his back. Each man tried to knock him from his seat with a single punch. It was a game they were playing. They had no questions for Logan, no statements, no news of his wife. It was painfully clear to Logan he may no longer be invincible, and for the first time in a long time, he was scared.

"Get in the chair," a man said, a thick, indiscriminate accent slurring the words; or perhaps it was Logan's head that made it hard to comprehend. He did as he was told, climbing into the tan, leather chair of the executive aircraft. Logan's hands were numb as he pinched them forcefully, trying to elicit a response. They were cold, he could sense that through his lower back as they pressed themselves against his skin when he sat in the chair. He took several breaths, tried to clear his head, trying to focus on the best plan of action when he met this mysterious man—a man who knew where his home was, a man who blamed him for the death of his son, a man who had limitless funding and resources.

As the wheels hit the tarmac, Logan looked out his window. He saw a hangar. The door was wide open and inside he saw four SU-35s parked nose forward, almost watching their plane decelerate and turn toward a second, larger hangar. As they wheeled inside, the engine noise reverberated off the walls, an anxious whine from the engines, knowing their work was almost complete. Inside this second hangar were dozens of helicopters, drones of various sizes, and a second private jet.

ND431DB, ND431DB, ND431DB Logan said over and over again in his head. He was trying to memorize the tail number of the second jet in the hangar; in case he made it out alive.

"Goodbye, Logan Falcone," a guard said as he climbed onto the plane. He was average build, nothing memorable, except for the sack he had in his hands. He quickly threw it over Logan's head. The men picked him up by his numb arms. Logan's shoulders screamed out for mercy, but he didn't make a sound. They carried him down the stairs, his arms bent behind awkwardly as they threw him into the open back of a cargo truck.

The engine rumbled, a diesel, Logan could smell the gas and hear the low idling RPMs. They began bouncing out of the hangar and into the open air. Logan worked his hands around his hips, behind his legs, then under his feet. Finally, his hands were in front of him and a rushing warm sensation cascaded down his arms and into his hands, bringing life to his extremities. He didn't mind the wet bag on his head. The cool, moist sack was almost soothing on his wounds, but soon, the bag began to collect dust, making it hard to breathe. He reached up with his hands, lifted the sack slightly, and saw a rifle striking down onto his face.

"Mr. Falcone," Karim said from across a stainless-steel table. "Mr. Falcone!" he said a second time, more forcefully than the first. Karim looked toward the guards, upset with Logan's current state. He was bloodied, his face swollen beyond recognition, eyes seemingly unable to open. But worse, he was severely concussed, and unable to wake despite being carried from the truck, slammed down into a steel chair and not even reacting to his own name.

Karim reached into his pocket, pulled out a small packet, and ripped the top off. He walked around the table, carefully avoiding the drops of blood that had fallen from Logan onto the floor. Gently, Karim took the packet and placed it just under Logan's nose. It took three inhalations, but Logan's head finally snapped upward and he scanned the room.

Logan squinted in the bright light, his head throbbing

in the rhythm of his heart rate. It was impossible to hide his current state of discomfort. He winced. The multiple assaults on the plane had made it difficult for him to stabilize his head. Each movement sent crippling spasms though his neck as he tried to remain in control.

"So, this is Logan Falcone. The American terrorist assassinator," Karim stated condescendingly as he returned to his side of the table, removing his suitcoat and placing it over the back of his chair. His shirt was wrinkled, his tie, undone, and his shoes were scuffed. "You realize Mr. Falcone, you have stepped out of bounds in this game we were playing." Karim bit hard down onto his teeth as he stared at Logan.

"I don't play games Mr.—"

"I ask the questions," Karim said and motioned for a guard to approach. He then gestured for them to remove the table, allowing empty space between the two. "You executed an attack in my compound Mr. Falcone. I was honestly impressed. I'm assuming the intelligence came from Candyman, but I don't care about that. He will pay for his foul as well. In time, you will tell me everything, and he will be next. How ironic that day will be."

Logan stared into Karim, unblinking through thick, swollen, eyes. Capillaries had burst within his eyes, creating a sinister, beastlike gaze. It was unnatural, a Hollywood trick, but one Karim was used to seeing.

"Where is Samantha?"

"Ah, to the point. Remember Mr. Falcone, I ask the questions. What happened to my son? I must know. You understand, as a father."

"Where's my wife?"

"I said I ask the questions!" Karim hollered and slapped his shoe down hard onto the tile, the leather and wooden sole echoing off the floor, piercing everyone's ears. "You realize I know your wife carries a child? Do you know how easy it would have been for me to take yours, like you took mine? I must admit it was a thought I had, to abort the child, to make you suffer as I've suffered. Do you know, in the *Quran* it says the son is punished for the sins of the father, if the son is at all part of the father's sin? But I ask you now Mr. Falcone. Who has paid greater? Me having suffered for my sons' losses? Or *their* deaths because of *my* sins?"

"You said one son was lost."

"I have no sons now. What is the difference?" Karim said, swatting his hand in the sky. "I like to think of your future child having suffered the greater loss. A child without a father, a child knowing a father had been taken captive, tortured, made to live years in confinement in atonement for his sins against another. Maybe that will save your child after all? Or maybe, they will be driven to revenge, and that will perpetuate the sin in your bloodline for generations."

Karim had shown his cards, emotion getting the better of him for the first time in decades. Logan, despite his concussion, his throbbing head, his nausea, knew the next move.

"I won't talk until she is free."

"I said too much," Karim stated, knowing he lost the battle. Karim would never harm the baby, and by default, Samantha would be safe as well. "Bring her in."

An eternity passed, but when the door opened, Samantha stood naked, shamefully covering her untouched body.

"Logan!" she shouted and covered her mouth. It was more a guess, his face had been distorted, bruised, bloodied.

"I love you," he said, emotionless.

"Stay alive. Don't you give up on us," she said sternly,

defiantly, as she grabbed her belly and stared at him.

"November. Delta. 4. 3. 1. Delta. Bravo." Logan said to his wife.

"What is this?" Karim said and motioned for them to close the door.

Logan regretted the moment. It was the last time he'd see her. At least told her he loved her.

"She'll go to the Embassy. From there, the Americans can send her home. Out of my hands," he said, wiping his hands together.

"I didn't kill your son. I was never in the compound."

"Who was?"

"Special ops. They secured the building and we blew it to hell."

"Who ordered the assault? Where did the intel come from?"

"No idea."

"Lies!" Karim said involuntarily reaching out and striking Logan before he could stop himself. Confused at his outward emotion, he sat back into the chair.

"How do you know we killed your son?"

"He was there. Holding the pilot, talking with him."

Logan had Karim. He answered a question. The momentum was shifting.

"Who else was there?"

"Your friend," Karim said, smiling, beginning to laugh.

"My friend?" Logan asked, already knowing the answer.

"Amir Qasmi, but he's gone as well."

"How do you know?"

"We found his body with my son, Taj. He was smashed in the explosion, but my son had a gunshot wound as well. Amir never left Taj's side." Karim said proudly, trying to build the moment in his mind, to imagine those fleeting seconds before their death, embraced as brothers. Logan knew the truth.

"I watched the bombs drop. I painted the target. I blew up your murderous sons, adopted or not. I laughed while the building crashed down around them. I screamed for joy when your helos erupted in balls of fire. I killed so many of your terrorists in the U.S. it's uncountable." Logan sat proudly in his chair, smirking, his swollen cheeks pressing up toward his bruised eyes, almost forcing them closed. He watched Karim, studied his reaction, saw his rage grow inside.

Karim leapt from the chair sending it bouncing off the tile behind him. In a fraction of a second his hands were around Logan's neck, thumbs pressing hard into his trachea. For the first time the hands that signed orders, hands that dictated dirty deeds, were now dirtying themselves.

"I could end you right now!" Karim said with wide, rage-filled eyes as he let emotion take control. He wanted revenge, respect, control. "You know nothing of the plans I have Falcone! Nothing!" he screamed as he nearly stood on top of the American hero.

Logan lost consciousness, his lifeless body fell toward the floor. Karim wasn't strong enough to support the weight, and allowed Logan to fall to the ground. Logan's body brought itself back to life, as time and time again his chest exploded in deep, desperate breaths.

In that moment, Karim realized emotion had won the day. He left the room, quickly exited the facility, and drove to his secret home in the mountains to recover, to gain control, to plot with a clear head.

Chapter 30
WORLD SERIES

Pittsburgh, Pennsylvania

Rami sat in his car at a shopping mall. He preferred using public wi-fi when checking his emails, especially lately. The entire country was paranoid after the event weeks earlier that left him a hero, at least for a moment. After his interview, people were even more polarized, and he was quickly forgotten. It was never his job to be a hero of the people. He was supposed to be an ordinary man, a leader in the Islamic community, someone to be trusted. His email finally opened, revealing a message he'd been waiting for. It was a picture of his wife, Dinah, her beautiful smile, her skin, the beautiful dress she wore on their wedding day.

He smiled as his heart ached to be back in that moment. It had already been three years since their souls were made one in the eyes of *Allah*, but it felt so recent. He thought of the past three years, how he was placed on SWAT, how he received his sharpshooter appointment, how they moved to a house, his new car, and now a baby on the way. So much can happen in such a short time. It made him nervous for Dinah and the baby.

Just the day before, Rami had been notified he would be a sharpshooter during the Pittsburgh Pirates game as they hosted the Chicago White Sox for game one of the World Series. The city was already a powder keg, and the FBI warned that terrorist threats were imminent, but they didn't know where or when. Rami wasn't going to be the only sniper, the FBI would undoubtedly have several, especially because Senator Waxman was throwing out the first pitch. He was a Sox fan, which could make the crowd even more unruly.

Rami started his car and pulled away, the rumbling from the engine made his heart quicken, the excitement of five-hundred horsepower gurgling through his pipes always made him happy. He needed the pick-me-up, because he would be having a very uncomfortable discussion when he got home.

Dinah was balled up on the couch watching television when Rami came through the door. She grunted but forced a smile as she sat up, his long shirt sliding upward from below her knees.

"Hey baby," he said, going to her and sitting, stroking dark hair from her face. "You still feeling terrible?"

"Understatement of the year," she responded. Her face was pale, her light brown eyes wrapped in dark haloes.

"We need to talk."

"Okay?" she said, pulling back and looking at her large husband.

"I need you to go to your parent's house."

"What are you talking about Rami? I can't even get off the couch!"

Rami paused, looking at the floor as if it were a crib sheet with the answers he desperately needed. "There might be an attack here tomorrow."

"What!" she said, grabbing her mouth with both hands, her eyes filling with tears. "We need to tell everyone!" she grabbed the phone and began to dial the mosque.

"No!" Rami said, taking the phone from her gently. "We can stop it Dinah, but in case we don't, I need to know you're safe."

"You'll keep me safe Rami. You're a hero, and you're all mine," she said, reaching around his waist and leaning in awkwardly to bring him close. The word hero felt like rot in his soul. He desperately wanted to rid himself of the association.

"Baby, listen to me. I'm not going to be here tomorrow. I'll be at the game."

"The Pirates' game?"

"Yeah. Waxman's throwing out the first pitch. They're worried someone's gonna do something stupid."

"Everyone likes him. Why would someone want to hurt him?"

Rami paused, frustrated. His wife would never understand. He grasped her by the shoulders gently and looked into her eyes. He loved her eyes. It was what drew him in five years earlier. They were almost golden, a shade of brown he'd never seen before, encircled with a thick black ring; and nearest the pupil, a touch of green. They came to life in moments like this, when the light from the window kissed them obliquely and they burned like fire. He had to look away.

"I'll help you pack a bag and take you to the airport. Let them know you're coming."

"How long, Rami?"

"For what?"

"Till I can come home to you."

"I'm always with you, baby."

The next day Rami was up early, packed his bag, and headed into the office, distracting himself from thoughts of his wife and baby.

"Rami Salim?" FBI special agent Marcus Latimore asked as he extended his hand.

"Yes, sir," Rami said with a smile as he set down his duffel bag.

"I hear you're one hell of a shot."

"I've been known to send it downrange."

"I also heard what you did a few weeks back. You ever serve in the military?"

"No sir, never had the pleasure."

"I have. Wouldn't call it pleasurable, but I understand what you mean. You move like a spec ops man. Glad to have you on board."

"Thank you."

"Don't thank me yet. You're on shit detail. FBI wants our guys in the good spots. You won't get to see the game, but you'll hear it. The Roberto Clemente Bridge always shuts down for Pirates' games, so we're going to take advantage of that. Senator Waxman will be leaving the game immediately, and exiting the stadium via the south exit, facing the Allegheny River. You'll be on the top of northeast tower on the bridge, overlooking the exit."

"Sounds good Mr. Latimore. Thanks for selecting me."

"You're callsign will be Hawkeye Three," he said, extending his hand.

"I like it," Rami said, returning the handshake.

It was 1700 hours when Rami reached the top of the northeast tower. He looked into the stadium, which already held a few thousand fans watching the teams warm up for the start of what promised to be a series nobody would soon forget. Rami set down his heavy bag, placed his long-range rifle onto the platform, and lay prone behind it, setting the range on the weapon. He was six-hundred yards from the chosen exit, elevated eighty feet over the bridge deck. The wind was strong out of the west so he'd have to monitor it as the night progressed.

Rami heard from Dinah the previous night when she got to her parents. She was still feeling sick, but at least she had two people to help her. Even better, her sister heard she was heading home to San Francisco, and decided to head home herself to see her pregnant sister.

Rami settled in and pulled out his cellphone. He began to read text messages from his wife, the I love yous, the emojis, the pictures that made him blush. She loved him as much as he loved her. His fingers began to type before his mind could stop him. He texted quickly and haphazardly, getting hundreds of characters into the digital message before his conscience could stop him. It was the least he could do in a moment like this. He sent the message and a selfie with the stadium behind him. He took his phone and threw it down into the Allegheny.

"Good evening Pirates' faaaaaans!" the stadium announcer hollered and the crowd erupted. "Please stand for the singing of our national anthem."

"Hawkeye Three this is command, over."

"Go ahead command," Rami said into the voice-activated comms. It allowed him to stay sharp behind the rifle instead of trying to reach for a button.

"Be advised, we're fifteen minutes out."

"Copy," Rami said and began to account for the current conditions. The river allowed for an aggressive west-to-east shearing wind that fortunately had died down considerably in the past hour.

The national anthem concluded and immediately

following, Senator Waxman began marching toward the mound, waving to boos and applause. Rami could barely see the senator, but he made out a big smile and a White Sox hat.

"Hawkeye One, eyes on SW."

"Copy Hawkeye One," the voice from command responded.

Senator Waxman threw a strike and the Pirates' catcher ran out to the mound to give him the ball. The catcher pulled out a Pirates' hat from his back pocket and handed it to Waxman. Waxman played nicely, and exchanged his White Sox hat with the player, placing the Pirates' hat on his head and waving to thunderous applause. The pillar Rami laid on shook in the energy. The noise was incredible and Rami's heart began to accelerate. He wasn't a baseball fan, but the environment was stimulating, the raw emotions were contagious, and he battled to get himself together.

"Hawkeye Three five minutes out."

"Copy," Rami said and began to control his breathing. He watched Waxman disappear into the home dugout and the clock began to count down.

He thought again of Dinah, the baby. He imagined it was a boy, and wondered what she would name him. He knew it wouldn't be Rami, and that was fine with him. The name wouldn't fit the boy anyway. In fact, it hadn't been his own real name.

Everyone called him Rami because that's what he told them to call him. His grandfather gave him the name when the family took a trip to visit their ancestral home in Syria where his father's father lived. "Sharpshooter," his grandfather said when they went into the country and shot rifles. "I will call you Rami, for that name means sharpshooter," his grandfather said, kissing him on the forehead. The young boy loved the name and he stayed in contact with his grandfather until he was killed in a bombing. It greatly affected Rami, leaving him scarred, hurt, searching for answers he never received—until a friend of his grandfather reached out a year after the bombing and began working with Rami, helping him find a way to get through his loss, and even, avenge his grandfather's death.

"Hawkeye Three, eyes on," Rami said into the radio.

"Copy."

It was twenty yards to a convoy of vehicles lined up in a row. It would take less than five seconds of overwatch before the group would enter the bulletproof government SUVs. However, it only took a fraction of that time for a round to fly.

Rami exhaled and squeezed.

Boom! The sound of powder exploding echoed through the river valley as Rami slid back the bolt, removed it from his weapon, and dropped it into the river below. He knew the round entered Waxman just above the left eye, blood and matter had sprayed rearward onto the secret service agent behind the senator, his new baseball hat obliterated with the force of the exiting metal.

"Shot fired!" he heard in the comms as he stood, dropping his rifle to the bridge below. Several moments passed before it finally struck the ground, bouncing erratically before settling in horrific silence.

It was ironic how the fans roared when the helicopters came screaming over the stadium, heading south in response to the shooter. The fans were naïve, stupid, their emotions high and everything was thrilling. They had no idea why the helicopters were flying over the stadium. If they knew, it would cause a panic.

"Hawkeye Three, do you copy?"

Rami ignored the radio but left his earpiece in. He removed his vest, his all-black gear, which he wore for the

Facebook picture Dinah hated. His muscled frame was easily discernable when the FBI spotlight shone brightly toward the northeast tower. Rami reached into his duffel bag, took out a rug, and placed it onto the ground. He then grabbed his *thawb*, a red garment accentuated with golden stitch work around the edges, a wonderful piece of clothing he wore for special events and holidays at the mosque. But this was a different sort of celebration.

"What the fuck, Rami!" someone screamed into the comms. By now, news helicopters began trying to encroach on the airspace around the stadium and over the Allegheny, but the FBI made it very clear they needed to stay back. Still, the news choppers had far reaching zoom lenses that immediately caught the spectacle. They didn't know Waxman had been shot, but they recorded the muscled man putting on his clothing, and watched as he bowed to the east on his rug.

"Rami, you traitorous son-of-a-bitch!" Rami recognized the voice of Marcus Latimore from earlier that day.

Below, dozens of vehicles began to approach. The bridge was easily accessible for law enforcement, and they came in by the dozens. He watched the lights, a strange Christmas-like dance of colors and activity below. Dozens of agents were climbing the stairs toward Rami. It was seconds from ending.

"Mr. Latimore," Rami said into the comms breaking his silence as the end became eminent. "You have no idea what's coming. This is the beginning. *Allahu akbar.*"

Rami never looked up, never reached for anything, but he did think of Dinah and the baby one final time, hoping she wouldn't hate him; but knowing she would likely suffer for what he's done.

A flash of light and the earth quaked as Rami was atomized by an explosion. The northeast tower collapsed, killing everyone inside, and the Roberto Clemente Bridge listed eastward, and rolled, hinting at a complete failure. The stadium lights dimmed, and the entire country went silent, unsure of what had happened. The video feed in everyone's home across the U.S. cut to commercial, but in Pittsburgh, there was no escaping the truth.

The stadium came back to life, but the screams of joy and happiness had morphed into terror and panic. Thousands rushed toward the exits and onto the field looking for a way out. Hundreds began to pour out of the stadium, thousands more pressed their way through the halls, punching, clawing, biting one another in an attempt to save their own lives before anothers. It was exponentially worse than the events from weeks earlier. Fights broke out in the parking lot, and in the stands, players on the field were being assaulted by panicked fans trying to get through the underbelly of the stadium and outside to the streets. Law and order was a false ideology. Everyone just hoped it would burn itself out. Only a few knew this was just the beginning.

Chapter 31
FALLOUT

Within days, the entire country erupted in chaos. Some called it anarchy, but others saw the social uprise as glue that brought America together. In the forty-eight hours since Senator Waxman was assassinated, terrorism swept throughout the country. Citizens who had been fighting with one another, fighting the police, screaming hatred, all came together. They took self-preservation over their disagreement, and fought back. Citizens were capturing terrorists before they could execute their plots by the hundreds. But, it hadn't been enough.

The entire country was under attack from the inside. Rami had begun a domino effect, hundreds, if not thousands, of sleeper agents who'd been entwined within the U.S. infrastructure mobilized. Medusa was gathering actionable intel, getting it through the proper channels seemingly instantaneously, but that was only catching one-tenth of the violence being committed. The majority of sleeper agents had become autonomous, waiting for a sign, their instructions memorized years ago. Rami had been the sign.

President Pierce and Secretary Smith hadn't slept a minute since everything began. They were in an undisclosed facility near Colorado Springs. There had already been separate attacks on members of the Senate and President Pierce's advisors. Of the twenty recorded assassination attempts, three more were successful: Senator Patrick McDunnough of Massachusetts, Senator Jason Reynolds of Montana, and Senator Grace Lions from Virginia. The others were given specific warnings thanks to Medusa, but barely.

A bombing at Oklahoma University, coordinated attacks on State Street in Chicago and Wall Street in New York's financial districts, shopping mall shootings, and attempts to hijack three separate planes were thwarted; once again thanks to Medusa. However, the latest numbers told the story: thirteen thousand died by shootings, explosions, or stabbings across the country, and the number was growing.

Secretary Smith sat at a large wooden table. To his left, a stunned and reeling President Pierce, to his right, General Anderson, and surrounding the table were advisors, generals, admirals, Chuck Renfro, FBI, and Bill Whiteside, CIA. The room was quiet, the men had talked for hours, coordinated responses for the terrorist attacks, which continuously and spontaneously erupted throughout the country.

They looked into Rami's history. Superficially there was nothing of significance, his background had been Syrian. But, upon digging deeper, they made connections. His grandfather had been a warlord in the Middle East for several years prior to Rami's father moving to the U.S. Rami's email records showed several communications a year with his grandfather in the time preceding the old man's death by drone strike. In fact, Rami hadn't been his real name, and he earned the nickname from his grandfather while on a trip to Syria with his family when he was young.

After his grandfather's death, Rami had been sending correspondence to several email addresses in the Middle East, but only in response to messages he had received. The last email he had was a picture of his wife. Strange to think, but they all agreed it was the go signal.

"Mr. President," Chuck said, breaking the silence. "Medusa had helped us dramatically, but we need to do something more aggressive."

"Martial law?" Secretary Smith responded tapping his pen on the table. Everyone had thought it at one time or another over the previous forty-eight hours. Putting the entire country on house arrest wouldn't be taken well.

"Yes."

"We could mobilize immediately," General Worthington said. He was a small, thin man, but his words were powerful. He'd been placed in charge of the U.S. national police force. For almost a decade the budget for this secret police force grew in response to the social unrest. It was designed as a fail-safe, a stop-gate to massive protests and riotous acts. Even the small precincts across the country didn't know about the nationalized police initiative, but hierarchy and structure had been made into law year after year, buried in other bills before congress, citizens not reading the fine print. Now it was time to mobilize the expansive, unified police force across the country.

"Chuck, you and General Worthington get your shit together quickly. We need to make sure the FBI knows what they're doing. They essentially serve as the officers on this. Make no mistake. This is effectively a declaration of war against our own people and I don't like it one bit."

"Understood Mr. President."

"We need to arrest anyone who seems suspicious, who's caught outside curfew, no matter what their demographics," President Pierce said, standing and leaning against his hands on the table. He stared at a graphic of the United States that was projected on the screen in the front of the room. It displayed red dots on all the locations that a terrorist attack had been committed, and green on those where one been stopped. The map looked like Christmas, but it was far from celebratory.

"We still don't know where Logan and Samantha are?" General Anderson asked in frustration toward Secretary Smith.

"No. And that makes me nervous," he responded quietly.

"Why?" Whiteside asked.

"Because if they were taken, then the enemy knows far more than they should, and I have no idea how."

Chapter 32
SONGBIRD

Sana'a, Yemen

David found a small apartment on a first floor in the bustling city of Sana'a. It was a quiet, poor area, one that promised a lack of wandering eyes and nosey neighbors. It helped that the neighborhood was often the location for fighting and illegal activities, so it allowed him to blend in. He purchased a couple of monitors from a back-alley vendor and quickly got his computer operational once again. Five days had passed relatively quickly, and he was grateful for it. The thoughts of Amal weren't far from his mind, but the conversation he had with Saad was drowning his conscious.

He'd been in Yemen for years, alone, absent any contact from his director. What little communications he had were directly with Washington. Even though Secretary Smith was passing along the intel he'd send, he still wasn't listening to the data David was collecting regarding internet communications. Admittedly, it hadn't led to anything actionable, but the locations of the dark web access were getting concentrically larger, the activity increasing, and he had no idea where it was going. He assumed the U.S., but also France, Great Britain, other areas throughout the Middle East, but he had no proof. What David needed was a way to track the messages, and that could come from Washington. But for now, he was occupied with a signal that kept popping up in Sana'a.

For three days David tracked a mobile device that had continued to access the dark web. He'd narrowed it down to the southwest portion of the city, relatively near to where he had his apartment. Whoever was on the dark web would stay active for approximately three hours in the middle of the afternoon, then shut down. He pinged the location repeatedly, and it was always the same place. David moved down the streets, the tall red and brown buildings bouncing his signal around like a pinball, as he'd done before. David meandered his way through the streets, down alleyways, even into buildings trying to narrow the search area. A day earlier he figured it had to be coming from one of three eight-story buildings, but that was as specific as his gear was allowing in the tall, dense city.

This day, David arrived before the time the signal began: 1030. He was conspicuous, making himself known to anyone who was entering or leaving the buildings. Several minutes passed, and like clockwork, he was able to ping an IP address accessing the dark web. For David, this was confirmation someone was trying to get his attention. Of the dozens of times he hunted IPs, this was the first time it stayed stationary, consistent, but it also threw red flags for David. After narrowly escaping in Aden, he knew he was being hunted, but he did not know by who specifically. David played the prey, allowing himself to be drawn in.

He scanned the windows all around him in the narrow street. The rooftops were impossible to see from where he stood, but that also made it difficult for a shooter to target him without being noticed. The street had moderate foot traffic, however, as the sun traveled toward its pinnacle, the pedestrians evaporated and he was alone. Soon, two hours had passed and David continuously pinged the IP address obsessively, ensuring he wouldn't miss the moment when the activity went dark.

Then it happened. A ping went out and it didn't immediately return. A digital wheel spun on his device while it tried over and over to communicate with the IP address which had been working just moments earlier. David pocketed his device, reached into his backpack, and pulled out a blowpop, his calling card, and waited.

It didn't take long before he saw a tall, dark man walk out of the building. His clothes were ragged, his frame was weak, thin, emaciated. He had thick stubble on his face and meandered slowly away from David, limping slightly on his left leg. David approached the man cautiously, but quickly. He felt he had to reach the mysterious man before the street corner, where an ambush may lie in wait. David's long strides made quick work covering the twenty yard distance.

"You've got my attention," David said from behind the man as he took out his freshly sharpened blade.

"It's about time," the man said, coming to a stop and slowly turning, his palms facing forward, fingers splayed out showing David he was unarmed. "I've got a gun in my waistband," he said, looking down toward his left hip.

David reached down and grasped the weapon, noting the fine mist of blood spatter that still painted the weapon's steel slide and barrel. "You do something you shouldn't have?"

"I've done quite a few things I shouldn't have. I've come

to turn myself in, Candyman."

"Why?"

"I've got one hell of a story, and I know you're the only one around here who can get it stateside."

"Who are you?" David asked, putting away his blade and placing the confiscated firearm into his own waistband.

"Sumeet Patel. But everyone calls me Amir Qasmi."

The apartment was dirty, uncomfortable, making the two men share a space meant for one. The tension was high as Amir sat close enough for David to cut him stem-to-stern with a flick of his spindly wrist. David was leaning forward with his forearms on his knees, throwing black daggers through pale blue eyes at the traitor so far from what he had once called home.

David had known the name, Amir Qasmi, but he hadn't ever thought the man would find his way into his care. No one knew where the former decorated Army hero had gone following his capture and there he sat.

"I know your story," David said, now spinning his knife in his hands. "Problem is, how do I know anything you say is worth looking into? I'm a wanted man myself, who's to say you're not here to draw me out?"

"We both know what you do. Let's skip the pleasantries," Amir said relaxed, leaning back in a steel chair, his hands and feet secured. "Give me the drug if you want, but you'll hear the same story one way or the other."

David stood, his long frame extending toward the ceiling as he turned and grasped a small black case from the desk behind him. He unzipped it, removing a vial of milky liquid and a syringe.

"You ready to sing?" David asked as he returned to Amir who waited patiently for the CIA agent to administer his drug.

"That's what I've been saying."

David was taken back at Amir's demeanor, his relaxed body language, his unwavering tone of voice. David reached for Amir's arm, chose a vein, and plunged the needle inside, delivering the drug. He allowed himself to hope Amir could unravel the web he'd been building for years.

Time passed quickly in the small room for the two men. Amir was open, honest with his answers; he had to be. The intel was overwhelming for David, finally finding a source worth bringing stateside for a full debrief with U.S. intelligence. After two hours, David decided enough was enough.

"Stay put," David said to Amir who remained confined to a chair.

David walked outside into a brisk evening. The days had been getting shorter, and the warmth was fleeting. A chill climbed up David's frame as he reached to dial.

"Mr. Secretary—"

"David! Tell me you've got something," Secretary Smith exploded into the receiver before David could speak.

"I do—"

"Things have gone from bad to insane, stateside," he said, cutting off the agent for a second time.

"Sir?"

"Senator Waxman was assassinated. Then all hell broke loose. We've lost four senators, and thousands of American lives. We've declared martial law. I need to know you've got some actionable intel."

The information was paralyzing. David, for a moment, forgot why he called the secretary. *Martial law? Was Amir trying to deceive him? Distract him? No, he couldn't be, his truth cocktail was unbreakable.*

"Shit," David responded, finding a word. "I've got Amir

Qasmi in custody. He came to me."

"Well I'll be damned. What's that asshole got to say?"

"He's got lots of intel. Willing to give it all to us. We need to get stateside."

"He's a goddamned liar. Don't trust a word of it. Where you at?"

"Sana'a."

"Get him to the Embassy. We'll get you guys stateside in forty-eight hours. I want his ass on our soil ASAP." Secretary Smith paused, his rage taking a backseat to nostalgia, to fear, regret. *Logan would love this shit,* he thought.

"Will get there tomorrow. Need Amir to come around a bit. Can't have him stumblin' around the city from the drug. He's hard enough to manage if things go south."

"David," Smith said, his tone sincere, almost nervous.

"Ask him about Falcone."

"He already told me."

"Good. Is Samantha with him?"

"I'm not sure what you mean," David responded, concerned for Logan, the man who'd become a distant brother-in-arms. The soldier who had become the long arm of action for David's intel.

"What the hell's going on!" Doyle responded in anger, the sleepless nights reducing his ability to think clearly.

"Amir told me he had a message for Logan, that he was the only one he'd trust with it."

"What's the message?"

"We're chasing the wrong threats, but it sounds like it's old news."

"What else did he say about Falcone?"

"Nothing. Why?"

"Jesus," Smith whispered with a sigh. "Logan and his wife are missing. Just get stateside for a full debrief, and bring all your intel. It's time we went through it with a fine tooth."

"Yes, sir," David said lazily as he allowed the phone to slide down his face. He had no idea what to say, confused at the overwhelming knowledge that for once, terrorism seemed to be two steps ahead.

Chapter 33
THE HUNTED

Logan sat in a cell, his bruised head leaning against the concrete wall of a room that seemed to tighten around him by the hour. The cool sensation allowed him feel as though his swelling was reducing. He had to move a lot, adjust his head position, but it helped him stay focused on something other than Samantha and the baby.

He already lost track of time, the concussion, the erratic noises, and the random bright lights limited the time he found rest. His body throbbed, aching in the events from the preceding hours and days, but, while he was interrogated, his mind was sharp. It was as if his body knew what was to come; and his brain hibernated during those moments in the concrete vault.

Since his first talk with Karim, he hadn't seen the leader. Instead, he was dealing with the captains, unintelligent and lacking tact, brutality was their chosen means of coercion. Logan took the beatings, the screaming, the scare tactics in stride. There was nothing they could take from him he cared about. Knowing Samantha and the baby would be safe had been his only concern. Physical pain was a welcomed relief. For years he'd battled emotional suffering, scars of the soul, but now he could wear physical badges and process physical pain. The difference between the physical and the emotional, was that he knew the physical pain would go away; he felt it change, saw the healing of tissues, the stoppage of blood, and reduction of swelling. He had yet to see a change in his mental anguish and it had been years.

"American," Logan heard someone say as light shone brightly into his cell. "It is time."

Logan crawled toward the opening and stood slowly, his whole body screaming as his stiff, swollen joints begged for mercy, but not a word let loose from his mouth. He walked slowly down a well-lit hallway that had become familiar to him; twenty steps left, then ten more steps, before turning right and entering the interrogation room. He counted them each time.

"Mr. Falcone," a voice said as he entered the overwhelmingly bright room. Light from above bounced off the tiled floor and walls, creating the illusion of being surrounded by lights on all sides.

"Come, sit with me."

Logan's eyes, despite the concussion, quickly adjusted to the brightness. There, in the center of the room, were two chairs and a steel table; on the other side, Karim.

"Logan Falcone," Karim said, smirking. "I have some news for you from the states." Karim stood, walked around the table pulling out the second chair.

Click, click, his ring rapped against the metal seat as he gently patted it, gesturing Logan to sit. Slowly, Logan approached while Karim returned to his seat, unbuttoning his coat, revealing the ornate 1911 he carried on his waist.

"*Allah* is good," Karim said, his eyes dazzling in the light from above and his smile, a straight row of eerily white teeth. "You must watch." Karim reached to the side, and snapped his finger. Within a moment, a large flat screen was wheeled into the room, already broadcasting the news from the U.S.

"Thousands reportedly injured, hundreds killed in the most orchestrated terrorist attack in world history."

Logan felt faint, he reached forward with cuffed hands, resting them onto the table, hoping to feel grounded. He tried not to listen but the news was too overwhelming.

"Rami Salim, a Pittsburgh SWAT team member and Muslim-American, seemingly was the catalyst that sent sleeper agents into action. Thankfully, not all hope is lost. The U.S. government has declared a state of martial law in order to combat the aggressors. As President Pierce stated, 'We have already had great success in stopping a tremendous amount of secondary attacks thanks to our government agents.'

"Remember, it is for your own protection. Curfew is set for eight PM, or 2000 hours. No businesses will be open, anyone out past this time will be arrested by military police. The president also went on to promise earlier today, 'this curfew will not last long, only until they have stopped the attacks indefinitely.' We will continue to broadcast updates on an hourly basis. It has been over twenty-four hours since the last attack had been attempted. Hopefully, the curfew will only be a few more days. Thank you America; God bless."

The news hit Logan harder than any physical assault he'd underwent in the previous days. He looked toward Karim, who met Logan's gaze, smirking.

"I told you Mr. Falcone. You have no idea the games I'm playing." Karim placed his forearms on the table, his silky white shirt sliding easily, silently across the steel. He leaned forward getting close to Logan. "I will bring the entire west to their knees, starting with America."

Logan was stunned, reeling in the one–two punch of the attacks and martial law. He didn't speak.

"I have something else for you to watch," Karim said and started a video of the World Series game.

Logan watched the events unfold. He saw Senator Waxman throw the first pitch, change hats to support the home team to thunderous applause, then exit the field. The shot abruptly changed to an aerial camera where he witnessed a large man standing on top of a bridge just moments before it exploded. Then, an emotional reporter delivered the final blow, "Senator Waxman was assassinated, and, following the senator's death, a suicide bombing which killed dozens of uniformed officers and FBI agents."

"Mr. Falcone. You're no hero. You haven't saved anyone I didn't allow you to save. Sure, you adjusted my plans with Alex Pines, but he was no prize. I'm still up big in the game, and I haven't even played my hand yet. How unfair this game must feel to you?"

Logan was trying to recover, trying not to let his emotions decide his next move; but he was losing. Logan too had a trump card, a fact that would cause Karim to reel. He wasn't sure if it was the right time to show his hand.

"I have secrets too. Secrets that would hurt you. Admittedly, you've won the battle, but do you think America is lost? Your arrogance is laughable. I pity you for the moment your world crashed around you. You've already shown me how emotional you can get. Karim Al Muhammad." Logan spit his name out with disdain.

Karim's eyes squinted, his body stiffened and he tried to hide the shock. *Had I said my name?* he thought as he stared at Logan. "A trick, Mr. Falcone. But it doesn't matter. My professional name is different. None of my money is associated with who I truly am."

"Are you sure about that? How would I know who you are?"

Karim was silent, reviewing conversations he'd had with Logan, ensuring he hadn't spoken his name. He had, after all, been incredibly emotional following Taj's death. "How then do you know my name?" he asked, genuinely interested.

"One of your own," Logan said, gesturing with his hands, both moving in unison as they remained tightly shackled together.

"No sir! He is a liar!" the guard begged as he approached Karim, palms facing his leader, pleading with him to think.

"Then how does he know me?" Karim responded to the guard. He was growing impatient.

"It wasn't me! *Allah* strike me down if I am lying. I am faithful."

"Grab every man who's been with Logan while he's been here."

The guard rushed away, hoping his speed would prove his worth.

Logan was focusing on keeping his emotions in check, but the idea of Samantha likely unable to get out of Yemen due to the attacks was continuously bombarding his thoughts. One saving grace was at least she wasn't in America, vulnerable to attacks at home without him to protect her. The Embassy would find a way to get her somewhere safe, but he'd never truly know.

A door opened, and Logan felt anxious. Not out of fear, but anticipation. Karim was emotional once again, but to what length would he go to punish an individual for an act they hadn't committed? It was, after all, Amir who told Logan about Karim by way of Alex Pines.

"Stand against the wall," Karim said, pointing directly to his right as a dozen men filed into the twenty-by-twenty foot room. He reached into his waistband, and, without a second thought, *bang!* His 1911 erupted, its noise echoing in the solid room, as if it was alive, cheering for the moment it had been designed for. The first guard lay dead on the floor, an entry wound in his head was evidence of Karim's emotional instability.

"Now. Who will tell me which of you spoke with our prisoner. Which of you said my name?"

Bang! Again, his pistol send a round into a guard; two now lying on the floor.

"I will execute every last one of you until I have my answer—and this will not grant you access to a martyr's heaven."

The remaining men scrambled, panicking, searching for an answer that didn't exist. They had no idea what their leader was referring to, none of them knew how to respond. Logan sat, watching silently as Karim fulfilled Logan's wishes of a retaliation.

Bang, bang, bang! Three more fell without a word from anyone.

"Please we don't know what you are speaking of!" one of the guards finally yelled out as he looked at Karim, whose face and expensive white shirt were covered in red particles.

"Someone spoke my name in his presence," Karim growled, pointing the gun at Logan, but his eyes remained transfixed on his guards.

"Ask him who. Ask him which one of us told him!"

Karim turned toward Logan. Their ears where ringing, the sound had been deafening. It was almost as if the gun was still firing in the room.

"Who told you?"

"I said one of your own."

"Which?" Karim asked, taking his weapon and slowly scanning across each of the fearful men.

"Amir Qasmi," Logan said, administering his own killshot.

"Impossible," Karim said mockingly, smirking in what he thought was a desperate attempt at distraction.

"Is it? Who found his body? Did you ever actually see it? He's still alive. In fact, maybe he's the one who killed your son. That's the story I was told."

"By who? This is not truth. One son would not kill another."

Logan sat back in his chair and took a deep breath, exhaling slowly. "What would you call it when a person does something in response to a stimulus? When it happens automatically?"

"What are you talking about?"

"If I were to reach out to strike you, like this," Logan leapt out of his chair toward the table and Karim responded by standing from his chair and pointed his gun at Logan, waiting.

"What was that response called?" Logan asked, sitting in his chair.

"A reflex."

"Mhm," Logan said nodding.

"I don't understand."

"You're a smart man, Karim. Think about it,"

The wealthy man did just that. He sat back into the chair, rapping his pistol against steel, and let the word replay over and over in his head: *reflex, reflex, reflex.* Reflex. It hit him. Karim stood from the table abruptly, looking at his men.

"Put him in his cell and clean this up. You will NOT speak of this to anyone." Turning to address Logan, his once calm eyes were accented in angry red tributaries filled with rage. "This is no longer a game Mr. Falcone. While you lay in your cell, I want you to reflect on one thing: your child, and the life I will not allow it to have. I will hunt Samantha now; I will end her life and any life that remains inside."

Karim took long powerful strides out of the room, and immediately outside to his car. Quickly, he called his lieutenants.

"We have two new objectives," he said to them each in turn. "One is to attack the Embassy in Sana'a where Samantha Falcone will surely be. Kill her, and anyone who tries to protect her. Second, Amir may be alive. Hunt him down and bring him to me."

Karim sat, taking deep breaths of dry, thin air. He'd fought for years to avoid direct contact with his old friend, a man who moved stateside to protect his most prized asset. It had been years since Karim felt the urge to call, but, he knew it was getting close to time. If he waited too long, all hope could be lost. Now, it appeared he had a crack in his lines, in the web of people he spun so closely around him. The thought of deception made him sick to his stomach. He needed to talk to his friend again, to hear, directly from his mouth, the current state of things.

He grabbed his phone.

"Hello," the lost, familiar voice said on the other line. A rush of memories flooded back to Karim's mind: Two small boys playing ball, running through the house, the sound of their laughter echoing through the halls of a small apartment, the smell of fresh baked bread, of summer air, of fire and dust filling their noses. He remembered the pain he endured, the bond it created.

"*Assalamualaikum*," Karim said after what felt like a minute of silence.

"*Assaalamu Aliekum wa rehamutallah*, my brother. Is it really you?"

"Yes. Time to bring him home."

Chapter 34
U.S. SOIL

The sun had risen into the afternoon sky by the time David and Amir set out. As was often the case, the candy stayed in the victim's system well into the following day. David needed Amir with a clear head, one that had to be on a swivel. David was a wanted man after all, and, Amir was easily recognizable. Both of the men stood out in a crowd at well over six feet tall, so it was in David's best interest to travel in the height of a day in order to insulate himself from searching eyes.

"How you feeling?" David said as Amir finally sat up on the floor, his feet and hands were still tied together.

"Like I'm hog-tied."

"Can't blame me, right?" David asked while he prepped his bag.

"Nope. When we leaving?" Amir asked, rotating his head around, trying to gain relief from the strain in his neck. He'd slept, unmoving for hours due to the drugs, and he was now paying the price.

David zipped the main compartment on his backpack,

placed the straps over his shoulders, and cinched up the vinyl, ensuring an immovable fit. "Now." He walked to Amir, took out his blade, and cut off the restraints.

"Trust me now?" Amir said sarcastically.

"Not a bit, but if you remember, they're hunting me. If you want to get stateside and tell your story, you're on protective detail."

"What do I do, throw stones?" he asked while miming a trigger pull.

David reached toward his hip, grabbing a 9mm. He depressed the release, counting the rounds inside the high capacity magazine. "This okay?"

"I think I can manage."

The two men moved quickly through the streets, not pressing the flow of traffic, but navigating the pedestrians like water around boulders. They were careful not to be memorable, not to draw attention, weaving through alleyways, main streets, shopping districts, all in an effort to remain anonymous. After just thirty minutes, the streets became quiet, foot traffic slowed, and they heard a scream.

Immediately, the two Americans froze, the crowd around them continuing forward, even pressing into the two tall men. Seemingly, nobody had heard the fear in the voice that echoed through the street, bouncing off building.

Pop, pop, pop—the sound of gunfire, nondescript, distant. The flow of people quickly began to stop, their conversations abruptly ending, only a few distinct voices of merchants and drivers could be heard in the strange silence of a bright, hot afternoon.

Three more bursts of gunfire rang out, and immediately, a flurry of screams. The river of people that had flowed around David and Amir, was now reversing, tripping over themselves, banging into the two men who still stood processing the direction of the gunfire. It was easy for them to see through the crowd, their height now an advantage.

"I've got nothing," Amir said as he scanned far down the street, looking for any sign of danger.

"Same. We've gotta move."

They ran, guns in hand, against the flow of panicked civilians. The chaos become contagious, like a herd of prey animals rushing from an unseen predator, instinctively they all had begun running. No one knew what happened or from where the shooting originated.

David finally grabbed a young man who was fleeing. "What's happened?" he asked as the man tried to break David's vise-like grip.

"Shooting!" he responded in Arabic.

"Where?"

"The U.S. Embassy."

David released his grip from the boy and looked to Amir.

"What'd he say?"

"The Embassy is under attack."

"What the hell?" Amir said, confused.

"What didn't you tell me!" David said, reaching for Amir and slamming him against a nearby wall. "You tracked me to Sana'a, you waited for me to dig in, plant a root, then came with this confession. Meanwhile, you set up an ambush for me at the Embassy."

"I told you everything," Amir said, unmoved by David's rageful attack.

"Lies on lies. I know what you've done. This is nothing different. You deceive."

"Trust me. I don't have anything to do with this. I'm done lying, I'm done looking out for me. I was trying to survive, for years I've been trying to just protect myself; from shame, from jail, from death. Now, I don't care."

David's bony forearm began to release the pressure

from Amir's chest.

"I don't have any other options," David said, releasing Amir completely. "But I swear to God if I'm captured, the last thing I'll do is end you with my bare hands."

Soon, David and Amir were only blocks from the Embassy, crouched in the shadows of a building, assessing the area. The streets were completely empty, quiet, except for sporadic gunfire and random shouting from men. They heard English from the American Marines who protected the Embassy. "Stand down," a voice was repeatedly saying, while another voice would yell the same in Arabic immediately after.

The two men moved slowly, one soft-footed step at a time, clearing corner after corner, alleyways, behind obstacles. Finally, two-hundred yards down the road, they saw the Embassy for the first time. It was difficult to see against the harshly backlit sky, the entire building appeared as a dark shadow.

Pop, pop! David grabbed Amir and pulled him quickly across the street as the road directly behind them erupted in a wave of dirt and debris from metal shredding the ground.

"Holy shit," Amir said as he sat with his back to a large wooden crate in the next alleyway. "Why the hell are they shooting at us?"

"I'm guessing they're to shoot anyone on site. We're late to the party."

"I never saw a muzzle flash."

"Been that long has it?" David said, trying not to smile. "Shit," he said, the urge to smile fleeing his mind; the sound of air whipping past propellers was unmistakable, even for someone who hadn't been familiar with them. What was a bit more tricky, was counting the individual number of aircraft, of which, David could make out four.

"Shit," Amir said, hearing the familiar noise too.

"We've got about fifteen minutes to prove we're not bad guys."

"Or what?"

"We won't get the option to explain. Move!" David said and hurled himself down the next street, hoping to find whatever insurgence was assaulting the Embassy.

David saw a man hiding behind a wall, his head craning around a corner, trying to get a look at the Embassy. Quickly, David's long, soft strides narrowed the distance to the suspect. In one move, David reached for his blade, lunged forward, and slid it across the man's throat. A second strike from David rendered the man's shooting hand useless as he sliced through the flexor tendons. He tried to reach for his radio, to call for help, but life fell in spurts from his wounds, leaving him worthless as he collapsed to the ground.

"Candyman is here," David said into the radio; slowly, as a poltergeist, haunting their thoughts.

"Who is this?" he heard a response in Arabic.

"Come and find me," he answered back, teasing the assailants. David then shot two rounds into the air from the dead man's AK-47, turned to Amir, and said, "Show time."

It took several seconds, but the enemy came running. From behind Amir, a lone soldier presented himself, rifle held high in front of him, searching for the ghost they call the Candyman.

Pop, pop, Amir shot the man without a thought. The rounds hit their target as the man's head snapped back and he dropped his gun.

Amir felt a rush of honor, of duty, of clarity like never before. The first time he killed was for America, the second for himself, avenging his father's death. From then on, he killed for others to save himself from prison, and used his desires as an excuse to hide the fact he didn't know who he was. But never had he felt good about taking a life; until this moment.

Amir raced to the rifle, grabbed it, and turned to his left to see David smiling next to him.

"Rock and roll motha' fucka'," David said, pulling the slide back on his AK and placing his pistol in his waist.

"You're on point," Amir said, feeding off David's energy.

"You need a lesson with that thing?" David asked, gesturing toward the assault rifle in Amir's hands.

"Just do what you do, and I'll do what I do."

Pop, poppoppop. David and Amir both fired at another target, putting him down before he even brought up his gun.

"Watch our ass Amir, I know you guys like to stab in the back," David said, scanning the street ahead.

"I can see when we get to the Embassy I'm gonna have to write it all down for you. I'm not so bad," Amir said, rolling his eyes.

"Explain it to the judge, traitor."

Pop, pop! Amir put two terrorists down.

"I could've let them kill you."

"They'd have shot at you first."

"Look," David said from behind a small shack attached to a building along the alleyway they were traveling. It had been some time since they saw the Embassy, and hadn't really kept track of what vector they were traveling in. Between sheets of metal and wood, David could make out five men approaching rather quickly, bounding from hide to hide, overlapping one another, providing cover for one another.

"They move pretty well," Amir said, catching up with David and glancing through the slits in the structure, while David watched their rear.

"You count five?"

"Yeah, five for sure," Amir said, concentrating, watching

their movements. "Well son-of-a-bitch."

"What?"

"Number two. I know him."

"Figures."

"That asshole beat me for weeks."

"You're one of those guys huh? Likes to get knocked around? Don't get all nostalgic on me."

"Oh, I'll kiss him alright," Amir said, raising the rifle.

"Whoa cowboy. As soon as you shoot they'll hit the deck. Then we got five targets to our east, and they'll call it in, box us in here for sure. I've got a radio, but that won't get us anywhere if they get us surrounded."

"What's your plan?"

"Work back to that street," David said, pointing where they had been a moment earlier.

"Then what?"

"Well, I'll go right, and you go left. Draw their fire. When they come barreling down the street, we'll have them in a cross."

"So. I'm the bait?"

"Appears that way."

"Just don't shoot me in the back."

"Me? Never," David said, checking the magazine. "I've got eight rounds left."

"We'll have to grab some clips from these guys—"

Amir was interrupted by the intensity of the downdraft from the helos overhead. In the heat of battle, the two unlikely allies had forgotten about the time, the reinforcements arriving nearly on top of them.

"Change of plans," David yelled with a wink and spun out into the alleyway, opening fire on the five terrorists working their way up the street. As David's gun sang its death song, black ropes descended from above, as if inviting the soon-to-be dead one last lifeline. But that all changed when a dozen Marines spilled from the helo just moments before their tethers touched the earth. David knew the helo would be a distraction, but Amir quickly saw the favorable timing as well. Within moments, their rifles were emptied and to Amir's surprise, only one terrorist remained uninjured.

They saw each other. Amir's heart began trying to leap from his chest, as if it wanted to kill the man itself. Over and over Amir felt the steady knocking, as if the large, smooth muscle would eventually achieve its goal.

"Get on the ground!" David shouted to Amir who was locked eye to eye with the man who assaulted him over and over those months in captivity, just a few short strides away. A year ago, Amir would have preserved his own life, choosing to live and fight another day, but things had changed.

"They'll shoot you without thinking twice," David yelled again from his knees, his hands locked together behind his head. The terrorist saw David, and did the same, dropping his weapon, placing his hands behind his head and dropping to his knees. He spat toward Amir, the saliva landing just short of Amir's feet.

Amir exploded, his feet never felt the ground as he shot toward the man. The guard had no chance, no time to move, before Amir's boot found purchase against the bearded face of the terrorist. Nearly unconscious, the man struggled to get to his feet, but quickly felt Amir's heavy hands crushing down on him over and over. Amir got behind the man, placing his forearm against his throat, not allowing the man a breath.

As the Marines' feet hit the dirt, the first six set a perimeter, while the rest moved in on David and Amir.

"Hands in the air!" one Marine yelled toward Amir, who continued to apply even more pressure to the guard's neck.

The Marine repeated the command in Arabic as he moved closer, his M4 unmoved from Amir's face.

Ignoring the Marine for a moment longer, Amir brought his face down close enough to feel the guards beard on his own cheek. "I'm going to tell them everything."

The guard began to laugh, despite the lack of oxygen and the pain it caused him. Amir released the guard and placed his hands in the air. A moment later, the guard fell forward placing his hands in the dirt. He gasped in large, long, life giving breaths of air. He coughed several times, but began to laugh.

"Amir, you are a wanted man," the guard said as the Marines threw him face down in the ground.

Amir was confused as the Marines roughly began searching him for any weapons, finding the handgun and throwing it several feet away.

"What's your name?" the Marine yelled to Amir.

"Amir Qasmi. I'm American."

Wham! The Marine punched Amir hard in the side of the head, his brain rattling against his skull. His head was whirling, voices, sounds, all blending together as dust blew into his eyes and nose. He felt numb, but safe, the familiar taste of iron dominated his palate. At least he knew he wasn't going into a basement, wrapped in a concrete box for months.

The Marines escorted their prisoners, three in all, to the Embassy. They walked into the lobby, and immediately were taken down several flights of stairs, deep within the compound. Quickly, the terrorist guard was taken from the group and ushered off.

"Like I've said several times now," David said, annoyed. "I'm David Westbrook, CIA. Secretary Doyle Smith told me to bring Amir Qasmi to the Embassy for safe transport back to the U.S. Call him for Christ sake!"

David was frustrated, annoyed. "This was supposed to be a relief, to hear an American voice again. Instead, I'm being dicked-around by ooh rah Marines." David took a deep breath, trying to relax and remember they were going by the protocol. After all, they had just been attacked. *But why?* David thought to himself.

"Jesus Christ," Amir said as he tried to stop and get a better look.

"Wow, from the mouth of a Muslim terrorist?" David said, looking comically toward his counterpart, his prisoner.

"Quiet," one of the Marines said without looking at them.

"Wanna know why they attacked?" Amir asked, knowing he'd get hit for it.

Whap! A second Marine struck Amir in the stomach, immediately his wind taken and nearly dropped to his knees, but he was being held up on each side by even more Marines.

"Her," he squeaked out between attempted breaths.

"I said shut the fuck up!" The Marine turned, finally addressing Amir. He was larger than Amir had anticipated, having never really looked at the man who stood in front of him. He was in full gear, hard to see his real shape, but the thickness of his neck told the story.

"No disrespect, but I know that woman," Amir said, preparing for another strike, this time from their large C.O.

"That's Samantha."

"Yut," the Marine responded, crossing his arms.

"Shit. That's Logan Falcone's beau," Amir said playfully toward David.

"What you just say?" David asked crossly, not understanding.

"Logan Falcone. That's his lady. She's why you were attacked. You need to listen to Dave here, and soon.

Otherwise this attack shit won't stop anytime soon."

The Marine looked toward Amir, then to David, then back. "Be right back."

The Marine walked toward Samantha. "I need you for a minute, ma'am, is that okay?"

"Sure," she said not asking why, her thoughts were flooded with distress. *Is the baby okay? Is Logan okay? Why were we attacked? What's going on stateside? Will I ever make it out of here?*

Samantha stared at the concrete floor during the short walk toward the prisoners, not actually knowing they had been there at all.

"Mrs. Falcone, do you know these men?" the Marine asked, pointing toward David and Amir.

Her eyes immediately found Amir's, despite his malnourished body and several days of stubble, she recognized him. She'd never forget his eyes, Logan told her it was the most important part of a person. She remembered the interrogation with Logan, how Amir belittled her.

She lunged at him, her actions speaking before her thoughts as she scratched at Amir's vulnerable face. He had no way of defending himself, and the Marines stepped back, allowing Samantha to exact whatever revenge she was craving. She made a noise, as if she were a lioness feasting on prey, and Amir fell back tripping over his own feet. He fell back and Samantha remained on top, as he slammed hard onto the concrete floor, his head once again being assaulted. Amir's hands were tied behind his back, unable to deaden the fall.

"You ruined my life!" she screamed at the unconscious terrorist.

"Okay that's enough," the thick-necked Marine said as he gently grabbed her from behind, raising her from Amir.

"That son-of-a-bitch!" she yelled into Marine Corps BDUs as she sank her face into the closest person to her. He placed his arms around her awkwardly, his gear getting in the way, but Samantha didn't care. She hadn't cried since leaving the compound where Logan replaced her as prisoner. It hadn't felt real until this moment, coming face-to-face with the one man who got away.

"Why couldn't it be Logan who got away?" she asked the Marine, who stood confused.

"Samantha?" David asked gently, still being held by two Marines who stood watching the events unfold, more curious now than ever.

"You're talking about Logan Falcone?"

"Yes," she said, suddenly feeling hopeful. "You know where he is?"

"No," David's shoulders rounded forward. Samantha was as desperate as he was.

"He's in a compound in the mountains," she said to herself, remembering how bloodied his face had been.

"How do you know?"

"He took my place," she began sobbing, the weight of it all taking hold for a second time.

"Can I please talk to Secretary Smith now for the love of God!" David said loudly, and with authority. "And give me my backpack," he said to one of the Marines who stood watching, his left-hand clutching the data David had spent years compiling.

Chapter 35
DECEPTIONS AND SECRETS

Seattle, Washington

The morning was still dark as Nassir waited patiently in his home. He watched the east, waiting for the sun to rise. That time would be 0724, and curfew would lift a short while later, at 0800. For Nassir, he didn't mind the later start, it allowed him time to relax, work from home, stay up a bit later and watch a show he hadn't been able to since Medusa really began working.

Washington promised a contract a week ago, since Medusa stopped so many attacks. She had proven her worth, and, handsomely. He would be a multimillionaire overnight. The innovative computer had been working non-stop for weeks, feeding the military, the government, and the local law enforcement instantaneous intel regarding possible threats. Medusa had saved an incalculable number of lives, and Nassir felt confident, almost inspired, to one-up himself.

Bzzz, bzzz, bzzz, his phone began to rattle against his desk. Again, it rattled before he acknowledged the call.

"Dad," he said, answering the phone and noting the time, 0735. Nassir glanced out the window and noticed the darkness losing the battle against the light, despite the cloud cover.

"Yes. Did you rise for the *fajr*, Nassir?"

"Come on, Dad. Why did you call? For that?" Nassir had openly discussed his lack of faith, and the two men had agreed for years not to discuss it.

"Can you blame a father for wanting his son to think of God? Are you well?"

"Very. We should talk. The government promised me many things." Nassir paused. "But I can't go into the details. Just know that I'm doing very well."

"I would like to see my son smile! I can hear it through the phone. I'm so happy for your successes, Nassir. *Allah* has blessed you. It is the computer thing I assume? No need to tell me details."

Nassir rolled his eyes. *Another God reference,* he thought. "Thanks, Dad."

"Can we meet for breakfast?"

"Is that why you called?"

"You've seen the truth, as always. My stomach speaks for me more than it should."

"I'd agree. Does the doctor still tell you to lose weight?"

"He does."

"Well I think you should listen."

"It's my only sin, Nassir. Give me that," he laughed into the receiver, a quick, young trill, which contagiously spread to anyone around. Nassir was no exception.

"I'll meet you," he responded with a smirk.

Washington, D.C.

Secretary Smith paced the office. It had been several days since the curfew went into effect, and the attacks had all but stopped. It was the silence that drove him crazy. He hadn't heard from David in over twenty-four hours, he hadn't heard an answer from the president regarding when they would lift the curfew, and worst yet, he hadn't heard a peep regarding Logan.

"Mr. Secretary," his phone broke the silence, the buttery voice of his assistant cut into his thoughts.

"Yes."

"Mr. President is on the line."

"Mr. President," Doyle said without wasting time. He was eager to hear any news.

"Well more shit is hitting fans."

"What now?"

"We've been attacked in Yemen. Our Embassy."

Shit! Doyle thought recalling his last conversation with David. "Any news?"

"We're all good. Here's the kicker," President Pierce paused a moment to gather his thoughts.

"Samantha Falcone was there. In the damn Embassy."

"How? What did she say? How?" Doyle sat, rubbing his hands over the stubble on his head. Nothing was making sense.

"Before I answer that, I've got a question for you," the president stated in an accusatory tone. "Did you have knowledge of the whereabouts of Amir Qasmi?"

Doyle sighed, a secret he wanted to keep until David

brought him stateside. "I did sir. An operative reached out to me, explained Amir had come to turn himself in."

"An operative. Is this your Candyman?"

"Yes sir. It is."

Knock, knock, knock! Secretary Smith's door swung open without permission.

"What are you doing, Nancy!" Doyle hollered at his assistant as she burst into the room.

"I'm sorry Mr. Secretary, but these men said it's a matter of national security, she said, flustered. Doyle had never seen Nancy anxious, her hands searching for something to relieve her nervous energy as her mind searched for the words to say; her eyes darting left to right, from the men entering, back to Doyle.

"Mr. President, I'm putting you on speaker." Doyle gestured for Nancy to leave, her eyes screaming, "thank you," as she left.

"What you got for me?" he asked, recognizing the two operatives immediately. They worked exclusively with the data coming in from Medusa, and were instructed to report directly to him had any immediate actionable intel reach them, specifically regarding high-value personnel.

"We just decoded an operation," one man said, glancing toward the other.

"Spit it out!"

"Nassir. Someone's going to kidnap Nassir."

"What the hell, Doyle!" President Pierce hollered over the speakerphone. "Do we have a security detail on him?"

"Yes. I'll make the call myself. Call you back." He pressed a button ending the call, and began dialing Nassir.

"You two, get your asses back downstairs. I want everything that comes in, and I want an action plan initiated before you tell me about it. This kid can't go missing. Especially not now."

"You've reached Nassir Ajab. Please leave your name and number and I'll get back to you—"

"Shit!" Doyle ground his teeth as he pounded again the desk again, redialing the number of their best hope for peace in the states. Again, he got his voicemail. He dialed another number, one to the secret servicemen who were providing watch over Nassir. The young engineer hadn't been told, but several weeks ago, a small group of men watched over him day and night, ensuring his safety. They were trained to always be ready, but Doyle knew a head's up wouldn't hurt.

"Hello," a voice said after three rings.

"Perseus is in jeopardy," Doyle said into the phone.

"What's the problem?" the steady voice responded.

"Someone wants to steal him away, but we can't let that happen."

"Time?"

"Assume it's imminent. Don't let the shit out of your sight."

"Copy."

The line went dead.

Seattle, Washington

"Nassir!" an old, bearded man exclaimed as he stood, a high pitched, vibrato of a laugh extending across the small café.

"Keep it down, Dad," Nassir said as he hugged his father, embarrassed that so many people now stared at the two men.

"What, I cannot love my son?" he said, attempting to cause guilt.

"Okay, old timer."

"I already got you coffee, decaf," he smiled. "A father

never forgets."

"It's not hard to remember."

"I'm an old man!" he said dramatically, and at high volume, laughing again. This time it became contagious and quite a few people in the café laughed with him.

"Just sit down," Nassir begged with a smile.

"So, your job? It is good? Finally getting money?"

"Be proud, Dad. You raised a good son." Nassir reached across the table and squeezed his father's hand, their skin tones differing slightly, but still neither as dark as the coffee inside their cups.

"I wish I could be like you, Nassir. So honest, so genuine, so gracious."

"Come on Dad. You're being emotional."

"You are being modest. You've worked so very hard Nassir. I remember when you were seventeen," he paused, staring out the window. Something had caught his eye. "You— uh—you, you came home and went to your room. I could always tell. You had a mischievous look, you smiled with your face, just like your father. I snuck up the stairs behind you, watched you reach under your bed for a wooden box. Later, I went to your room and opened it."

"You did? Why did you never tell me?"

"I didn't want to know where all the money came from."

"Why tell me this now?"

"I'm not sure," he said, still watching out the window as three men walked across the street toward the diner, splitting off toward the multiple exits.

"Do you want to know where the money came from?"

"No," he said softly, his eyes now looking into Nassir's.

"People used to pay me for cheat sheets. Then it was to help them program apps. Nothing illegal Dad."

"That's a relief," he said softly, looking into his coffee. His chin began to quiver as he stared. "I'm glad your soul isn't as dark as mine."

"Dad, what's going on? Talk to me?" Nassir said as he watched several tears slip quickly out of his father's eyes, and hid inside his thick salt and pepper beard.

"Nassir I've loved you as a son for so long I don't know what else to do. Please don't judge me in this moment."

Nassir sat frozen, unable to process what his father had said. "Dad?" he managed to say, softly, searching for his father's eyes, but they wouldn't look up from the coffee. He sat slumped forward, unmoving, seemingly lifeless except the tears and the steady rise and fall of his chest. "Dad?" Nassir said again, this time standing and walking around the table.

"Do not move," a voice said from behind, as something firm pressed into Nassir's back. "Walk out the front door, and into the black Suburban."

Nassir froze, staring at his father who only sunk lower into the booth.

"Walk," the man from behind said, pressing harder into Nassir's spine with the gun. Nobody in the restaurant noticed what was happening, and, in a moment, it was all over.

Nassir was outside and into the seat behind the driver, the man with the gun to his right. The rear of the SUV had two additional men, both with large capacity mini-machine guns, and the passenger seat held an eagle-eyed rifleman, who began shouting orders. Immediately, the car pulled off at a tremendous rate of speed.

Nassir was panicked as the SUV swerved through traffic, avoiding other cars, quickly turning back and forth down several streets to lose a car that was very clearly following them. Nassir refused to look back, afraid of what he might see, but also, he was already feeling nauseous from the erratic movements. He grasped the door, the handle above, but nothing helped him get a firm hold, and he continuously found himself struggling to stay put.

Bang, bang, bang! Three shots rang out and Nassir felt a cold rush of air. Curiosity got the better of him, and he turned to find the source of the wind. The two men in the rear of the SUV had opened the rear window a small amount, and were firing toward another black SUV. Instinctively, Nassir rolled forward into the floor space behind the front seat. He grasped his knees with his arms, buried his head within his body, and began rocking back and forth, humming songs in an effort to block out the noise. He was stable, jammed between the seats, no longer feeling nausea from the thrashing physics of the screeching car.

Wham! Nassir was thrown toward his seat as something struck the rear of their vehicle. Wham! Again, this time forcing Nassir out of his Zen-like state. How could my father do this to me? The thought leapt to his brain, despite the terror that surrounded him in the moment.

Wham! A third collision, this time from the driver side, sent the entire SUV spinning. The G-force caused the men inside the vehicles to slam against the doors and side panels, and forced Nassir's hands from his knees. In a fraction of a second, his head snapped back, and struck the door. A moment later, the friction from the screaming tires decelerated them rapidly, the immutable laws of physics once again played havoc with the men inside, forced Nassir's head toward his own knees where immediately the impact rendered him unconscious. There he sat impossibly still, infantile in his inability to steady his own head, bleeding uncontrollably from his face. But everyone in the car was looking elsewhere.

Chapter 36
IMPROVISE, ADAPT, OVERCOME

Sana'a, Yemen

David sat in a conference room on the main floor of the Embassy. He had just hung up the phone, having tried to call Secretary Smith for the second time with no answer. Frustrated, but remaining calm, he sat, letting the light from the windows bathe him in warmth. It was odd feeling— the sun—which was even more awkward considering he usually sat in a small, cramped office alone, dead to the world, and never considered being around other Americans while he worked. Nonetheless, it was the condition the local intelligence chief insisted upon. "You can do whatever you damn well please, so long as I'm sitting right there with you,"

Rafael, "no last name," had said hours earlier.

"Can I have my bag?" David asked the station chief, staring at him from across the table. *I could cut his throat from here,* he caught himself thinking. The deal they struck didn't sit well with the recluse agent who'd worked alone for half a decade, reporting straight to the top of the food chain.

"What for?"

"I've told you already. It has everything I've worked toward for five years inside. Be part of the solution, let me work," David said, slamming his fist firmly into the wooden table separating the two men.

"Touchy, touchy," Rafael smirked as he stared condescendingly. "I haven't heard about you, David Westbrook, or what you're doing in country. Explain it to me again? You work directly for Secretary Smith, but now he won't answer your call?"

David sat silent, provoked, but resisting the urge to attack the man.

"Sounds to me, if what you're saying is true, you've maybe gone AWOL. Why were you with the group attacking the Embassy?"

"I've said it before. Not repeating myself again."

"Amir Qasmi, right, right. Well, I can't argue. You surely had the man in your possession. But I find it hard to believe after a year of evading agents all over the globe, he suddenly finds you, an unknown agent in Yemen, and decides to tell you everything."

"Where's Amir?" David asked, changing the subject. It had been nearly twenty-four hours since seeing him. He had seen Samantha here and there around the compound, but she rarely talked, mainly stared at inanimate objects, oblivious to her surroundings.

"Safe. Once we get a green light to travel stateside, he

and Samantha will be outta here."

"I'm going stateside too. With. My. Gear," David stated in staccato fashion, ensuring Rafael understood.

"I have no doubts you're going stateside. But maybe not the way you'd prefer."

"You're so damn stupid."

"Excuse me?"

"You're career's gonna be over. You have no idea what you're interfering with," David said, shaking his head and smirking, his long arms tied securely behind the chair.

"Until I know who you are I'm treating you just the same as our friend Amir. A prisoner."

"Please, listen to me. Grab my gear. I'll tell you everything but we don't have long."

Rafael left the room. Upon returning, the large backpack was slammed on the table. David cringed, praying the drives hadn't been destroyed. They'd survived years of abuse, moving several times, hand-to-hand combat, and firefights. If they were destroyed by an American agent, he'd likely kill Rafael.

"Open the main compartment. You'll see three redundant drives." David read into the look Rafael was giving him. "Jesus, at some point you're going to have to trust me. Turn the wi-fi off on the laptop, disconnect it from the motherboard. If there's a virus, then destroy the computer afterward, but I promise, you'll like what you see."

It took only moments, but Rafael went the extra step, opening the laptop, removing the wireless antenna and Bluetooth, finally attaching the drive.

"Look at us now," David said, tilting his head sideways. "Becoming friends after all."

"What now?"

"The encrypted file, titled 'War Games.' Open it."

"Holy shit," Rafael said out loud, unable to control

himself as a map of the Middle East covered the screen and thousands of datapoints began flying in from all angles, and pinning themselves into cities. The more pins, the larger a red dot would appear.

"What you're watching is what I've collected for years. Access points into the dark web. You're likely seeing a timeline of the access, starting from the earliest data, and gradually sweeping toward new. The larger and more red, the more activity in that particular month. You can see a trend, right?" David asked as he watched Rafael take it in.

"Yes. The data points toward the mountains. The larger points almost walking themselves toward them."

"I noticed that too," David said. He was relieved, almost gracious now for Rafael's approach to the situation. It led to someone finally seeing what David had been observing for a while now, but not understanding the meaning.

"What's this mean?" Rafael said, looking to David for the first time since opening the file.

"No damn idea," David admitted, sighing heavily and wincing, the cuffs digging into his wrists.

"Tell me everything."

"I'll tell you what I know," David responded.

"Fair enough," Rafael leaned onto the table in anticipation, as if David was whispering.

"But if you don't take these cuffs off soon, I'll be the last person you ever see."

It took about an hour, but David never stopped speaking. He told Rafael about his interrogations, how it had been leading to critical operational intel back stateside. He told Rafael about Logan and his team, how they were the enforcing arm back home, and how they recently lost one of their own. David went on to tell Rafael about Alex Pines, the rescue mission, and how Amir escaped with a message for Logan.

Rafael had heard the rest directly from Amir's mouth. How a man named Karim Al Muhammad was the leader of a multi-billion dollar terrorism group, and had built several massive compounds in the Haraz Mountains in Yemen, as far as he knew. Karim possessed surface-to-air capabilities, owned Russian-built aircraft, including SU-35 Terminators, and a variety of helicopters, land vehicles, as well as artillery and long range weaponry; and that was all for defense. Amir, admittedly, had no idea what his offensive weaponry was, but assumed it primarily involved the soldiers they trained in the mountains.

"Why capture Samantha? Why Logan? If you and Logan were doing his bidding, so to speak, as Amir had said, why capture him?"

"I have no idea."

"And then why attack the Embassy? What the hell's going on?"

"I don't know," David said, rubbing his wrists. "Thanks for this," David said, raising his hands, sarcastically.

"Hurt a bit?"

"I'm a big boy."

"Yeah, don't be a bitch. So, what's your plan Candyman?" Rafael said, smirking at the name.

"I need to talk to the secretary. We can't go stateside until we have Logan."

"Sounds to me like you've got a crush."

"He's a good man. I told you already, he risked his own ass to save Alex Pines. No way I'm not gonna risk mine for a guy like that."

David sat for a moment, deep in thought, rattling idea after idea around in his mind. He hadn't planned a mission in some time, lately his life had been more improvisation, reacting to each new situation as it had come. He wasn't thinking about the conditions in the U.S., how they were faring with the attacks, or if things had died down since martial law was enacted. Thoughts like that were worthless, the actions there, far out of his control.

"Where's the third man you brought in with us?" David asked, remembering what Amir had said about the man.

"In a cell downstairs."

"Near Amir?"

"Yes."

David smiled, "I've got a plan. But I'll need something from my bag."

"Take it," Rafael said, sliding the black bag across the table.

David's bag had seemingly infinite pockets, but there were few he used. This pocket was deep within a larger compartment. He reached inside, his fingers wrapping firmly around a metal tin.

"Altoids?" Rafael asked confused.

"These little tins are great to mod for any use," David said, opening the small metal box. Inside, a kit with two syringes, several needles, and a vial of milky white liquid.

"Well shit, that's the candy, isn't it?"

"Ready to work Mr. 'No last name'?" David asked as he prepped the drug. "We're gonna need Amir for this."

The two specters descended the stairs, their shoes echoing louder with each step below the earth, the firm walls reverberating the sounds more efficiently. David quickly got his bearings once they were below, entering the large room at the bottom of the stairs. He looked left, noting the hallway with several cells, and right, along the wall, the bench where he first saw Samantha.

"Don't get sentimental," Rafael joked watching David scan the basement.

"Amir first," David said without reacting.

Rafael walked down the hallway, a moment later

returning with the tall, dark man.

"You get this shit figured out yet?" Amir asked David who stood with his long arms crossed awkwardly over his chest.

"Not quite. I need you to show me more loyalty first. Don't worry, you'll love this shit."

"Lovely, can't wait."

"Oh, don't be bitchy. You get to talk to your friend again."

Amir understood immediately. "You can't be serious," he said, his heart banging in his ears, his hands flexing in anticipation of knuckles to flesh.

"Hang on now boy," David said, sensing Amir's excitement. "We need information first."

"Why does Karim want Logan?"

"He wanted to give him to me as a gift, so to speak."

"To kill?" David asked, Amir nodded in confirmation.

"So, what now? He think's you're dead, right?"

"I don't know how he couldn't. Taj is dead, I made sure of that, and I placed one of the guards near him, the tallest one, the best replacement for me."

"We need to find out where Falcone is."

"I'll beat that bitch bloody, but he won't talk," Amir said, looking down the hallway, knowing behind one of the steel doors lay one of his many tormentors; one of the men that made it hard for him to sleep at night.

"Amir, I don't come to parties empty handed." David uncrossed his arms and held the syringe in the air, shaking it back and forth.

"My kind of party," Amir responded smiling.

Three men walked down the hall toward the only closed door in the depths of the compound. The metallic clank was noisy as the lock released, the door opened silently, revealing the battered man.

"Sweetheart, what happened to your face?" Amir joked without smiling as he saw the swollen and bloodied face of the man who used to drag him around by the hair, punch him in the stomach for flinching, or strike him in the face for a wrong answer to an impossible question.

"Amir Qasmi, *assalamualaikum*" he responded. "He called you son."

"Jealous?" Amir quickly shot back.

The man looked to Amir, his eyes full of rage and absent fear. The guard began to stand, and Amir took a step forward, but David and Rafael quickly grabbed him.

"Make this easy, tell us where Logan Falcone is," David said, holding onto Amir's arm.

"Amir, you must have told them," he said, chuckling.

"I did. But they insisted."

"You'll talk," David said gently, releasing Amir.

"Physical pain means nothing to me," the man said, smiling, raising his arms out to the side, inviting the beating.

"No, no, we're not starting there my friend," David said, smirking.

"We'll finish there," Amir said, approaching the guard, quickly grasping his arm, and slamming him hard into the wall, opening up the wound on his face. He held the guard's arm behind his back firmly, pulling upward on his wrist, causing the man to grunt as pain exploded into the front of his left shoulder and across his face.

"What was that sweetheart?" Amir asked him, close enough to smell his rancid breath from nearly a day without food or water.

"You cannot intimidate me my friend. I will bleed out, you could cut me one piece at a time and I will never cry out, never talk. *Allahu akbar.* It's my calling."

"Here comes the Candyman," Amir sang the words into his ear, ignoring the ramblings.

David approached, injecting the poison into the enemy. Amir released him, allowing the guard to fall to the floor.

"Amir. I knew you were alive before I saw you."

"Oh? And how is that?"

"You are too emotional Amir," he said, smiling. "Karim knows as well."

"Lies."

"Truly? I was instructed to hunt you down. To bring you to him so he could ask you how you lived and Taj died."

Amir looked to David, asking with his eyes what his mouth could not.

"Tell us where Logan Falcone is," David asked, testing to see if the drug had worked as quickly as it appeared. The man, after all, had been dehydrated, starved, and bleeding.

"Amir knows the place. Don't you Amir? Do you remember the place we met? Where I first made you bleed? Where I made you cry out for your mother, where you told me about your father's death, how you begged for your own? Do you remember that place Amir?"

Amir was trembling, his knuckles white, and he failed to control his breathing. For a moment, he was back in that room, white tiles all around, three guards standing around him asking questions, meaningless inquiries mostly, but anxiety always won him over.

"Ah, there you are Amir, a scared little boy, American. That's what Taj would call you, right? Even after you became his brother." The guard spat the word out, an insult, an accusation, a reminder of who he had become.

"Amir, do you remember the place?" David asked.

"I don't know its coordinates, but I remember the place."

"Where's it located?"

"In the Haraz Mountains."

"How do we get there?"

"Only access by vehicle."

"Can you show us on a map?" Rafael asked, realizing he brought his laptop down.

"It's possible."

Rafael approached, placed the computer in front of the guard and opened it, revealing David's map. He scanned to the wide area of Yemen, and the Haraz Mountains.

"There," the man said, pointing to the screen. "In that valley, two-days drive from Sana'a." He looked to Amir once more. "You want your revenge now, don't you?"

"I want a lot of things."

David and Rafael looked toward each other, then stood back, allowing Amir to approach the guard.

"Do you know why I killed the drunk for Alex Pines?" Amir asked as he removed his shirt, throwing it to the floor behind him. David and Rafael counted scars by the dozen as they watched Amir's back contract and relax with each breath.

"Jesus," Rafael said quietly toward David, who just stood staring, almost cheering for Amir in his moment.

"I killed the drunk so Alex remained pure, unlike me. I've killed for so many reasons, for so many people," Amir paused, his own words causing him to reflect on his past. Amir took a deep breath as a tear rolled down his face. "So, my friend, now that you're unable to tell a lie, you are jealous he called me son, aren't you?"

"How could I not be? I've done so much for him, but he favored you."

"Yeah, that must hurt," Amir kicked the man in the stomach. "Wrong answer," Amir said.

"What is Karim's plan? He told me details, maybe he made changes after I left."

"I don't kno—"

Smack—the sound of knuckles on flesh as Amir struck the

man before the answer left his mouth.

David looked to Rafael and the two men slid out of the room, allowing Amir some privacy with the man.

"We're gonna need an immediate action plan," David said to Rafael. "Damn it! Where's the secretary?" he slapped the concrete wall in frustration.

As David and Rafael discussed possible special ops scenarios, Amir walked out of the room, closing it behind him, the lock engaging. He was covered with a spattering of red, quickly wiping it away with his shirt. He was breathing heavy, but for the first time since David met Amir, he saw calm in his eyes.

"I've got a plan," Amir said, wiping his face.

"I've heard about your plans in the past. I think I'll pass," David said, ignoring the terrorist turned witness.

"Hear me out David. Have I done anything wrong since we met? Have I lied, on or off your truth serum?"

David stood, once again crossing his arms, his real planning taking a back seat as he listened to Amir.

"The answer is no, I haven't. If Karim thinks I'm alive, then you're in. He's not going to turn away his own son."

"What if he kills you on sight?"

"He'd have to see me first, and even if he does, you'll have your target, if nothing else."

"So now you're a martyr for our cause?" Rafael asked, annoyed.

"I've never been a martyr. I've always been looking out for number one. I've learned something since Saint Louis." Amir became uneasy in his vulnerability in the moment. "I—I'm trying to be who I wanted to be years ago. I got lost along the way."

"You're still gonna pay for the shit you did stateside, no matter what happens out here."

"I know, and I'm okay with that. Just let me do this."

"So, you want to drive to the compound by yourself, snatch Logan, and get out?"

"Something like that, yeah."

"We're gonna have a backup plan, just in case your wild idea doesn't work, Hollywood," David said, looking to Rafael.

"Let's keep trying the secretary," Rafael said already walking down the hallway.

Chapter 37
OPERATION RAM

Washington, D.C.

Doyle arrived a moment after Nassir at the George Washington University Hospital. Nassir had been unconscious, for nearly two hours after the trauma from the rollover accident, but everyone else in his vehicle had been killed. The secret service members had stopped the attempted kidnapping, and in return, kidnapped his father as he left the diner.

A physician in Seattle signed off on what the U.S. government deemed "critical for national security," insisting Nassir needed to get to Washington, D.C. as quickly as possible. In the meantime, several squads of special forces operatives placed themselves around and within Nassir's company headquarters, ensuring Medusa would remain operative and safe while Nassir was unable to access his invention.

"Nassir," Doyle asked gently as he saw the young engineer stir in bed. "Nassir," he repeated and stood, placing his hand on the injured man's shoulder.

"Mr. Secretary?" Nassir asked, his eyes squinting in the soft light of the room. They had turned the lights out in anticipation of his concussion.

"Yes, how are you feeling?"

"Dead, are we sure I'm not dead?"

"Quite positive. I'm sorry to do this to you Nassir, but do you know who tried to take you? Did they talk at all? Ask you any questions?"

"No," Nassir responded, his head beginning to throb as nausea completely consumed him. "My dad, why?" Nassir asked as he remembered the moment in the diner before he was abducted.

"I don't know anything either Nassir, but I promise we'll get answers. Rest. Call me when you feel you can talk."

Secretary Smith quickly returned to his office, where several messages were waiting. *Shit*, he thought as he saw four calls from Yemen had been missed. He picked up the phone and dialed.

"Hi, this is Secretary Smith," he said into the phone when someone at the Embassy in Yemen answered.

"Please hold."

"About damn time, Mr. Secretary!" David hollered into the phone. "Do you know there was an attack on the Embassy?"

"I've heard, yes. Things haven't been wonderful here. Nassir Ajab was abducted, but we got him back. He's beat up pretty good. We need you stateside pronto—"

"Mr. Secretary, with all due respect, shut up for a moment." David waited for the shock to clear. "Samantha Falcone was here when we arrived. We think that's why they were attacking the Embassy. She was kidnapped, and

Logan exchanged himself for her."

"Thank God. What do we need to do? Where is he?"

"Luckily, Amir saw a guard he recognized. It's been a real shitstorm here Mr. Secretary, but we know what compound he's in."

"I'll coordinate an op with General Anderson."

"Okay, but that's plan B."

"Stop dicking around David. Out with it."

"Amir. He had a plan."

"Fuck that traitorous bastard! I know what his plan is, to escape."

"I agree with you, but he hasn't lied to me, yet. To tell you the truth, it's the best shot we've got. Karim Al Muhammad apparently thinks Amir is still alive, and wants to see him."

"So what?"

"So apparently, Logan was supposed to be a gift for Amir before we snatched Alex and killed Karim's son, Taj. Plan is to get Amir inside, and have him bring Logan out. From there, any ops are on the table, but if we go in full assault, the concern is they'll execute Logan without prejudice."

Secretary Smith squeezed his eyes shut, trying to process it all. It was difficult to compartmentalize everything, to see the big picture. He was fighting a two-front war between Nassir and the martial law, and now he was trying to coordinate a rescue mission to get Logan home. He needed David stateside to interrogate Nassir's tight-lipped father. He wasn't speaking, wasn't drinking or eating either. They were on a limited timetable with getting intel out of him, his deconditioned body and diabetes would likely kill him soon.

"I'll call General Anderson. Get him up to speed. He's gonna want to get his boy home just as bad as we are. Luckily, we've got a team that's already assaulted a compound so they should be familiar with the terrain."

"I'm going to ride in with Amir until we're half a day out. From there, I'm going on foot," David said, giving the secretary more confidence in the plan.

"We'll have a SEAL team waiting for you there. Take GPS so we can have them group on you."

"They have SAMS, and Amir ensured me Karim would likely be on site, so they'll have a shitload of defense systems ready to go. We're walking into one badass compound."

"Let's hope Amir's plan pays off."

"If it doesn't, he'll likely be the first to die," David said, sighing, the operation was moving quickly.

"If it does, we're gonna bomb those bastards straight to hell. Make sure Amir knows he's not off the hook for America."

"I did." David said, pausing. "Doyle," David asked, his tone softening. "You think Alex is up for a ride?"

"Doubtful. His injuries are bad. He'll likely never fly again."

"Shit. Would have been poetic to have him drop a bomb."

"Gotta run, David. Get on the road. Bring the sat-phone."

"General Anderson," Doyle said into the receiver, waiting for a loud response.

"Mr. Secretary. Heard about my boy yet?" he asked, getting directly to the point.

"Yes, sir. It's why I'm calling. We've got Amir too."

"Fan-fucking-tastic. Can't wait to see him rot."

"Thing is General, we need him to get Logan. We need an op."

The two powerful men talked for several minutes,

Secretary Smith giving Anderson the long, exhaustive details in quick order, leaving out the fluff. It was clear General Anderson was uncomfortable, but conceded to the idea that Amir's plan was the most likely option to get Logan out alive.

"Op name is Ram," General Anderson said.

"Fair enough," Doyle said, understanding the reference to Saint Louis, the Rams football game where they caught Amir.

"Good luck, General. Keep me posted."

"We don't need luck, Mr. Secretary. We're the best damn fighting force in the world, and now we've got a reason to loose the hounds."

Chapter 38

THE PRODIGAL SON

Solomon was eager for battle. He knew Logan, watched how passionately he fought for Alex, a man he never met, and it forced Sol to stay as sharp as he could. His ranks were once again reinforced with Lonnie and Dubs, both of whom had proven their worth just weeks earlier. Solomon took a liking to Dubs after their physical match up in the mountains, and now interacting with him for a second time, he knew the man meant business. Dubs hadn't smiled, hadn't even talked since the debrief on board the carrier just hours earlier.

Under the cover of darkness, the SEAL team had descended into a valley thirty miles from the compound, by way of HALO jump. It had proven its effectiveness already once before. They buried their gear on site leaving no trace of their presence. The team sat, waiting for a solitary vehicle to approach from the south, carrying Amir and David.

The sun was low in the sky as Amir drove on top of a ridge that formed a peak between two deep valleys on either side. To his right, the slope descended into a bottomless darkness; to his left, a million hues of orange, red, and brown, reflecting the setting sun. It was just as Amir's life had been, one side dark, the other brilliant, and now he was stuck somewhere in between. He knew he'd never be free, but at least he'd be in control for once.

"What you thinking about?" David asked from the rear of the truck as it bounced without ceasing over the ancient terrain.

"My lines," Amir joked.

"Hope you got 'em down, cause otherwise, you're fucked."

"Don't I know it."

"We got a while, why don't you tell me why you turned?"

"Which time?"

"This time."

"Alex Pines. We have a lot in common. Both lost our dads, both served, both were given the opportunity to avenge a death."

"Okay?"

Amir paused, forming words he hadn't thought of. He knew the sensations he felt when he looked at Alex, when he reflected on the young pilot's life, both in and out of captivity.

"I saw who I could have been if I made different choices. I'm embarrassed about who I've become. Huh," he smirked. "I guess I'm envious of Alex. I didn't want him to become like me."

"That's why you killed that guy."

"Yeah, that's why I killed him. So Alex couldn't, but he still got to see that asshole die. That was the moment I decided I was done. I didn't give a shit what happened after that, but I knew then, I wanted out."

"Can't say that's a bad story, Amir. Almost admirable."

"What about you Mr. Candyman? What's your story?"

"I keep my secrets," David said, thinking of Amal, the boy who died protecting his secrets.

"This is gonna be a boring-ass ride," Amir said, rolling his eyes. He continued to drive as darkness encroached on the vehicle, quickly changing the landscape as the sun descended below the mountains.

It was dark, quiet, and uncomfortable when Amir hit the drop point in the mountain pass. As planned, Amir exited the car, grabbed fuel containers from the top of the truck, and began filling the tank.

"Catch ya' on the flipside," David said, throwing his bag on his back, putting on a pair of NVGs, and quickly sliding down the western edge of the ridgeline into darkness where the SEAL team lay in wait.

Amir smirked, then sighed, knowing he was now alone, vulnerable to whatever end Karim would find appropriate.

Bang! Amir was struck from behind and thrown against the SUV.

"Figured I owed you one. In case you get your ass killed in there, mother fucker."

"Chill out," Amir said as best he could, his face pressed against the steel door.

"Chill out? You're lucky it's Logan we're saving. He's about the only reason I wouldn't kill you right now!"

Amir felt the unexplainable pressure release, allowing him to turn and face his attacker. Dubs was much larger up close than he had been through the rifle scope a year ago in Saint Louis. It was no wonder the man survived. Three shots from a high-powered rifle, not just one, was needed to take that beast down.

"I volunteered to give you an intel update. You've got two roadblocks ahead. He'll know you're coming from a long ways out." Dubs placed his heavy hand onto Amir's shoulder. "I really hope you make it outta this alive."

"Appreciate that big man. No hard feelings," Amir said, adjusting his shirt.

It took everything Dub's had not to jump the man who shot him through the abdomen barely one year earlier. His chest rose and fell, the air entering his massive airways was audible in the silence of the ridgeline.

"Get my boy out. Then we'll talk again."

"That's the plan."

Dubs disappeared from sight, and Amir knew the twenty-man assault team was on their way.

Amir turned the headlights off on his car, something Taj had done while they traveled to one of the compounds, stating, "They're watching us." Amir smiled at the thought. He knew Taj had been right, and at that moment more than one satellite was orbiting overhead, tracking his movements, as well as those men navigating the mountains through the darkness. It was beautiful without headlights, it allowed the half-moon from above to illuminate the earth as he bounced his way down the ridgeline.

Amir drove for another hour before stopping to sleep. It was something the team strategically planned. It would allow the SEALs to navigate at night, approaching the compound before Amir arrived. What help would they be if they weren't even on site when Logan was brought out? It also gave Amir one last night of freedom, before death or imprisonment. He was grateful for that. Freedom had been the only thing he craved for years.

Solomon led his team through the unsteady terrain for miles under a bright, cloudless evening. They had the latest reports, they knew where Karim had his SAMS' sites, where outposts were, roadblocks, and even the geographical impasses that would leave them unable to proceed. A cartographer had given them a detailed map of the quickest route, allowing them options if they encountered possible threats. Their first objective: to get on site without being seen or heard, which in these valleys, was a lot more difficult than one would imagine.

Along with the stationary weaponry and manned outposts, there were sporadic, aerial reconnaissance flown by Russian-made helos, scanning the area for anything abnormal. It was the primary reason Solomon and the men had to bury their HALO gear after landing, the O2 tanks, masks, and flights suits would have been a dead giveaway.

Whap, whap, whap! The team heard the echo through the valley, causing each man's heart rate to increase dramatically, flashbacks from their previous missions playing in their heads.

"Zeus we've got unfriendly noises, you seein' anything in the air?" Sol asked, signaling his men to get down and spread.

"We've got two tangos approximately fifty mikes from you, no immediate threat," responded a voice from the E-3 Sentry.

"Thanks, keep us informed," Solomon said, instantly letting the men know it was time to move.

"That's why we're here, sir."

Eventually the prop noise faded, allowing them to focus on the ground and to remain unseen. Their forward position was just within a mile of the compound on a southern slope. It was the easiest access point for them to manage, based on the need to pick up David on the way.

David was holding his own, sweating his ass off, but the runs he took most evenings had paid off. They gave him some BDUs, and an M4, which felt as familiar as an ex-girlfriend in his hands. He fell in line with the SEALs, placed in between Ghost and Blue, both of which wouldn't hesitate to put David in his place if need be. It was daybreak when they arrived on site, just in time to see Amir driving down into the valley, throwing up a trail of dust on the road toward the compound.

"Whiplash, get the drone ready," Solomon said calmly, watching Amir approach the gate. The guards on location hadn't been increased, which was a good sign. They expected twenty outside, six of which would be at the main gate, and God knows how many inside the compound. There was also an airbase within fifteen minutes by helo, should they call in more reinforcements.

"Count six at the gate," Blue said, staring through his scope, the .50 caliber poised at his shoulder, waiting for the moment Logan was spotted.

"I can't believe this shit," Lonnie said, looking at Dubs, who knelt behind a boulder, his eyes locked on the seemingly infinite space between him and his friend.

"I know. He's right there and we can't do a damn thing about it," Dubs responded, still fuming over his interaction with Amir.

"Halo, be advised, possible tangos entering the airspace. ETA thirty minutes."

"Copy, Zeus. Alright everyone. We've got some aircraft inbound. Stay low."

Karim was emotionally overwhelmed. The roadblocks had radioed ahead, explaining Amir was traveling alone toward the compound, and was hoping his father would see him. Deep inside the facility he waited for Amir's arrival, his thoughts confusing, replaying the conversation he had with Logan over and over again in his head. *Amir killed Taj.*

Karim sat at that same metal desk when he heard those painful words, the same desk where he sat watching Amir shoot the drunk driver, the same place he sat while Amir shot the guards. Karim smirked, surprised at how many people had been killed by Amir in little white rooms like this.

A door opened, and in stumbled Logan Falcone, or at least a shell that resembled the man.

"Mr. Falcone," Karim smiled as he stayed seated for their greeting.

"You ready for another round of emotional overreactions?" Logan asked, spitting a pinkish hue on the floor.

"You've been lippy with more than just me lately I take it?"

"You know it's funny you say that."

"Why's that Mr. Falcone?"

"That's what the sergeant said at my SERE training. You know what SERE training is, don't you?"

Karim nodded and gestured for Logan to continue.

"Here's how mine went. We were supposed to hide, try to evade capture, but I knew it was only a matter of time before they found everyone; and I wanted to test myself. So, I didn't hide. I let them find me."

"Why?"

"To see how hard I could make them work to break me. The first time I did SERE I broke after a few days. But, that was because I was tied to a chair with my hands behind my back, and when the Marine kicked me in the chest, the chair tipped back breaking my wrists. But after that, I felt strong. Not physically strong, God no. I was down nearly twenty pounds, unable to use both hands effectively, but mentally I was impenetrable. So, I requested to do SERE again because I wanted to see if *I* could break *them*."

"Let me guess, you did?"

"No. Those assholes are tough. Broke me for a second time, but it took quite a while longer. You know what they asked me after a week?"

"Enlighten me, Mr. Falcone."

"They said, 'been lippy with the last few guys have you?'"

"I remind you of your sergeant? Should that make me feel good?"

"No, I hated him more than you. He's the one who broke me. If you think you've got anything here that can make me talk, you're sadly misguided. I love this game, Karim. I can play it much longer now than I could when I was a twenty-two-year-old boy. I've been on both sides of the playing field. I know the tricks, I know what works. I've even made you blush a few times, and I'm supposed to be playing defense."

"So, what to do now?"

"Tell me where Samantha is."

"Unfortunately, she's safe and sound. My plans are often full of patience and timing."

"I'm gonna level with you, Karim," Logan said, plopping down with a hard sigh, relief spreading through him as he rested his weak legs. "I don't think I *can* be killed."

"Oh, well that's bravado now, isn't it?"

"I've never said it out loud before. It's something I've thought for a long time. Watching friends die does that to a man. Why me? Why do I always get to live?" Logan said openly, the words flowing therapeutically out of his mouth. It made him a bit uneasy, but in the moment, he was beyond giving a shit.

"Well today just may be your day my American friend. Since we're on the subject, how would you greet death? With open arms, perhaps? It sounds to me you struggle with the topic," Karim unbuttoned his jacket and smiled condescendingly.

"I'll put it to you this way," Logan said, leaning forward onto the table. "It would have to be an act of God to take me out. I can't find any other reason I'm alive."

"You think you're alone in seeing death Mr. Falcone? I, too, must be immortal," Karim said, raising his arms into the air. "How many have you lost, three? Maybe four? I've lost dozens, sons, my wife, brothers; watched them die by so many hands I cannot even tell you which fell to whom," Karim said, his eyes enraged.

"I can tell you who killed Taj," Logan responded without hesitation. "But we've gone down that road, haven't we?"

"It's a funny thing, hearsay. You witnessed the disgraceful way I reacted when you spoke my name, but I held back when you told me who killed my son."

"You're an emotional guy."

"Logan, I've made a lot of money being able to read people," Karim continued through the interruption. "I base most of my business in person, reading their body language, their eyes, the physiological effects during questions. You my friend," he said, pointing at Logan and shaking his finger, "are admittedly impressive. I haven't seen a flaw in you. Which is why I'm so very glad we have a visitor. Someone I have been able to read for quite some time. Someone, in fact, who might get you to respond."

"Well I can't wait," Logan said. Inside he was a storm of misguided rage, as if his body already knew what his mind couldn't possibly. A scent, a pheromone creeping through Karim's language, through the structure of the building, straight into Logan's physiology.

"I'm actually a bit excited for this moment," Karim said and shivered, smiling at Logan and laughing. He turned toward the door to his right. "Send him in," Karim said loudly, and Logan's heart raced, his throat dried, unable to swallow.

In through the door walked a tall, dark man. His hair was short, but clearly professionally cut. His frame was leaner now, allowing the muscles to ripple as he moved to embrace the terrorist leader.

"Amir, you embrace me," Karim said, pulling back and gesturing toward Logan who waited at the table, his eyes transfixed on the man who haunted so many dreams.

"I do Father. Glad to see you."

"But," Karim said, reeling back and looking at Amir. "Are you here as the Prodigal Son? Or as Cain reincarnate?"

"I was in Sana'a. After I ran from our compound I was scared, tortured by the visions of men like this who killed Taj." Amir said, pointing to Logan. "I ran from that place, vowing revenge, but I never imagined seeing this man when I arrived."

"He says you killed Taj. He says Alex Pines witnessed you. He says you told Alex you had a message for Logan, one that included my name."

"Lies," Amir said, looking Karim in the eyes, unwavering.

"Hm," Karim looked toward Logan, smiling.

"My son," Karim embraced Amir a second time. "*Assalamualaikum.*"

"*Assaalamu Aliekum wa rehamutallah,*" Amir responded.

"It is good you are here to clear your name."

"A name that's already shit everywhere else in the world," Logan said, interrupting their reunion.

"How does it feel?" Amir said, turning his attention to Logan. "I don't actually need you to tell me," Amir responded before Logan could. "Did you know this man put a plan in place a long time ago to get you here? In front of me? *For* me?"

"How's that?" Logan asked, playing along. He read Amir's body language from the moment he entered the room: the false embrace highlighted by a vanishing smile as the two men hugged, the grinding of Amir's teeth as Karim spoke about Taj, how Amir immediately turned his entire body to address Logan, rather simply turn his head. Logan knew Amir was uncomfortable, and he'd rather engage Logan than get caught in a lie.

Amir smirked, and stared at the floor. "My father got me out of the U.S., trained me in these mountains, showed me I was a prince, and not a lowly servant like I had been in the Army. I'll admit, several months were rough, but it made me harder, more focused."

Amir paused as his traumatic time in captivity hijacked his thoughts: the beatings, the guards, how he fell apart emotionally and physically; something Alex Pines never did. Amir was envious of the young American pilot, and embarrassed of himself. He felt uneasy standing near Karim, he wanted to move, to push the man away, to kill him. Instead, he spoke once more to Logan.

"My reward? You."

"What was so bad about your first few months? I've had a pretty good stay so far. Me and Karim here have become good friends, swapped stories. We even got emotional together, right?" Logan asked, smiling at Karim, who nodded his head and smirked back.

"Amir, I'm glad you've returned," Karim said, deflecting the jab, and grasping the tall Pakistani man on both shoulders. Logan saw the subtle move Amir made, his shoulders tightening, leaning back from the physical contact, once again grinding his teeth, and this time, clenching his fists as well.

"I told you I'd bring him for you. Take your vengeance, if you wish. Otherwise, I'll take it for Taj." Karim reached toward his hip, grabbing his handgun once more in the small, confined room.

"I've never thought to harm him. I mean, I've never imagined it would really be an option. This man imprisoned me. I had no option but to run, to kill Jenkins, to reach out to you," *and then you had me beaten, starved, broken, used me for your cause,* Amir didn't say out loud. Rage built inside Amir as the events of the previous months began to overtake him. His head began to throb and his body ached, memories becoming alive in flesh and blood. *It all started with Logan,* Amir thought as his body began to respond before his mind.

Amir reached a hand toward Karim, who placed the gleaming 1911 into his hand. Amir pulled the slide back and walked toward Logan.

"Do you know how I got away?" Amir said, sitting in a chair opposite Logan.

"Never figured it out," Logan sat staring, admitting his defeat.

"I pulled off a piece of the trolley car's hand rail, used it to get into the storm drain. I bet you check those trolleys again, you'll find the spot where I took it. Matter of fact, you pop that drain open, you'll still see the pipe about fifty feet down stream."

"Bullshit. We had the whole city covered. You had help," Logan had been convinced for the past year that Amir hadn't been alone, that someone helped him get out of the city, likely had a mask just like they did for their attacks in Paris and Chicago.

"I wouldn't lie to you, Logan. Not when it's time for you to go," he said, pointing the gun at the Marine.

"So, this is your revenge? Shooting me thousands of miles from home in a damn basement? Come on. You've gotta do better than that? I kicked your ass more than once, and this is how you repay me? Pretty anti-climatic," Logan responded, shaking his head. Inside Logan knew Amir wouldn't shoot, that he couldn't die. But still, he wanted answers for how Amir got away, he wanted to know what he missed a year ago.

"I guess that's true," Amir said, gesturing with the gun and shrugging his shoulders.

Wham! Without warning, Amir reached across the table, striking Logan in the face with the barrel of the pistol, opening up a wound on Logan's cheek. The unexpected assault left Logan unable to process the next few moments as he fell, his chair slamming against the floor, shattering several tiles.

"I want him to feel my pain," Amir said to Karim who nodded in approval, both men wanting Logan to suffer. Amir walked around the table and picked Logan up from the floor. Logan groaned, his shoulders burned from being tied and affixed to the chair that Amir was lifting, forcing Logan back upright.

"Feel familiar, Marine?" Amir asked, recalling the moment when Logan pistol whipped him outside of the hotel in Saint Louis.

"I've never been bitch slapped before," Logan said, smirking through the blood entering his eye. "Do it again?"

Amir looked confused, but hit him again nonetheless. It was no different the second time, Logan went to the floor, a bit more blood this time seeping from his open wound, finding a resting place on the white tile. Amir lifted him a second time.

"I'm still not sure I felt that," Logan said, spitting, the smile was gone, a brimstone rage beginning to fill him with energy. His hands pulled aggressively at the handcuffs, willing them to snap. He saw the same look in Amir's eyes, the desire to kill, the pain, the humiliation.

"Is it me you want to kill?" Logan asked as he squinted, trying to clear the blood from his eyes, the viscous matter causing them to burn.

"I'd say so."

"Make it worthwhile. Take these handcuffs off. Don't leave it on the table, don't kill me and wonder later, 'Could I have taken that old, beat up Marine?'"

Amir walked to Karim, who gestured for a guard to enter. Amir was focused, blinded to his mission at hand, his past coming full circle. He hadn't predicted this reaction to seeing Logan, the hatred he had for the Marine was palpable. It had only taken a moment, but Logan was detached from the chair.

"I whoop your ass, you tell me what really happened after DuPont Circle," Logan said, swinging his arms back and forth, shaking his hands to regain the ability to squeeze. He didn't care that his hands lacked sensation, it was better that way.

"That's confidence. If I win, you tell that big asshole outside to back off."

Amir had said it quietly, only the two of them could have heard it. Logan dropped his hands, confused. Amir rushed him, taking him down hard, the two men sliding to the far corner of the room.

"Guh!" Logan grunted from the blow, the wind escaping him as his diaphragm went into spasm.

"Don't fucking talk," Amir said softly. "Your boys are outside. Follow me closely, or we're both dead."

Amir stood, grabbing Logan by the shoulders, standing him up. "Sorry," he said quietly, punching Logan in the abdomen once again, then taking him and throwing him across the room toward Karim. Amir took large confident strides in pursuit. He gestured for the guard to enter.

"Grab him," he said to the guard who responded quickly, grasping Logan firmly, both arms behind his back.

"Are you ready?" Amir asked Logan, who nodded, still unable to breath from the blows.

Bang! Amir struck the guard hard. Immediately, Logan felt his grip loosen a moment before the man collapsed. Amir turned to Karim, and before the leader could react, Amir had grasped him firmly by the suitcoat, slamming him against the wall.

"You're not my father, you're not my leader, you're a fucking monster," he growled. "I want nothing more than to rip out your heart and stomp on it—but I can't. Not now."

Logan walked up behind Amir, and hit Karim, sending him to the ground hard, knocking him unconscious.

"We've got about thirty seconds before the second guard comes in," Amir said to Logan as he moved to the wall, out of sight.

"I don't owe you shit for this, you realize that?" Logan said, picking up Karim's gun and doing his best to clear his eyes of the blood.

"I'm not asking for anything. Just stay close."

Bang! The door swung open hard and hit the wall just beside Amir. In a flash, Amir was on the guard, choking him to the ground silently, while Logan closed the door, then watched.

Amir picked up the guard's rifle and radio, then ran toward the door Logan had been brought through a short while earlier; the same door that led him back to his cell. He hesitated to follow.

"I've gotta get out of here just as bad as you do," Amir responded, reading Logan's body language.

"We need to get Karim. Take him out of here. End this today."

"You don't think we've got a plan for that? Your boys are topside. An airstrike is coming as soon as they see us."

I can't die, Logan thought, but didn't say. Logan ran to Karim, attempting to lift him.

"They rotate a guard down here every five minutes! We'll never get out if we try to haul his ass outta here. Trust me."

Logan strained to lift the small man, but his body was failing him. The months of depression and imprisonment left him lacking strength.

"I saw Samantha. Remember her? She's waiting for you. You've got a baby coming, man! Let's get you the fuck outta here," Amir said forcefully, trying anything to snap Logan out of his myopic view. He was envious of Logan, his unabridged loyalty, his ability to think through the panic, the fatigue, the hatred they both shared for one another.

Logan stood, slowly, the achiness throughout his body screamed for rest, for a moment of silence. "I won't be merciful if you're lying to me. You think this shit was tough? It's child's play."

The two men raced through the endless concrete bunker, Amir leading the way. He'd been familiar with this specific compound, it was the first place he was allowed to roam free once Karim let him out of his cell. After several turns through the mazelike, concrete sublevel, Amir saw a large, steel door.

"Shit," Logan said, slowing to a stop. "Great plan."

"No faith?" Amir asked, smiling, placing his hand on the keypad, striking the four-digit code without looking. The door unlocked and Amir smiled at Logan. "After you?"

Logan stood, frozen. "Where's this go?"

"A back door." Amir began to jog through the corridor in almost complete darkness.

"These—are—everywhere?" Logan asked between breaths, his fatigue was incredible as he barely pumped his arms, his heavy legs causing his bare feet to slap against the concrete floor. He was numb, but surviving.

"There's one at every compound," Amir responded, remembering how he got away; Logan also recalling the moment when he saw Amir emerge from the compound in darkness, limping away into the mountains.

"I saw you run," Logan said softly as the neared the end of the tunnel. "When we saved Alex. I saw you limping away. What the hell is wrong with your leg?"

"Old war wound. Up this way." Amir paused for a moment. "You first."

They climbed the makeshift ladder in complete darkness. Amir knew it was far, about seventy-five vertical feet, and was unsure Logan would be able to do it. Logan ascended, slowly, grunting and sweating profusely, despite being severely dehydrated.

"Shit," Logan said softly, shaking his hand about halfway up. "Hands are cramping."

"Just climb, Marine," Amir responded, and moved up just behind Logan, pressing into his thighs with his upper back. Amir continued to push from below, each rung becoming synchronized without the need for verbal communication.

As they reached the top, the radio Amir had stolen began to broadcast white noise. The sound echoed through the vertical chamber and both men secretly held their breath.

Bang! From above, and a sliver of light entered the tunnel, allowing the odd couple to see they only had three more rungs before fresh air. Even the small amount of light entering was blinding, disorienting, forcing them to squint.

"Wait," Amir said, doing his best to peek around Logan and investigate.

"We got men up there?" Logan asked, understanding someone likely opened the hatch.

"Not that close. About a mile south, in the mountains."

"They know we're coming out here?"

"Yes. It was the plan."

"Is it Solomon?"

"I think that's his name, a SEAL team."

Blue, Logan thought as his heart quickened. "We'll be alright. I'm movin'," Logan said as a new-found energy surged through his body. He knew if he got topside, he was free.

Chapter 39
RAPTURE

Blue was scanning the compound. It had been over an hour since Amir drove through the gates, however, in the last five minutes, the compound came to life. Dozens of armed men began sweeping the grounds, several had moved off the compound and toward what the team knew to be the back door, as David had told them. Amir explained the layout of the compound to David, who then relayed the exit strategy to the SEAL team during their night's hike to their current location.

"Seems like something's stirred the nest," Blue said over the comms as he watched. "We've got three targets approaching the primary exit area."

"If they pop that hatch, we don't have a choice," Solomon said in response, his heart quickening in anticipation of a fight.

"Halo be advised, you've got tangos entering the airspace above your location," the aerial support stated.

"Any more info?" Solomon responded, clenching his teeth. They had come a bit more prepared this time, sporting two FIM-92 Stingers, a man-portable surface-to air-missile, capable of tracking and destroying a helicopter.

"Appears to be four helos, and at least two fast-moving aircraft."

"Copy."

Solomon looked toward his men, each having heard the news.

"Zeus, what's the ETA on our support?"

"Fifteen minutes once we hit the go."

"Copy."

Solomon looked toward Dubs. He was staring down into the valley, the flat plain where the compound was nestled into high-ridged walls, hidden from the world. "We'll get Logan," Solomon said to Dubs directly, not through the comms.

"Fuckin' right we will," Dubs said without taking his eyes off the exit point, staring at three nondescript moving objects, their form wavering in the atmosphere from a mile away. Suddenly, the waving figures started to run.

"You've got three targets Blue," Solomon said confidently. "Put 'em down."

Blue immediately stopped scanning and focused. The range was one mile, the wind, three knots right to left, in a relatively open and still valley. The sun hadn't yet risen high enough to cause a large change in temperature, so the wind was low, predictable. Blue had already dialed in on the escape hatch, his reticle was primed for the shot. He didn't need just one, but three critical shots downrange.

"Zeus, how long till tangos are on location?"

"ETA is five minutes for fast movers, and fifteen for the helos, all coming from the northeast."

Blue removed the comms from his ears. He took a long breath, watching the three targets come into frame. He waited a moment for them to settle in. He knew the one-mile distance would allow a substantial delay to target, nearly two seconds to impact. One mile was also near the Barrett's effective range limit. He placed his finger gently on the trigger, focused on the first target, the one who was reaching down for to open the hatch, and flexed his index finger against the hardened metal.

Boom! The SEAL team watched in anticipation as Blue fired a second shot downrange at the initial enemy. He went on to fire three more shots, acquiring the second and third targets rapidly, while they froze in the horror, their comrade nearly blown into two pieces.

"Three down," Blue said, beginning to scan the area for any further approaching terrorists.

"It's opening," Lonnie said as he watched the hatch begin to rise, only to fall under the weight of two dead men, pinning it closed. The whole team watched in horror as the hatch continued to rise and fall, over and over, seemingly impossible to lift.

"We need to do something," Dubs said, looking to Solomon, fighting every human instinct to run, to help his friend, to throw Amir back down into the hole and watch him die in the imminent airstrike.

"Targets on the move," Blue said as he watched through his scope. "Five."

"Let's roll," Solomon said before his concerns could catch up with him. "Get those Stingers ready, we can at least take out the helos. Blue—"

"Stay here and overwatch," the sharpshooter said before Solomon could finish, as he placed the comms back into his ear.

Dubs was the first to move, jumping from his hide and running with all his might across the open terrain. He was faster than he should be, his large frame and heavy gear should have slowed him down, the thin, dry air should have made his lungs scream for mercy, but he pushed those thoughts down deep, and pressed forward. Soon, the earth seemed to jump up from beneath him, trying to grab his ankles, slow him down; but his fearlessness, his loyalty, his brotherhood refused to allow him a moment of clarity, as round after round pierced the air striking the red ground in puffs of dust.

Dubs was the first to the hatch, and heaved the bodies from it, allowing it to open. Lonnie knelt behind the open steel hatch, and began spraying fire at the approaching enemies. From the south, several other rifles cut the silence, their own hellish sound ushering enemy after enemy to their own versions of the afterlife.

"Take him," Amir said as he pushed Logan from below toward the apex of the opening. Dubs reached down, grabbing Logan by both wrists, and hauled his emaciated friend into the light of day.

"Got ya' brother. Let's get you home."

Amir climbed out of the hole and Dubs was on him quick. He pushed Amir hard, throwing him back toward the dark chasm. Amir fell to the ground, his momentum surely would have placed him into the tunnel had he not.

"Get your ass back in that hole," Dubs said, his rage completely overwhelming him.

"That's not the deal," David said, finally on the scene. "We need him stateside, help us all figure out how to handle this terrorist group."

"Listen to this guy," Logan said as forcefully as he could, the gunfire ringing in his hears, the sunlight scorching his skin, and blinding his eyes. "We need him."

Dubs turned to Logan who rested on an elbow, his eyes completely closed, and exposed to the firefight.

"Come on," Dubs said, grabbing his mentor, hoisting him over a shoulder, and running back to the south.

"Zeus, Operation Ram complete, we are go."

"Copy Halo, sending in the hornets, ETA fifteen minutes out."

A rumble from above stopped everyone's heart.

A rush of dust and debris spun in the air as high-caliber rounds dug deep into the ground all around them.

Whoosh! Two SU-35 Terminators came swooping down, peppering the area where the SEAL team had grabbed Logan.

"Everyone pop smoke!" Solomon said as he threw the first canister, several more following shortly after. "How strong is this door?" Solomon asked Amir.

"Strong enough to stop the machine gun fire, but not ordnance."

"Everyone down the hole!" Solomon yelled, his voice like pure thunder echoed in everyone's ears.

Solomon waited, hiding in the white smoke, ready for any combatant to attack them while the team worked to get underground. One by one the men descended into the only option they had for survival. Finally, Dubs reached the hold, Logan still on his shoulders. He lowered Logan to the ground, climbed into the hole, and reached up to his friend.

"Just put your weight on me," Dubs said to Logan, whose eyes were nearly shut, his lungs, searching for clean air. Logan did just that, barely able to hang onto the rungs, he placed his life in Dubs' capable hands.

Solomon grabbed Amir just before he tried to enter the hole. "How effective will our comms be from inside?"

"If you've got something to say, do it quick," Amir said, both men hearing the screams of the SU-35s approaching for another pass."

Solomon reached for the large, steel door, and slammed it down, leaving himself and Amir vulnerable. Amir understood and backed away, hidden in the smoke, creating separation between the two men.

"Requesting immediate air support at target. We're inside the compound, I repeat, we're inside the drop zone. Be advised. There are two SU-35s above. Forced us inside the exit point."

"Copy Halo, we've got four hornets supersonic, heading your way. Nobody's dropping anything until you're in the safe zone. ETA six minutes."

Bang! Bang! Bang—from above came high-caliber rounds, ricocheting off the steel door and spraying the ground around Amir and Solomon. But the fighter pilots were shooting blind, the thick smoke on the ground made it impossible to see anything, including where the secret entrance lay.

"You've got more incoming," Blue said. "Five helos, at least three of them full of bad guys."

"Do not engage. We've got air support incoming. Going down, we might lose contact. Don't let them drop shit on us till you hear from me."

"Alright."

Solomon quickly grabbed the steel door, Amir was there to help, both men quickly going inside and shutting the door, entering the darkness.

"We've got helos incoming. Blue says at least three are full of troops. We're going into the compound, clear it out, till we hear otherwise."

It took several minutes, and lots of strength from Dubs, but finally everyone was down the ladder, and into the passageway leading to the compound. Solomon was the last inside, closing the door behind him.

"This blast proof?" he asked, staring at Amir.

"The door? Yeah, but not bunker buster proof," he responded, nervous the inbound super hornets may get trigger-happy.

"Blue, you got me?"

"Copy Sol."

"Glad to hear it. What's the story up top?"

"Targets on the ground, thirty at the compound, ten to the shaft."

"How long's this hallway? Any exits?" Sol asked Amir.

"No rooms, exits, or cover. It's a few hundred yards." Amir's thoughts shifted, remembering Karim was still in the compound. "Solomon, ask your man if anyone was taken out?"

"Any exfils on the helo?" Sol asked, a look of concern and frustration overcoming his battle-hardened face.

"Hard to say," Blue responded, the comms creating white noise from his men inside. He remained prone, his breathing becoming more rapid, uncontrolled, the reality of the moment setting in. Blue took his eyes from the compound as two helos flew away, and he focused on the escape hatch.

He saw several men around the opening, slowing lifting the door. Three of the targets threw something inside, then quickly closed the hatch. "Incoming!" Blue yelled as he watched them hold the steel door closed.

Blue then lifted his head from his focused, limited view. The world was infinitely larger, brighter, clearer than the haziness he was focused on a mile away. Something primitive took over, his body insisted on him turning away, but when he did, he began to scream.

"Yeah!" he yelled knowing nobody would hear. The noise of gunfire, of rotors spinning, of engines whining couldn't mask the sounds of victory. He saw the first SU-35 explode as two FA-18s flew in tight formation behind the debris, banking hard to the north, and coming back around with vengeance.

From behind, he heard the whine of another aircraft, quickly causing him to turn and look skyward. It was the second SU-35, just a few hundred feet above, turning hard toward the west, a hiss escaped the fighter as it expelled bright flares into the air, while an American made AIM-9X Sidewinder chased. Blue knew the Terminator wouldn't last long with Navy pilots in hot pursuit.

Before Blue even saw the first two FA-18s return, he watched missiles fly in from the east, quickly turning two helicopters into confetti. He finally saw familiar warbirds sporting the Blacklions mascot on the tail wing. *Brrrrrap! Brrrrrrap!* the echoes of their rapid .20 caliber Vulcan cannon was incredible, unmatched by any weaponry Blue had heard before. He promised himself he'd forever remember the sound of the Super Hornet's gun, as quickly two more helos were eliminated, sending them to the ground in horrific fashion.

"Air support cleaned up. Get topside," Blue said as he watched through his scope once again. A moment later, the final helo was destroyed, but Blue's heart dropped when he noticed all ten terrorists near the door of the escape hatch had descended into the hole.

"Copy, Blue. On our way topside," Sol said and signaled for them to move.

"You've got ten incoming from the shaft." They all heard Blue say through the comms.

"Whiplash, Lucky, Ghost, you stay here, watch our ass. We're gonna take the main compound, make sure Karim didn't get out. Amir, get up front. Dubs, take Logan in the back. He's your responsibility."

Amir jogged down the hallway toward the thick, steel door. He was scared, unsure of what may lay in wait. His safety was no longer a concern for anyone, having gotten Logan, and potentially trapping Karim, his stock wasn't high any longer. The last fifty feet he slowed, decreasing their foot noise, not tipping off anyone listening on the other side.

"Flashbang," Amir said, looking back toward Lonnie, who stood just steps behind. After a brief moment, Lonnie reluctantly handed the canister to Amir, making the terrorist work a little to remove it from his grasp.

"We'll all shoot your ass," Lonnie said, reaffirming Amir's suspicions. "You don't have friends here."

Amir crept his way down the hall, reached the door, placed his hand on the handle. He paused, taking a deep breath before he input in the code for entry. He knew Karim may have one more card he hadn't played, and that was the thought that made him most nervous. Amir struck the last number, freeing the door. He opened it a crack, threw the grenade into the void behind the door, and waited the longest three seconds of his life.

Before he opened his eyes, the SEAL team was on top of him, pressing him out of the way. *Bang!* The grenade detonated, and quickly, Solomon's team was opening the door, throwing two additional grenades inside, slamming the door shut.

"The locks will reactivate!" Amir said, shoving his way to the panel, inputting the numbers. The door unlocked just as the two frag grenades exploded, and inside the SEALs went, Amir, Logan, and Dubs bringing up the rear.

Amir heard shots echoing from the hall behind them. He froze, not sure which way to continue. The team was working quickly, clearing room after room, but an attack from behind would threaten their primary objective. He knew if he heard shots this loud, the door must have been opened; the problem was that Lucky, Whiplash, and Ghost didn't know the code.

"Go," Amir said to Dubs as he held Logan up, supporting him from falling. Logan was spent, the emotional and physical toll finally catching him.

"What the hell you gonna do?" Dubs responded.

"Something's wrong. They got in back there."

Dubs searched down the long hallway, seeing flashes in the checkered darkness.

Bang, bang, bang, they heard AK fire, an explosion, and silence.

"Like Lonnie said." Dubs stood staring at Amir while holding Logan's nearly incapacitated body.

"I'm not trying to be a hero," Amir responded and crouched as gunfire began to come down the hallway, striking concrete, sending sparks and debris toward the three remaining men.

Amir ran a few yards down the hallway and froze, the gunfire overwhelming him. He reached a dark spot in the hallway, a place where the lights from above couldn't quite cover. He laid prone, his heart racing, every part of him wanting to turn and run to the SEAL team that was now likely working their way to the second level of the substructure. Amir's spine shivered when he heard Arabic, rather than English, accompanying the sound of boots on concrete. He stared down the iron sights of the AK he had stolen from the guards. Amir wanted to be done killing, done running, done with the anxiety that ruled his life. To do that, he needed to get out; to get out, he needed to go through whoever was running toward him.

Bang, bang, bang! The sound from his gun deafened him to the oncoming men. He fired again, this time barely hearing the cartridge being struck, erupting gunpowder and lead. For now, that sense was dead, but what hadn't been lost, was the ability to feel.

Without explanation, something clamped onto his calves, causing a searing pain in his left leg, his old wound revealing his weakness. He turned to see Dubs was yelling at him, trying to communicate, but Amir couldn't hear. He saw the walls sparking all around Dubs, from above, from the left and right, but the man never flinched. He was dragging Amir back down the hallway but Amir couldn't understand why.

Then, Dubs dropped Amir's leg, quickly reached for his M4, and began shooting it down the hall with his right hand, while grasping blindly for Amir's leg. Amir turned to face the oncoming targets, and sprayed supporting fire for the man who was dragging him out of danger. Finally, Dubs reached the door, and with one last strong pull, slid Amir inside, closing the door behind them.

"You big ass," Amir said, pointing to Dub's left shoulder. "You're bleeding pretty good."

"So—are—you," he responded slowly through deep labored breaths.

"They're dead," Amir said, realizing the fight wasn't over. "We gotta get the hell out ourselves."

"Grab an arm," Dubs said as he moved toward Logan.

"I know the quick way, follow my lead," Amir said over Logan's drooping head, as Amir and Dubs both walked with Logan's arms draped over each of their tall shoulders.

They moved quickly, Amir tracing steps he thought he may have forgotten, but realized he likely never would; even after the place was blown sky high.

"Did they find Karim?" Amir asked as they turned toward the interrogation room.

"Haven't heard."

"Cut through here then," Amir said, gesturing right with his head, and Dubs responded, entering the bright, white room.

"Mother fucker," Amir said softly as his heart sunk.

"Shit. We need to go," Logan said, speaking for the first time.

"What's wrong?"

"Karim's gone. He was right there. Logan put him down. Thought we'd make it out before he woke up. Come on, through that door."

"Shit," Dubs said, hearing rapid footsteps and the sound of yelling echoing through the concrete maze.

"Listen to me," Amir said, releasing Logan. "Go straight down this hall, do not turn. At the end, you'll see a staircase that takes you topside. After that, head south through the gate and toward the rendezvous."

"I'm not letting you escape again," Logan said, reaching weakly toward Amir.

"Explain it to him later, please," Amir said, pushing Dubs. "This is the last bottleneck. After that, who knows where they'll be coming from?"

"You gonna be a martyr?"

"I'm done running from my problems. If I make it out I'll see you soon. Take me to the U.S. and put me on trial. I don't give a shit anymore. I'm already an embarrassment. Make this trip worthwhile, and get that asshole to the surface."

Dubs, supporting Logan with an arm wrapped around his waist, his rifle ready, raced down the last long hallway to freedom.

Logan was angry, but couldn't express it in the moment. Amir had been the reason he was depressed, frustrated, having nightmares again, and now they allowed him to be left alone, in the basement of a compound no less. It was eerily similar to DuPont Circle. *Who really knew what Amir was up to? Was it another game? Another way for Karim to get what he wanted? Part of the longer play? Where was Karim?*

"Jesus," Logan said as they began working up the stairs, gunfire exploding behind them, unsure of the outcome, but both men were satisfied that it continued. At least that meant Amir was still able to shoot. With each step, Logan was forcing his body to work, sheer willpower and training from decades earlier finally being put to use. It was inspirational, but slow, Dubs decided to pick him up and sling him over his shoulder.

"You're bleeding," Logan said as his chest landed on Dubs left shoulder.

"I heard."

"It's a lot," Logan said, watching the trail his friend was leaving in their wake.

"That's helpful," Dubs responded as he took two stairs at a time.

Bang! He kicked the outside door, sending it open in a rapid swing. Instinct caused his knees to buckle, as he saw three guns pointed in his face.

"Ugh!" Logan said as his body slammed hard into the earth, the sun once again temporarily blinding him.

"Where's Amir?" a voice from above asked the two men on the ground.

"Inside, where he belongs," Dubs responded, his eyes finally adjusting, recognizing Solomon and Lonnie.

"What happened?" Sol said as he lowered his weapon.

Dubs stood, grabbing Logan and hoisting him back over his shoulder. He shook his head, not knowing what else to say to the SEAL team leader.

"Damn it," Sol said, shaking his head subtly. "Blue paint the target."

"Zeus, we're five minutes to safe zone, over."

"Copy. Operation Ram. Incoming in five mikes."

"Let's scoot," Solomon hollered to the men.

But Solomon became distracted, quickly raising his weapon toward the door as it slowly opened. *Bang, bang!* He quickly shot two rounds into the top of the door. From the bottom of the door, a bloodied hand reached out, two fingers held out peace. Lonnie circled toward the crack and saw Amir prone on the ground. He opened the door, grabbed the injured Amir and hoisted him over his own shoulder.

"We'll aren't we a pair?" Lonnie said as he caught up to Dubs. "You know you're bleeding, right?"

"If one more damn person tells me that I'll kill 'em," Dubs responded without looking to his friend as they all raced toward the southern range.

A minute later, two FA-18s dropped heavy ordnance onto the compound, the ground expanded, then rumbled beneath the men's feet as they continued to run from the location. None of them looked back, their focus was ahead, all nearly expending their reserves, but they had been made to ignore the sensation of exhaustion; replacing it for an unquenchable urge to survive.

As the ordnance dropped, the letters A-L-E-X could be seen, as each bomb was hand painted with a letter. The Blacklions all wanted Alex Pines to release the powerful devices, but he wasn't whole, mentally or physically. He likely wouldn't fly again. It was inspiration nonetheless to see his name associated with the final blow to the largest and most successful terrorist group in history.

Finally, the SEAL team, including David Westbrook, Amir Qasmi, and Logan Falcone, all gathered near Blue. Seemingly moments earlier, they had moved on Solomon's command into the open, vast valley, now filled with dust, oily smoke, debris from wreckage, and fire. At the center of it all, a collapsed remnant of where a compound used to be. In retrospect, it all happened in the span of just over sixty minutes: Blue firing on the three men, the first wave of FA-18s taking out surface-to-air sites, allowing the second wave of fighters to enter the airspace, shooting down the SU-35s, the helos, and finally, the third wave of fighters taking out the compound.

"I'll tell you what," said Blue to David. "If Karim was on a helo for exfil, he's dead now either way."

"Yeah? Well *he's* not gonna last long," David said, grunting as he stood to approach Amir, placing pressure onto a chest wound.

"You think I'm done?" Amir said, looking toward David and smiling, blood providing the contrast between his teeth and gums.

"I'm no doc, but I shouldn't hear you breathing through a hole in your chest." It was an eerie and mortifying sound. David turned as he heard something drop next to him on the ground.

"Pack the wound. Then let's get the hell outta here," Solomon said, looking down at the two men. "Ghost was our medic."

Nobody said a word, opting to look toward the earth, their three fallen brothers on their minds.

"How you doin' big man?" Solomon asked, walking over to Dubs.

"Ooh rah," he said, supporting Logan, trying to get his friend to drink water, ignoring his own needs as blood ran the length of his shirt, painting the ground below.

"Let me see," Solomon said, reaching toward Dubs' shoulder. "Went through the back. Big ass shoulders got in the way of a bullet."

"Don't be jealous," Dubs said finally taking his eyes off Logan.

"You ready to move? I'll take Logan for a while, we can switch off."

"I'm good. I got 'em," Dubs said, standing and reaching down to help his friend.

David picked up Amir, threw him over his shoulder, and began heading south. Amir was too weak to say anything, but his mind was uneasy. He hadn't seen Karim since the moment he laid on the floor. He knew the compound, and the SEAL team cleared every room. Amir thought, *where did Karim go?*

Chapter 40
MIT

David, along with Amir and Logan's team, took a private jet stateside. It was cramped, loud, and stressful. Two doctors from Landstuhl Regional Medical Center accompanied them with a wide variety of medical equipment. The three injured men received care the entire flight home. By far the worst of them had been Amir, but everyone in the states demanded he get to the U.S. immediately, even if he died on the flight. Despite the two-doctor team expressing their concerns, Amir was placed on the flight, coding twice on the way.

David Westbrook wasn't physically hurt, but mentally he was breaking. His mind replayed an erratic range of memories before his eyes. The only problem: he wasn't sleeping. David hadn't slept the entire flight. In fact, he barely slept in the last week, between tracking Amir, interrogating him, the Embassy attack, and the operation to rescue Logan, he hadn't found the time. He sat in the plane, watching the medical monitors as they beeped, rattled, and flashed for the three men resting in reclining seats, IVs attached to their arms. Twice he stood back and observed the two doctors bang onto Amir's chest in an effort to keep delivering oxygen to his brain, using an AED to shock him back to life. Both times it worked, and both times David said a silent prayer of thanks. Amir was still the only person alive who could link his data to possible future threats.

David closed his eyes as the sun rose over the long, bubbled, purple and orange landscape beneath a blistering light. It was too bright to look out the window, but too beautiful to close the slide. The piercing light eventually forced him to close his eyes, allowing him a momentary pause, a chance to sleep. In a moment, he was.

President Pierce, along with Secretary Smith and General Anderson all waited inside of an aircraft hangar as a chartered jet to taxi inside. There were three ambulances as well, and a full medical team to evaluate the injured on site, before sending them to the hospital; Amir likely going into surgery.

The SEAL team had already been debriefed through General Anderson, getting the rundown on how they lost three men, as well as gathering the mission details. Everyone was happy Logan and Amir were coming home, but the three leaders were waiting for David Westbrook.

The twin engines on the jet whistled loudly as it entered the hangar, the pitch slowly lowering as the pilot slowed their rotation and began to shut down. The hatch popped open several seconds later, and a tall, spindly man exited first, followed by Dubs and Lonnie carrying Logan, and finally, Amir being carried by the two doctors.

"Mr. Secretary," David said, walking toward the group of three men, shaking his hand.

"David. I'm realizing I've never actually seen what you look like before," Secretary Smith said, taking in the exhausted agent.

"I'm not myself at the moment, sir. Mr. President, it's an honor. I didn't expect to see you."

"Pleasure is mine," he said, extending his hand and forcing a smile. "I understand we owe a lot of our intelligence to you. Thank you for your service to the country." He paused, glancing toward Secretary Smith.

"How you feelin'?" the secretary asked David.

"I'm good," he lied.

"You get enough rest?"

"Amir coded twice. No. Not much, but I can manage." The group turned and looked toward Amir who was being placed in an ambulance, the medical team discussing the care he received in flight, the two doctors clearly exhausted, and relieved.

"David, as we said over the phone, I need you to work right now. Are you capable?"

David removed his backpack, opened a small pocket. "I've got everything I need."

"Good, you handle the interrogation. I'm heading off with my boys. Doyle, let me know what you guys get," General Anderson said, jogging off to catch the ambulance that Logan was being hoisted into. Dubs, very clearly, refused to ride in a separate vehicle, climbing in with Logan and Lonnie.

"How's he doin'?" General Anderson asked as he reached the ambulance.

"He's drugged pretty good. Haven't talked to him since we got him out."

Anderson looked to Logan and clenched his teeth. "You got room for one more in there?"

Dubs extended his left arm, drawing it back. The pain had finally begun on the flight home, the adrenaline wearing off. General Anderson saw Dubs draw back.

"I can manage son," he said, climbing into the

ambulance quickly, shutting the door behind him.

President Pierce insisted on being present for the interrogation for the mysterious father of Nassir Ajab. The FBI and CIA had both taken turns talking with the man, but weeks passed and he hadn't spoken, hadn't made a noise, hadn't eaten, and drank very little. He did sleep, soundly in fact, seemingly unfazed by the situation. Once, they brought Nassir in, but all it did was cause Nassir to react aggressively and emotionally when his father simply stared, refusing to speak, or even show emotion.

"Clear the room," Secretary Smith stated boldly as the president and David walked into the observation box adjacent to the room that held Nassir's father. They waited several moments while the two FBI agents grabbed their gear and left.

"All we know is his name is Irfan Ajab. He came to the states twenty-five years ago from Saudi, with his wife and only son, Nassir. He's an engineer, no ties to the Middle East as far as we can tell. We've looked into him for days now, pulling out nothing. Clean as we ever find. We previously vetted him for our work with Nassir, and came back clean then as well. The guys in the vehicle, the men who took Nassir, we connected them to Yemen. We know they're affiliated with Karim's network."

"Okay, let me work," David said, leaving.

A moment later he was with Irfan. David quickly fell into his old ways, reading the older man's body language, his face, and essentially, his thoughts.

"You don't know me, but I know you," David said, sitting in the chair opposite Irfan. Sitting made him feel instantly fatigued, craving rest. He lazily blinked, hoping the flash of darkness would be enough, promising himself when this was over he'd sleep for a week.

"Is Nassir your son?" The man stared, emotionless. "Do

you know Karim Al Muhammad?" The man continued to stare. "Who is Karim Al Muhammad?"

David smirked, and pulled out his kit. "Do you know Karim is dead?" David watched the man swallow. *Got him,* he thought, as he opened his metal tin containing his truth serum.

"Yeah, the bastard was tough, but I finally caught him," he looked down at his two broad palms, and the alien-like digits that extended from them. "Grabbed his throat with these hands here. Pretty sure I haven't washed them since." David watched him blink as he showed his hands to Irfan.

As fast as a lizard's tongue, David reached across the table, grasping Irfan's wrist, squeezing tightly. The man squinted from the pain, but erased it as quickly as it came, remaining passive, not fighting David's vise-like grip.

"What I don't understand," David said while injecting the drug into his suspect, "is why you continue to protect him, even though he's dead? And why give up your son?" David stared at the man for a moment before speaking.

Irfan closed his eyes, took a deep breath, tried to calm himself. David's drug had begun to work, seeping into his bloodstream. With each beat of his heart, more of the drug was ushered toward his brain, taking down defenses and lubricating his tongue. David released the man's wrist and sat back in his chair, waiting. Irfan finally opened his eyes.

"Who is Karim?" The man smiled, still not talking. "We'll give you some time, but eventually, you'll talk."

David left Irfan and re-entered the room with Pierce and Smith.

"That's it?" Secretary Smith asked, disappointed. He heard legendary things about David, and often wondered what his true techniques could be.

"For now. He's relatively healthy, and clearly loyal. It might take another half hour, but he'll eventually let go."

"Then what?" President Pierce asked.

"Then we find out whatever we want to know. He already gave me some clues. I know he's got something he's hiding."

"What do you think is happening?"

"I think you need to get Nassir down here. Keep him in a separate room."

"Why?" President Pierce asked, frustrated. "The kid's been through quite a bit. He's been vetted out by our team more than once, he's provided endless intel against the terrorists. He's already tried to talk to his father, and that ended because of his emotional outburst. David, he tried to kill his own father! Tried to choke him out."

"When I talked to Amir, when he told me everything, he said Karim was allowing us to find things. He wanted us off his bigger plans."

President Pierce stared through the one-way mirror, observing the bearded man. Irfan had begun shifting uncomfortably in his chair, his eyes darting around the room, he even took a long drink of water from the glass that had been placed on the table for him hours earlier.

"Mr. Secretary, I need to talk to Nassir anyways. He needs to see my data, compare it to where his data is coming from. We can likely build a map of where the good intel is coming from. My stuff is right here," he said, taking off his backpack and placing it on the table. "We can get anything this asshole says, then use Nassir's intel, as well as mine, to find any remaining high value targets in Yemen, and throughout the Middle East. Let's get this over with."

Smith nodded his head, a stern look on his face. "We haven't had any retaliatory intel following your op for Logan, and that likely means Karim is in fact dead. Clearly the hierarchy is disturbed, nobody knows what steps to take. They're on the run Mr. President, time to strike," Secretary

Smith said, turning his attention to the Commander-in-Chief. "I think we do exactly what David's suggesting. Strike them while they're weak. End this and lift the martial law."

President Pierce looked away from the glass and toward David. "You're confident this could work?"

"Mr. President, with all due respect, I've worked for this country for a long time. I've been in Yemen for over five years, working on getting you guys actionable intel, all the while, collecting data for dark web access as possible communication networks. I haven't heard an American voice, let alone seen an American face during that entire time. Nobody, including you Mr. Secretary, seemed to have the time or the concern to look at my data. It's here, now, and I think it's about damn time we compare it to what we've got from Nassir, given our current conditions in the country. So, no Mr. President, I'm not supremely confident, but I think it's worth investigating."

"Okay, David, calm down."

"Mr. Secretary, isn't this exactly why you said I needed to come stateside? You expressly told me to bring my hard drives, along with Amir. Well, I'm not confident we all know the story here, but Amir isn't likely going to make it, so this might be our only shot."

"Okay, David, we both see your point. Doyle, get him down here quickly. Let's put the pieces together."

"Just don't tell him about me yet. Say you wanted him to bring his data regarding where the communications originated. Tell him you've got some intel of your own recently, and want him to cross check the points. I'll introduce myself when I'm done with the dad."

David turned to the room and smirked. "Turkey's done."

David entered the room with Irfan. The man was sweating, fidgeting in his chair, his red eyes blinking several times as he raised his hands to wipe them. His chin quaked as he looked toward David. His gaze was filled with doubt and sorrow, a silent plea for mercy.

"Who is Karim Al Muhammad?"

"A nightmare," the man spoke for the first time. He folded his hands, interlocking his fingers and squeezing, his knuckles whitening.

"And why is that?"

"Because he's a specter, a ghost, a man who cannot be killed."

"I assure you he's dead."

"Is he now? Where's the body? I don't see it? I've witnessed him survive more than you could even imagine. I see through you. I know you didn't kill him with your own hands. He wouldn't allow you to get close enough."

"Why did you give up your son?"

"You make assumptions."

"What are the assumptions I've made?"

"That I gave up my son."

"Let's take it slowly. Clearly the lack of nutrition has got your mind confused."

"No. You are confused," the man said, pointing at David, his laughter which was once contagious and awkward, now seemed sinister as it echoed through the room. "Nassir was my duty, not my son."

"Explain," David knew the storyline before the man even opened his mouth. He'd witnessed extreme loyalty over the years, watched as men chose to die rather than give up a friend. He'd seen lifelong commitments made without hesitation, witnessed men kill another for honor, for friendship, for loyalty, knowing full well they would be retaliated against. It wasn't commonplace in the U.S., a society that favors self over others.

"You Americans will never see."

"He's not your son."

"This is true."

"He's Karim's son, isn't he?"

"Yes. And he will soon know his father. Whether you'd like to believe it or not, Karim is alive. He will find his son, he will take him home, he will be his father once again. *Allah* will see to it."

"Why did you do it?" David couldn't understand the loyalty, the commitment to raising a child that wasn't his, to love him, to nurture him, only to give him up in a moment.

"We were barely friends. I was ten, he was eight. We were bad, stealing from a few vendors in town with several other boys my age. Karim was smart. He convinced us all to do it, explaining how to distract the workers, it was like a game. We played this game for weeks, testing each other, seeing who could take more, risking more, and after each heist, Karim would always win. He insisted on splitting things equally, and rarely took his share. Then we got caught," Irfan paused, recalling the painful memory.

"He took the entire punishment. From six fathers, he was beaten. He convinced them he was the one to blame, that he tricked us all into playing an evil and deceitful game. I'll never forget the sounds of the wood on his back. I lost count how many times he was struck, but he never made a noise, despite the tears running down his face and the blood staining his shirt. He stared at us the whole time, and when it was over, he mouthed the words, 'for you my brothers.' I pledged my loyalty to him that day. He's sacrificed so much since then, and become so successful."

"How did he get in touch with you? How often?"

"I hadn't heard from him in over twenty years."

"Why did he call you?"

"I don't know. I just knew it was time to get Nassir to his father."

David got up and began searching for Secretary

Smith. It took several minutes, but he found him in a second interrogation room, a tech associate was setting up several large computer screens, along with a desktop.

"Don't let Nassir see my work," David said, grasping the secretary behind the arm, his firm grip startling the thick-armed African-American.

"What's going on?"

"Karim is Nassir's father."

"Bull-fucking shit. That guy's a liar."

David stood, staring at Secretary Smith.

"What's going on?" Smith said confused, unable to put this new info together.

"Let me do my job. Follow my lead. We'll know soon enough."

It had taken two more hours, but Nassir arrived, nervously clutching onto his messenger bag as he entered the small room. He hadn't shaved in days, his eyes appeared as though they were scorched, their dry, red condition hinting at many hours in emotional anguish. His typical magnetism and confidence had vanished. He was lost, physically clutching the only thing he still knew was his.

"Nassir, glad you could come down," Secretary Smith said, rising and placing a hand over the young man's shoulder, ushering him toward a chair. On the table, a four-screen display, awaiting his latest intel from Medusa.

"Thank you, Mr. Secretary. Have you heard anything from my father?" he sighed heavily, his lungs quaking slightly as his bronchioles spasmed, an artifact of his emotional state.

"Nassir, I can't—"

"I understand," Nassir cut him off before the answer shook him again. The FBI told him after his outburst, it would be the last time he'd be able to hear any information regarding the investigation, due to its national security implications.

"Nassir, I want you to meet someone. It's why I've called you here. He's been working in the Middle East for quite a while, and he's recently come across intelligence which could mesh well with yours."

"Okay," Nassir responded as he slowly began removing his hard drive from his bag, wiping his eyes.

"You okay, son?" Smith asked. *No way this kid knows anything about his father, the real one or the fake,* he thought observing the young genius.

"I'll be fine. You wanted the source map? The location of where we're pulling the dark web info from?"

"Only the ones which have been proven true attempted attacks."

"Give me a few minutes," Nassir said, staring at the screens, digging through file systems, setting parameters to pull only those specific files requested.

"I'll give you a minute. I'm going to grab David, the man I want you to meet."

Secretary Smith left the room, and entered the observation suite where David sat waiting, reading Nassir.

"I don't do interrogations, but I have serious doubts about Nassir knowing anything. It doesn't fit."

"Nothing ever does, Mr. Secretary."

"What's next?"

"Don't interrupt me when I'm in there. No matter what happens, I'm not going to hurt him, but I *am* going to inject him. We don't have time to dick around."

"Fair enough. Just get whatever info you need."

"Nassir, this is David—"

"Nassir Ajab," David said, interrupting Smith. He approached Nassir, who leaned back nervously in his chair, ducking away from the tall, intimidating man who just walked in.

"What the hell is that?" Nassir said, leaping from his chair and fleeing to the corner of the room. He began to panic, his back pressing into the wall. He thought to run, to try and sneak around the spindly man, but he froze, his feet failed to unglue themselves from the floor.

"Nassir, we think the kidnappers poisoned you when you were unconscious in the car."

"What?" he asked, the confusion forced his guard to lower.

"I've spoken to your father. The plan was if the men couldn't successfully take you, then you had to die. They injected you with a substance which is hard to detect, but luckily, we have an antidote."

"I don't understand—"

"Have you felt tired, weak, confused?" David asked quickly, forcing Nassir to focus on him, rather than the logic in his own mind. "How about pain, have you had headaches? Nausea?"

"Yes."

"Shit. Headaches are part of the latent stages. We need to administer the drug now, before it's too late."

"How can you be sure?"

"I can't, but we also know the cure doesn't have any nasty side effects. It's a win-win."

"Fine. Do it, just do it!" Nassir said, quickly walking toward the table and rolling up his sleeve.

"I know Secretary Smith told you who I am, but he didn't really tell you what I do," David said, sliding the needle into Nassir's forearm. "I talk to people for a living, I find things out. Now, before we go any further, before we share what we both know about the dark web, about the terrorist communications, we need to talk about your dad."

"Mr. Secretary, what's going on here?"

Secretary Smith grimaced, folded his hands, and stared

at Nassir for a moment, before David turned, drawing his attention. David then gestured with his head toward the door, and Smith responded with a nod, closing the door behind him.

"Doyle!" Nassir yelled, his voice cracking slightly in the terrifying moment. He was left alone with a man he didn't know, who just told him he was poisoned, given a drug he didn't understand, and now began feeling lightheaded. His breath quickened, the lights in the room seemed to dim, and he felt himself leaning forward, almost falling from the chair.

David grabbed Nassir by both shoulders, sitting him up, and gave him a quick and forceful shake. "Don't you go anywhere Nassir."

"What's going on?"

"You're gonna be just fine. Who is your father?"

"You know who he is," Nassir said, blinking hard, then opening them wide.

"His name?"

"Irfan Ajab."

"What does he do?"

"He's an engineer like me."

"Is that all? Have you ever witnessed him do anything else?"

"No."

"Do you talk to your dad often?"

"Yes."

"How often?"

"Uh, around once a week."

"Is that a question or an answer, Nassir?" David said, slapping the engineer gently on the cheek several times.

"Do you remember any trips he took, any unexplained absence."

"No. He never wanted to leave."

"Strange, isn't it? He never wanting to leave?"

"Why is that?"

"I don't know."

"What do you know?"

"He was a great dad," Nassir said quietly, staring at the floor. "He was there for me, for everything."

"In what way?"

"He listened. He gave me space to grow, to expand my knowledge, even though sometimes I took money for things I shouldn't have." Nassir looked confused. "Please, don't tell anyone. Is someone watching?" he asked, staring at the one-way glass for the first time. "Who's in there?"

David placed his hand firm into Nassir's chest, guiding him back down into his seat. "It's just me and you, smart guy. What did you do for money?"

"Cheated. On tests, exams, on papers, I programmed phones, calculators, tablets. I rewrote coding, developed apps for people, stealing their ideas and reworking them later, for myself. It's how I got my seed money for Medusa."

"Who invested in Medusa?"

"One-Star. An investment group out of New York, but I've already paid them back with interest."

David looked toward the glass, then back to Nassir. "Did they ask for anything in return?"

"No. They didn't know what I was building, or what for. They knew it was computer tech, and they liked what I had to say about its potential."

"Nassir, what if I told you Irfan wasn't your real father?"

"I'd call you a liar. It's impossible."

"Maybe, but that's what we're here for. I need to make sure you're right, and your father is wrong. Why would he say he's not your father?"

"I don't know," Nassir began to cry, tears striking the floor one by one, a metronome of sorrow.

"What about you is worth protecting by a lie? Don't you see what I see?" David said, getting up from his chair and squatting down in front of Nassir, trying to grab his gaze. "I need you to think back, Nassir. To your early childhood."

David paused, allowing Nassir to draw out his past. He watched as Nassir shut his eyes, witnessed his face soften, to smile.

"I remember my dad, Irfan," he said the name sternly, opening his eyes to meet David's, then closed them to re-enter the memory. "We were on the beach in the Puget Sound. We played all day in the water, throwing stones, hiking. We pretended we were on another planet. And then the sun began to set." Nassir's eyes opened.

"The tide began to come in quickly. We were at least a mile down the beach from where we began, and the cold ocean was rising quickly. Soon we were pinned against the cliff that marked the edge of the beach. The whole afternoon it had been the sidewall of our Martian trench, but now it was a wall preventing our escape. It wasn't a game anymore. Luckily, a couple of fishermen came around the curved wall from the north, and pulled us inside the boat. We were safe. He took me out for a hot dog after that. He hadn't eaten a hot dog before or since. Maybe it was something he'd always wanted to try, but religion wouldn't allow it."

"How old were you?"

"Couldn't be more than five or six."

"Before that Nassir. Something long ago. Do you remember your trip to the U.S.?"

"Yes."

"Who was with you?"

"My dad . . ." he paused, wiping his hands against his thighs over and over. "I—I remember being afraid," Nassir said as he placed his hands over his face. "Oh my God. Oh my God!"

Nassir stood and began to pace the room, David watched, reading his emotions.

"It's okay, Nassir. It's not your fault—"

"I remember now. I remember a truck chasing us. Dust was everywhere. A woman screaming at a man driving—my mother!" he hollered, the sounds was piercing. "Uh—she kept screaming at the driver, but the truck kept gaining. I moved to the floor. The sound of the engine, the screams, the erratic movement scared me. I covered my ears so I couldn't hear."

Nassir closed his eyes and began to hum while David sat in silence. He hummed for several moments, rocking forward and back in his chair.

"Who else was with you?" David said, breaking Nassir's rhythmic rocking.

"My brother."

"No father?"

"Yes." Nassir began to cry, holding his face in his hands. "My father was driving the truck. I was young, very young. I think my mother was trying to take us away. The truck finally caught up. I don't remember how but he eventually forced us to stop. I remember nothing from that point until waking up in the hospital."

"Do you remember a man there? What happened to your brother. What was his name?"

"There was a man there. Taj. My brother's name was Taj but I can't remember what he looked like. I thought this was just a dream I had as a boy."

"You alright?"

Nassir stopped crying, and instead, stared at David. "How does someone suppress something like that?"

"The mind is a difficult thing to understand. But Nassir, we need you to be the man you've been your whole life. I needed to know you weren't against us. Needless to say, we're in a tough place, and I had to vet you out personally before I showed you what I've got." David pulled out his hard drive. "I heard you went to MIT?"

"Yeah."

"Me too. Maybe after this we can talk shit about the program. You ready to swap notes?"

"Whatever it takes to make me forget all the shit we've talked about already."

Chapter 41
A NEW BEGINNING

Logan woke up. He saw Lonnie and Dubs sleeping in chairs next to his hospital bed, but it was difficult to make out details. He couldn't see out of his right eye, the swelling had increased over the last forty-eight hours and the pressure was unrelenting. His head throbbed, but the aching in his body soon allowed him to forget his head. He tried to adjust himself silently, but immediately Dubs responded.

"I've got it Dubs," Logan said, holding up a hand. "You've already done enough."

"How you feelin'?"

"Invincible," Logan said, forcing a smile, attempting to wipe away the grimace.

"Yo', big man," Lonnie said, waking to the conversation. "Logan this guy was crazy," he joked, gently grabbing Dubs on the shoulder.

"How's the shoulder?" Logan asked.

"Flesh wound."

"You bled a lot. I remember that much." Logan thought of Dubs carrying him through the compound, how he felt the blood from Dubs on his own abdomen as he bounced on the big man's shoulder. In the moment, Logan thought it was his own, like somehow he'd gotten hit and didn't feel it. Secretly, Logan had given up, conceding to the idea he wasn't invincible, that it was finally his turn, passing the torch to Dubs. It was a confusing time for Logan in those hours, his body failing to work, his mind twisting events. Even now, the twists of reality gave him anxiety.

"The last one was worse," Dubs said, patting his abdomen.

"Where's Amir?" Logan remembered how close the terrorist was to death during the flight back home. The doctors said more than once his lung had collapsed, he'd lost several pints of blood in flight, his heart stopped twice, and they were confident he had several blood clots.

"Surgery. I doubt we'll be hearing anything until Secretary Smith comes by. He's with David, trying to get his intel in the right hands."

"Just rest Logan. Samantha'll be here soon," Lonnie said, grabbing his hand.

Samantha was rushed to the hospital once they knew Logan was safely stateside with no chance of harm. She herself was still suffering from anxiety, malnourished, but the doctors said the baby was safe. She ran through the hospital, erratically, not knowing where to go. "He's alive, he's alive," she kept saying softly as she raced, holding her stomach. The moment she last saw him flashed to her mind, causing her to freeze, her heart sunk once again, the loss seemed imminent, undeniable. She remembered the number Logan told her, *November, Delta 4, 3, 1, Delta, Bravo.*

"You alright, ma'am?" her escort asked from behind, finally catching up with the emotional FBI agent.

"Tell me where he is?"

The man pointed down the hall. "Take a left at the end

of the hall. You'll see two guards."

Time froze as she ran around the corner, her shoes landing hard on the linoleum floors, but she heard nothing except her heart racing. She imagined his face, the strong jaw, his eyes which always told his true emotion; at least with her. In a moment of weakness, she allowed herself to imagine being a single mother, that Logan wouldn't make it back despite her final wish. The guards at the door immediately recognized her, opening the room and allowing her inside.

"Oh my God," she said softly and froze. Both hands trembled as she covered her mouth. When she saw his face her eyes released a wall of tears that had formed. In the years she'd known him, she had never seen him hurt. She talked with him, when he allowed it, about the emotional scars, the pain of loss, the guilt, what he could have done differently; but she never dealt with any real physical damage. She told him for years how the emotional scars were worse than the physical, but looking at him now, she wasn't confident about that.

"Hey baby," Logan said as strong as he could.

She ran to him, jumping in the bed, leaning into him, and feeling his warmth. She missed how his body radiated heat.

"Jesus, Sam," he said, trying not to scream in pain, but laughing anyway as he put his arms around her.

They laid entwined for hours, sleeping—the three of them, the baby moving and kicking the whole time, seemingly trying to reach out and touch Daddy as well. Dubs and Lonnie stepped outside the room, standing watch over the door, giving the two duty guards a much needed break.

"Hey Dubs," Lonnie said, nodding down the hallway.

"This guy doesn't have a life," Dubs responded sighing heavily, referring to Secretary Smith who came barreling through the hallway.

"How's he doin'?" Secretary Smith asked, quickly addressing Dubs and Lonnie.

"Sam's inside. They're sleeping," Lonnie responded, looking to Dubs.

"He needs rest Mr. Secretary."

"I'm not here for a job guys. First things first. You'll be happy to know that terrorist son-of-a-bitch is gonna make it. Amir came out of surgery alive."

"Logan should hear this, he's been asking. Give me a minute," Dubs said, peeking into the hospital room.

"Logan, what the hell are you tryin' to do?" Dubs yelled, laughing at Logan who was trying to climb over Samantha.

"Shit. I was trying not to wake her up you loud piece of shit," he said, laughing at how insane it must have appeared.

"Sweetheart, I don't think you're ready for sex yet," Samantha said, waking up and laughing as her husband straddled her.

"Baby, you don't know what I'm capable of," he bent down to kiss her, but his myopic vision forced him to miss slightly. "Ugh," he grimaced, the inflammation in his head clamping down like a vise.

"You know, if you keep that beard," she said, tugging at the hair on Logan's face, "kinda sexy."

"Hurry up old man, the secretary's here. If you wanna know what's what, he'll come in. But not till you two are decent." Dubs closed the door and waited.

"I take it he's ready to listen?" Secretary Smith asked.

"What's the word with Amir?" Logan said, opening the door and spotting Doyle Smith.

"That's why I like you Logan. No bullshit. Let's go inside."

The men all entered the room, while Samantha slipped out. Smith allowed the door to close behind her before he spoke.

"Amir made it out of surgery safely. They had to take a lobe of his right lung, but he'll survive. When he's out of the hospital, he'll go to trial. A quiet one. We don't need more terrorism talk on T.V. President Pierce has lifted the martial law, no attacks made in the last five days. No retaliatory response after rescuing you Logan, nothing coming in from Medusa either. That being said, David's intel was incredible. I just wish we had the opportunity to evaluate it before. He and Nassir are compiling a list of locations we're going to be looking into. Solomon and his boys are gonna be busy."

"They're good guys." Dubs looked toward the floor, the moment in the tunnel playing fresh in his mind, three fallen SEALs thinning their ranks. "I wanna go. They're gonna need help."

"Yeah, they're three men down," Lonnie said, agreeing. "I'm gonna help too."

"Me too," Logan responded without his brain thinking through the risks.

"You're not going anywhere," Secretary Smith said and the other men nodded in agreement, looking awkwardly toward their team leader.

"Head wound's worse than I thought," Lonnie said without smiling.

"You're not going anywhere," Samantha said from around the corner, quickly closing the gap between them and grasping Logan's hand, placing it on her stomach. "You were this close to leaving me. This close to making me a widow. Your responsibility is here now, not there. It's always been here. We never agreed—"

"Okay," Logan said as he felt the baby roll around inside her. "Okay."

"As for you two, you're staying stateside too," Secretary Smith said. "For now, we need you guys here. We can't afford to break this team apart. Plus, have you seen yourself Dubs? You're not exactly in good fighting condition. I'm not having that on my conscience. I'll keep you guys up to date with everything. Good to see you boys are ready to fight already. I'm sure we'll need you stateside sooner than I'd like to admit."

Secretary Smith reached for the door to leave. "You two, give them some alone time. They need to get reacquainted," he said as he left, smiling. "I'm going to get some sleep myself. Been quite a few weeks."

Yemen

Karim laid in darkness. The concussive blast of the four bunker-busters shook his insides, causing him to hemorrhage internally. Blood leaked from his nose and he vomited viscous fluid, the taste of iron adding nausea to the list of symptoms. He continued to crawl down the tunnel toward the escape hatch. His body was weak, and broken, the smell of sulfur burning his lungs. He couldn't see, but felt the walls, the ground, and the dead bodies as he made his way down the long corridor. It was unknown how long he remained unconscious after the blast, but he knew he couldn't hear. Even the blast door he closed just moments before the ordnance fell couldn't stop the massive vacuum the explosion created, as it sucked the oxygen toward itself from every conceivable space, including Karim's lungs and ears, the delicate tympanic membranes erupted from the negative pressure. He never heard the bomb detonate, but he felt it.

Karim thought of Taj, of Nassir, of Amir. He remembered his loyal friend Irfan, his own wife who fled in fear. Karim was destroyed physically and emotionally, but, he was now free from distractions and weakness. He had nothing to hold him back any longer. He also had an advantage, no one knew he was still alive, and, even if they knew his name, they did not know his businesses. He never used his real name professionally, and always kept himself well insulated. Karim's plan was still unfinished, and unsullied. He hadn't told a soul about his last chapter. He owed it to himself to finish, he owed Nassir an explanation.

Karim urged himself on, knowing someone would be topside looking for him. It was only a matter of time, a minor setback, before his plan could come to completion.

| OTHER WORKS |

| CONTACT |

Join Mike's email newsletter at his webiste for the latest information regarding new releases and upcoming work.

Web: **michaelreidjr.com**

Instagram: **authormichaelreidjr**

Twitter: **@michaelreidjr1**

Facebook: **www.facebook.com/Authormichaelreidjr/**

| COLOPHON |

Book designed and laid out by
a.r. merlo, July 2017.

The cover and back covers designed by
John Apostolopoulos Digital Ink Group.

Interior text is set in Univers LT Std family and
Twentieth Century MT family.